"Eerily recalling today's headlines, Diane Noble spins a tale of innocent young women gone missing in exotic locales…and you will adore the heroine who makes it her business to solve the riddle of their disappearances. Harriet MacIver is a woman for our times, and *The Butterfly Farm* is a pulse-pounding adventure."

—ANGELA HUNT, author of *Uncharted*

"Diane Noble has created an intriguing mystery and delightful heroine in *The Butterfly Farm*. Harriet is wise, intelligent, and compassionate, solving the crime with a spunky determination that kept me up way past my bedtime. A terrific and versatile writer, Ms. Noble had me alternately laughing, holding my breath, and cheering as Harriet followed God's leading when almost everyone else thought she was a bit barmy. I can't wait for the next book!"

—SHARON GILLENWATER, author of *Twice Blessed*
and *Standing Tall*

"A masterpiece of fiction with cleverly arranged twists and turns from a most unique heroine."

—DIANN MILLS, author of *Leather and Lace*
and *When the Lion Roars*

"I want to be Harriett MacIver when I grow up! She's a fresh, faith-filled, and feisty heroine ready to take the mystery world by storm."

—LYNN BULOCK, author of the Gracie Lee mysteries
and *Less Than Frank*

THE
BUTTERFLY FARM

OTHER BOOKS BY DIANE NOBLE

The Last Storyteller
Heart of Glass

The Harriet MacIver Mystery Series:
The Butterfly Farm
Those Sacred Bones (coming May 2007)

The California Chronicles:
When the Far Hills Bloom
The Blossom and the Nettle
At Play in the Promised Land
The Veil

Novellas:
Phoebe
Come, My Little Angel

Other Fiction:
Tangled Vines
Distant Bells

Written as Amanda MacLean:
Westward
Stonehaven
Everlasting
Promise Me the Dawn
Kingdom Come

Nonfiction for Women:
Letters from God for Women
*It's Time! When Your Children Have
Grown, Explore Your Dreams and Discover Your Gifts*

THE BUTTERFLY FARM

A Harriet MacIver Mystery

DIANE NOBLE

WaterBrook
PRESS

THE BUTTERFLY FARM
PUBLISHED BY WATERBROOK PRESS
12265 Oracle Boulevard, Suite 200
Colorado Springs, Colorado 80921
A division of Random House Inc.

Scripture quotations and paraphrases are taken from the following versions: Holy Bible, New International Version®. NIV®. Copyright © 1973, 1978, 1984 by International Bible Society. Used by permission of Zondervan Publishing House. All rights reserved.

The characters and events in this book are fictional, and any resemblance to actual persons or events is coincidental.

ISBN 1-4000-7039-2

Library of Congress Cataloging-in-Publication Data
Noble, Diane, 1945-
  Butterfly Farm : a Harriet MacIver mystery / Diane Noble.— 1st ed.
    p. cm.
  ISBN 1-4000-7039 2
  1. Travel writers—Fiction. 2. Caribbean Area—Fiction. I. Title.

PS3563.A3179765B88 2006
813'.54—dc22

Printed in the United States of America
2006—First Edition

10 9 8 7 6 5 4 3 2 1

Gus is the Cat at the Theatre Door.
His name, as I ought to have told you before,
Is really Asparagus. That's such a fuss
To pronounce, that we usually call him just Gus.
—T. S. ELIOT,
Old Possum's Book of Practical Cats

At 11:38 a.m. on day three of the spring-break adventure cruise, Carly Lowe was ready to make her escape. She tramped down the gangway, a crowd of passengers growing around her like a giant ameba and adding to her annoyance. The rattletrap ship was too small, the stuffy lectures too boring, the same old group she hung with at Shepparton College too predictable. Why should she spend another day with any of them, especially today, lurching along by aerial tram through a drizzling, bug-infested rain forest?

Drifting toward the back of the group, she turned her thoughts to Julian Mendez. The fiery-eyed Latino had asked her to meet him just before noon in front of Club Bolero. It was a date she intended to keep. He was totally sweet…and hot. Capital *H* hot. And he played guitar. She'd heard him play onboard and loved the sound.

Following Ricki Ross, the ship's naturalist, the group trailed into the deserted main street of Parisima. Harriet MacIver walked beside Carly, but the older woman was paying no attention to her. Harriet had whipped out her notepad and was writing down some bit of scientific trivia imparted by the man to her left, Dr. Jean Baptiste, the onboard guest lecturer on the scientific wonders of the human body. Bo-ring.

Ricki Ross walked backward, holding high an unfurled umbrella as she shouted last-minute instructions about splitting into two groups—one led by her ecologist husband, Gregory; the other by Ricki herself. The umbrella thing was weird because it wasn't as if they were surrounded by hordes of other tourists. Parisima was practically deserted.

For several minutes Carly pretended to hang on Ricki's every word, but as the group rounded a corner, she ducked behind a potted palm. She waited, peering through the fronds, as the last of the passengers straggled along. If Harriet or any of the others noticed she wasn't with them, they would assume she was with the other group.

Carly had not invited her roommate, though now she was having a few guilt twinges. Zoë had glanced up when Carly left the room, but only to shoot her a sad look. Not many people liked Zoë. Truth be told, Carly didn't either. Not much. But Zoë was on Carly's list of things to work on in her new be-kinder-to-others self-improvement campaign. Her class-mate wasn't part of the "in" crowd, and Carly felt sorry for her. Part of her crusade on this cruise was to help the poor waiflike creature dress better and improve her image so she might gain acceptance from their peers. Carly didn't even grimace when they were assigned to the same stateroom on the ship, but she was dismayed when Zoë rebuffed her every effort to help her improve her looks and interact with Carly's friends.

She'd also been surprised to find something comforting in Zoë's solid, studious, no-nonsense ways. Here they were on the sun-kissed eastern coast of Costa Rica—well, *sun-kissed* might be a stretch; more like insect-infested swampland with lonesome gray beaches, straggly coconut palms, and air so heavy it dripped—and Zoë was holed up in their stateroom with her nose in a chemistry textbook. Too bad. This would have been a great opportunity to impart a few wise tips about social graces to her roomie.

Not that Carly didn't appreciate Zoë's hard work and the sobering realities that went with good grades. But work was work and play was, well, essential to one's well-being. Most of Carly's friends saw her as a fun-loving airhead who knew more about Kate Spade than Albert Einstein. It was true that she loved a good time, but she also got a kick out of things that fed her intellect and soul. She just didn't advertise it.

She watched the last knot of passengers disappear around another corner, their voices fading until only silence remained. The *Sun Spirit* brochure said that this village was known for its Latin music and native art, but from what Carly had seen so far, Parisima was more sleepy than artsy. Now that the tour groups were gone, she realized how empty the town was. Maybe she should have done the buddy-system thing after all and insisted that Zoë come with her.

She pushed aside her creeped-out thoughts. After all, she was here for simple pleasures—a cold lemonade in an outdoor café, a tour of Julian's village, a bit of dancing at Club Bolero while he played his guitar. Her only concern was getting back to the *Sun Spirit* in time to meet Harriet for dinner.

Leaving her hiding place and stepping out into the sunlight, Carly glanced up and down the cobbled street. It was flanked on both sides by sun-bleached, pastel-colored buildings. She wondered where the photographer had found the beautiful spots featured in the *Sun Spirit* brochure. From what she could see, Parisima was a ghost town. She half-expected to see tumbleweeds blowing through the streets.

She almost sighed with relief when she caught the faint strums of an acoustic guitar drifting on the heavy air. She squinted toward the sound, barely making out the hand-painted name on the building's facade: CLUB BOLERO.

Squaring her shoulders, she strode down the street toward the club, halted in front of it, and swallowed a laugh. The so-called club was little more than a faded, crumbling storefront. Maybe she had misunderstood Julian. He had said there was no better place for dancing and meeting people than the Bolero. She suddenly pitied the town if this was all they had to look forward to on Saturday nights.

Then she grinned, thinking of what Harriet would say: "Honey, some folks, desperate to find happiness, try to find happiness in the most desperate places. The harder they look, the more desperate the places. And all along, happiness is in the simplest place of all—right smack in the middle of their hearts."

That was Harriet, her philosophy in a clamshell. A wave of affection for the older woman washed over her. And she wondered at the chill that overtook her as she gazed at this desperate place. She thought about turning around and heading back to the ship, but the call to adventure was too strong.

On the outside patio a few plastic tables and chairs had been placed near a faded terra-cotta fountain. Dried palm fronds covered the ramada, providing shade over the patio. The sound of trickling water joined with the strums of guitar music, and the balmy wind tickled the dried tips of the fronds. A cockroach the size of Carly's fist crawled up one of the supporting poles. She shivered.

Julian sat to the right of the fountain, chair tipped against a stucco wall, his hat pulled low. As Carly took a seat, he lifted his guitar in a friendly salute, then once more let his fingertips dance across the strings. Jazz. A smooth, liquid jazz with a Latin beat.

The village no longer seemed so empty or scary. Julian didn't take his eyes off her as he sang, and she lost herself in his music. And when he began "Bésame mucho" she leaned forward, elbows on the table, and shot him a flirty smile.

She wasn't surprised when, after a few more songs, he put aside his instrument, sauntered over, pulled out a chair without asking, and sat across from her. He wore khaki pants with a brilliant white shirt, tucked in, sleeves rolled up, unbuttoned enough to see the tan of his chest. When he smiled, his teeth matched the white of the shirt. He looked even more delicious than he had onboard the *Sun Spirit*.

"You came."

"You thought I wouldn't?"

"I have watched you on the *Spirit*. You are smart and cautious, not one to take chances. I thought you might have second thoughts about meeting a stranger." His tone was teasing.

"Are you a stranger?" She matched her tone with his.

"I worried that you might think so." He reached for her hand, turned it over, and gently stroked her palm. She pulled it away, but not before a 5.3 tremor shivered up her spine. "Now that we are no longer strangers, I have questions for you."

"And they would be...?"

"How do you like this place, my little village? How is it you prefer an educational adventure cruise to a party ship? How is it you prefer meeting me to soaring by aerial tram through the rain-forest canopy? How is it you travel on a ship about to 'go under,' so they say?"

Carly countered, "And how is it you work on such a ship instead of on a five-star, two-thousand passenger party ship where the tips would be two hundred times what you get now?"

"Your spirit matches your flame-colored hair."

"And you speak beautiful English, but in clichés."

He threw back his head and laughed. "You very adeptly sidestepped my questions. Most American students travel only as far as Mexico to party. What makes you different?"

"I'm not most students."

His gaze traveled down her frame. "So I have noticed."

"To return to your first question, your village certainly doesn't match the pictures in the brochure. As for your second, I'm on this cruise because my mother gave it to me as an early graduation gift—plus I need the credits to graduate. She thought the whole package would be more suitable than partying."

He leaned closer. "And what about you? Do you think it is more suitable?"

"A ship with so few passengers is a bit limiting, but not unpleasant."

"You do not mind one lone guitar player instead of clubs that rock all night?"

"I'm not that kind of girl."

"You are intelligent, then? A serious student?"

"I like to think so, but why should you care?"

He threw his head back again and laughed. The sound of his laughter was almost as beautiful as his singing. "I treasure women with brains."

Carly's cheeks warmed, and she let her gaze drift away from him, enjoying the moment. She felt him watching her and turned.

There was a new look in his eyes, perhaps admiration for something more than her figure. "When are you due to board the *Sun Spirit*?"

"The same as you. This evening." A mosquito landed on her arm, and she brushed it away. Another took its place.

"Ah, what you say is true…to a point, and I will explain later. But this also means you can stay to see me perform tonight at the Bolero—at least for a little while. But we cannot have you waiting around here. I think you might enjoy a personal tour of Parisima, yes? What you see here in town is nothing. It is out there where the magic begins. Beyond Parisima." His gesture took in the outskirts of the village, the ocean to the east, the rain forest to the west, the banana plantations to the north. "You can trust me. What I tell you is true." His teeth flashed in the sunlight.

Julian seemed to sense her indecision. He removed his hat, raked his fingers through his hair, and leaned forward intently, his eyes never leaving hers. "We can stop by the ship if you would like. Captain Richter will vouch for me—even though he is no longer my boss." His smile was wide and confident.

"Don't you sail with us tonight?"

"That is what I need to explain. I am sorry to report that my contract ended with last night's performance. Does this mean you will miss me?"

Carly didn't answer. It bothered her that he no longer worked on the *Sun Spirit.* She felt as if she was stepping close to the edge of something dangerous, unable to help herself, yet unable to move away. It was the same feeling she once had when standing too close to an overlook at the Grand Canyon. It had made her toes ache.

"I will be at the Bolero every night for the next six weeks. And as for the five-star super ship you so glowingly described? That is the reason I ended my contract with the *Sun Spirit.* I will be performing onboard the *Empress Catalonia.*"

"A step up. Congratulations."

"You do not sound sincere."

The boldness of his gaze was beginning to bother her. And the way it darted now and then to the dusty cobbled road, as if he was looking for someone.

"I would like to return to the ship before our tour, if you don't mind."

"Of course I do not mind. The captain knows me well—"

"No, no. It's not that at all. It's just that I was supposed to meet someone later tonight."

Julian's eyebrow shot up. "Someone I know?"

"No, just a friend. But I want to let her know I may be late."

"Of course. We'll head to the ship first." He rose, bowed slightly, and took her hand as she stood. "I will tell you about our beautiful country and my little village as we walk." His obsidian eyes glinted as he adjusted his hat brim. He tucked her hand in the crook of his arm as they walked toward the edge of the village. "I will start with butterflies, something Costa Rica is known for. They are so abundant we claim ten percent of the world's species. One of our butterflies—the blue morpho—has a wingspan the size of a saucer." He laughed. "A very large saucer—nine inches to be exact. And it is a vivid, electric blue. The bright color serves as a warning for predators to stay away. Is it not a shame that beauty cannot always do that in nature? So many innocent creatures would be spared." He smiled, but he obviously didn't expect an answer.

They stepped around a wooden cart filled with overripe bananas. Flies buzzed around the fruit, and a sickening scent hung heavy in the air. An old man sat nearby in the shade of a dried-palm shelter. He held out his hand, palm up. *"Por favor, señorita, ¿quiere comprar de fruta?"*

Carly dug into her pocket for a coin. She placed it in the man's hand but waved away the fruit. Almost before she had finished, Julian cupped his hand beneath her elbow and guided her to a path flanked by tall, leafy plants. "And did you know the blue morpho is poisonous?"

"No," she said. "I've never heard of such a thing."

"It is true. Though intended for predators, its venom is so strong it can kill a human being." She shivered visibly and he laughed. "You do not need to worry. These rare and beautiful butterflies do not sting. You will die only if you eat one." He laughed again.

"Their feeding habits are especially interesting. They suck in the juices of everything from the bodily fluids of dead animals to fermenting fruit." He stopped walking and looked down at her. "Strangely, it is when they become inebriated and wobble in flight that they are most easily caught." He paused again, his dark eyes fixed on hers. "For you see, their beauty makes them valuable. Their wings can be used to grace exquisite pieces of jewelry for the wealthy or to decorate masks for carnivalgoers. Not even the most precious gemstone can duplicate the color of their wings."

His tone was beginning to frighten her. It was as if he knew he was tormenting her by describing in detail the eating habits of this poisonous, beautiful butterfly. She drew in a deep breath to calm herself as he went on.

"It is also strange that, in some species, morpho caterpillars are cannibalistic." He shrugged, half-smiling. "Can you imagine such a thing in nature? But it gets even more intriguing. If disturbed, the blue morpho butterfly secretes a fluid smelling of rancid butter."

"A warning to its predators," she said.

He shot her an admiring glance. "Exactly."

As they continued to walk, he moved on to other oddities having to do with the flora, fauna, and climate zones of the area.

Carly brushed away another mosquito, concentrating on his words instead of the nervous twinge in her stomach. Trees now obscured her view, but to her reckoning, they were heading away from the harbor.

As he spoke, he lengthened his stride.

She halted, glanced back the direction of the village, also obscured by foliage, and then turned again to meet Julian's gaze. "I'm not comfortable with this. We seem to be heading away from…the ship. And the town." She laughed lightly, as if she knew better. "Let's go back." She laughed again, nervously, and turned away from him.

He reached for her arm. "Oh no, you do not understand. This is—

how do you Americans say?—a shortcut. You must be patient. We are almost to our destination."

She stepped backward. "This doesn't feel like a shortcut. I'd like to return to the ship—the way I came with the others. Let's go."

"I think not." His fingers tightened around her forearm. He took a step forward, but she dug in her sandals and held her ground.

"I want to go back. Now."

"I'm sorry. It is too late."

"What do you mean 'too late'?"

He jerked her forward without answering.

"Please, let me go." She forced herself to breathe, to keep her wits about her. How could she have been so naive?

She pulled away from him, throwing her weight backward.

He looked at her, amused. "So you think this is child's play?"

She was too frightened to think of a smart-mouth comeback. She tried to swallow; her mouth felt like cotton.

Still smiling, he twisted her arm.

She yelped. "Please," she cried, praying for the pain to stop.

He twisted harder and jerked her toward him again. She stumbled, then caught herself. She bit into his upper arm and tasted blood. He grunted and ground his opposite hand against her face. Her neck bent backward, and searing pain shot through her. He cut off her air supply, and she melted to her knees.

"Ah, you are a lively one. When I read your profile, I thought you might be."

Carly gasped for breath, then whispered, "Profile? What profile? What do you mean?"

He said nothing else until they reached the coconut trees. Bile stung her throat as he dragged her into the underbrush. Even if he released her, her knees were shaking too hard to run.

Two men waited in a clearing. Julian shoved her toward them. She spit at his face as he stepped away from her.

"Adios," Julian said, wiping the spittle from his cheek. His voice was low, menacing, and what he probably thought was seductive. "Adios. Until we meet again…" He hummed a few bars of "Bésame mucho" as he walked away from her. He turned, laughed, bowed, and then he was gone.

"Not on your life," she called out. "You can't get away with this. I'm an American, protected by—"

Her words were cut off by more laughter.

An hour later, wrists bound in front of her, Carly stood silently on a dilapidated dock as one of the men untied a faded blue fishing boat. Around them was a lava-rock-strewn beach ringed with palms. The second man held a pistol against her temple. The tide was coming in, and the boat rocked against the waves.

Carly pressed her lips together, drawing in deep, silent breaths. She saw only one chance for escape. And she planned to take it. The man with the gun gave her a small shove toward the boat.

She stepped in, twisted hard to the left, then immediately to the right. The boat rocked abruptly, upsetting her balance. She flipped overboard. Water rushed around her as she sank. She panicked, her arms immobile, her clothes soaking up water and becoming heavier by the second. For a moment she couldn't think.

A sound above her brought her back to action. She wriggled eel-like through the water, heavily, awkwardly, until she was beneath the boat, the only place she wouldn't be seen.

She waited, utterly still, her lungs ready to explode. She needed air...
and fast.

Heart racing, she propelled herself toward the shelter of the dock.
Muffled gunshots exploded around her. She came up for air, gulping
wildly.

A hand closed around her neck. She struggled, clawing at the clamped
fingers, as her head was forced underwater by a second hand. The water's
rippling surface teased just inches above her nose.

So close, but unreachable.

Beyond the two shadowy figures above her, she could see the bright,
shimmering tropical sky mocking her.

She tried one last time to reach the surface.

Then her body went limp and her bound hands floated upward as if
in supplication.

I thought my first assignment would be a dream job. A Caribbean Sea adventure cruise, fewer than three hundred passengers, hidden ports of call most world travelers only fantasize about. Lazy afternoons basking in the sun, sipping lattes at sidewalk cafés, going on jungle treks under the watchful care of a naturalist. Capped off with an overnight stay at a luxury spa. A perfect recipe for adventure and pampering.

And as my editor, Tangerine Lowe, pointed out, a great way to mend my broken heart

Or so I thought. As is too often the case, expectations and reality can miss each other by a mile. A hundred miles. Make that a million. Or more.

From the morning I boarded, the *Sun Spirit*—a rusting ship with a stabilizer that tossed us around like beans in a beanbag—limped along the Central America coast, seasick passengers hanging over the railings, their faces as green as the Caribbean. We had missed two ports already with no explanation from the captain. Someone overheard a crew member say that the ship's parent company, Global Sea Adventures, couldn't pay the port fees or cover the cost of taking on new supplies. Now there were rumors that the GSA was headed for full-blown bankruptcy. Belly up, which isn't a comforting visual for a cruise ship.

My name is Harriet MacIver, and I am a travel writer.

I am afraid to fly, which complicates my job somewhat, but we'll get into that later. For now, suffice it to say that I specialize in rating cruise ships of all kinds, from bare-bones adventure cruises to hoity-toity five-star, five-diamond ships longer than a football field—or two. Around the globe. From the Amazon to the Antarctic, from Easter Island to the Antilles.

At least these are the destinations Tangerine mentioned just before she said, without missing a beat, "By the way, you wouldn't mind keeping an eye on my Carly while you're in Costa Rica, would you?" But that's another story.

Travel writing wasn't my first career choice. But achingly sad circumstances changed everything. When loneliness settled into my heart and threatened to take up permanent residence after Hollis was killed, I sniveled my last snivel, tossed aside my box of Kleenex, and set off to sell myself to my local newspaper, the *Town Crier*. Some of our locals affectionately call it the *Town Liar*, but you never heard it from me.

I'd known Tangerine, editor in chief, since our stint on the PTA board when our now-grown children were in grade school, so we go back some. Tangi and I were often on the opposite sides of issues, but, well, that's to be expected in a small town like Bender's Point. For instance, I wanted to use our bake-sale profits to send the year's perfect-attendance winners on a hot-air-balloon ride; Tangi thought we should give the money to the students so they could start a school newspaper. Come to think of it, just a few weeks after we voted her idea down, she set aside space in her garage and started the *Town Crier*. We all thought she was nuts, likely reacting to some midlife crisis because her husband had just left her for his floozy secretary. But after some fits and starts, she began turning out a good little paper. It won all kinds of awards, which went to her head, according to some of our more envious peers. But word got around, and soon subscriptions were pouring in via the Internet and snail mail from all over the country and one province in Canada.

Critics caught wind of her work, comparing her to Garrison Keillor and her paper to his news from Lake Wobegon. One major difference: Garrison's news is made up; Tangerine Lowe's is not. She has even been interviewed on NPR, much to the dismay of our town's mayor and his cohorts who think NPR is run by communists.

So when I trotted into Tangi's office with my travel-column idea for the *Crier*, she went for it. Her eyes glistened as I talked, and I could see that she was ready to go for an even larger readership. Maybe international attention. Another NPR interview. She didn't even ask whether I could write. Nor did she glance at the highlighted journalism classes on my yellowed and wrinkled college transcripts. She didn't ask if I could sound as folksy as the other *Crier* reporters. Or how I was going to get myself on an airplane after what had happened to Hollis.

Instead, she pulled out a world map and started plotting my trips, a half smile that looked suspiciously like greed playing at her lips, eyeglasses propped on top of her spiked, flame-hued hair like eyes on a fuzzy orange bug. After a minute she looked up, a flicker of affection warming her gaze. "Cruises," she said, "will be your specialty."

So she understood about my fear of flying. This wasn't like her. Everyone in Bender's Point knew what a hard-nosed, no-nonsense, unfeeling woman she had turned into. I grinned. "Cruises are good."

She glanced down at the map again and narrowed her gaze at Central America. "Costa Rica will be your first assignment," she said. "The weather's mild, the people friendly, the political climate safe for Americans. I recently heard about an upscale spa experience that's included with an adventure cruise package—Global Sea Adventures out of Nassau. You could rate the whole deal—cruise, jungle tours, aerial trams, spa, the works." She smiled. "We'll put you on the Internet. Website with flash media. You'll be the Dear Abby of the travel world. Plus, the trip would do you some good. Give you new vistas. How about it?"

I blinked, astonished. A second later a nagging doubt flitted around the edges of my mind. Hollis always said that if it sounded too good to be true, it probably was. "What else have you heard about the spa?" I pictured something nefarious. Maybe this hadn't been such a good idea after all. Maybe she was going for the sensational to draw even more attention to the paper. I would be the bait. (This was still before the oh-by-the-way-would-you-mind-watching-Carly bit.)

I almost chuckled at the nefarious spa thought. I'd obviously been watching too much FOX News.

Tangi shrugged. "The spa is run by a health-nut guru. He specializes in gourmet vegan cuisine and an exercise regimen suited for your, uh, individual body type."

She had the grace not to glance at my expanding middle. When I'm depressed, éclairs turn into the singing sirens of the frozen-foods section at the Village Market. And since Hollis's passing, the sirens seem to commandeer my cart even as I valiantly try to steer to fresh produce.

"And there's yoga, of course. It's ubiquitous at spas touting the sort of good life that caters to the upper crust. This spa's called *La Vida Pura*. The pure life."

I gulped, picturing myself in a leotard, or whatever it is they wear. "Of course."

"You'll need to rate their exercise program right along with the rest of the cruise package."

I stifled a laugh. I get short of breath just bending over to feed my cat, Gus. And yoga of all things. Pointy hands above my head? Face reflecting some sort of ethereal ecstasy? I could see it all now: Silvery-blond bun atop my head. Round grandmotherly face. Laugh lines firmly set. Holding a graceful pose even as my arthritic joints ache, humming while I converse with the universe. We were getting close to Granny Clampett does Club Med. "I might have to skip the yoga lessons," I said.

"The *Town Crier* can't pay you much. Expenses only."

It was more than I'd hoped for. "Add enough to cover Gus's fare, and you've got yourself a deal."

"I'll watch Gus for you."

"He bites."

Tangi barked out a laugh. "So do I. We'll get along fine."

"No, he's gotta go with me. Seriously." Since Hollis died, I've needed Gus to drape his warm body over my ankles at night. When I dare to wiggle or stretch my feet, he pounces on them, but my complaints are halfhearted. I need the feel of life in the bed beside me. "Where I go, Gus goes."

"I don't think they charge for animals you bring along," Tangi said. "You just stick him in a little carrier—"

"Big carrier. He's over twenty pounds. A ferocious-looking feline, all muscle and fur."

She grinned, enjoying the visual. "Big carrier, then. Tuck him under the seat in front of you, and away he goes. I honestly don't know how the folks who operate the ship will feel about it, but I'll find out for you." She paused. "It's fairly loosely run. Small adventure ship that's going after the spring-break market by offering condensed-credit courses on ecology and oceanography. A few fluff classes to round it out—snorkeling, scuba diving, kayaking, that kind of thing."

Kayaking? With college kids? I pictured the thing spinning—with me in it. I'd seen it happen on the Travel Channel.

This didn't sound like the sort of exotic travel the public was panting to read about. "Carly needs the credits to graduate? The cruise is this May, right?"

Tangi looked at me without blinking for a minute, then she laughed. "You always were a quick study. Yes, she needs the credits—and some time away. She's been wound tighter than a yo-yo ready to spin. I want her to relax and have some fun—plus get those six credits she needs." She paused. "And you remember, of course, how she tends to, well, seek her own adventures—no matter how heavily supervised?

I'd always adored Carly. Something about her quirky ways, even in third grade, had lassoed my heart. And my son's, too. He was a world away, but he was still half in love with Carly. But through the years Carly had given her mother plenty of reasons to hide her gray with Clairol Hot Lava number three.

"Of course," I said, hoping she'd grown up some by now. "I'll be happy to keep an eye on her."

As if knowing I couldn't resist, Tangi stood and reached across the desk to shake my hand. "Welcome aboard, Harriet. I'm glad you came to me with this." She paused as I pushed myself up from my chair. "You'll be ready by the sail date, yes?"

I patted my hair, straightened my skirt, and gave her a wide smile. My passport was current, but I had some work to do on a travel wardrobe. Sensible trekking clothes were in order and, of course, whatever it was I needed for my yoga lessons. And a photojournalist's vest with all those little Velcro pockets. I'd always wanted one of those. "You got it, Tange. You tell me when and where, and I'll be there. With Gus."

For the first time in months, I almost forgot my grief.

So here I am, Harriet MacIver, recently widowed, nothing on my résumé but loving wife of thirty-six and a half years to Hollis MacIver and mother of two grown sons and a daughter who no longer need me.

I thought travel might force me to look—to live—outside myself instead of dwelling on my loss. I was still mad at God for taking Hollis from me, especially in such a tragic way. Not that it would have been easier if slow-moving cancer or even a heart attack had taken his life. It's just that accidents are so abrupt. One second you're thinking about taking something out of the freezer for dinner that night. The next, a black-and-white police car pulls up in front of your house and two men get out and walk slowly to your door. You see their faces, and you realize what they have come to tell. You also know life will never be the same.

And it wasn't.

The ship dipped and rolled, pulling me away from my thoughts of Hollis. The stabilizer still hadn't been repaired. But somehow I'd developed a growing affection for the rusting hulk. It had seen the world, and then some, and like some people I've known, it was a bit worn around the edges. But then, aren't we all?

Through the porthole window, the Costa Rican coastline disappeared into a twilight haze as the *Sun Spirit* headed south to its next destination.

My stomach did backflips as the last twinkling lights of Parisima faded, and I saw nothing but the darkening sea. I wondered whether I was up to the task ahead. Wondered if I still had the guts and savvy I'd always counted on. When the wind is in your face instead of at your back, even taking a single step into the unknown seems daunting. And here I was leaping—not stepping—into a world beyond my imagination.

I stood and peered into the mirror.

Harriet MacIver, travel writer. The Dear Abby of the jet set…well, make that ship set because of the flying thing.

I pulled my hair through the back of my ball cap, grinned at the "You Go, Girl!" stitched above the brim, and headed to my stateroom door. I didn't want to be late for my dinner with Carly.

I scated myself at a table for eight. On an ocean liner, tables are assigned, and you're attended to by a server in a tuxedo who treats you like you're related to the princess of Wales. Candlelight glows across linen table-cloths, reflecting in crystal goblets and gleaming silverware.

Not on this bare-bones bucket. No maître d' with a white cloth draped over his arm to lead you to your table, no symphonic music playing in the background, no smiling waiter making food and wine suggestions from a menu of endless choices. Here, instead of roasted pumpkin-and-apple soup for an appetizer, mahi-mahi tempura for an entrée, and a custard-nut parfait with warm caramel-fudge sauce, almonds, and macadamia nuts for dessert, you have the choice of tricolor tortilla chips with green or red salsa or shoestring potatoes with ketchup for a starter, hamburgers or tacos for an entrée, and a scoop of vanilla or chocolate ice cream for dessert.

And instead of classical music softly playing in the background, you have the roar of laughter and shouting provided by college students, their professors, and the adventurous, brave souls—mostly golden agers—who dared to travel with Global Sea Adventures.

I scooted my chair closer to the round Formica table and smiled at my seat partners, the Browns, the Doyles, and the Quilps. Carly's chair beside me was still empty. I rather liked dining with people who weren't trussed up in tuxes, party dresses, heels, and jewels. And although I missed the elegant desserts on cruise liners, this fare suited me fine. I reached for a tortilla chip, took a bite, salted the whole basket, then reached for another chip.

"Are you saving this seat?" Adele Quilp seemed perturbed that I was alone.

"Actually, yes. One of the students, a friend, will be joining us shortly." Adele raised a severely plucked eyebrow. "Hunh."

It was an us-versus-them *hunh*. I'd heard it before. Some of the passengers were put off by the college students and gave them a wide berth. So to speak. Some of the passengers even talked of demanding their money back at the end of the cruise. Adele Quilp was likely one of the disgruntled few.

"Carly's a sweetheart," I said to get Adele to lower her eyebrow. "I've known her for years. Since she was in grade school actually. I have a son the same age, and I'm still holding out hope they'll get together. She was his first girlfriend."

"Well, now. That's the sweetest thing I've heard about any of these kids," Ed Brown said, his Oklahoma drawl thick as sorghum.

His wife, Betty, laughed. "That's about the only sweet thing you've heard about these kids."

Adele looked pained and said, "Hunh." Her husband looked down at his plate. So far he hadn't uttered a word.

"You ought to sit in on some of the classes," Barbara Doyle said. "These kids are bright. I attended one of their lectures yesterday—Dr. Baptiste's talk on the intricacies of the human body. It was incredibly complex stuff, but he had the kids soaking it up like deep-sea sponges. And the classroom was crowded. Standing room only."

Betty Brown reached for a chip. "I hear he's up for a Nobel Prize for his research."

"No, he's not," Adele said. "There's talk of it, but no formal announcement."

"What I'm getting at," Barbara said, "is that those who are upset with the invasion of the Shepparton students ought to sit in and listen to what they're here to learn. They may be boisterous and annoying at times, but overall they're good kids."

Her husband agreed.

I glanced at my watch. It wasn't like Carly to be late. The girl might be petite, but she had an appetite. I tried not to worry.

Some of the students were earning extra credit by working in the kitchen and dining room. Breakfasts and lunches were buffet affairs, but dinners were served family style by the student waiters. One of the students, a tall, thin kid who'd told us the night before that his name was Max Pribble, walked toward us with a platter of tacos in one hand and a platter piled with hamburgers in the other. The condiments were already on the table.

I thought about how I would word my article for the *Town Crier* as I rated the cuisine, but I drew a blank, just as I had from day one. I sighed and reached for another tortilla chip.

Max set the platter of tacos in the center of the table, then with a wobbly hand, he set down the heavy plate of hamburgers. The cook must have thought the golden agers onboard had appetites equaling the students'.

"Do you know Carly Lowe?" I ventured as he wiped his hands on his apron.

"Sure, everybody knows Carly." Max gave his hair a shake. It was shaved even with the tops of his ears and worn long and straight on top. It made his head look like a cantaloupe with a corn-silk toupee. It made me want to smile.

"She was supposed to join me for dinner. I'm surprised she's late."

He shrugged. "With Carly, who knows. She never does what you expect her to."

I laughed. "Or what she's told to do."

He shot me a surprised look. "How'd you know that?"

"We go back a ways."

"Then you can probably guess she's just changed her mind." He grinned. "Probably got a better offer. No offense."

"None taken. If you see her later, let her know I asked."

"Sure." And he was off to wait on another table.

"Kids are so undependable these days," Adele said. She picked at her taco with a fork, pulling out the chicken pieces and setting them in a precise pile at the far side of her plate.

Her husband sighed and bit into his hamburger.

"I disagree," Ed Brown said, reaching for a taco. "I've got grandkids who are the smartest, most responsible teens you'd ever want to meet. One's a summer lifeguard."

"That's my point," Adele said. "These kids are no longer teens. Used to be we worried about teenagers. It's a proven fact that kids run about a decade behind in their level of maturity than our generation did. It's the kids in their twenties you have to worry about now. When they hit twenty or twenty-one, it's all downhill until they reach thirty. I pity their parents." She shook her head.

"You have any kids, Adele?" Ed wanted to know.

"No," Adele's husband said. I figured he was thinking it was a good thing. The replication of Adele was no doubt too scary to consider.

It was the only word he said all evening.

That night I awoke to the light of a full moon spilling through my window.

Something was different about the ship. Startlingly different. Usually the *Sun Spirit* almost seemed to cavort through the swells between ports each night. But now it was utterly still. Silent. As in no engines humming, no tropical winds whistling. I turned over and closed my eyes against the bright moonlight, wondering why my heart thudded in alarm, wondering what, besides the silence, had awakened me. All I could see on the back of my lids was the pale hull of the ill-fated ghost ship in *The Rime of the Ancient Mariner:*

> *Day after day, day after day,*
> *We stuck, nor breath nor motion;*
> *As idle as a painted ship*
> *Upon a painted ocean.*

Then the image of Carly's face replaced that of the ghost ship. I sat up fast and flicked on the lamp beside my bed. I'd have to find my own bottle of Clairol by the time this cruise was over if I couldn't keep my imagination under wraps. Carly was a big girl. She'd pulled her share of disappearing-slash-looking-for-adventure acts before. Just because she'd missed dinner with me didn't mean she'd missed the ship. But telling myself not to worry wasn't helping.

Gus sat up on the end of the bed and began vigorously licking his left paw in a patch of moonlight. The *scratch-scratch* rhythm of his tongue brought me back to reality. I patted his head and heard his tail thump in response. Then somewhere in the bowels of the ship, the engines coughed and sputtered. Within minutes they were humming as if I had imagined their earlier silence. And maybe I had.

I was just about to drift off again when a knock at my stateroom door made Gus sit at full attention, ears cocked, and my heart threatened to jump from my chest. I obviously hadn't fully recovered from my earlier alarm.

A muffled whisper floated from the other side of the door. "Mrs. MacIver? I know it's late, and I hate to disturb you..."

I fumbled for the clock on the bedside table, drew it close to my nose, and peered at its face: 12:42 a.m. With a sigh I found my slippers, pulled on a light cotton robe, and padded to the door. "Who is it?"

"Zoë Shire."

I unlatched the lock and swung open the door.

The young woman stood there for a moment, her large gray eyes peering at me through thick glasses. She was a thin girl, small boned, a bit mousy, but only because she seemed not to care about her appearance. She was wearing baggy sweatpants and a Shepparton T-shirt, and her hair was slicked back into a ponytail. She looked like who she was: a bookish science major trying to get into med school, a wannabe activist for the downtrodden in society who maybe cared more about the fate of others than the latest fashion fad. Commendable, but she might get on in this world better if she shampooed her hair more often. A smile now and then wouldn't hurt either.

I had overheard some of the cattier students snickering about how Zoë had once made a big deal out of how she was going to chain herself to the White House fence to draw attention to Alzheimer's patients. Then she chickened out. I knew from their guffaws that she had never lived it down. Worse than openly teasing her, the other students seemed to have chosen ignoring her as the best punishment for being "uncool."

"Zoë, come in. Please…" I stepped back from the door so she could enter. She slouched onto the small sofa across from the bed and stared unblinking at me as I took the barrel chair by the window, facing her.

Gus lost no time hopping onto her lap. She pushed him away. "Allergic." She pulled out her inhaler and took a couple of puffs as if to emphasize the point. Gus hopped back onto her lap. I patted the seat beside me, but he stared at me as if he had no idea what I meant. I reached across the distance between us and picked him up, bringing him back to my lap. He hopped down and stared up at Zoë as if hers was the only lap in the world he wanted.

She blinked at him. "I'm sorry."

Gus turned his back to her, stretched, and sauntered to the bed, his tail waving lazily. He hopped up and circled several times before curling into a ball, his back still to Zoë. Apparently he didn't accept her apology. Cats are like that.

I waited for her to initiate the conversation, then finally said, "What is the problem, Zoë?"

"The note you slid under our door? The one for Carly…?"

I nodded and waited for her to go on, swallowing a yawn that made my eyes water.

"I didn't open the note, but I know you were supposed to meet for dinner tonight. I figured you were worried about her."

Premed student, social activist, and mind reader. "A little," I lied. "Do you know where she is?"

I reminded myself again of Carly's guts and brains. I was worried over nothing. I was certain. Sort of. Besides—I glanced at the clock—it was still early for students to be tucked into their staterooms. Carly was no exception.

"She's usually in by now." Zoë leaned closer. "I wouldn't think too much about it, but I haven't seen Carly since everyone left for the onshore excursion."

My heart crept into my throat. "You didn't go?"

"No one asked." She twisted a stringy lock of hair around her finger. "After we left port, I got worried."

I took a breath. "The students get together in the evenings, don't they?"

She nodded. "Yeah, they do."

She looked embarrassed again. She'd probably never been invited to one of those confabs either. "Look," I said. "I don't think you need to worry. Carly's pretty good at taking care of herself. I've known her a long time. She's a pistol."

Zoë pushed up her Coke-bottle glasses and stared at me with those mournful gray eyes. "A what?"

"Self-sufficient. Feisty."

"But what if she missed the ship?"

The moon reappeared, casting a silvery glow across the water. The engines hummed below us, and the rhythm of the swells was gentler now.

"There's something I should tell you…"

I frowned as her voice trailed off. I guessed she didn't want to bad-mouth her friend—or she might have been dramatizing for effect. I sighed, suspecting the latter. "I raised two sons and a daughter. You can tell me anything." Well, almost. There are certain topics today's young people discuss quite openly that I'd rather not hear. But this wasn't the time to get picky.

Her eyes caught mine.

"What is it?" I asked.

She settled back into the sofa and tucked one foot beneath her. She reminded me of a baby stork. Big eyes set on a pale, elongated face. The mother in me wanted to gather her into a big hug. "She's been a little angry that her mother asked you to spy on her. A couple of days ago, she said she had to get off the ship."

Spy on her? I almost laughed. I'd raised three kids. They love drama. I didn't correct her. "Look, Zoë, maybe she did need to get away." I gave her a reassuring smile, though my own apprehension was growing by the minute. "Why don't you go back to bed? She may be in your stateroom by now. If she hasn't shown up by morning, we'll talk again and decide what to do."

She nodded, unwound her leg, and stood. But she didn't make a move toward the door. "Carly is one of the only kids onboard who treats me like I'm somebody."

"She's a caring kid," I agreed. I sidled toward the door, hoping she'd take the hint. I stifled another yawn when she didn't.

She shrugged. "I'm just worried, that's all. There was that groom who disappeared on his honeymoon on a Mediterranean cruise... Do you remember?"

"Yes, it was tragic."

"They think he fell overboard—or was pushed." As she voiced her fears, her eyes widened, seeming too large for her face. "His poor bride," she whispered softly. "What if—?"

"Hey, kiddo," I interrupted. "You're letting your imagination run off like wild horses." As if she had a corner on the market.

"And then there was that girl in Aruba..."

I sighed and softened my voice. "If you're that worried, go check your cabin, and if Carly's not there, come back and tell me. Then we'll go see the captain."

Zoë gave me an appreciative look. "I'll be right back."

I pulled on my sweats and ran a brush through my hair. Ten minutes later, Zoë was back. "She's still missing."

"*Missing* is a bit over the top," I said. "She may be in one of her friends' staterooms."

"I asked a couple of kids I saw in the hall. They said they hadn't seen her."

"How many students are on the ship?"

"Ninety-seven. There was supposed to be hundred, but at the last minute three students dropped out. Health reasons." When I frowned, she went on to explain. "I work in the registrar's office on campus, which carries over to taking care of administrative details for the program here onboard." She flushed and lifted her chin a notch.

"How about the head of the program, the dean—what's his name?"

"Dean Williams. Guy Williams."

"Shouldn't you let Dean Williams know your concerns?"

"What if I'm wrong, which, of course, I hope I am. But if I am, I would look like such a fool."

I sighed. The girl was a bundle of neuroses. "What I was getting at is that out of ninety-seven students, Carly could be in one of several staterooms."

She shrugged. "I suppose."

"But we'll take a look around anyway. Where do you want to start?"

"How about contacting the captain? Maybe he could do a search."

She'd be embarrassed to be wrong in front of the dean, but not the captain? She read my expression. "You could be the one to raise the question. You're her friend, charged by her mother to keep an eye on her. She didn't meet you for dinner tonight…"

Her reasons were well thought out, which surprised me. There was more behind those Coke-bottle-covered eyes than I'd first thought.

"No, it's too soon," I said, "and there's no evidence that she's actually missing." I could picture Carly's embarrassment if the captain announced an all-out search for her and she was merely having an all-night yak-fest with her girlfriends. "Let's start with Ricki. I would hope she counted noses when the excursion folks came back onboard."

I took the lead as we headed out the door. The ship rolled slightly in the swells. I grabbed the railing for balance as we descended the metal staircase, Zoë right behind me. As we stepped onto the lower deck, the wind, still balmy and warm even at this time of night, whistled past my ears. A chain clanked against the side of a lifeboat that hung over the side of the ship.

We were alone on the deck. The moon gleamed across the water, turning it into a surrealistic mirrorlike surface. I shivered and moved away from the railing.

We had almost reached Ricki's stateroom when I heard a small cry. I turned to Zoë.

She had stopped dead still. Her face looked paler than ever in the moonlight. Her hand shaking, she pointed to a small pool a few yards away. It had once been a decompression pool for deep-sea divers. When Global Sea Adventures purchased and refurbished the ship, they turned the pool into a dipping pool, just for cooling off when passengers wanted to sunbathe.

At first glance, nothing seemed amiss. Then I saw what Zoë had seen in the moonlight.

A body floated facedown in the pool.

THREE

Before we had taken a half dozen hurried steps toward the pool, two crew members raced from the bridge, shouted, and plunged into the pool. In the same instant the captain slammed through a doorway on the far side of the pool. The first mate followed on his heels, the hotel manager was next, then Ricki and her husband, Gregory. Trailing after the others was Dr. Baptiste. A few steps behind him came the white-bearded Dean Williams himself. They all huddled together, speaking in hushed voices, their faces white in the moonlight. I hurried toward the group, Zoë on my heels.

She whispered, "Who is it? Surely it can't be—"

I spun around, glowering. "Don't even think it. And certainly don't say what you're thinking." It wasn't Carly; it couldn't be. My trickle of fear was swelling to a torrent in response to the girl's apprehension.

I moved closer to Ricki. "Who is it? Do they know?"

Ricki turned to me, glanced at Zoë who was sniffling loudly, then shifted her gaze back to mine. She shook her head. "The captain has radioed for instructions from headquarters in Nassau. I heard him say that deaths onboard ship can be a nightmare. He needs to find out who has jurisdiction. Nassau will want to play it down for obvious reasons."

"Bad publicity?"

She nodded. "He may just want to wash his hands of the whole thing—act like it never happened."

"Shouldn't the Costa Rican authorities be involved?"

"Depends on whether we're within territorial waters. And then there's Canada, who's in charge of the day-to-day operations of this ship." She shrugged. "It gets messy."

I knew the United States traditionally claimed twenty-four nautical miles from its shores as territorial waters and that the UN had sponsored the Law of the Sea Treaty, which gave all sea-bordering nations territorial waters of twelve nautical miles. But I had no clue how fast we had been traveling when we left Parisima or whether our heading had kept us within Costa Rican territorial waters. I had also discovered in my research that although Global Sea Adventures was a Canadian company, its fleet of ships—including the *Sun Spirit*—was registered in Nassau, the location of its headquarters. But I had no idea as to the jurisdiction involved here.

The ship's running lights were on now, and I watched the men trying to pull the body from the pool. As they lifted the body to the surface, I could see that the figure was slight, wearing clothing appropriate for either gender—khaki bermuda shorts, tank top, Velcro sandals. In the dark, the hair—short and of an indistinguishable color—could also have been that of a man or a woman. I tried to remember what Carly had been wearing when I last saw her, but nothing came to me.

Two men knelt beside the body and began CPR, their backs to us. I still couldn't make out the identity of the victim. A man I recognized as the ship's doctor hurried toward the group and knelt beside the others.

I commanded my fears to hush their ugly voices and turned to Ricki. "We were on our way to your cabin to ask about Carly Lowe—find out if she's safely back onboard. I was with your husband's group this afternoon. I saw her briefly when we got to town, then I lost track of her. I assumed she was with your group."

Ricki frowned and shook her head. "She had signed up to be with me, but she disappeared by the time we got to the rain forest." She paused. "That's not unusual when we have college students along. Many like to seek out their own adventures. We treat them like the adults they're supposed to be. I've made it clear they're responsible for getting themselves back onboard before we sail."

So she doesn't count noses. I didn't bother to hide my irritation.

Her husband, obviously eavesdropping, stepped up. "If she missed the ship, she'll catch us by the time we get to the spa this afternoon. Kids these days are resourceful. I wouldn't be too worried." He paused. "You've heard about canal travel on the coast?"

I nodded. Gutsy, brainy Carly. More resourceful than most, my head said. My heart didn't agree.

"We've done these spring-break cruises more than once. Believe me, when kids miss the ship, they take to the Canal de Tortuguero. Taxi skiffs travel between villages several times a day. She'll probably get to Playa Negra before we do." He shrugged. "Though there's also the possibility she's onboard, just busy elsewhere, if you know what I mean."

I did, and I didn't like the implication.

I focused my attention on the men still laboring over the body by the pool. After a few more minutes, they stood and backed away. We now had a clear view of the body.

The body was ashen and a substance, dark and bloody, trickled from the man's lips and pooled on the deck below his head. I turned away, feeling sick.

"I think it's Harry Easton," Gregory said. Frowning, he swept the palm of his hand into his receding hairline. "He's from San Francisco. Nice guy."

I vaguely remembered seeing him around mostly hanging out with the students. The first day out, I had assumed he was one of the professors. "Did he have anyone with him? A wife?"

Gregory shook his head. "I talked with him a few times, but he didn't ever seem to relax. Pretty uptight. Made me wonder if he was here on doctor's orders or something. You know, maybe a forced vacation."

The attention of the captain and crew was fixed on something the doctor was saying. I sidled closer, listening intently. Zoë, sniffling, started to follow me. I held up my hand and gave her a stern shake of the head. She backed away.

The doctor's voice droned quietly. I've been blessed with sharp hearing, which, I must admit, is disconcerting to people who think they need to shout at anyone over sixty. Even from several yards away, I could hear every intonation as he spoke, even the click of the doctor's ill-fitting teeth. Dr. Mortimer-Beldon is older than I am by a pinch. Or two.

We'd had breakfast together the first morning out, and he told me he had the greatest job ever for a widower: a free cruise anywhere in the world in exchange for treating a few passengers suffering from bee stings and seasickness. He'd also waggled his eyebrows and asked if we might take a moonlight stroll together sometime. I'd stared at him, gaping, too dumbfounded to utter a word. He finally winked, squeezed my hand, and said he'd be in touch later. He'd obviously misunderstood and thought I was tongue-tied because of his unexpected—and "welcome"—attention. I'd steered clear since.

"I suspect he had a heart attack," he was saying to the captain. "The man was out of shape, short of breath the last couple of days. He hadn't been feeling well, and I recommended he get more exercise. I'd say he was probably down here for a late-night swim, fell in before he got his clothes off, became disoriented. The fear got him. And likely, the strenuous activity just getting out of the pool got the old ticker out of rhythm." He tapped his chest. "Sadly, it took him before he could call for help."

"The blood," I said, stepping forward. "What about the blood?" I glanced at the body and felt my stomach quiver.

Dr. Mortimer-Beldon gave me a faux smile—half arrogant, half pleased to play the role of the expert. "Likely caused from a burst blood vessel in his esophagus. Maybe from the stress of trying to reach the side of the pool while dealing with the chest pain. Might have been from, uh"—he glanced at the crew members who had administered CPR—"overzealous efforts to revive him."

Dr. Baptiste stood off to one side, silently, ever the gentleman. He didn't overstep the bounds of professional courtesy and offer his expert opinion, either to agree or disagree.

A jewel-like flicker near the body caught my eye. I slipped around the huddle of crew and passengers who were still firing questions at the doctor. I was about to suggest an autopsy be performed but stopped before the first word left my mouth. I didn't want to draw attention to myself. Not yet. First I wanted to take a closer look at the strange yet familiar object by the victim's right hand.

I ignored my arthritic knees and stooped beside the body.

I felt someone watching me and looked up to meet Ricki's curious gaze. I motioned her over. A moment later she knelt opposite me. "You seem to recognize this," she said.

"My late husband was a butterfly hobbyist. He didn't collect them; thought it was too cruel to kill such magnificent creatures and stick pins through them. But he had books scattered around the house on the delicate little creatures."

"Have you seen one of these before?"

"It's a blue morpho." I tried to remember other characteristics beyond the unique color and size. Nothing came to me. I always figured that only so much information could be packed into my brain. Not much room left for trivia.

Ricki reached for the dead insect and, with the practiced movements of a trained naturalist, cradled it in her hand. "This is a beautiful specimen, nearly perfect." Carefully, she stretched one giant wing outward.

The glittering lights above us caught the iridescent, almost electric blue of the nine-inch wingspan. The wing dazzled and shimmered, its lacy edges trembling in the sea breeze. Unexpectedly, tears welled in my eyes, and not just for the butterfly. "Such a magnificent creature shouldn't die," I said. "Not here, like this." I paused. "How could it have traveled so far over water?"

She gave me the butterfly, and I held it, wondering how it happened to be at the side of the pool where Harry Easton died.

"It may not be as far from home as you think. This one might be an escapee from the preserve. This rare species of morpho is raised there, mostly because of its unique beauty. And its unusual size. The rain forests boast dozens of similar species—eighty altogether."

As Ricki rejoined the huddled group of whispering passengers, I returned the insect to the place where it had died. I stared at it for a moment, something important nagging at the edges of my mind. I couldn't fathom what it was. After a moment I stood and stretched the kink from my back. Surrounding the ship was the ink-black sea. Dead center was a body, a magnet for sleepy-looking passengers, who stood about, speaking in hushed tones.

Interspersed were clusters of students, some yawning, others looking wide-eyed and worried.

Carly wasn't among them.

Knowing the crew had bigger things to deal with than a passenger we weren't sure was missing, we headed back to our staterooms.

"I knew Mr. Easton," Zoë said as we climbed the metal stairs.

"You knew him? How?"

"He'd been talking with me and some of the others."

My antennae went up. "About what?"

She shrugged. "I don't know. Just friendly stuff about school. He said he has daughters in high school. They're not sure about where to go to college. He wanted to know all about Shepparton. That's all."

The antennae retracted. She went up ahead of me, trudging as if the weight of the universe rested on her shoulders.

"He was really cool about the whole fast-track spring-break thing. Wanted to know what else kids do when they're onboard and what clubs they hit when they're in port—that sort of thing."

I sighed as my antennae shot up again. "Why would he want to know something like that?"

"He called it research for his girls. Places to let them go—or not go." She wiped her nose with her shirt-sleeve.

We reached her stateroom door, and she halted in front of it. "It's so sad," she said. "I mean, what will his daughters say when they find out about their d-d-dad?" She pulled off her glasses and buried her face in her hands.

After a moment I gave her a hug. "Maybe we can find out their

address. You can tell them how highly their dad spoke of them." I hesitated. "I'll talk to the captain in the morning. For now, young lady, you
need to first check to see if Carly's back, then get some sleep."

I waited impatiently while she sniffled, wiped her glasses on the hem
of her T-shirt, and gave me a watery smile. Finally, she unlocked her door.

"Thanks, Mrs. MacIver," she said. "This has been a terrible night.
One of the worst I can ever remember." She looked inside, called Carly's
name, and turned back with a shrug.

"She still may be in someone else's cabin," I said and told myself to
believe it.

She gave me a pitiful look and closed the door.

A flash of something in her face reminded me of the Sarah Bernhardt
impression my Janie would adopt for dramatic effect when she was a teen.
My daughter always did love drama, and no matter how mousy Zoë
seemed, I was beginning to suspect that she did too.

On the way back to my stateroom, I turned my thoughts to Harry
Easton. Nothing I had heard about him added up. No matter what Dr.
Mortimer-Beldon said, Harry didn't look out of shape. And from the
questions Zoë said he had asked the students onboard, I doubted the story
about his daughters.

I changed direction midstep and headed back to the pool area for
another look around. Hollis always said I worried too much over niggling,
unimportant details, like a dog worries a bone.

Maybe I was doing it again. All I knew was that I couldn't help myself.
It was the tiny, unimportant detail of the out-of-place butterfly that
nagged at me.

I just didn't know why.

FOUR

B y the time I arrived at the pool, the body had been removed, I assumed to Dr. Mortimer-Beldon's clinic. I didn't want to consider what happened to people when they died onboard a ship this small. The only refrigeration system big enough for a body was in the kitchen. Now that was a tidbit of trivia I could use to liven up my article. I wondered if anyone planned to tell the chef before he arrived to fire up the grills and pour water and pancake mix into the industrial-sized KitchenAid.

The trip to the Sub-Zero for sausages was going to catch his attention, to say the least.

I imagined his expression, then tried out a few headlines, finally settling on "Frozen Find near the Flounder." It didn't help that I was scheduled to tour the kitchen and observe the chef in action in the morning. I only hoped he discovered the body before I stepped foot inside his domain.

The ship's running lights had been turned off, but moonlight still flooded the deck, so I could easily make out details around me. I stooped near where the body had lain. Poolside lounges and chairs were in scattered disarray, hiding whatever might be underneath them. Frowning, I went down on my knees and peered under the deck furniture.

Harry Easton had been too young to keel over from a heart attack, no matter what the ship's doctor had said. I went through a mental list of other reasons he might have been asking about the students' hangouts. Drugs? After all, we were in Central America. That wasn't so far-fetched. Maybe he was a trafficker checking out new sources for transport. What better way than a group of unsuspecting kids on a fast-track, spring-break cruise?

Though I hadn't the slightest evidence this was true, I grew angry as I felt my way around the deck. I didn't know exactly what I was looking for. A syringe maybe, or dust particles from some sort of powder. Even if Easton hadn't been involved in such a trade, it infuriated me to think that thousands more were.

My anger toward the hapless man finally spent by my overactive imagination, I stood up and brushed off my hands. Besides, who did I think I was—Miss Marple? I turned around. Harry Easton probably died from a heart attack just like Doc said.

"Out for an early morning stroll, Mrs. MacIver?" A low voice rumbled from the shadows.

Startled, I squinted into the darkness. My fantasies about some sort of drug deal gone bad made me want to run in the opposite direction. But I stood my ground, knees shaking, and told my heart to slow its off-kilter rhythm.

"I'm sorry." The voice moved closer. "Did I frighten you?"

Finally I could make out the shadowy figure as it moved toward me. "Not at all," I lied. I shaded my eyes against the moon and blinked. "Who is it?"

"Adam Hartsfield."

Adam. I breathed easier. We had spoken a time or two in passing, but I was surprised he remembered my name. I guessed him to be in his sixties. He was handsome in a craggy, lean, Clint Eastwood kind of way. As I watched him walk, I noticed a limp—something I hadn't observed before. Perhaps it was a recent occurrence caused by a nighttime skirmish with a man who ended up dead? I was chilled by the thought and tried to put it out of my mind.

"A lot of excitement tonight." He stared down at the pool.

"Yes. I was out here earlier."

"So was I, but the captain seemed to have everything under control."

"Heart attack, they say." I waited for a reaction, but the man seemed to have about as much emotion in his face as a dead barracuda.

"That's what they say." He sauntered closer to the pool, kicked back a couple of plastic chairs with his sandaled foot, squinted into the water, and shrugged.

"The man's name is Easton," I said. "Harry Easton. From San Francisco, I hear."

Adam glanced up quickly as if about to say something, perhaps to correct me, then seemed to change his mind. "I'm certain the captain will make all the proper phone calls, notify all those who need notifying."

Cold.

"Harry Easton was someone's son, perhaps someone's brother or father, or spouse. He didn't die in a vacuum." I swallowed hard, remembering the "notification" that had been delivered to me. How it had altered my life. Unexpected tears filled my eyes. Without another word, I turned away from Adam and headed back to my stateroom.

At the top of the metal stairs, I turned to see if he was still standing by the pool. But he had disappeared as silently as he had arrived.

❦

I slept fitfully the rest of the night and woke at dawn, my head throbbing from too little sleep. I pulled out my miniature coffee maker, added water, and waited for it to boil while Gus laced around my ankles. The coffee's deep fragrance calmed me as I scooped it into the top section of the pour-through receptacle. I knew from experience that this headache would require at least three strong cups before I would be ready to meet the world.

"Okay, buddy, your turn," I said to Gus. He purred, arched his back, and waved his tail elegantly, acting cute so I would hurry up and feed him. I gave him fresh water and a scoop of sensitive-stomach food. He continued to purr as he ate.

The ship's engines droned on as we moved through the water. The coastline of Playa Negra was even more deserted than that of Parisima. A few scattered huts were visible in the rolling hills and, closer in, a sagging wharf that had seen better days. From the ship's brochure, I knew the *Sun Spirit* would anchor in the harbor, and the passengers would be shuttled to shore in little boats known as tenders. I found it a stretch to believe a five-star resort spa was anywhere in the vicinity. But so far nothing on this cruise matched what was advertised.

I planned to tell the truth about it in my article, from the bucket-of-bolts vessel to the missed ports of call, from the dead body in the pool to my suspicions of drug trafficking. The more I thought about it, the more inspired I became. I would pull no punches. These students were in danger—the thought hit me like a bullet train traveling faster than sound.

Students?

What about Carly? The bullet train slammed into my heart, and I sank into a chair, almost breathless. What if Zoë was right? What if Carly was really missing?

When my kids were still under my roof, I had kept to the old adage that ninety percent of the things you worry about never happen. I'd found it mathematically correct. More or less. And usually working out closer to the 99.9 percent. Of course, there was the time Joey dyed his sister's hair fluorescent orange two days before her first piano recital. Though the box said the dye would wash out in three shampoos and we scrubbed Janie's hair at least a dozen times, she performed "Spinning Wheel" with hair that could have stopped trucks at a hundred feet.

I took a quick shower and pulled on my bermuda shorts, camp shirt, multipocketed vest, high socks, and sensible walking shoes. I would find Carly, and we would laugh over the fright she'd given me.

I stepped to the window to whisper a prayer for a calm spirit, something that would take some doing on God's part in my present state.

Ribbons of gray mist and fog clung to the dark water. The faint drone of a private plane echoed in the distance. I would know that sound anywhere. I squinted through the mist trying to see the plane as it came in closer, then headed toward the rolling hills. Realization dawned. Not all La Vida Pura patrons arrived by sea. Many flew in, of course. If the spa lived up to the description on its website, the runway length could accommodate fixed-wing aircraft or corporate jets.

The little plane, a Cessna, disappeared from sight. I thought of Hollis and turned away from the window. Too often the ache in my heart lurks just below the surface and little triggers—sounds, images—bring a sharp clarity that threatens to double me over with grief. This was one of those moments.

Grimly, I stared into the mirror as I donned my "You Go, Girl!" cap and laced my ponytail through the back opening.

Taking a shaky breath, I sang a few measures of the old Helen Reddy song: "I am woman; hear me roar."

The sound was so pitiful I couldn't help smiling. I tried it again louder. My heart lifted in spite of my worries as I hurried through the door.

I stopped by Zoë and Carly's stateroom, knocked once, then again. No answer. I tried once more before heading downstairs. When I arrived, I hurried toward the dining room, now set up for a breakfast buffet with an array of the usual nondescript fare: scrambled eggs, sausage, bacon, fried potato wedges, and canned fruit. I didn't think it wise to mention to the chef how I thought he could improve his breakfasts. And lunches. And dinners. I was even willing to tie on an apron and help him out. Well, except for the frozen surprise in his Sub-Zero.

Cooking was once my hobby—no, make that my passion. But ever since Hollis died, I hadn't had the heart to put on a dinner party. He had been a chef par excellence. I like to cook, try out new recipes, that sort of thing. But my Hollis, he made a study of it. I'm hoping that by interviewing chefs on my journeys, my passion will reignite. But I'm not holding my breath.

I made a beeline for the hot oatmeal, ladled out a generous scoop, topped it with butter and maple syrup, then headed to a window table. It was still early for most passengers, and the dining area was all but empty. I'm not good company until after I've had my third cup of coffee, so I hoped that no one would bother me.

So much for wishful thinking.

"Ms. MacIver?"

I turned to see a group of Shepparton College students lolling at a table toward the back of the room. Behind them, the early morning mist was rolling back in off the ocean, settling deeper and thicker close to the water, turning the ocean a murky gray green.

Three of the young people I'd interviewed for my article were scattered among the others. A pretty, dark-haired girl leaned forward. I remembered her name was Kate. "Ms. MacIver?" she called again.

I glanced at my oatmeal, worried for a second about how quickly it would cool, then nodded to her as I stole a quick spoonful.

"We need to talk to you," Kate said. "Do you mind?" They were already standing and heading my way. Max Pribble, our dinnertime server, brought up the rear.

I was savoring that first sweet, nutty bite and couldn't answer. "All right," I said after I swallowed.

Kate looked distressed but gave me a slight smile as she sat down next to me. The boys, sloppy as they looked with their baggy pants and untucked shirts, were surprisingly polite. They pulled out two chairs across from me and sat down.

"Did you hear about the dead guy?" This from a baby-faced boy named Price Alexander III.

"Yes, I did."

"He was hanging around us a lot, you know?" Kate's face was pale, and her large green eyes looked frightened. "I've never known anyone who died before? I mean, like, talk to 'em just before they died?" I swallowed an impatient sigh. Every sentence the girl uttered ended in a question mark.

"Yeah, it's weird," Max said. He was thin and tall, a beanpole of a young man. He looked as if he would be a lady-killer when he grew into his feet and hands. "Like one minute he's sitting here talking to us about his kids, like where they're gonna go to school, then he up and dies." His hand trembled as he swept a blond shock of hair away from his forehead. Death has a way of changing even the most self-confident.

I went after another scoop of oatmeal, making sure it was laced with melted butter and syrup. Savored the taste, then washed it down with coffee. I was almost ready to talk to someone other than Gus.

Max leaned toward me, elbows on the table. "You know, you asked me last night if I'd seen Carly?"

"Have you seen her?"

Kate broke in. "She was talking to the dead guy a lot before she got off the ship? You know, Mr. Easton?"

"Before the shore excursion?"

Baby-faced Price slouched back in his chair, his knees propped against the table edge. "We didn't think much about it until the dude died. I mean, it was just another conversation. But we've all been talking just now about how weird it is that the last one we saw the dude talking to was Carly. Then he died."

"And none of us have seen Carly since yesterday." Kate's eyes were wide.

My heart stuttered and threatened to stop. So much for my 99.9 percent theory. "You've asked around?"

Kate nodded. "Nobody's seen her."

"We didn't put it together until just now," Max said. "That she's gone missing and was the last one to talk to the dead guy." He shivered visibly.

"Did anyone overhear their conversation?"

Price and Kate exchanged glances, then looked at me again. "None of us did," Kate said. "But we could see they were arguing."

"Carly has a temper," Price said with a laugh. "Matches her red hair."

Original.

"There was someone else with them?" Kate's lip curled. "Zoë Shire?"

I felt my forehead furrow into a frown. "Zoë?"

"Yeah." Price lolled back in his chair again. "Zoë heard every word."

As if on cue, Zoë hurried through the swinging doors into the dining room. She went straight to the coffee machine without looking to her left or right. I wondered if this was how she always dealt with her peers. Act like they didn't exist so their indifference wouldn't hurt so much.

I glanced longingly at my still-steaming oatmeal, then pushed it aside. I had to catch Zoë before she got away.

"Excuse me," I said to the kids at the table and headed toward Zoë, who was pouring coffee into a paper cup.

"Zoë?" I spoke softly so I wouldn't startle her. When she turned, I could see she'd been crying.

I poured another cup of coffee, number four, one beyond my limit. "Mind if I join you?"

She shrugged one shoulder, slouched over to the condiments table for a sugar packet and a stir stick, then joined me at another of the round plastic tables. She sat across from me with a heavy sigh.

"I take it Carly didn't come back last night."

She shook her head.

I got right to the point. "I just heard that Carly and Easton talked before she went ashore."

She looked up at me, her gray eyes large behind her thick glasses. "I told you, he was talking to everybody." She shrugged again, letting her gaze drift away from me. "I didn't think it mattered."

"Maybe it didn't...until last night. Now it does."

She tore open the packet of sugar, dumped it into her coffee, and stirred.

"I heard they argued."

"It didn't mean anything."

I studied her as she stirred her coffee.

"Yeah, she talked to Mr. Easton just before she left to go onshore. I was there. He told her not to go, like he was playing dad or something. I don't know what she had planned, but what he said really made her mad."

"What exactly did he say when he tried to stop her?" Mr. Easton certainly was full of surprises.

Zoë launched a Scud missile.

"He warned her that things might not be what she thought. That you couldn't trust everyone you met—especially on spring break." She paused. "Isn't that weird? Why spring break? And then he said something else weird."

"What's that?"

"He said she needed to be on hyperalert here—in Costa Rica. That's the word he used. Hyperalert. Carly laughed about it afterward. Called him 'Hyper Daddy on Alert' behind his back."

I took it all in. Could he have been DEA? Killed because he was hot on someone's trail? I was beginning to feel sick. It seemed that Carly was connected somehow, that Harry knew something specific and had tried to warn her. I was more alarmed than ever.

"And you were aware that she was the last person to talk with Easton before he died. Why didn't you mention this last night?"

"I thought the doctor said Mr. Easton died of a heart attack. Why would it mean anything that he talked to Carly?" There was a hint of defiance in her voice, and a glimpse of something I didn't understand flitted across her face. Something dark. Hard. It struck me that I didn't know much about this girl. Parents. Siblings. Background. She was an outsider; that much I knew. Few, if any, friends. Tucked in beside the hard places in her heart, I suspected, might be a longing to be accepted.

"It could just be a coincidence, you know," I said, softening my voice. "Carly missing the ship and Easton dying of a heart attack."

She sniffed. "So you think Carly will show up at our next stop?" That dark place behind her large gray eyes made me suspect she knew more, but the set of her jaw said no amount of prying would get it out of her.

I excused myself and headed to the galley to reschedule my appointment with the chef. I had changed my mind about the tour. The chef looked disgruntled, said that he was too busy to see me anyway and that he doubted another time would work. That's all I needed. A prima-donna chef in a rusting galley with a body in the freezer. Now that I thought about it, maybe he was disgruntled because of his lack of usable freezer space.

I left the galley and hurried toward the bridge to inform Captain Richter about Carly, unzipped vest flapping. When I rounded a corner on deck three, I ran into the man himself.

"Just who I'm looking for," I said, halting in front of him. "One of the students seems to be missing."

The captain barely blinked. His eyes were red rimmed and deep circled, and he smelled of alcohol and mints. "It happens all the time," he said. "Students take off on their own—out from under the supervision of their chaperons. They're big kids, most of them legal adults. I wouldn't worry if I were you."

"You need to have your crew conduct a search."

He rolled his eyes. "If she doesn't show up today, we'll do just that. Now if you'll excuse me—"

"What if her disappearance is connected to Easton's death?"

He blinked. "What do you mean?"

I pulled out my notepad. "Sir, do you mind if I ask you some questions about last night?" I flipped over the cover of the pad and clicked my pen.

"Wha—?" His mouth dropped open in barely disguised irritation. "There's nothing to tell." He looked at his watch. "Besides, I have more important issues awaiting me on the bridge."

"My readers will want to know the details," I said. "If I recommend this cruise, I need to let them know what happens in cases like this." I met his icy blue eyes. "In the event of a passenger's death."

He shot me a hard stare, then threw back his balding head and let out a mirthless laugh. "Recommend this cruise?" He laughed again and tried to brush past me. I stepped in front of him. He sighed heavily, started to move around me, then thought better of it. "Costa Rican authorities removed the body by helicopter earlier this morning. That's all I can tell you."

I must have been dead to the world to have slept through the racket. "Will they perform an autopsy?"

"I suggest, Ms.—"

"MacIver."

"Ms. MacIver, I suggest you put away your notebook and go have breakfast with the rest of the passengers. Have a nice little omelet or doughnut or something, and then get ready for the shore excursion. Today is spa day, you know. You're in for a lovely, relaxing time. Believe me, it will be the highlight of your trip." He gave me a condescending smile. "Leave the unfortunate death of Mr. Easton to those of us who know best how to handle such things." He put his arm under my elbow to propel me toward the stairs leading to deck two.

I didn't budge. Hollis learned a long time ago that nothing could make me dig in my heels faster than an attempt to play the condescension card, the don't-worry-your-poor-little-head approach. My hackles were standing tall as I glared at Captain Richter. "First of all, I've eaten. Second, you didn't answer my question: Is an autopsy planned?"

"I have no idea." He shrugged. "Please, Ms. MacIver, return to the other passengers. Leave the handling of all this to—"

"To those who know what they're doing," I finished for him. I took a few steps away from him, then turned. "You might also want to find out what Harry Easton was really doing on this cruise," I said. "I don't think he was who he led us to believe."

"What do you mean?" The captain looked puzzled, then shook his head and exhaled noisily.

I stared at him, considering whether to tell him what I had surmised. I had no proof that Easton was DEA or involved in any way with Carly's possible disappearance. And if I was right, who was to say Richter himself wasn't involved?

Now I was really going off the deep end. "Just think about it," I said.

I clambered down the metal stairs to the deck below and, leaning stiff-armed against the railing, stared out at the rolling swells. I thought about Carly. If the captain didn't start a search soon, I would knock on every stateroom door myself and examine every inch of the ship from the top of the smokestack to the bottom of the holds.

"Good morning."

I turned to see Adam Hartsfield heading toward me. He was wearing a lightweight jogging suit and earphones plugged into a small piece of electronic equipment in his pocket. The sunlight hit him squarely in the face, and I almost gasped. I knew him from somewhere other than the cruise. Or at least I thought I did.

He came closer, his craggy face guarded. With one hand he removed the earphones; with the other he lifted a paper coffee cup to his lips and took a leisurely drink, watching me. It was as if he knew that I recognized him and was challenging me to figure it out.

In my mind's eye, I could see the grainy face set in newsprint, the sloped shoulders of a man brought down by criminal charges, the defeated look in his eyes. Front-page stuff. Important enough to make the headlines. But the story behind the photos didn't come to me.

He leaned his back against the railing, crossed his feet at the ankles, and studied me. He wore the earphone headset around the back of his neck. "Have you come up with the answers?"

For a split second I thought he meant about his identity. "Oh, you mean about Easton?"

He nodded, then took a swig of coffee. I noticed he liked it black. A silly thing to notice about someone, but I did. I had always teased Hollis about liking a little coffee with his cream and sugar.

"I talked to the captain a few minutes ago, but I couldn't wheedle any information out of him."

"Doesn't surprise me. He's in charge of this ship. The company image is at stake. I'm sure he'll play this close to the vest."

"We're talking about a human life, not how such an event might affect business."

He raised an eyebrow, and I thought I saw a smile. Then he uncrossed his ankles and turned to look out at the ocean. Gulls swooped by, wheeled upward, only to dive again, calling out in mournful cries. A breeze kicked up, and a few wisps of hair blew across my face. I tucked the longer strands behind one ear, still trying to remember what I'd read in the paper about Adam Hartsfield.

"Mozart," I said, causing him to turn and smile. "Cecilia Bartoli."

"You've got good hearing." He reached into his pocket to turn off his MP3 player, or whatever it's called. "And good taste."

"I adore opera—from Mozart to Puccini—especially when Cecilia

Bartoli is performing." I smiled, unwilling to divulge anything more of my eclectic musical tastes, especially my secret passion for old Beatles hits. No one but Hollis knew how I liked to dance around the kitchen while concocting a favorite meal for friends, "Hey Jude" blasting from the stereo. I resisted the urge to hum a few bars of "Yellow Submarine." I had a sudden longing to dance in my kitchen again the way I did before Hollis died. I blinked and turned away.

Adam tossed his empty cup into a trash container a few feet from us, reached for his earphones, and put them back in place. Then he turned toward me, started to say something, but changed his mind.

In that split second, with the sunlight accentuating the craggy shadows of his face, I knew his identity.

With a gasp, I took a step backward.

stood in front of Adam, staring. His eyes narrowed as if he knew what I was thinking. Before I could say a word, the captain approached. It had been less than fifteen minutes since my encounter with Richter. For a split second I wondered if he had news about Carly. But it wasn't me he was after.

"Detective," the captain said.

It didn't matter that the earphones were still in place. Adam's hearing was excellent. At the word, he tensed, and the hand nearest me clenched, its veins becoming visible as he tightened it into a fist.

Detective Adam Hartsfield, San Francisco PD.

I'd put the puzzle pieces together. But somehow, I found no satisfaction in it. Adam had been suspended from duty during an investigation into an episode a few years ago in which he almost killed a man with his bare hands. I remembered reading that the charges were later dropped, but it was rumored he'd made a deal with the department. He took an early retirement. I felt an almost palpable tension radiating from him.

He stared at the captain without speaking.

Captain Richter wasn't intimidated. "I'd like for you to look over some information that just came in from our headquarters. Has to do with Harry Easton."

"You're asking the wrong man." Adam turned to walk away.

I followed him, the words slipping from my mouth before my brain could stop them. "How can you just ignore a plea for help? You know more about this sort of thing than all the rest of us put together."

"This sort of thing?" He laughed. "What sort of thing might that be?" He gave me a cold gaze, shook his head, and kept walking.

"Don't bother," the captain said as Adam disappeared through a doorway. He stared after him with a bitter expression, then he shrugged and turned to leave.

"What did you find out?" I called after him.

His look told me that I was about to get the don't-bother-your-pretty-little-head lecture again, then he stopped and grinned at me. "You don't give up easily, do you?"

I smiled and stepped closer. "Not usually. Actually, not ever."

"Harry Easton was a PI in the Bay Area. I had GSA Nassau run a check on him. He was here on a case."

My heart slammed into my rib cage. "What kind of case?"

"I'm sorry. I'm not at liberty to say."

I glanced around at the milling passengers, some gazing out at the port, others chatting, a foursome playing table tennis just inside the glass doorway. A couple of the college students I'd spoken to earlier, Max and Price, sauntered to the bow, snickering, heads together. Now that we had dropped anchor, a few bright orange kayaks were in the water, students calling to one another as they paddled through the waves. I wondered again if the students, especially Carly, might be involved. I turned back to the captain. "Do you still think that Harry Easton's death was from natural causes?"

The captain let out an audible sigh. "I hope so."

"And if Carly is missing, I have to wonder if there's a connection—just as I mentioned earlier." It chilled me to consider it.

"Who?"

"Her name is Carly Lowe. The missing student."

He looked embarrassed. "Before the Global budget cuts, we had a system. Computerized. Everyone was given a key card to check in and out every time we docked. The kids, being kids, abused it. Forgot or lost their cards, traded them, bullied their way on and off ship, laughing at any security precautions we'd set up. GSA got tired of reissuing the cards and resetting the equipment, and we finally gave up."

"So there's no way of knowing whether a passenger has been left behind?" The lack of security on the cruise ship was appalling.

The captain shrugged. "We try our best to get them to stick together. The buddy system, you know." He looked out at the small port beyond the kayakers. "Believe me, I've done this milk run up and down Central America more than once. College kids are always missing the boat and catching up with us later. You've heard about the—"

"Canal system? Yes, I've heard." I started to turn away, then changed my mind. "You said you heard from Nassau."

"By satellite phone. We've got ship to shore, of course, but we use the satellite when we can get a signal. There's always a good connection here."

"I should call Carly Lowe's mother. Would it be possible to borrow the phone?"

His tone turned condescending again. "Look, Ms.—"

"MacIver." I was getting tired of filling in the blanks.

"Look, Ms. MacIver, why don't you wait until we've done a search? I'll announce it after our morning lecture. After that, we'll see if she made it to Playa Negra by canal boat. Believe me, this sort of thing happens with the students all the time." He gave me a sympathetic look. "No use worrying her mother without reason."

His reasoning was sound. But I found no comfort in his assurances. Besides, I don't take condescension well.

The ship's daily bulletin had announced the previous morning that a lecture by naturalist Ricki Ross would precede our disembarking for the butterfly farm, the morning excursion. Those who had signed up for the overnight side trip to La Vida Pura spa would receive last-minute instructions immediately following Ricki's talk. After a blast of static, Ricki announced over the PA system that her talk would begin in five minutes in the Clipper Lounge just off the dining room.

I ducked into the dining room for a bottle of water to take with me to the adjoining lounge. There, standing near the stacks of bottles, was Jean Baptiste.

He looked up and smiled. "Good morning, Harriet."

He was known for his good rapport with the students. His rapport with a certain female passenger wasn't so bad either. I'd always admired a well-trimmed goatee streaked with silver. I smiled back.

Rumor had it that he had given generous grants to Shepparton College, especially to fund this program, so he was welcomed with open arms whenever he could spare the time to come aboard. He made his home in Costa Rica, so he was a frequent passenger and guest lecturer. Though he was brilliant, he was an easy man to be around.

"So today we say good-bye to the good Dr. Baptiste." I started to tell him I would miss him but changed my mind. I didn't want him to get the wrong idea. A widow has to be careful about this, I'd heard. And the hand-some, charming Jean Baptiste was single. I had an idea that women fell all over him, and I didn't want him to think I was standing in line.

I remembered what Aunt Tildie once said about a fellow inmate, as she called him, at Green Acres Retirement Home. A tall silver-haired wid-ower started bringing her handpicked flowers every morning. She was tickled pink but said she didn't want to find his slippers under her dining-room table.

Flowers were fine, but I, too, wasn't looking for anything permanent. And because of Hollis, I probably never would.

I felt my cheeks warm when Jean interrupted my thoughts. "You make it sound so final. I hope our paths will cross again." He tucked his water bottle into a pocket and gestured for me to accompany him to the lounge. "And how about you? Are you going into town today?"

"I wouldn't miss it."

I briefly considered telling him my suspicions about Easton's PI work, then I thought better of it. I did, however, think he might shed some light on finding Carly. He lived in the area, knew the town officials; maybe he could help me get the word out—providing Carly didn't show up onboard or on a canal boat.

I hesitated before stepping through the open doorway into the Clip-per Lounge. "May I ask you something?" He listened intently as I told him about Carly.

"Carly Lowe? The petite redhead?"

I nodded. "We were supposed to meet for dinner last night, but she didn't show."

He laughed lightly. "You don't think she might have gotten a better offer."

I rolled my eyes. "That's already been mentioned. My self-esteem's taking a nosedive."

He laughed again. "There's the canal—"

"Don't tell me."

He gave me an understanding smile. "It's obviously been mentioned before."

"Half a dozen times, at least. First the canal mode of transportation, then the order not to worry."

"I'm sorry if I sounded flip," he said. "You have every right to worry. I know what it's like to lose a child."

"Oh dear. I'm so sorry."

He swallowed hard and looked away from me. We were still just outside the entrance to the lounge. In the background I heard Ricki tap the mike and say, "Listen up."

I touched Jean's arm. "Was it recent?"

His charm and self-confidence seemed to crumble. "It's only been a couple of years, but it seems like a lifetime. The irony is, Nicolette suffered from chronic myelogenous leukemia, the same cancer I'm working to cure."

"That explains your passion for research."

An inner light seemed to burn deeply in his eyes as he nodded. "I'm so close. So very close."

The irony wasn't lost on me. By the time he finally made that breakthrough, it would be too late for the one cancer victim who probably mattered most in this world to him—his daughter. That fact alone must have threatened to break his heart. If it was true that he was a Nobel Prize contender, his cure—when it happened—would save countless lives. Yet he would probably trade it all just to have his daughter back. I understood that kind of grief.

"Your work has a greater chance of success because of Nicolette."

"I like to think so. I do it for her—and for many others who will some-day benefit from my research."

"I've heard that your research has to do with stem cell transplantation."

He smiled gently, seeming glad to turn the topic to his research. "That's one of the reasons my lab is set up here in Costa Rica. Less government interference."

"The jury's still out on the morality of such research."

His expression turned dark, and sarcasm laced his words. "Due to ignorance in most, if not all, cases. People who make such judgments simply do not know the facts."

"It's a hot-button issue." I thought of the recent debates in the States, the polarization of beliefs. Some people were so passionate about their opinions they seemed ready to kill researchers just to make a point—the same way abortion doctors and nurses were targeted. The other side was just as unyielding. Sometimes violently so. I had always been pretty confident about my opinions on the issue, but I had to ask myself, what if my sons or daughter were dying of cancer or a loved one was suffering from dementia and could be helped by stem cell transplantation? It would give matters a different spin.

Jean's face softened. "I'm sorry," he said. "I get a little overwrought sometimes. Ignorance is the one thing I cannot abide."

"I understand loss," I said. "I haven't lost a child, but I know what it's like to lose someone you love."

"Yes," he said and met my eyes. It was as if he were looking into my soul. "I can see that you understand."

"About Carly," I said. "If she doesn't show up today, is there any way you can help? Perhaps direct me to the proper authorities in Playa Negra?"

"I don't live near town, but I do know the locals. If she disappeared in Parisima, those are the officials we need to contact."

I remembered hearing the students talking about Jean's private island. They were obviously in awe of the man, from his private island, which they had built up to Donald Trump proportions, to his scuba-diving expertise. "I know you're a distance away, but anything you can do will be so appreciated."

"Do you have a photo?"

I shook my head. "I can ask her mother to e-mail one to you—or to the police in Parisima."

"That's a start. They can put out a bulletin up and down the coast."

We turned to enter the lounge, but I touched his arm lightly to stop him. "Thank you," I said simply. "Just talking with you has been a great stress reliever. I really am worried about Carly."

"I'm happy to do what I can."

He stepped aside to let me walk through the doorway. The lounge was full. This was obviously a popular lecture. But only a smattering of students were in attendance, sprawled toward the back of the room, backpacks scattered around them. I couldn't imagine the kids were that interested in butterflies, and I wondered why they were here.

The lecture had already started, and there were no two chairs together. Jean gestured for me to take the first one we spotted. Unfortunately, it was in the back row next to Adam Hartsfield. I was still steaming over his attitude toward the captain. The contrast between Adam and Jean hit me full force. One gave new meaning to the words *honor* and *gentleman*. The other seemed to have rewritten the book on porcupine behavior. I glanced at the porcupine beside me and gritted my teeth as I sat down.

As soon as I had settled into my chair, I leaned toward Adam and whispered, "Why didn't you tell me you knew Harry Easton?"

He stared at me, his eyes cold. "What makes you think I knew him?"

"I saw a flicker of recognition in your eyes."

"Sorry to disappoint you." He turned back to Ricki's lecture.

I stared at his profile, mildly irritated that I liked the strong set of his stubborn jaw. "Aren't you the least bit curious about why he was here, what he was working on?"

He muttered without turning, "I figured he was on vacation. Same as me."

"You're kidding, right?"

"Yeah. Whatever."

"There's this girl, the daughter of a friend…" I explained about Carly, then waited to see if he connected the same dots I had.

He at least had the courtesy to turn to me when he said, "Sorry, I can't help."

"Don't you care? A girl missing. A man dead. What if he was murdered?" My whisper turned into a growling hiss. "What if she were your daughter? And don't you dare tell me that kids miss ships all the time."

"I didn't know Easton personally, so there was no reason to recognize him. Plus, he had an unsavory reputation around law-enforcement circles. He was an expert on cults. Parents from the U.S. and Canada paid him big bucks to find their kids."

Something inside me twisted. The guy had been hired to find missing kids? That blew my theory about Easton to smithereens. And the theory that replaced it chilled me to the bone. "Cults?" I croaked. "I thought they were a thing of the eighties and nineties. I didn't think today's kids got caught up in them."

"They're out there," he whispered. "Cults a generation ago. Now it's gangs, neo-Nazis, paramilitary, that sort of thing. Even girls get caught up in the romance of such idiocy."

"You said Harry had an unsavory reputation. Sounds to me like this was an honorable thing he was doing. Getting kids out of trouble and bringing them home."

Adam's ice blue eyes met mine. "The word was that he was more show than go. Charged exorbitant fees. Made a big production out of plucking kids out of danger, deprogramming them at some five-star resort in the Caribbean, handing them over to Mommy and Daddy—with full media coverage. He liked media attention. Always played the big hero." Disgust laced his voice. "Nine times out of ten, the kids ran back to where he'd found them as soon as Mommy and Daddy weren't around, which was the case most of the time."

Ricki stopped her lecture and looked pointedly at us. I settled back in my seat, Adam's words whirling like a tornado through my brain. A young person disappears. Harry Easton, hunter of missing kids, is hired to find her. She's from a wealthy family; he's getting paid big bucks. Then he's found dead in a swimming pool. Natural causes? Maybe. But what if it wasn't?

And what about Carly? Had she been planning to jump ship all along…to join some fringe group? Was that what her argument with Easton had been about?

I hated to admit it, but it did sound like something she would do. I sat back to let that thought sink in.

"We've got a busy day ahead, folks," Ricki said, "so listen up. First of all, we'll board the tenders—there will be two launched today—and head to shore. Each holds fifty, so there's no need to push and shove when you head to the gangway. There's plenty of room for everyone." She smiled, and several people tittered. "We'll be met by a bus that will take us to the butterfly farm—forty kilometers or so through the most beautiful terrain you'll see on this trip.

"Sometime around sunset, we'll arrive at La Vida Pura. Those who signed up for the spa package will remain at the resort when the rest of us head back to the ship. The bus will return tomorrow evening to pick you up and return you to the ship. Don't forget your spa clothing—bathing suits, yoga togs, warmup suits—and, of course, your paperwork, showing that you're prepaid guests. Everything else will be provided."

Ricki paused as she pulled out a sheet of paper. "Now I'm going to read the names of the prepaid guests who are signed up for the spa. If there are any errors—if you signed up and I don't read your name—raise your hand."

Then she proceeded to read the list, which was surprisingly short. Strange, Adam Hartsfield was listed. So was Harry Easton. Ricki seemed embarrassed as she read his name and corrected herself immediately. I wouldn't have expected either Harry or Adam to be a spa kind of guy. My antennae zoomed high. The only students staying at La Vida Pura were those I had talked to at breakfast—Kate Rivers, Max Pribble, Price Alexander, and Zoë Shire. Also listed were my dinner companions, the Browns, the Doyles, and the Quilps.

Ricki got to the M's but didn't read my name. The image of me in full yoga attire flashed into my head, and I considered letting the error stand. After a moment of arguing with myself, I waggled my fingers halfheartedly.

Ricki noted the correction, then looked out at the crowd. "Any questions before I tell you more about what we'll see at the butterfly farm?"

A hand shot up in the back of the room. When Ricki nodded in that direction, I turned. It was Kate Rivers. She stood and cleared her throat. "Is it safe for us to get off the boat?"

Ricki raised an eyebrow. "Safe? How do you mean?"

"Well, with Mr. Easton dying and all? It just makes me wonder…"

"Wonder what?"

Kate was picking up speed. "It occurs to me that we might have a murder on our hands? And if that's the case, no one should be allowed to get off the ship. The perp might still be onboard."

The perp? She sounded like she was trying out for a part on *CSI*. Ricki must have thought so too. She leaned toward the microphone. "Whoa. You're jumping to some pretty serious conclusions."

Kate shrugged and sat down. Price gave her a high-five for her performance, and she grinned.

That was when Captain Richter strode to the podium, tapped the microphone, and cleared his throat.

"I want to assure you all that we are investigating Mr. Easton's death. As you have probably heard, the ship's doctor judged that he died from natural causes. We have no evidence to believe otherwise. None of you is in any danger. But this brings me to another point..."

He spent five minutes reviewing safety procedures—the need to watch out for one another, to travel in groups, and to keep an eye out for unsavory characters who might be lurking about.

Several students snickered at that and called out each other's names as examples of unsavory characters. They had suddenly regressed to junior high. I knew the symptoms; I'd seen it before.

"Another item of possible concern," Richter said, "is the whereabouts of Carly Lowe."

The students fell silent.

"Members of my crew are currently inspecting the ship to see if she is onboard, though at this time my bet is that she missed the ship in Parisima. Just as many others before her have done, she'll no doubt catch up with us via canal boat. But I wanted to take this opportunity to ask you if you've seen Carly since the shore excursion yesterday."

No one spoke up.

Richter glanced at me and shrugged. "Seems not," he said, looking toward the students again. "But do us all a favor, okay? Watch for her in town. She knows our itinerary and will probably show up sometime today. According to your dean and others, she's a smart young woman and can take care of herself." He scanned the room. "Got it?"

There were murmurs of agreement, and he left the lectern to Ricki.

"Now, let's get back to what we'll see in the tropical rain forest," Ricki said as she pulled out a chart.

As soon as the lecture concluded, I headed for my stateroom at a trot, put enough food and water in the feeders to last Gus for two days, and added fresh sand to the litter box. Before I slathered on sunscreen, I adjusted my ball cap, picked up Gus and rubbed my face against his whiskered jowl. His innards rumbled into a purr. "Hey, bud, you be good while I'm gone, you hear?"

I thought he did, but then you never know with cats. He squirmed from my arms and hopped down and turned around until he found just the right spot to face me in a classic sphinx pose, his big yellow eyes unblinking. His tabby markings were distinctive—gray, black, and white with touches of rust. He sported a black necklace that looked like it held a half star in place at the center of his white throat and face stripes that included Elizabeth-Taylor-as-Cleopatra eyeliner.

"You know I'll be back, bud. Meanwhile, you're on bug patrol." I blinked back a sting of tears. Hollis had said the same thing to Gus that last morning.

A half hour later I headed to the bridge for an update on the search for Carly, only to hear the disappointing news that the search hadn't turned up a trace of her. She simply wasn't onboard.

Fighting off my concern, I trudged toward the gangway on deck one, amidships. Zoë appeared at the bottom of the stairs as I descended and looked up as if she was waiting for me. She was dressed in ratty jeans, a T-shirt, and flip-flops. Her hair was pulled back in a tight ponytail, and a frayed backpack sagged from her shoulders.

"Shouldn't you wear sturdier shoes for this outing?" I pictured insects the size of armadillos drawing a bead on those bare little toes.

A hint of a smile lit her eyes. She seemed to appreciate someone caring. "It's all I brought. I hadn't planned to get off the ship that much." She brightened slightly. "Besides, this is the tropics. I thought these would be fine." She looked down at the worn rubber thongs.

I sighed. "Just watch out for bugs."

She frowned. "I put on bug spray. They won't bother me."

I drew her to one side before joining the knot of passengers stuck at a standstill on the gangway. Up ahead a crew member was helping them, one at a time, into a mustard yellow tender. Some passengers had already boarded and rounded a little spiral staircase and were sitting on the open-air top deck.

"Hey, Zoë," I said. "Did Carly ever mention an interest in paramilitary groups…or fringe groups of any kind? Religious cults, anything like that?"

She studied me for a few seconds, her expression blank. "The only group I can see Carly joining would be an excursion to a Kate Spade factory outlet."

I couldn't help smiling. "You know her well."

She didn't smile with me. "I don't know her at all." There was sarcasm in her voice.

"Seriously," I said, "was there any hint that she planned to leave the ship on purpose?"

She shook her head, then surprised me by touching my hand. "I'm being too hard on Carly with the Kate Spade thing. You're right. She's the type to take off on a whim—maybe for a romantic encounter of some kind. Or for a guy. Maybe for some exotically romantic group." She gave me a rare smile. "If the uniform is stylish enough, I could see her joining a weird paramilitary group. She once told me she'd love to be on the cover of *Women & Guns.*"

Women & Guns? Carly? I mulled this over while we stood in line to board the tender. If she was involved in some such a thing, I only hoped that she would come to her senses before we left Playa Negra. I wanted to see her literally leap off that canal boat.

As soon as I was helped aboard, I headed to the top deck. Zoë shadowed me every step of the way. I went to a narrow metal bench near the railing-encircled bow. Zoë scooted in beside me on my left. I looked across the deck and saw Adam between two chatty women. One was Adele Quilp. He wore a pained expression.

He caught my eye and grinned. The chink in his tough-guy armor surprised me. I smiled back.

The pilot revved the little craft's engines, turned in a slow circle, then headed to shore. As we drew closer to land, I noticed a surprising number of small yachts anchored among the dilapidated fishing vessels. One supersize yacht, a gleaming white motored craft, towered above the others. Across its stern, elegant scrolled lettering spelled out *Sea Wolf.* It flew an American flag.

Even after we chugged by, I craned to see more. Adam stood and sauntered toward me, grabbing the railing to keep his balance. He fixed his gaze on the magnificent ship. "I'd say it's about a hundred footer, runs at speeds up to twenty-five knots, has a crew of twelve or so, maybe a dozen luxurious staterooms, state-of-the-art galley. Gourmet, of course."

The wind riffled his hair, blowing a tuft of it off his forehead. He looked years younger than he had onboard the *Sun Spirit*.

I stood and moved to stand beside him. "You know your yachts."

"Always dreamed of getting one. Never could on a cop's salary."

"She's a beauty."

"If it were me, I'd have chosen a sailer." When I gave him a quizzical look, he explained. "Primarily powered by the wind, but with auxiliary motors in the event you need them. Can't beat the beauty of those towering sails." He squinted at the *Sea Wolf* as we moved away from her. "But then if I were sailing long distances, I'd probably go for the motored yacht." The American flag was fluttering and snapping in the wind. "Whoever owns her traveled a long ways to take the waters at La Vida Pura."

"My thoughts exactly," I said. I wondered if a love of the open seas had prompted Adam to take this adventure cruise. He didn't strike me as the type who would go for a party ship that flitted up and down the Mexican Riviera or for that matter, a luxury liner that sailed the Med. I turned to ask him why he had decided on the *Sun Spirit* cruise, but my attention was diverted as the tender neared a ramshackle building at the end of a sagging wharf.

The captain of our small craft eased back on the throttle, and we glided closer. A crew member on the lower deck lassoed a post and pulled the tender to a standstill. Then he jumped to the wharf and fastened the stern with a second rope. The passengers queued near the gangway and within minutes stepped onto solid ground.

As soon as I was on the wharf, I looked around for Carly.

As if reading my mind, Jean Baptiste appeared at my elbow. "I don't see her."

"I really was hoping she'd be here."

He strode across the wharf to one of the uniformed officers and spoke to him in Spanish. I followed. After their brief conversation, Jean turned to me. "He says the water taxis from the south have been delayed because of canal work. They will resume later today. Or maybe tomorrow." He shrugged. "There is definitely a mañana culture here. I'm sorry."

Zoë stood nearby, watching our exchange, her gray eyes wide. Perhaps because she was an outsider among her peers, she had decided to cling to me. Every time I turned around, she was at my elbow, listening quietly. It was hard not to be annoyed; it was harder still to ignore a young woman without friends.

"Hey, kiddo." I draped my arm around her shoulders and gave her a quick squeeze. "Wanna hang out with me? I could use the company."

She nodded eagerly.

A group of students had gathered as they awaited the tour bus. Jean was standing just to my left. He glanced at Zoë, a slight frown creasing his forehead as his gaze lingered a bit too long on her face. The look she gave him in return seemed almost arrogant.

I was puzzled by the silent exchange and dropped my arm to peer at the girl, wondering if I had been mistaken about what had passed between them. But my thoughts were interrupted when a sleek black car pulled up and stopped at the Playa Negra end of the wharf. It parked immediately behind a white stretch limo.

"Ah, my ride," Jean said. I wondered which car he meant.

"So, Baptiste, you gonna drive to your island?" Max Pribble guffawed and looked around for an audience.

He found one.

Price Alexander sniggered. Kate Rivers giggled. Others joined in. The adults rolled their eyes, except for Adele Quilp, who said, "Hunh." Only Zoë remained silent and aloof, her expression pinched.

Jean laughed with the others. "Just heading to the airport, my friends.

I'll 'drive' home from there. Before I go, I'd like to take this opportunity to thank you for your attentiveness this week. I hope you've enjoyed the lectures and gained knowledge from them as well. The other professors and I have been impressed by the caliber of students this time out. You are incredibly talented, even gifted, people. You can make a difference in this world—through whatever field of science you pursue. We need more people like you with the passion to make things happen, with the desire to remove any obstacles that might block you from achieving your dreams."

The students broke into applause. Although Max, Price, and others in their circle played the empty-headed jocks, I'd seen them poring over their books while we were at sea. I'd also been impressed with the snatches of more serious conversations I'd picked up.

Jean smiled and nodded his thanks. Then he stepped again to my side and steered me slightly away from the group. "If you need to get in touch with me"—he pulled a business card from his jacket pocket—"I'm a phone call away. I can get to the mainland in a matter of hours. Please promise me you'll call tomorrow and let me know about Carly." He wrote a number on the back of the card. "My cell," he said, then handed the card to me.

I tucked it into one of the myriad pockets in my vest and thanked him again. He stepped into the waiting car, nodded to his driver, and was gone. I was pleased the limo wasn't his.

I turned and headed for the waiting bus, Zoë again at my elbow. Just before we boarded, loud voices caught my attention. I looked back to the wharf. A smaller craft had just pulled up alongside the *Sun Spirit* tender, and its captain was shouting for the tender to get out of the way.

It was a curious development. The smaller vessel's captain obviously thought he had priority status. I stepped closer. Adam appeared beside me. "I should have known," he muttered, his focus on the altercation.

"Should have known what?"

"It's the owner of the *Sea Wolf.*"

"The one doing the shouting?"

"Oh no. He leaves that kind of unpleasant detail for others. He's sitting in back."

I moved to one side to get a better view, away from a cluster of *Sun Spirit* passengers lining up to board the bus. Even above their chatter, I could still hear the shouts of the two captains.

Then I spotted him—the multibillionaire whose photograph had dominated all forms of media for the past decade, from the *Wall Street Journal* to *Entertainment Tonight,* from the *Economist* to *People* magazine.

Lorenzo Nolan.

The woman next to him, Elsa Johannsen, was reportedly in his sights as wife number four. I recognized her from the news accounts of the engagement soiree that Nolan had thrown in his Manhattan penthouse, with a guest list that had included the president of the United States, a half dozen influential senators and congressmen, plus European politicians and royals.

Not that I pay much attention to such rubbish. But I do read *People* magazine when I'm getting my roots tinted.

Nolan's small tender had now reached the wharf, and the man himself was moving toward the makeshift gangway, bodyguards nervously scanning the knots of tourists nearby. Elsa wobbled behind him in heels too high to easily navigate the worn, uneven wharf. She was beautiful. Even from this distance I could see her gleaming, sun-streaked hair, pulled into a knot at the base of her neck, and her elegant movements as she stepped onto the wharf. She was every inch the Scandinavian businesswoman I'd read about. Albeit, Scandinavian businesswoman on vacation. She was dressed in a white, gauzy skirt and blouse; a mix of shell-like pastel stones and thin golden chains graced her neck and dangled from her ears. Her transparent sunglasses screamed designer label. She was tall, towering a good two inches over Lorenzo. Now that she was on solid ground, she walked with feline grace. Even without the visual cues of Lorenzo, her fiancé, at her side or the white stretch limo by the wharf, she utterly oozed money and power.

Not wanting to confirm the drenched-in-DEET aura I oozed, I resisted a glance down at the knobby knees just below the hem of my Bermuda shorts, the sturdy walking shoes and knee socks, and the Velcro-pocketed vest that sagged around my middle. The logo ball cap was my crowning glory.

I was still thinking about God's system of distributing genes and dreams when a movement at the back of Nolan's tender caught my attention.

A third member of their party was now being helped to the gangway. A child. In a wheelchair. A heavyset, gray-haired woman, perhaps a nanny or a nurse, hovered nearby as two crew members lifted the chair onto the ramp, then wheeled it toward the waiting Lorenzo and Elsa.

Within a few moments the entire party was whisked into the limo by their attentive bodyguards, and the vehicle glided away, darkened windows shutting out voyeurs like me.

A low whistle escaped Adam's lips. "Now, that was something to see."

"So you think the *Sea Wolf* belongs to Nolan?"

He nodded. "I would bet on it. I should have made the connection when we spotted her."

"What do you mean?" We turned and walked to the bus. The last of the passengers were boarding just ahead of us.

"Nolan owns La Vida Pura."

I stopped dead in my tracks and frowned up at him. "I researched the spa before I left home. That never came up."

"He likes to keep his connection to the place low profile. Big-name world figures fly in and out of here regularly." He stood back as I hoisted myself onto the bottom step of the tour bus, just inside the door. "I think he tries to protect their identities."

The bus was idling with the air conditioning on arctic blast. I shivered as I reached the top step and looked down the aisle. Toward the back, Zoë held up a hand and motioned that she had saved me a seat. I stifled a groan and headed toward her, Adam following. There was an empty seat on the other side of the aisle. He sat down, half-facing me as I settled into my seat.

"He craves media attention," I said, keeping my voice low. "Why should this be any different than the sordid details of his life that he parades before the media in the States?"

"Who?" Zoë asked, leaning in.

I gave her a withering look that I hoped reminded her she shouldn't be eavesdropping, then I turned back to Adam. "Who?" she repeated.

With a sigh I turned to her again. "Didn't you see who just walked by to get into his limo?"

"I guess I wasn't paying attention."

"Lorenzo Nolan."

She stared at me in disbelief. "*The* Lorenzo Nolan?"

"The same."

"What's he doing here?"

If I had a quarter for every time I had to remind my kids not to eavesdrop, I'd have taken ownership of my own yacht long ago. I gave Zoë a hard stare. She got the hint and turned away.

My maternal instincts were starting to bug me. Suddenly I wanted to turn off the mother-of-all-humankind switch, get up, and sit somewhere else. Then I took in Zoë's profile—the Coke-bottle glasses, the stringy hair, and slump of her shoulders—and I stayed right where I was.

When I turned back to Adam to continue our conversation, he was engrossed in something his seat partner was saying.

With a sigh I leaned back in my seat. At the front of the bus—or coach, as these Mercedes-made vehicles are called—Ricki stood and tested the mike. Beside me, Zoë had slouched into what looked suspiciously like a royal pout. I knew the position well. My Janie could have written the ultimate how-to manual on pouting when she was fifteen. Although I suspected that Zoë was at least twenty, she personified the worst of adolescence ninety percent of the time. Again I thought about changing seats.

Ricki tapped on the mike again and the chatting quieted. "I thought it would be good to give you a refresher course on the Garden of Eden we're about to enter," she said, "for it truly is one of the most diverse and spectacular places on the planet. Although Costa Rica lies directly in the tropics, it has twelve distinct ecological zones—from tidal mangroves to dry deciduous forests, from tropical rain forests to subalpine grassland. Cacti grow in the northwest, and in the wetlands, crocodiles bask in the sun."

She grinned. "Bet you didn't know that, did you?" I appreciated her mix of humor and science. The laugh lines at the corners of her eyes said she enjoyed it too.

Beside me, Zoë tensed. "Crocodiles?" she whispered.

"This is a veritable hothouse of biodiversity," Ricki continued. "About five percent of all known species on earth slither, skip, or swoop through the varied habitats, including one-tenth of all birds known to man."

She paused as the driver pulled away from the wharf, then sat down in the seat behind him still holding the mike. After he had driven a few miles out of town, Ricki went on with her refresher course. "This extraordinary biodiversity stems from the fact that Costa Rica is at the juncture of two continents. And over eons, life forms from both have migrated across the narrow land bridge and adapted to the varied terrain and climates. It's no wonder travelers flock here like migrating macaws to see jaguars, quetzals, and three-toed sloths." She laughed and turned off the microphone.

Thankful for the momentary quiet, I closed my eyes, considering God's amazing handiwork in this place. After a moment my thoughts drifted to what I'd witnessed at the port: Lorenzo Nolan and his entourage, his fiancée, and the child in a wheelchair were interesting enough. But nagging thoughts about Adam that had been simmering on the back burner since I ran into him last night suddenly moved from simmer to stage one boil. What was his interest in all this? What was a man doing alone on an adventure cruise? I didn't know whether he was married, and frankly, it didn't matter. Whether he was single or married, this kind of vacation didn't make sense for a man by himself any more than it made sense for Harry Easton.

Who was Adam, and why was he here? The headlines that had screamed accusations against him were fixed in my memory. He had almost killed a man with his bare hands.

I shivered as my thoughts turned even darker.

What about Carly?

My Janie was a world-class screamer. Still is, if the truth be told. Growing up with two brothers—her twin, Jeremy, and her baby brother, Joey—could try the nerves of the most tomboyish of young women. But Janie never got used to the beetles hidden in her bed, the spiders hanging from a silken-strand of web dangled in front of her, or frogs tossed into her shower over the top of the shower curtain. So when Zoë let out her first warbling squeal not more than three minutes after we entered the rain forest, it didn't annoy me as much as it might have.

By Zoë's fifth scream—when Ricki gently placed in her hand the larva of a swallowtail, the *Papilio cresphontes*, that looked forevermore like the head of a viper attached to a stick body—the other passengers were rolling their eyes and moving cautiously away from the young woman. Everyone, that is, except Kate and Price. I suspected their actions had more to do with entertainment than camaraderie. I shot Price a warning glare, remembering how Jeremy and Joey were egged on by Janie's squeals.

Price's expression was one of wide-eyed innocence, which worried me more. He might be a college senior, but I suspected that with his round, freckled baby face and spiked sandy hair, he could get away with murder. Or thought he could.

"And this, ladies and gentlemen," Ricki said, "is the cream owl butterfly, the *Caligo memnon*, whose six-inch wings provide superb camouflage." She gently but firmly held the butterfly in one hand and pulled out one wing with the other, holding it so the underside of the wing faced the group.

I pulled out my miniature field glasses. The passengers, now clustered around Ricki, let out an appreciative sigh. The butterfly suddenly took on the look of an owl. From a distance I wouldn't have known the difference. The upper wings were a pretty blue gray, but the underwings were mottled brown and gray with spots that resembled yellow eyes, complete with black pupils and white dots that for the life of me seemed to reflect sunlight.

"These little guys are usually pretty quiet by day, but when dusk falls they take to the air and flit about the forest in search of rotting fruit." She placed the insect on a nearby leaf. "We're lucky to have seen him."

Ricki brushed off her hands and continued down the path. When she reached a small rope bridge, she stopped and looked back at the group. "Before we cross, I want to tell you more about the swallowtails we will be seeing once we reach the butterfly farm.

"As you know, Costa Rica has some 1,250 species of butterflies—more than in all of Africa, and is home to one in ten of all known species in the world. Most of these winged insects are magnificently beautiful—from the *Riodinidae Calephelis* with their metallic gold wings to the majestic electric-blue morpho, the neon Narcissus of the butterfly world. Which, I might add, isn't really blue. Morphos are brown, but their scales have a complex structure that absorbs all colors of the spectrum except blue, making them appear blue."

She paused. "Truly, folks, if you're here at just the right time, the Costa Rican countryside can look like a storm of dancing sweet peas." She laughed lightly. "You'll have to pardon me if I wax poetic about these creatures from time to time." She leaned against the curved trunk of a giant rubber tree. "But it's the swallowtail I'd like to focus on for a few minutes. Most of us have seen them around the world. Pretty common, right?"

There were nods of agreement. Standing next to me, Kate said something about seeing them in Pacific Grove, near Monterey, California, when she was a child. Price muttered something with a smirk, but before he could go on, Ricki held up a hand to quiet the group.

"One of the most exotic—and uncommon—creatures you'll see at the farm is the *Papilio antimachus*," she said. "That's its rather musical scientific name. It's more commonly known as the *antimachus* swallowtail. Originally from Uganda, they are endangered, so they're being raised here in captivity as part of a worldwide effort to reintroduce them into their native habitat.

"You may wonder why there's so much fuss over this butterfly. For one thing—and you'll see what I'm talking about in a few minutes—with a nine-inch wingspan, it's the world's largest butterfly. Although certain species of the blue morpho give them a run for their money sizewise." A few murmurs of appreciation mixed with the chirps and buzzes of the insect and bird life around us.

Zoë swatted at an insect near her head, then reached down to scratch her ankle and peer at the ground near her foot as if looking for whatever had bitten her. I was sure she wished she'd worn anything but flip-flops.

"It's also the most extremely poisonous butterfly in the world." Ricki paused, letting the information sink in. Then she grinned. "It's true. But again, the blue morpho runs a close second. 'Pretty is' is not necessarily as 'pretty does.' These guys—either one—can cause serious damage to the unsuspecting predator."

"The blue morpho is like the one that was next to Mr. Easton's body." Zoë almost breathed the words.

Adam and I locked gazes for an instant, then he looked away.

The world stood still. I had seen pictures of the beautiful blue morpho in Hollis's books, but I hadn't known of its poisonous qualities. Information hit my brain almost too fast to process: Harry Easton, finder of lost children, dead. One of the world's most poisonous butterflies next to his body. Carly Lowe missing.

All the platitudes I'd been given about her leaving for this reason or that, about her finding her way back to the ship, flitted away like so many swallowtails. Reality settled in full force.

Carly was in danger. I felt it in my bones. The enormity of this realization threatened to suffocate me. I hadn't experienced claustrophobia in years, but I felt its hot breath lurking.

The jungle seemed to close in on me, the towering mahoganies and strangler figs breathing hot, humid air. The dangers that had been flitting at the edges of my mind wrapped around me, a too-real version of boa shoots on giant fig trees. I struggled to breathe.

"I saw it," Zoë said and brought her hand to her mouth. "The blue morpho near his body."

Ricki shook her head. "I know what you're getting at—and I'm sorry to disappoint you—but it would take several of these butterflies to kill a person. And they'd have to be eaten. As far as I could tell, the butterfly near the body was untouched."

I stared at Ricki, my what-if questions refusing to die. And still I struggled to breathe.

She turned to the bridge. "Now listen up, all of you. As soon as you cross the gorge, immediately to your right on the far side, you'll see a secondary footpath. Take it, head to the clearing just a few yards down the path, and wait for the rest of the group. The entrance to the butterfly farm is just beyond the clearing, but we'll all enter together."

I gulped and looked around for something to get my mind off the panic attack that lurked just beyond my consciousness. Off to one side, Adele Quilp glowered at a cluster of students who blocked her view of the bridge. Arms crossed, she tapped her foot and murmured, "Hunh." I pictured a *Jurassic Park*–sized butterfly swooping down to pick her up and felt immensely better.

"I'll stay on this side of the bridge," Ricki said, "until everyone's crossed. We'll proceed one at a time. Spacing is important. Wait in line until I indicate that it's your turn to step onto the bridge. Do not look down—I repeat, do not look down—and hold on to the rope sides with both hands. The bridge is perfectly safe, though it may feel unstable. I've been over this particular bridge dozens of times, and it's quite well made compared to most."

Zoë sidled into line next to me. She was immediately followed by Price and Kate, who was twisting her dark hair high into a clip. Price's baby face had paled somewhat, and he wasn't sporting his usual swagger. Behind them, a cluster of giggling coeds stepped into line, and farther back Adam was sandwiched between the Quilps and the Browns.

I turned back to watch Ricki help the first trekker onto the bridge. The going was tedious, but Ricki was a pro. She knew exactly the mix of banter and serious instruction to put people at ease. Before ten minutes had passed, most of the first group had crossed to the other side.

It was Zoë's turn. Ricki gestured for her to take her place near the bridge. With a visible gulp, the young woman scurried to stand beside Ricki. I started to move forward, but Price touched my arm. "I'd like to go next if it's okay." He was fiddling with his Swiss army knife, a habit I'd noticed over the course of the few days we'd been together. It hadn't struck me as chilling until now. And there was a look on his baby face I didn't trust.

I shook my head. "Actually, I'm ready to go."

But before I could take a step, he'd grabbed Kate's hand and hurried to the bridge, cutting me off.

By now Zoë was taking one trembling step after another, slowly moving toward the middle of the gorge.

"Don't look down!" Price shouted, which of course made Zoë look straight down into the frightening depths below her. Her lips moved as if she was about to scream, but no sound came out.

"You're okay, Zoë," Ricki said quietly, then narrowed her eyes at Price.

The bridge creaked and groaned beneath Zoë's weight. White knuckled, she clung to the ropes on either side. Even from this distance I could hear her asthmatic wheezing. With the damp heat of the jungle closing in on me and insects biting at my ankles, I clamped my lips together impatiently. It was as if my skin itched someplace inside itself, someplace I couldn't reach. It occurred to me that at this nanosecond of time, I could throttle someone just to get to the other side, to get out of this claustrophobic sense of life pressing down on me. As Zoë clung to the rope bridge, Hollis's betrayal slammed into my heart for the millionth time since his death. That bridge was like my life, and I was desperately hanging on. Afraid to look too closely at the past for fear of what I might find. But scared to death to move forward.

When it was his turn, Price stepped up to the bridge and waited until Ricki said it was time to go. He exchanged a triumphant look with Kate, then took a long wobbly step. And another. On his third step—with Zoë still several feet from the far side—he jerked the ropes. The bridge swayed dangerously. He stomped and jerked again.

Zoë let out a howl that could have been heard back on the *Sun Spirit*. In the forest around and above us, monkeys screeched, parrots squawked, and birds of every species cried out and fluttered en masse. The explosion of sound startled Price, who tripped over his Nikes and lost his footing. The bridge tipped precariously to one side, bumping and creaking like it had come to life.

As Zoë dropped to her knees and whimpered, every heartache, every betrayal, every selfish human act I'd ever witnessed seemed to fly at me at once.

I straightened my vest and marched toward Price as if he were that poisonous butterfly, as if he were Hollis. It didn't matter that he was just an overgrown kid picking on a classmate, just like all of them had been doing since the cruise began.

I effectively cut off Ricki's movement toward the bridge. She saw the wisdom of letting me go first and stepped aside. Maybe it was because of the look in my eye. Maybe it was because the bridge couldn't stand up under the weight of three people. Though that was a thought I didn't want to consider.

"Young man, apparently your mama didn't teach you any manners," I said to Price's back. "I've seen quite enough of your disrespect for others. You think you're some rare part of society that can do anything to anyone without consequences. You and your friends set yourselves up as judge and jury. You mentally vote on who's cool and who's not, who to talk to and who to ignore, who to invite into your little social circle and who to shut out. Who to ridicule.

"Well, mister, I've got news for you. If I see you so much as blink at Zoë in the future…" I halted, realizing I'd painted myself into a corner. I wasn't his mother; he wasn't sixteen. I couldn't ground him or take away the keys to his Mercedes convertible.

But the bridge obviously frightened him more than I did. The tendons in his neck were rippling with fear. He stared into the river and trembled. His feet seemed glued to the bridge. I might be as mad as a wet cat over what he'd done to Zoë, but right now I needed him to move. For both our sakes.

I needed him to think about something other than falling into the precipice below. Though it had worked for me, now probably wasn't the time to mention *Jurassic Park*–sized butterflies.

Instead, I growled, "If you ever threaten Zoë again, I'll call the president of Shepparton College, who happens to be a personal friend. You ever pick on anyone again in my hearing, I'll have you out of that school so fast your mama and daddy won't know where to mail your allowance."

Behind me, the other jungle trekkers had fallen silent.

Price still didn't move.

So I squared my shoulders, lifted my chin, pictured Clint Eastwood in *Dirty Harry,* and growled, "Now, get! Get off my bridge."

The boy marched toward Zoë, who had catapulted herself into a crumpled, wheezing lump on a sodden bed of decaying leaves. On the opposite bank, a smattering of applause grew into cheers and louder clapping.

But I took no joy in it. The boy's shoulders were slumped as he skirted Zoë's limp form and moved down the path. I had just humiliated him in front of his peers, which probably hurt his psyche in ways he would not soon forget. And though no one knew it, I had lied. I didn't know the president of Shepparton College from Arnold Schwarzenegger.

I stepped off the far side of the bridge and, kneeling beside Zoë, brushed the girl's hair back from her damp forehead. "You okay?"

Zoë had been crying. "Why did you do it?" She sounded angry.

Incredulous, I asked, "What do you mean?"

"Price. He was just teasing, that's all." Zoë's eyes were watery behind her thick glasses. "It was like I was…finally one of them. That's what they do to each other. I've seen them. If they like you, they tease and joke and do dumb stuff." She covered her face and wept.

I couldn't speak. It was as if the air had been pumped right out of my lungs.

Slowly, I stood, feeling every piercing ache in my arthritic knees. I followed Ricki and the others to the clearing and left Zoë in a sniffling heap.

After we caught up with the others, I kept to myself. To their credit, Price and Kate made an effort to be courteous to Zoë and at the same time kept their distance from me. Zoë, her eyes red-rimmed and watery, held her chin in a lofty way as she tramped along, alone as usual.

We came to the clearing, sunlight filtering through a thinning canopy of tall trees. Several yards ahead, across a savanna of grass and tropical succulents, stood the gated entrance to the butterfly farm.

I edged to the rear of the group, pulled my Nikon 35mm from its case, and made some light adjustments. I hadn't yet entered the digital, computer-friendly, point-and-shoot age. Give me an old-fashioned, solid, weighty Nikon any day.

I lifted the viewfinder to my eye and turned the lens, bringing the entrance gate into focus. I frowned as I read the sign that arched above the gate:

THE BUTTERFLY FARM
PROPERTY OF LA VIDA PURA SPA AND RESORT
ENTRANCE DENIED WITHOUT PERMIT

"It seems our Mr. Nolan has an interest in ecology."

I recognized Adam's voice and looked up from the viewfinder. "It does indeed."

Ricki had circled back to round up some stragglers and now joined us. "So this is also owned by La Vida Pura," I said to her.

She paused. "Oh yes. We're here only because they allow a few tourists each year."

"I thought this was government run."

She shook her head. "Used to be, but the Costa Rican government just didn't have the money to operate it. They have another big farm over near San José, and now all funding goes there. From what I hear, they jumped at the chance to sell this facility when La Vida Pura made the offer. The only stipulation from the government was that so many thousands of tourists must be allowed in per year. They are determined to continue educating the public about endangered species, ecology, and the environment."

"Why would La Vida Pura want a butterfly farm?" I squinted at the sign.

Ricki laughed, shrugging. "Who knows? The funny thing is that locals call the spa the real butterfly farm. Rich people come here expecting a metamorphosis—from ordinary to beautiful, from ill health to vibrant new life."

I lifted my camera to get another shot.

Adam cleared his throat. "I've heard there's a medical clinic associated with La Vida Pura. Is that true?"

I fiddled with the f-stop and took my shot. Then, letting the camera again swing from its strap around my neck, I looked up at him. His eyes were fixed on Ricki, his expression unreadable.

"It may be," she said, "but we won't be visiting that part of the facility."

"Do you think we might get a tour of the whole campus? Perhaps speak to the doctors if there is such a clinic?"

"We've had others in the group ask the same question," she said. "But we're contracted for the spa-resort tour only. I'm sorry."

As we entered the preserve, I felt an odd sense of discomfort similar to that which had swept over me in the rain forest. We were surrounded by mesh enclosures filled with a froth of colorful flying insects. I still had my questions about the deadly swallowtails and blue morphos and wanted to see their enclosures, so I wasn't about to turn around and run. But it was tempting.

"Are you okay?"

I turned as Adam walked toward me. He carried a walking stick, and again, I wondered about the injury that had caused his limp. Had it been connected with the headlines I remembered?

I saw no cruelty in his face this time. Only concern. I drew in a deep breath and shot him a weak smile. "Yeah, I'm great."

"Great?"

I laughed. It felt good. "*Great* might be a stretch. Let's go back to *okay* and settle there."

He fell in beside me as we walked along a dirt path, butterfly enclosures on both sides. Other insects were apparently in the same enclosures, for the buzzing surely didn't come from butterflies. It sounded more like the roar of cicadas at home. I shuddered, an involuntary reaction to stress that seemed to have happened too often in the past couple of days.

"I don't know what happened back there," I said.

"The kid had it coming. Any of us would have done the same thing to get him off Zoë's back. And off that bridge."

"I don't know where all that emotion came from. It seemed to fly out of the trees and land squarely in my heart."

"Gut reaction. I understand."

Equating my flying at Price with his barehanded pummeling of a criminal? That made me feel worse. "And to top it off, Zoë didn't even appreciate my coming to her rescue."

He stopped and looked at me. "That's not why you did it, though, is it?"

I stared at him, wondering how he knew. I shook my head. "There was something about the sweltering rain forest that brought it all back. In a way I was lashing out at the unanswered questions from when Hollis died, I suppose. But it was bigger than that even. I was going after everything from social injustice down to rich bullies like Price Alexander who pick on geeks like Zoë."

He smiled, a rare expression for him. "Geeks are chic these days." I shot him a quizzical look, and he added, "I read that somewhere."

We resumed our walk down the path. A few stragglers from the main group trekked along ahead of us by several yards, and two middle-aged couples were closing in from behind.

I stepped to one side to let them pass and asked Adam, "Did you see the butterfly by Easton's body?"

"It couldn't have had anything to do with his death. For one thing, it doesn't make sense that if Harry Easton was murdered—which we don't know—the killer would have left a calling card."

"They do that, though, don't they?"

"Sometimes. Usually to thumb their noses at the cops. A sort of catch-me-if-you-can taunt and 'Here's a clue to help, you dummies.' If Easton was murdered, it's an international incident, which makes it impersonal. Which authorities would he be taunting? And why?"

"Maybe the killer, or killers, didn't think it was impersonal."

"Still doesn't make sense. One poisonous butterfly when—from what I understand—it would take a multitude of the creatures to cause death. And they would have to be ingested."

"Or the venom injected."

"Even then, the poison would have had to have been in Easton's system for twenty-four hours to bring him down. He would have felt the illness coming on, probably have been in extreme pain, with vomiting, dizziness, and episodes of passing out. Not the sort of thing that would go unnoticed, then hit him after he decided to treat himself to a midnight swim."

"You know a lot about butterfly poisoning."

"I know a lot about death," he said, "but not from the perspective you think."

We came to a fork in the path. A giant swallowtail enclosure, the size of an aviary, rose directly in front of us. Another enclosure filled with blue morphos was to our left; Heliconids and Lepidopteras to the right. Adam took off to the left. The hurried pace of his gait and the set of his shoulders told me our conversation was over. And he didn't want me to follow. He also didn't like what I'd implied.

I adjusted my cap to shade my face, then walked to the giant swallowtail area. I looked up in wonder. Sunlight was filtering in through a stand of giant ficus trees with their otherworldly buttress roots. The trunks were literally covered with newly hatched insects, their wings stretched wide, drying in the sun. Other swallowtails were flitting, almost soaring, on wingspans wider than I had ever seen on a butterfly. Larger than my Pottery Barn sunflower bread plates, they rose toward the sun, away from the dark shadows of the canopy shade. From caterpillar to chrysalis, they had been transformed and were now free to rise with the wind.

I stood there, wanting to cheer as they flashed golden and glorious in the sun.

Then a sign on the mesh enclosure came into focus. I stepped closer. First in Spanish, then in English, the sign listed the species names, the factual information about both the swallowtail and the blue morphos endangered status, and the regions in the world and in Costa Rica where these giant butterflies could be found. But as I read, my concern grew. Everything Adam had told me about their deadly venom was true, down to the minutest detail—though the references to killing by butterfly poison on the sign had to do with nonhuman predators. Adam's information had to do with humans.

How did he know? And more important, why did he know? Why had he taken the time to find out so much about how a man would die by butterfly poison?

I didn't like the answer that came to me.

I started back down the path to catch up with the rest of the *Sun Spirit* trekkers. A movement behind the cream owl butterfly enclosure caught my attention. A flash of cloth made me think it was one of the students. I thought about the captain's admonition to keep together and began to move closer. Then I halted midstep.

Price Alexander stood in the shadows watching me. The look on his face was venomous. The hair on the back of my neck stood on end.

SEVEN

The motor coach pulled slowly through the elaborate gated entrance to the spa. A large guardhouse stood beside the outer gate, and just inside the gate on either side, waterfalls cascaded into reflecting pools. Ferns and wild orchids lined the road, tall bromeliads and palms towering behind them.

At first I could see no man-made structures, only gently rolling hills covered with lush lawns and flowering plants. The coach wound among the hills, beneath a canopy of trees, then into the sunlight again. Then we rounded a final corner, and the bus driver brought the coach to a halt to let the passengers take in their first view of the resort.

A chorused gasp filled the vehicle. Before us lay the most lush setting I could imagine. In the distance the sun was setting over a shadowy range of mountains, and closer in a small lagoon lay alongside a slow-moving river. Buildings seemed to rise from the shores of the lagoon as if placed there by nature. Some were on stilts, rising to nearly the height of the mangrove trees that edged the water. They looked like luxury tree houses. Other buildings, made of stone and sticks, blended with the landscape.

Still others, tucked in among the surrounding hills, were platform tents. The whole setting evoked an atmosphere of peace.

For me, peace lasted all of thirty seconds. That's how long it took me to notice the fencing at the borders of the property—ornate, scrolled iron-work that blended with the soft pastels of the buildings. Every ten to twelve feet for as far as I could see, monitoring devices that looked like cameras with wide, horizontal lenses sat atop the crossbar. The cameras were pointed toward the inside of the compound, not outward as one might expect for security. It was puzzling.

I glanced at Adam, who was again sitting across the aisle from me, and he was staring at a nearby section of the fence. He must have sensed my scrutiny, because he turned, looking perturbed. At my stare, I wondered, or had he noticed the cameras?

Everyone started talking at once. Ricki was besieged with questions, mostly having to do with how those who hadn't signed up for the spa could do so now. I pictured Granny Clampett doing the Club Med thing and for a few minutes argued with myself about raising my hand to give up my spot. But I couldn't. Not now, when I needed to find out why Harry Easton—and Adam Hartsfield—had signed up for this outing.

The driver started down the last half mile or so leading to the resort, crossed a stone bridge, pulled up in front of a building designed with a massive stone motif, and came to a halt. The doors swished open, and the passengers tumbled out.

Ricki instructed those who would be returning to the ship to stretch their legs, use the rest-room facilities inside the reception area, and then return to the motor coach within ten minutes. The rest of us—including the Browns, the Doyles, the Quilps, Adam Hartsfield, Zoë Shire, Price Alexander, Max Pribble, Kate Rivers, and me—were escorted to the reception desk. Ricki handed over our paperwork, including copies of our passports, to a young Costa Rican woman behind the desk. A name tag on her lapel announced her name was Carmen.

Ricki greeted Carmen warmly, the two exchanged a few words in Spanish, then Carmen set about checking us in.

I hadn't thought to request a private room and now chided myself for the oversight. I held my breath as assignments were made. The married couples were easy; they each received private rooms.

Then Price, Max, and Adam Hartsfield were assigned a room that Carmen said was a luxury dormitory. I could see Adam working his jaw in annoyance. Price exchanged a glowering look with Max, who merely shrugged and gave his blond hair a shake.

It didn't take me long to do the math. Only Zoë, Kate, and I remained. I stepped to the counter. "I am a writer and need the work space. I really do require a room to myself."

Carmen looked sympathetic. "Oh dear. I am so sorry. You are Mrs. MacIver, is that correct?"

"Yes."

She stared at the screen. "I am so sorry," she repeated. "We are fully booked." Then, still scrolling down the screen and clicking her mouse, she brightened. "But I see you are in a suite. One of our finest, the pagoda. You will have a room to yourself with a common room between you and Miss Shire and Miss Rivers."

"We're rooming together?" Kate's whine sounded more incredulous than usual.

From the corner of my eye, I saw Zoë turn pale, and Kate exchange a high-eyebrow glance with Price. Strange bedfellows, all. I stifled a smile. A little social discomfort would do them good.

We said our good-byes to the passengers who were returning to the ship. They filed out the spotless glass double doors to the waiting coach. Ricki blew us kisses, bowed with a merry flourish, and said she would see us the following evening. Then she headed through the doors to join the others. I turned back to Carmen who was handing out keys and maps to the members of our group.

The Browns were first in line. Judging from the manners I'd observed in the past few days, I figured it was happenstance rather than a position gained by elbowing and tackling. Although Ed Brown, a tall, broad-shouldered man, looked as though he could elbow his way through anything, whenever he chose to. The Browns signed their registration card and stepped aside to let the Doyles take their place. Barbara Doyle, a delicate, pretty woman with short auburn hair, smiled at Carmen, and said a few words in Spanish. Earlier I had overheard the Doyles and the Browns talking about Barbara's recent stint as a travel agent.

Next, Adam, Price, and Max stepped to the counter. Price's shoulders were in a slump, and he leaned on the wooden surface with a heavy sigh. "Any way to get a room alone?" he asked pointedly. Max lolled against the counter, his grasshopper legs crossed at the ankles. He looked studiously bored.

Carmen gave Price a patient smile. "I'm sorry, sir. We're completely booked."

He shot a glance through the glass just as the bus pulled away from the hotel entrance. With another grunt of a sigh, he signed the registration card, then sauntered to one side while Adam and Max did the same.

A few minutes later, keys, maps, and printed schedules in hand, we exited through the back double doors, also made of inch-thick glass, and stopped on the terraced patio near a massive three-tiered water fountain to orient ourselves to the layout of the compound. The sun had since disappeared behind the mountains to the west, and dusk had fallen. A twinkling of lights dotted the landscape in the distance and, closer in, squat solar-powered lamps illumined the pathway leading from the patio. The balmy air was heavy with fragrant blooms.

Crickets chorused nearby, and from the rain forest down the road, faint nocturnal cries carried on the breeze. Some sounded human. I tried to purge my mind of the thought. No need to let my imagination work more than it already was. The *Jurassic Park* butterfly thing by the rope bridge was quite enough for one day.

Zoë trudged ahead of Kate, and I brought up the rear. No one spoke.

The others in our group had trooped off to their various accommodations, and as the sounds of their voices disappeared into the night, I felt strangely alone. There was something about the atmosphere of the place that was causing my antennae to rise. And it wasn't just the guarded gates and the surveillance cameras.

"There's no one here but us," Zoë pointed out as we headed down the path.

Ah, that was it. I looked around. She was right. The compound seemed oddly empty, especially considering Carmen had said they were booked solid.

"They may be holding yoga sessions or talks on nutrition before dinner," I said, hoping I was right.

"Feels weird," Zoë said in a hushed voice. "Spooky."

"Spooky? As in Halloween?" Kate punctuated her words with a sarcastic sniff.

"Okay, girls," I said a few minutes later. "Here's the place." I held the map to the light and pointed to a bungalow slightly away from the other buildings. Kate looked bored.

We climbed the stairs to the front door, and my mouth dropped open as we stepped inside. The suite was in a class of its own, with a sunken living room, a king-size bed and Jacuzzi bathtub in my room, twin beds in the girls' room, and a Bali-style outdoor shower in their bathroom. A wraparound deck framed the entire bungalow, and come daylight, I knew the views would be spectacular.

Seemingly dumbfounded, Zoë and Kate didn't utter a word as they explored.

"Wow," Kate finally managed several minutes later.

"Wow," Zoë said.

I suspected it was the first time the two had agreed on something since the cruise started.

I stepped out onto the deck and closed the sliding door behind me, leaving the girls to their riveting conversation. Squinting into the deepening dusk, I surveyed the compound, mentally comparing the buildings in front of me to the features on the map we'd been given at the front desk.

I pulled the map from my vest pocket, unfolded it, and held it to the light streaming through the sliding-glass doors. I might have been turned around because we arrived near dusk, but it struck me as odd that the brightly lit building in the distance wasn't on the map.

If I had my bearings right, the bungalow was in a more secluded section of the compound, the least populated side of the resort. I suspected it drew its fair share of writers and artists. Maybe those who simply wanted to be left alone.

I dug into my vest again, this time for my field glasses, lifted them to my eyes, and brought the building into focus. Nothing unusual about it. Only that it was unmarked. It probably housed La Vida Pura's business offices or maybe classrooms. From what I understood, the resort welcomed tours from around the world. Many I'd seen advertised on their website were led by world-renowned yoga instructors and the like.

Or maybe the building was a hangar. I hadn't yet spotted La Vida Pura's landing field, but perhaps it lay farther west. I scanned the terrain with my binoculars but saw nothing that resembled a tower. Or a plane, for that matter.

I scanned back to the building, wondering if it might be the clinic Adam had asked about. Inside the pagoda Zoë and Kate chatted somewhat amiably, or so I hoped, but outside, only the chirp of crickets and the songs of a few night birds could be heard.

I was about to put away the binoculars when another sound drifted toward me on the wind.

A car engine. Coming from the direction of the unidentified building.

Lifting the field glasses back to my eyes, I peered through them.

Seconds later a white stretch limo glided into view. A chauffeur got out first, rounded the vehicle, and opened a side door.

Lorenzo Nolan was the first to exit. When the second man stepped out, I blinked and refocused, not willing to trust my eyes. I waited, but the others in the Nolan entourage I had seen earlier in the day were either absent or staying inside the limo.

The second man who exited the car appeared to be Dr. Jean Baptiste. I blinked and looked again to make sure I'd gotten it right.

I sailed through the buffet line in record time that night, trotted over to Adam Hartsfield, and sat down across from him. "What made you think a clinic might be part of this compound?"

The rest of our group was seated on either end of the long table. Scattered smaller linen-covered tables in the room were empty. Apparently we had arrived too late for the first seating. The wall opposite the buffet was lined with windows, but because darkness had fallen outside, only the in-side lights reflected back at us, creating a lonely, bleak atmosphere within the room.

"Why do you ask?" He seemed more interested in chasing a veggie burger around his plate than in answering my question.

Clint Eastwood looks or not, he was beginning to annoy me. "Do you always answer questions with questions?"

He bit into the pseudoburger and chewed for a moment, looking pained. I didn't blame him. He seemed the type who would rather dive into a charbroiled steak, juicy and rare. Out of nowhere came the image of dining with him at home. Candlelight, Puccini wafting from the stereo, the works. Just as quickly I thought of Aunt Tildie's slippers-under-the-table philosophy and blushed. I didn't even like the man; why would I want to fix him dinner?

"Many health spas in Central America are connected to clinics, some-times run by U.S. doctors. Most Americans can't get healthcare coverage on certain treatments—experimental surgeries, cosmetic, the like. Costs big bucks in the States, so coming here can save them a truckload of money. It was an obvious question to ask, that's all."

"Makes sense, then."

"What does?"

"I saw Lorenzo Nolan's limo pull up to the entrance of a building that's not on the map they gave us."

I watched Adam carefully, gauging his reaction. I didn't trust him. I felt that he was somehow involved with Easton's death and also somehow tied into this place. I just didn't know how or why.

He put down his fork and frowned. "Was the child with him?"

I shrugged. "I didn't see him."

His ice blue eyes hardened. "Why the sudden interest?" He picked up his fork and poked at something that looked like tiny rocks on a bed of steamed spinach. I resisted the urge to tell him couscous was good for him.

"In the clinic or in Lorenzo Nolan?"

"Both."

Adam had succeeded in turning the tables. I'd planned to find out what he knew, and now I was the bug pinned to a board under a magnifying glass. I could feel the intense scrutiny of his gaze.

"It's what I do," I said, putting down my fork. "When presented with a puzzle, I connect the dots." When he looked as if he didn't believe me, I went on. "My digging for details, no matter how insignificant they seem, used to drive my husband to drink—well, not anything that smacked of substance abuse, unless you consider caffeine a—"

"Mrs. MacIver," he said with a sigh. "You don't have to elaborate. I believe you."

"You don't understand," I said. "When I care about people—*especially* when I care about people—and when life's dots don't connect—"

"Life's dots?" There was a tiny quiver at the corner of his mouth.

I nodded. "Every human being has them. Sometimes they get out of whack, disconnect, short out—"

"Short out?" This time he rolled his eyes. And he almost smiled.

"That's where I come in," I said. It was true. Harriet to the rescue— for Hollis when he was alive, for my kids when they were under my roof. For everyone except me. I suddenly didn't want to explain anything more about the dots. I'd already told him more than I'd ever told anyone about my dot ministry. Even Hollis.

We finished our meal in silence.

I scanned the room before excusing myself. Zoë was at the far end of our table, firmly planted between the Browns and the Doyles, looking happier than she had in days. Price, Max, and Kate were at the other end, huddled in private conversation. Off by themselves were Orris and Adele Quilp. Adele was talking; Orris was studying the chandelier above their table.

Before I scooted my chair away from the table, Adam surprised me by gesturing for me to stay. "I have a warning for you." He wiped his mouth with his linen napkin, folded it, and set it beside his plate.

My hair stood on end. "Warning?" I couldn't hold back the sarcasm.

"I suggest you ask for a tour, not just barge into the place."

"Barge into what place?"

"While you're busy connecting dots, you also plan to snoop around. Am I right? Get into places you don't belong? Get into danger you can't get out of?" He leaned forward, his face hard, his eyes cold. "I am warning you, Mrs. MacIver. Stay out of this. Stay out of this deadly game."

The room seemed to hush, except for the unbearable pulsing in my ears brought on by the rush of blood. I gaped at him. "Is that a threat?"

His eyelid twitched, his expression remained hard. "If that's what you want to believe, then yes, it is."

"What do you know?" I kept my voice low, and the words whooshed out in a hiss. "How are you involved in this? Did you kill Easton?"

His eyelid twitched again. "Don't go where you aren't wanted, Mrs. MacIver."

I leaned closer. "What about Carly Lowe? Is she part of this?" It was a stab in the dark, but I had to ask. I expected him to laugh at the ludicrous question, but he didn't.

"That I can't tell you. I'm sorry."

My thought processes screeched to a halt. "What do you mean *can't?*"

He didn't answer.

"You're implying there could be a connection." I narrowed my eyes at him. "Tell me what you know."

At the end of the table, murmurs of conversation continued, interspersed with quiet ripples of laughter, mostly from the Browns and Doyles. The lighthearted banter seemed surrealistic in view of my conversation with Adam.

"You're in over your head."

"What are you talking about? All I'm doing is trying to find the missing daughter of a friend—someone I'm close to and care about. I've asked a few questions, pondered some strange connections, and done nothing to 'get in over my head.' " I paused, feeling my cheeks heat with anger.

"I saw how you reacted today with the kid who tried to scare Zoë. You leaped in without thinking. What if the kid had turned around and dumped you off that bridge? You act first, I suspect, and think about it later." He leaned closer. "What if you do that again? I think you're wound a little too tight, Mrs. MacIver, and should you fly into something bigger than you are, embarrassment will be the least of your worries."

"Those without certain health care coverage, Mr. Hartsfield?"

"You haven't heard a word I've said."

"You said people without coverage for procedures such as experimental and cosmetic surgeries might come to an offshore clinic to save a truckload of money."

"So you were listening."

"You left out something."

"And that would be?"

"Illegal procedures, Mr. Hartsfield. Wouldn't patients also visit these clinics to have illegal procedures performed?"

"If you're talking about doctors who aren't licensed, yes, that happens. Too often, I understand."

I leaned closer. "I'm talking about unethical practices, surgeries and treatments not approved by the FDA or other medical-specialty societies. Performed by either licensed or unlicensed doctors. Who's to stop them?"

Adam studied me without speaking. "That same thing can happen even in our own country. Under wraps, of course. Why would doctors spend the time or money setting something up in Central America when they can set up the same kind of clinic in South Central L.A.?"

"Tit for tat."

"What?"

"Cooperation, Mr. Hartsfield. Or maybe I should say the lack thereof. I sit down and spill what I know; you tell me I'm in danger if I snoop. I take a stab at making a connection between Easton's death and Carly's disappearance, and you send me off McBernie's Point. You owe me."

"McBernie's wha—? Owe you?"

"As in it's your turn to spill the garbanzos."

He surprised me by laughing. "You think I know something about this place that I'm not telling, but I don't. You think I'm somehow involved in something shady—perhaps in Easton's murder, and who knows what else. I'm not. I'm sorry to disappoint you, Mrs. MacIver, but I'm not who you think I am. I have no information to give you."

Criminals can be charming. And he was beginning to charm me. Criminals can be convincing. And he was beginning to convince me. Criminals can be likable. But that was going too far. If he had something likable lurking below the surface, I had yet to find it.

"That's what worries me," I said.

He pushed back his chair and rose. "May I walk you back?"

We left the dining room and headed down the path to the pagoda. The sense of safety I felt with Adam by my side was laced with a vague sense of danger. I wondered if I was wise to be alone with him. Maybe his earlier warning had more to do with himself than with anyone else.

We came to a length of trail darkened by foliage on either side. Palm fronds filtered what artificial light there was, and thin clouds dimmed the light of the nearly full moon.

"You remembered the headlines," he said. "I saw it in your expression."

I nodded, my heart racing. Why had Adam chosen this moment to confront me? No one was around to hear me cry out should I need help.

"I'm not going to deny my wrongdoing. I lost my temper. I deserved to lose my job."

I willed my voice not to shake. It didn't, but my knees were a different matter. They didn't feel connected to my brain. "There's a difference between losing your temper and nearly beating someone to death."

We stopped in the darkness just outside the pagoda. I hadn't turned on the porch light, worried that it would draw all shapes and sizes of flying critters. Now I regretted the decision. A giant flying horned beetle would be easier to handle than the criminal standing in front of me.

I looked up at him. "Why did you do it?"

For a moment I didn't think he was going to answer, then he said, "I'd been called in on a domestic-violence case. Not my usual beat, but we were short-handed that night, so I was assigned the duty. The guy had beaten his wife till she was unrecognizable." His gaze drifted away from mine, and in the light of the moon, I could see the muscles in his lean jaw working. "That was bad enough, but when I saw his kid—just a little guy, probably no more than eight—and what he'd done to him..." He didn't finish the thought. He didn't need to.

"The perp took off while I was checking out his boy. I gave chase. Caught up with him. I maybe would have killed him if I hadn't come to my senses. There was this guy, a PI with a video camera. Caught the whole thing on tape. It led on the evening news and was repeated day after day."

"It was a setup."

"No way to prove it. But I was wrong. I shouldn't have done what I did. End of story."

"When you wrestle with a pig, the pig wins, and you get muddy, Hollis always said."

Adam cocked his head, his eyes bright with interest. "What did you just say?" I repeated it and he laughed. Then he said, "Who is Hollis? I think I like this guy."

I didn't say.

"I'm sorry," he said after a minute. I wondered if he remembered what I had told him at the butterfly farm about my husband's death. I didn't want to talk about it, so I didn't ask.

Sometimes we think no one else fights the same emotional battles we do. There's comfort in knowing we're not alone even as our hearts ache for others, understanding their pain. I wanted to reach for Adam's hand but didn't.

That night as I tucked myself into the huge king-size bed, I realized I still didn't know why Adam Hartsfield was on this cruise, why he had signed up for the spa excursion, or whether I believed his story.

Unable to drift off, I opened *The Big Sleep* and tried to get lost in Raymond Chandler's 1930s Los Angeles. It didn't work. I stared at the bamboo ceiling, my mind aflutter with brilliant but deadly butterflies, the trickle of blood from Easton's ashen lips, the mysterious ex-Detective Hartsfield, and the missing Carly.

I heard Zoë call good-bye to someone outside the pagoda. Seconds later the entry door clicked shut, and after a few padding footfalls, the girls' bedroom door did the same. I had just turned out my light when the front door opened again. This time it was Kate, I assumed. I was right. A moment later she knocked lightly on my door.

"Could we talk a minute?"

With a sigh, I flicked on the light. What was it with these kids and their nocturnal habits? "Of course," I called out, then slipped on my cotton robe and followed her into the adjoining living room.

She tucked one leg underneath herself and sat down across from me. Her usual snooty arrogance seemed to have momentarily disappeared. She was prettier without it. "I just wanted to tell you I'm sorry?"

"Sorry?"

"I was in on what Price did to Zoë? I mean, I didn't realize how dangerous it was to cross that bridge until I got on it?"

"Zoë's the one who needs to forgive you."

"I asked her, and she said it's too late?"

I softened my voice. "She's the queen of drama. I know the type. I've raised kids of my own."

Kate looked relieved. "Do you have any ideas about what I could do for her? Maybe I could buy her a little something just to let her know I'm sorry? I thought you might have some ideas?"

"The best thing you could do is be her friend. She doesn't have anyone."

"She's always been a loner? She had one close friend our freshman year? They roomed together in my apartment complex. They were totally alike. Both geeks, you know?"

"Labels can hurt," I said quietly.

"I'm sorry." Her cheeks flushed, and she looked away.

"What happened to the friendship?"

"The other girl left after our freshman year. She got real sick and needed to live at home, so she transferred to another school."

"It's friendship and acceptance Zoë needs. That's the greatest gift you could give her."

The bedroom door flew open. Zoë stood there glaring at us through her thick glasses. For a moment the room was as still as a morgue.

"I heard every word," she said. "Get this straight. I don't need your sympathy or your charity. And I certainly don't need your friendship." She breathed heavily through her nose as if she was ready to explode or break into sobs. Maybe both. Two bright spots colored her cheeks.

"Zoë," I said, stretching one hand out to her. "It's not what you think…"

"I've got friends," she said. "Just because I don't hang with the imbeciles at Shepparton College doesn't mean I don't have close friends."

Kate stood, looking crestfallen. "I just wanted to apologize for what happened on the bridge, but you're too busy feeling sorry for yourself to listen."

"Feeling sorry for myself? You don't know what it's like to be me. Would you give up being beautiful for one day—how about one hour?—to trade places with me, a lowly, despicable geek?"

Kate looked ready to cry; she didn't answer.

"Like I said before, your apology is too late." Zoë stepped back and slammed the bedroom door. The windows rattled.

"I'm so sorry," Kate said again. "I feel terrible."

"Just be her friend." I paused. "Remember what I said?"

"Queen of drama?"

"You got it." But inside I worried. I had wanted to take Zoë under my wing, and all I'd gotten in return was anger. And since we'd arrived in Playa Negra, her demeanor had worsened. First her reaction to my help at the bridge, now this. She seemed to be pushing us away, daring us to care for her, in spite of who she knew herself to be. Maybe the dank, dripping rain forest had breathed its oppressive vapors on her as well.

Zoë probably had her own demons to battle, and this place had brought the worst of them out from the shadows. That I could understand.

I prayed especially hard for Zoë that night, that she might find peace. God's peace. She was a little girl lost, and I worried about her.

At 3:35 in the morning, I awoke with a start. The pagoda was quiet, but something—or someone—had awakened me. I lay still, listening.

For a moment my heart pounded in fear. Sounds from the distant rain forest—night animals—added to my discomfort. The air was thick, oppressive. Even my sheets were damp.

In the bedroom across the pagoda, someone stirred. Two puffs whooshing from the inhaler in the living room told me it was Zoë. Next I heard the soft pad of footsteps moving toward the front door. It opened, then closed with a dull thud. I sat up, swung my feet to the floor, grabbed my robe, and stepped out on the balcony to see where Zoë was headed.

I thought about the scene at the bridge and her spiteful words to Kate and me. Truth be told, I was still a little upset and perfectly willing to give her the space she seemed to want. She didn't want anyone to care for her, to watch out for her. So why should I traipse into the night—wild animals prowling and who knew what else going on in this place—to watch over someone who was likely to turn on me and chew me out for it? Why should I bother? I should just go back to bed and pray for deliverance from the whole maternal-instinct, caring thing I'd had going on since boarding the *Sun Spirit.*

I moved closer to the railing and peered down. Zoë came around the corner and, without looking up, headed onto the path leading toward the large building I'd been watching earlier. She was almost running, perhaps in fear of what might lurk in the shadows or because she was on her way to meet someone. She made her way along a few twists of pathway, then skirted a stand of date palms, and her shadowy figure disappeared.

I'd raised my own children, given them pieces of my soul throughout the years. I was the quintessential velveteen rabbit, rubbed and worn, but at this moment determined to keep intact whatever fur was left.

I looked after Zoë with nagging worry, fighting to keep my feet from sprinting to the door. Instead, I got back in bed, fluffed my pillow, and with a sigh started counting the lengths of bamboo in the ceiling.

I'd reached eleven when curiosity got the best of me. That and a burning need to explore the grounds while the rest of the compound slept. And, of course, there was that rabbit business. I guess I wasn't ready to keep the rest of my fur after all.

had left my clothes on a nearby wicker chair, planning to nose about the compound before daybreak. As I pulled on my shorts, T-shirt, and baggy vest, I tried not to think about the animals that might also be out roaming. Costa Rica is known to have a healthy population of jaguars. Nocturnal. I shivered as I tied my walking shoes in the dark. Without so much as a glance in the mirror, I put on my "You Go, Girl!" ball cap and pulled my hair into a ponytail through the opening in back.

In four minutes flat I stepped onto the balcony outside my bedroom and scanned the compound. With only starlight and a scattering of safety lights on the various paths, it was difficult to make out images. But in the distance, a slight figure was making her way toward the unmarked building.

It was Zoë. I was sure of it.

I gathered my courage and headed out the door after her, at first determined to coax her back to safety. Then, judging her speed, I realized that she knew where she was headed. It was time to follow.

She wound in and out of my field of vision, behind trees and night-flowering plants, around fountains and waterfalls. Their splashing masked the fall of my footsteps behind her. I hoped. The sounds of water again brought to mind the beasts that might have wandered here from the nearby forests and savannas for a drink. I picked up speed.

Zoë arrived at her obvious destination and seemed to hesitate. She didn't look back, but her movements were jerky as she sidled a few feet one direction, then back, all the while staring up at the now dimly lit windows of the building. I sensed she was nervous, perhaps aware she was being followed. Or worried about what she was attempting. She moved to a large stand of ferns and disappeared.

I faded into the shadows of a canopied tree and waited for her to come out.

Instead of Zoë, though, two armed guards stepped into the night through the heavy doors. One of the guards—a burly man—lit a cigarette, its glow reflecting on his face, and the other, slightly taller, stretched his shoulders as if he'd been sitting a long time.

They spoke to each other in Spanish, then laughed. After a few minutes of conversation, the taller man pointed to the corner of the building and shook his head with a shrug. The larger man dropped his cigarette and squashed it with the tip of his shoe. No smoking on the premises. Even for the staff, I assumed. And these two knew they were being observed; that much was obvious. It was probably part of their job, watching a panel of video-camera screens in some secure room deep in the building's guts. I studied the exterior facade, moving my gaze from the camera behind the guards to other surveillance devices—at least a dozen that I could see—lining the roof.

The building was much larger than I'd thought when I saw it from a distance. It was two stories, with larger, tower-like edifices on each corner rising still higher. With no balconies and no open windows, its design was similar to those in high-rise buildings. Sealed shut.

The guards turned and walked to the front door. One punched in a code on a keypad, and the door swung open. Seconds later it closed with a click. A whirring sound followed. Then a decisive thud shook the ground as a another heavy-sounding metal device on the inside further secured the door.

I stared at the building, looming gray and massive against the starlit sky. Whatever was housed behind those doors must be valuable indeed to La Vida Pura. And to Lorenzo Nolan.

I was torn between finding out what Zoë was up to and getting her back to the safety of the pagoda or taking the risk of entering the building. I decided to take care of Zoë first and sleuthing second. So I skirted the tree I'd been hiding under and, hoping I was out of sight of the cameras, moved silently to the stand of tall ferns she'd ducked into.

"Zoë?" I whispered, stepping closer. "It's okay to come out now." I waited, but there was no answer. "Zoë?"

All that greeted me was silence. "Zoë?" I called again a little louder. "Zoë!"

Still no answering movement or sound.

I crept into the ferns, willing from my mind the image of the three-inch-long rhinoceros beetle. Pulling back the lacy fronds, I peered into the darkness. "Zoë?" The small, dark area in the center of the ferns was empty.

Backing out of the fronds, I batted their tendrils away from my face. Zoë must have slipped away while my attention was fixed on the guards, the building, and its heavy security. I fought a growing sense of annoyance.

I crept around the building, squinting into the darkness and trying to ignore the sounds of the night creatures, the hoots and cries, the fluttering of insect wings as I neared the safety lights. I kept clear of the cameras, at least those I could see. I didn't call out to Zoë, but every few minutes I stopped to listen for voices.

Nothing. No human sound, at least. The other sounds, I didn't want to dwell on.

It took only minutes to completely round the building. I stopped at the entrance, hiding in the shadows where I hoped the cameras couldn't pick up my image. I stared at the heavy door and whispered a quick prayer.

I ducked beneath the surveillance cameras and crept to the entryway. The whirring of movement caught my attention, and I looked up. The camera, apparently sensing motion, was swiveling toward me. I dropped to my knees, heart thudding, and waited for the device to return to its original position.

I had just pulled a miniature screwdriver from my pocket when the camera did its whirring thing again. I tucked and rolled out of its way. Then I held my breath as it whirred away from me.

I peered at the keypad. Any tinkering would undoubtedly set off an alarm somewhere in the innards of the building. I thumped the pad with my screwdriver handle, trying to remember scenes from *Law and Order* that would help me out. Nothing came to me.

I had pathetically little experience breaking and entering, except for the time I smelled smoke and thought Joey was sneaking a cigarette in his room. I jimmied the lock and burst through his door only to find out that he was trying to pop a bag of Orville Redenbacher's over a 500-watt light bulb.

I was about to give up on the present B&E when I heard a sound from the backside of the building. Strangely, it sounded like a dozen trash cans being rolled down a hill. I started forward, then halted with an annoyed sigh.

The camera was grinding toward me again. I wasn't as quick to drop and roll this time, and the security lights blazed on, blinding me. I heard no wailing alarm, maybe because it was silent. I was almost certain I was drawing plenty of attention from security inside. I took off at a dead run, racing around to the back of the building.

I plowed into some ferns and dropped to my knees, panting.

Nothing happened. No guards raced out of the building. No horns or sirens. No searchlights crisscrossed the compound.

I waited in the ferns until my breathing returned to normal, then I slowly pulled back a couple of fronds and peered out.

I stared in disbelief. What appeared to be a dock for truck deliveries was right in front of me. Door wide open. No one in sight. If I hurried, I wouldn't even have to pick a lock.

I wondered how I had missed it when I rounded the building the first time, then remembered the sound I'd heard before diving into the ferns. Not trash cans. It had been a roll-up metal door opening. Slowly I emerged and duck-walked toward the dock.

All was silent now. Even the insects had stopped their cacophony.

I held my breath and climbed up eight steps to a rough wood-planked floor, straightened up, then moved deeper into a dimly lit cavernous room.

I brushed off my shorts and congratulated myself on my first successful B&E.

Then I saw a figure standing dead still in front of me.

NINE

wanted light, dazzling light, to illumine the shape that blocked my way. But the warehouse was dim, and all I heard was the soft, steady sound of breathing. It wasn't mine.

Not one to be kept in the dark too long, I managed to whisper, "Who's there?"

"I thought I warned you off," came the reply.

I didn't know whether to be more frightened than I already was, or relieved. I chose relief. Hollis used to say the enemy you know is always better than the enemy you don't know. I didn't know for sure that Adam was an enemy, but the deck was certainly stacking up that way.

"Adam," I said, still whispering. "What a pleasant surprise."

He slowly limped toward me. "In the flesh."

"What are you doing here?"

"I might ask you the same thing."

"Zoë got up in the middle of the night. I followed her here...well, to the vicinity. She disappeared, and I got worried. Thought she might have come inside." I paused. "And you?"

Silence fell between us. "We may be overheard," he said. "I suggest we get out before we're discovered." Or before I found something he didn't want me to see?

I glanced around but didn't see any surveillance equipment. I shook my head. "Not before I check on Zoë. I need to look around."

"She's not here. This is a clinic, but empty right now. I suspect it's set up for plastic surgery, lipo, that sort of thing, for certain high-rolling clientele."

"I'd like to see it myself." I still didn't trust him.

He gave me an annoyed stare. "I suppose even if I said no, you'd insist."

I smiled. "Especially if you said no."

With a heavy sigh, he motioned for me to follow him, which I did—through a door at the rear of the capacious room, down a long, dark hallway, and into the innards of the building's first floor. The place did remind me of a hospital, stark walls of an undistinguished color, polished linoleum floors, framed prints of flora and fauna—Costa Rican, I presumed—hung between closed office doors.

The room was silent except for the tread of our rubber-soled shoes on the gleaming floor. No white-noise hum of office equipment or fluorescent lights.

Adam led me through a maze of twists and turns until we arrived back at the warehouse entrance. "Satisfied?"

"Not really," I said. "There wasn't anything much to see."

He shot me an "I told you so" look.

We made our way through the dark room to the edge of the dock.

"How'd you get this door open?" I asked as I clambered down the short flight of stairs behind him.

He waited at the base of the stairs and held out his hand to help me to the ground. Gallant. The man was full of surprises. I rested my hand in his and started to smile…until I realized he had no intention of telling me. With a shiver I thought of the black-humor line "If I tell you, I'll have to kill you." I also figured he knew that if he told me, I'd be back to explore on my own before the squawk of the morning's first macaw.

"What were you looking for?" I challenged as soon as we were away from the building.

He stared at me without answering.

I blew out a loud, impatient sigh. "Has anyone ever asked why you can't answer a direct question? Is it a phobia or something?"

He surprised me by laughing.

"Look, there's something going on here that's far from funny. I'm worried sick about Carly. I'm trying to find Zoë. There's the whole business about Easton. Which reminds me, why in the world would he sign up for a health spa? Why did you, for that matter? Why are you here?" I should have zipped my lips, not presented him with the opportunity to give me another nonanswer answer.

This time he surprised me. "Hey, I'm sorry," he said, stepping toward me. "It's better you don't know anything more about me than you already do. Please believe me."

I blinked. His voice was husky, sincere.

"Have you thought of checking your suite?" he said. "Maybe Zoë's back, slipped in while you were…preoccupied."

"You could be right." I paused. "But you still haven't answered my question. About why you're here."

He stopped in the middle of the pathway. Toward the east a pearlescent predawn light had begun to show in the navy sky. I could barely make out Adam's features, but I saw enough to see his seriousness, his concern.

He studied my face for a moment without speaking, then he said,

"My reasons for being here are more important to me than life itself. But I can't say more without endangering you—or anyone I come in contact with."

"So you're staying mum out of a chivalrous sense of protection? Or is it a lack of trust?" I wasn't going to let him off the hook.

"Perhaps a little of both. After all, I really don't know you very well." He did that quiver thing at the corner of his mouth again.

I wanted to believe this was a good man, an honorable man, even though the ugly headlines and grainy photographs were still firmly fixed in my mind.

We reached the pagoda, and I hesitated at the door.

"Do you want me to come in with you?"

I am woman, hear me roar.

I shook my head. "No, I'm fine. I'll see if Zoë is here, then decide what to do after that."

He nodded and started back down the path. I stepped over the threshold, flipped on a light, and blinked in surprise.

The place had been tossed. Or whatever it's called when furniture is overturned, backpacks emptied onto the floor, clothing scattered everywhere. But I was bunking with two fairly immature coeds. Maybe this was their modus operandi. I never put up with such disorder when Janie was at home, but not all mothers make their kids toe the line like I did.

But this looked different. Dangerously different.

I hurried to the girls' bedroom and flipped on the light. Zoë's bed was empty.

So was Kate's.

My first reaction was anger. My kids knew that's how I handled fear. Whenever one of them had done something that scared me to death, I yelped, catapulted over whatever was between them and me to snatch them out of harm's way. Today they laugh. I never thought it was funny. When they have kids, they'll understand. Payback's another word for it.

So when I saw the empty beds, my first thought was that the girls were playing a trick on me, or simply being thoughtless and ignorant of the dangers that might be lurking outside the walls of the pagoda. Maybe they had run off to visit Price and Max, or… I went over the list of where they might be at this hour. It was a short list.

The girls were missing. Period. I'd followed one, only to lose her in the forest of fronds right in front of my nose. Now the other was missing as well.

First Carly Lowe. Then Zoë. Now Kate.

I slumped into the nearest easy chair, letting my racing heart slow, trying not to hyperventilate. "Oh, Lord," I breathed, "this isn't what I signed on for. All I wanted was a little part-time job to pass the time after Hollis's death. Now here I am in a Central American jungle, worrying over three missing girls and a dead PI whose rumored job was searching for girls nabbed by cults."

I drew in a deep breath. There had to be a logical explanation. For all I knew, Carly would show up at the wharf today to board the tender for the trip back to the *Sun Spirit,* and Zoë and Kate, fast friends by now, would barge through the door, laughing about their middle-of-the-night adventures.

Pure fantasy.

Outside, the sky was turning from dark gray to hazy, damp pearl, and a twitter of birdsong from the palms mixed with the rustling of their fronds in the breeze. I glanced at the clock: 4:58. Morning was coming.

And it was time to alert someone. But who? I wondered if any of the

La Vida Pura staff was at the desk this early. I suspected not. It was important to find Price and Max, to see if Kate and Zoë were with them.

I quickly ran a brush through my hair and put on my ball cap again. A quick glance in the dressing-room mirror was something I should have skipped. My wrinkled bermudas looked like I'd slept in them. My drooping vest had seen better days. Even my ball cap looked pitiful.

The air was turning balmy again as dawn approached. I remembered Adam's dormitory suite was an A-frame named Zahur. I pulled my wrinkled map from a vest pocket and located the building just northeast of the reception area.

I trotted along the winding pathway, passing other early morning walkers. I had noticed on the schedule that the first yoga lessons were offered at 5:30, so it didn't surprise me to see I wasn't alone. Some were dressed in white robes; others in designer workout clothes. Most were friendly, smiling as I passed, but silent. I wondered if there was an unwritten rule about not talking before sunrise.

I reached Zahur and tentatively stepped to the door. I was about to knock when I heard Adam's voice behind me.

"Well, this is another surprise," he said.

I turned to watch him approach from the path leading from the reception area. He was dressed as before in lightweight sweats, rather worn, I noticed in the lightening dawn. He carried a paper cup of what I assumed to be coffee in one hand, and a folded newspaper under the opposite arm.

He grinned. "Cost me an arm and a leg to get someone to make a pot of coffee for me. Seems they don't like to serve it before breakfast." He handed me the cup. "You look like you could use a sip."

The coffee soothed my frayed nerves. I didn't bother to tell him his comment was second only to telling a woman she looked tired.

"Something tells me Zoë wasn't there."

I shook my head. "It gets worse. Kate's gone too. And the place is a mess—like someone had quite an altercation there. Have you seen Price or Max since you got back?"

He frowned. "They were both asleep when I left to get coffee." He unlocked his door, then stepped back so I could enter. The interior of the A-frame consisted of a great room, bath, and small kitchenette on one end. Price's bedclothes were rumpled, but his spiked hair was visible at the top of his cotton blanket, just below the padded headboard. In a bed against the opposite wall, Max snored softly.

We exchanged a glance. "I'm worried, Adam," I said when we had stepped outside. "I've let my concerns about Carly go long enough without taking action, and now that these girls are missing—"

He held up a hand. "We really don't know that they are. There may be a perfectly logical explanation. And as for taking action, don't go beating yourself up. There's really been no action to take."

My heart seemed weighted with worries heavier than a ship's anchor. "If Carly doesn't reach the ship on her own today..." I shook my head slowly, unable to complete the thought.

Around us, the spa was coming to life. A gong sounded in the distance. A tour group of what looked like pilgrims from Nepal slowly, gracefully, moved toward a large open-air pagoda on a grassy hillside. A thirty-something couple trotted by in designer workout togs, and a woman in her seventies moved serenely by as if walking to some inner music. Somewhere on the other side of the compound a macaw squawked. It was answered by a flurry of bird calls and flutters in the jacaranda trees overhead.

"Maybe I should have a look at your suite. Did you leave it as you found it?"

"I didn't touch a thing."

We headed down a foliage-lined path to my pagoda. We'd taken only a few steps when Zoë came flying around a clump of low-growing palms. Her eyes were red-rimmed, her thin, sallow face paler than usual. She collapsed onto a nearby iron bench and stared at me. "Where's Kate? Have you seen her?"

"We were hoping she was with you. What's going on?"

Zoë was visibly trembling. "She was gone when I got back…and our room…it's a mess. Have you seen it? Someone's been in there…looking for something."

I exchanged a glance with Adam.

"When you got back from where?" I asked Zoë.

She swallowed hard and let her gaze drift somewhere over my shoulder. "I-I was going to meet somebody. Last night, in the middle of the night."

"Who?"

"Price Alexander," she whispered.

"Price Alexander?" I was incredulous.

She nodded sadly.

"So you went on this walk," Adam said, stepping closer, "and when you returned, Kate was gone. You haven't been too concerned about what she does or doesn't do before this. Why now?"

She pushed up her glasses with her middle finger and nibbled on her lower lip. Not a pretty habit.

The Browns and the Doyles jogged by at a slow clip, huffing labored breaths. "Greetings, y'all," Ed wheezed with a wave. "Beautiful mornin'."

They were decked out in matching workout clothes—the Browns in violet, the Doyles in dark salmon, racing stripes in all the right places. I wasn't sure that Ed and Don were too happy with the colorful hues, but their wives seemed delighted.

"You going to yoga lessons later?" Barbara called out as they passed.

"Not sure. I have to rearrange my sock drawer."

"Do y'all good." Ed grinned at Zoë. "You especially, sugar. You need to put some roses in those cheeks."

When they were gone, I turned again to Zoë. "The last I knew, you two weren't speaking. You and Kate, I mean."

"We talked last night after you went to bed. She said I shouldn't be mad, that you were just trying to help, and that we needed to put aside our differences. Start over again." She shrugged. "I still don't like her, and I'm pretty sure I'm not on her list of favorite people. But she seemed really sorry for what they did yesterday."

I didn't comment.

"Kate said Price wanted to talk to me. To apologize for scaring me on the bridge. He was supposed to meet me at a place where we would have some privacy. She even told me which path to take. I did what she said, but Price wasn't there. I looked around for a while, then finally came back here."

"Why would you believe her?" Adam said. "It was probably another practical joke."

"Maybe I shouldn't have. But she seemed so sincere. Plus, I'd overheard what she said to you about being sorry—I didn't think she'd lie to you. So I believed her." Her eyes teared. "She was asleep when I left the pagoda, but when I got back"—she shuddered—"it looked like she was in a hurry to get out of there...or maybe she'd caught someone breaking in. I can't tell you why, but it scared me. Now I'm worried about her."

"Do you have any idea where Kate might have gone?" Adam seemed to dismiss the idea of foul play. "Did she mention anything, any clue at all, last night when you talked?"

Zoë shook her head.

I figured out where Adam was going with this. Before we went to the resort manager, we needed to make sure Kate hadn't just slipped out to have a good time.

Adam turned to me. "You and Zoë check to make sure she hasn't returned to your suite," he said. "I'll wake the boys, see if they know anything."

We met at the reception area a few minutes later. Price trailed along after Adam, rubbing his eyes. Max looked dazed. "What's the deal?" he mumbled with a yawn.

Zoë glared at Price. "Why weren't you there last night?"

He rubbed his hair, mussing it even more. "Why wasn't I where?" He yawned and scratched his ribs.

"Kate said you wanted to talk to me."

"You're crazy, woman," he said, his eyes watering with another yawn. "I haven't seen Kate since dinner last night. She didn't say anything about you, and I certainly didn't either. Why would I?"

She narrowed her eyes at him. If looks could kill, he would have been dead.

TEN

The La Vida Pura manager was a fresh-faced, healthy-looking man in his forties who sported long, wavy hair tied into a rather thick and brushy ponytail. His eyes were luminous and his expression said he knew something about the world the rest of us could never comprehend. Slight of build and not terribly tall, he was almost a caricature of what I would expect a health-spa-and-resort manager to look like.

He smiled as he walked toward the counter to greet us, introducing himself as Brian Carrington. When he spoke, I guessed he was American, or perhaps Canadian. This job seemed like something an American would go for, though, so I put my money on that. And probably a Minnesotan seeking warmer climes.

"How can I help you?" His tone was pleasant and hushed to the point of making me strain to hear him. And me with perfect hearing

"A young woman who was staying in our suite last night has disappeared."

He tilted his head, a calm expression still fixed in place. "Disappeared?"

Zoë stepped to the counter and began to explain about her middle-of-the-night walk, the invitation that prompted it, and how she thought it was Price who wanted to meet her. She cast a hurt glance his direction. He looked confused with all the commotion this early in the morning.

"I can and will, of course, alert security," Mr. Carrington said. "Let me have the young woman's description."

Zoë and Price provided the details, which the manager wrote down. Max looked bored. When Price had finished, he stepped back and gave me a bitter stare. He was still angry about the episode on the bridge. I hoped my return stare conveyed that he wasn't my favorite person of the morning either. The trick played on Zoë last night had his fingerprints all over it.

"I know it's probably useless to tell you not to worry," Carrington said. "But let us work on this, and you try to enjoy the rest of your day here. Very often these sorts of things resolve themselves."

I ground my teeth. If I heard one more such platitude, I thought I might scream. I stared at him, hard. The Look, my kids called it. "You're right," I said. "It's useless to tell us not to worry. If she hasn't turned up within the next two hours, I want the authorities called."

Still smiling, Carrington said, "I think that's a bit premature, Ms., uh…"

"MacIver," I said without returning his smile. "I'm afraid I must insist, Mr. Carrington. I need a phone, cellular so I can take it to my room for privacy."

"We don't allow guests to bring cell phones to La Vida Pura for obvious reasons," he said. "But I do have one for emergencies." He reached beneath the desk, pulled out a flip-top cell phone, keyed in a code, and handed it to me. "You will be billed for usage, long distance and local."

"Thank you," I said.

"Way to go, Mrs. MacIver," Max said when we'd exited the office. He held up his hand to give me a high-five, but I wasn't in the mood.

I left them standing by the fountain and beelined to my suite. I'd been put off one time too many, and considering the dangers these kids might be facing, I wasn't about to be put off again. I needed a plan. And quick. I would start with a call to Tangi.

When I reached the pagoda, I punched in her number. After eight rings, I got her voice mail. "Hi, Tangi. Your daughter is missing" wasn't the sort of message one leaves on an answering machine. So I disconnected.

Sitting down, I searched my multitude of pockets for Jean Baptiste's business card. If ever there was a need for pulling strings with the local authorities, it was now. It didn't matter that I had some nagging suspicions about him. Finding Carly was more important.

I pulled out a small spiral notepad, two mechanical pencils, a click-down eraser, three BIC pens, my stateroom key, a high-intensity emergency light, nail clippers, four rolls of 35mm film, a canister of DEET (travel size), a tube of sunscreen, a small hairbrush, a pot of lip gloss, a tube of Vaseline, my Swiss army knife, an emergency police whistle, a battery-lighted magnifying glass, and a few other odds and ends.

I couldn't find the card.

My brain had turned to fuzz from too little sleep. I patted the pockets, opening and closing the Velcro strips. Still no card.

Where had I put it?

I sank back into the chair and closed my eyes.

The sun was long past rising, and my stomach was definitely complaining about a lack of food. I was fighting fatigue and a brain-splitting headache, and I was worrying myself sick over this brood of kids. Just when I thought my kid-worrying days were over.

And now I'd misplaced the number that would connect me to the one lifeline I thought I had in this maze of dead ends.

I sighed. "Lord, it's me again. I've muddled it up. My brain's gone into reverse mode, and I need some help here." I started to mention the card and how much I needed that phone number, then I halted in midthought.

Praying to find a business card felt a little peculiar, like I was one of those people I'd heard about who pray for a parking space nearest the entrance to the mall. I was vaguely ashamed and started over.

"Lord, it's Harriet again. What I really need here is your strength, your peace. You know how I take everybody else's burdens on my shoulders? Did it with Hollis. Did it with each of the kids, even after they were out of the nest. I don't think they knew I was praying so hard for them that my knees got calluses.

"I know I'm supposed to lay my burdens down at the foot of the cross, but you know how hard that is for me to do. I know I don't need to bear them alone, but I just can't seem to help myself." I sighed. "I guess you already know that, though, don't you?"

I stood, walked over to the glass door, and looked out at the lush landscape, gleaming jewel-like in the morning sun. A coffee plantation created a darker green hue on the distant hills, fading into a pale tropical sky. I thought about God's mercy, his love. The problem I had, as always, was taking other people's problems on myself, then resenting it because of the burden it represented.

Some people were called to serve God in safe places—at least to me they seemed safe. But recently I was feeling kicked out of my comfortable little nest into a dangerous new world. I wasn't sure I liked it.

"I thought I was done with all this heartache over others, Father," I whispered. "All this pounding the doors of heaven." I sighed heavily. "But I guess the calluses on my knees are going to be permanent."

I started refilling my vest pockets with the items I'd set on the coffee table. I thought about the parking-lot miracles I'd heard about through the years and held my breath, hoping for a tiny miracle of my own. But no business card appeared amid the clutter.

A knock sounded at the door. I rose to answer it.

Adam stood there, leaning against the doorjamb, ankles crossed, and looking a little uncomfortable. He held two dark, fruity muffins on a paper plate. "Can I come in?"

"Of course." I stepped back.

"How about if I have that look around?"

I gestured toward the chaos. "Be my guest."

He placed the muffins on the coffee table between the canister of DEET and the Vaseline. "I'll start with the girls' bedroom."

I followed him through the doorway.

He crossed the room and, frowning, picked up a folded piece of paper from Kate's pillow. "Have you seen this?" He unfolded it and held it to the light.

I walked over to the bed and read the handwritten note over his shoulder:

> To whom it may concern,
>
> Please don't worry about me. I need to get away for a few days.
>
> This wild place is calling me to adventure, something I've always dreamed of. I will rejoin the cruise farther south, maybe take a ride on the Canal de Tortuguero and catch the ship before the cruise is over. Tell my parents not to worry about me.
>
> Kate Rivers

found Jean Baptiste's business card beside the coffee maker. I had no inkling of when I had put it there. My aunt Tildie once mistook a bottle of vanilla extract for a bottle of aspirin and poured it into her hand. I sighed. Jean's card today, a handful of vanilla tomorrow.

"Jean?" I said into the cell phone.

"Yes, this is Dr. Jean Baptiste."

"Jean, this is Harriet MacIver. We met on the ship?"

His voice turned from clinically cool to warm. "Harriet! Of course."

I was alone in the suite. Adam had left to shower and change, but he planned to be back in a half hour to accompany me to the local police station in Playa Negra. I appreciated his willingness to help, but I couldn't rid my mind of the chilling look he'd given me right after we read the note. It was as if he knew something dark and desperate that he wasn't willing to tell me.

"You said to call if I needed you." I crossed my fingers, hoping he was still in Playa Negra. It had been less than twelve hours since I'd seen him emerge from Nolan's limo.

"Yes, yes, Harriet. And I meant it. Have you heard anything about the girl…Carly Lowe?"

"Another of the students disappeared last night. You probably remember her. Kate Rivers."

There was silence on the other end of the line.

"Are you there?"

"Yes, yes, I am. I'm just stunned to hear it. Are you certain she's gone? I mean, could it be a coincidence?"

"She left a note telling us not to worry, but I can't help thinking there's more to it than that." I related Zoë's account of events, then added my own thoughts about the rooms being searched.

"I wish I'd known before I left Playa Negra. I had business there until quite late last night and flew out at dawn."

I instantly felt guilty. If only I'd thought of calling him earlier. "I'm so sorry—" I began.

But he cut me off. "Not a problem. This is important. The weather's clear. I can be there in an hour."

"I hate to pull you away from your work."

"Don't say another word. I'll get there as quickly as I can. Plan to come into town with me; bring photos of the girls if you can get them. We have to move fast."

Relief flooded through me. "Thank you," I whispered.

"Can you meet me at the airport?"

I hesitated as old fears whirled up from the pit of my stomach. Airports, especially those housing private planes, were the settings for my worst nightmares. Finally, I said, "Of course."

"Good. I'll send my driver to pick you up."

"Adam Hartsfield has been helping me out on this. Is it okay if he comes with us?"

Silence. I thought the signal had dropped and was about to ask if Jean was still there when he finally spoke. "I've been looking into Hartsfield's background. Found out some pretty disturbing facts you ought to know about him. I'll fill you in when I see you. Meanwhile, for your own good, you need to stay away from him. He's a dangerous man."

"I know about the charges brought against him, if that's what you're referring to."

"No. I'm talking about something entirely different. Our Mr. Hartsfield, ex-detective, is about to be picked up by Interpol for murder. Please, Harriet, for your own safety, steer clear of the man."

I sat back, trying to make sense of the words. Denial is part of my modus operandi. When hit by sadness, sorrow, or betrayal, I push that emotion to somewhere deep inside my heart, assuming that when it slips out later, it won't hurt so much. The trouble is, the pain is just as bad—and maybe worse—when it does surface. That doesn't keep me from trying, though. Like now.

Unfortunately, my emotional MO didn't kick in this time. I believed every word, even though I didn't want to. I felt sick.

"Gotcha," I said into the phone.

Adam appeared on my doorstep several minutes later. I stared at him, taking in his ice blue eyes, his craggy face, the hard set of his jaw. Criminal? He certainly looked the part. Bitterness and hard times were etched into his face.

He seemed to sense the chill in my demeanor and gave me a quizzical look. A suspicious, knowing look. I willed myself not to shiver visibly.

"I want to go alone," I said. "This is my doing, and I really don't want to get anyone else involved."

He stood his ground, adopting a police officer's stance. Which frightened me even more.

I cleared my throat. "I have this thing I hum to myself. Sometimes."
He waited.

"I am woman, hear me roar."

That twitchy thing happened at the corner of his mouth. If he smiled, it would kill me. I was beginning to enjoy his smile, especially when it was in response to something I said. I couldn't think of him as dangerous and like his smile at the same time. It made no sense.

"Helen Reddy," he said.

I grinned. I couldn't help myself.

"Hey, I'm here if you need me," he said, backing down the walkway. "You go, girl."

I didn't even have on my ball cap. Unexpected tears stung my eyes as he disappeared around a clump of palms.

I took a shower, towel-dried my hair, and fluffed it with my fingers. I had stuffed a lightweight gauzy skirt and pullover top into my backpack the day before. Luckily, they were supposed to look wrinkled. After I put them on and slipped my feet into some sparkly, beachy flip-flops, I glanced in the mirror. My hair looked droopy, so I scooped it up with a clip, leaving a few wispy bangs, added some dangly earrings, and hoped I looked presentable enough to be picked up by Jean's chauffeur.

As I waited for the car, I tried for the third time in an hour to reach Tangi. Her answering machine clicked on. This time, I said, "Hey, Tange. It's me. Harriet. Where are you, girlfriend? I've been trying to get a hold of you. Call me onboard, ship to shore, later tonight. It's important."

An hour later I was seated in a comfortably air-conditioned car, making the short drive to the airport just two miles west of the compound. It was so well hidden from sight I didn't spot the landing strip until we were almost on it.

The Playa Negra airport, if you could call it that, consisted of one large hangar and a scattering of private planes tied down near a grass runway. I'd landed on a grass runway only once. I was at the controls, and Hollis was beside me. We were on a cross-country trip and had stopped to refuel in northern Texas. It was like landing in a cornfield. Bumpy, optically challenging. Frightening.

And that was years before I slid into a serious clinical phobia. That was before I swore I'd die before crawling into the cockpit of a private plane again. That was before Hollis's death.

The closer we came to the airfield, the harder my heart needed to work. I looked down and held my forehead with my hand, unwilling to see the kind of plane I used to fly, the kind Hollis died in.

If I looked up, I was sure I would see the most common of all Cessna models, a red and white 172 Skyhawk. I would cry and likely wouldn't stop. After Hollis's crash I even tried biofeedback training to get over my fears. The therapist said to think of the good times, the joy we took in flying together, instead of the accident. It didn't work then. It wasn't working now.

"Ma'am?" the driver said. "We are here, but Dr. Baptiste has not come in yet." He spoke with an unidentifiable accent. Northern European perhaps.

I met his gaze in the rearview mirror.

"Would you like to wait in the car—or inside?"

"Inside?" I glanced at the hangar, which was closed.

"Dr. Baptiste owns the hangar. He has set up a little waiting area for passengers to relax. A kind of lounge. It is quite comfortable. We have refrigerated soft drinks, coffee, snacks."

"Yes, please. That sounds lovely." I smiled into the mirror.

He drove nearer to the large metal building, got out, and opened my door. We entered a sectioned-off portion of the hangar, air-conditioned and nicely furnished.

"May I fix anything for you? A ginger ale perhaps? Or Coke?"

My stomach was still jumpy, and with the faint acrid smells of airplane fuel, oils, and engines drifting from beyond the partition, it could use some soothing. "Ginger ale, please."

I settled into an easy chair facing away from the window. As I took my drink from the chauffeur, though, I heard the low hum of an incoming aircraft. Curiosity got the best of me, and I turned to watch Jean enter the landing pattern downwind.

He was piloting a private luxury jet. White, it gleamed in the morning sun. Judging by the length, I guessed it to be a seven-seater Citation, which made it easier for me to watch without falling to pieces. I stood to move closer to the window as he turned into base, then a few minutes later into his final approach.

A bright object on the floor near the window caught my attention. I looked down, hesitated, then stooped to pick it up. It was a bracelet.

I had seen it before.

It was distinctive, a unique Brighton design. A leather strap that buckled. In its center was a tiny silver-embossed motif made up of three hearts. Tiny engraved letters in each smooth center spelled the words JOY, HOPE, COURAGE. A small chain linked a quarter-inch solid silver heart in place to the buckle. In its center was the word LOVE.

I closed my fingers around it, held it tightly in my hand, and drew it to my chest, almost afraid to breathe. I had seen the bracelet only twice before: the night my son Joey gave it to Carly—and the day before she disappeared. When she noticed me staring at the bracelet, she'd raised her hand into a fist with a "yes" punch in the air, and winked at me.

I looked out the window in time to see Jean bring the Citation in for a perfect landing. The reverse jets roared, then quieted as the plane slowed. He swung off the runway to the taxiway and headed toward the hangar.

I quickly reached for my handbag, tucked the bracelet inside, and snapped it closed.

Carly had been here. I was sure of it. But why? And how did she get here from Parisima? The canal had been temporarily closed, or so I had been told. Was she brought here against her will? By plane? I watched Jean taxi closer, his face barely visible behind the cockpit glass. Was he a man I could trust? I had thought so. Now I wasn't so sure.

I was still mulling over these unanswerable questions when I heard a section of hangar behind me open with a rattle and a bang. Apparently the chauffeur doubled as a ground pilot. After Jean stepped down the ramp, the chauffeur climbed into the cockpit, and a few minutes later, the Citation disappeared inside the hangar.

Jean strode through the doorway, concern etched on his face. I noticed again his elegant good looks, from his silver-streaked goatee to his Armani loafers. "Has there been any word?"

I shook my head. "Nothing."

He walked to the wet bar and took a soft drink from the refrigerator. "Can I get you anything?"

I held up my ginger ale. "I'm fine, really."

He took a long swig, then joined me in the sitting area. "I'm worried," he said. "There are too many coincidences in all this. I've had some suspicions, but I needed to find out more before I mentioned them to anyone."

We sat down opposite each other. He leaned forward, his expression troubled.

"About Adam Hartsfield," I ventured.

"Yes. And, please, what I'm about to tell you is confidential. I've contacted Interpol, but I haven't said anything to Captain Richter or to the Shepparton staff. Before I leave today, I'll need to go out to the ship and let them know to keep Hartsfield from boarding should he try."

"Wait a minute. What are you talking about?"

"You said you know about the charges against him."

"Yes, yes, of course. But what does that have to do with any of the rest of this?"

"Did he tell you he knew Harry Easton?"

"Adam said he'd never met him, but knew of him—by reputation. A rather unsavory reputation, from what he said."

"He did know Easton, and well. It's true they may never have met formally, but Easton was closely tied to our Adam Hartsfield."

My anxiety meter was hovering to the far right of center. "Go on."

"Easton was on to him, out to prove that the rumors about excessive violence in the force were true, all of them. The night Hartsfield was caught on film, it was Easton behind the camera. He took the video and the stills."

"It could have been a setup," I said, surprising myself by coming to Adam's defense.

"There's more."

I didn't want to hear it. I was feeling sick enough already. I nodded for him to continue.

"There was a big fight between Hartsfield and his wife after his arrest. Because of what had happened with the video, every time he wiped his nose it was news. The man I hired to investigate said this was no different. The wife finally leaves, taking the girl with her. Then there's a knock-down, drag-out custody fight over their teenage daughter."

"What does this have to do with your contacting Interpol—other than Hartsfield possibly being a suspect in the Easton death? Which, I remind you, is still officially an accident."

Jean studied me for several moments, then said, "Two things connect. First, I have friends in the San José coroner's office who faxed me the preliminary report. Easton died of a poisonous injection."

I stared at him, unable to think of anything except Adam Hartsfield standing near the pool where Easton died the night I returned to the scene. I remembered his chilling demeanor, the look on his haggard face.

"You said two things."

"His daughter."

The room suddenly seemed to swell to an enormous size, while at the same time I seemed to be shrinking. Once when I was a little girl, perhaps four or five, I witnessed a puppy being run over by a car. I was standing on the sidewalk, holding my mother's hand, and was helpless to do anything about it. She pulled me toward her, holding me close, so I wouldn't see the little dog's body or hear its last whimpering cries of death.

But I saw anyway, and I heard. And the whole world swelled to an enormous size as I realized my tiny size, my powerlessness, in comparison. I had nightmares for years, vivid nightmares, of the same sensation.

The same as now.

"Don't tell me she disappeared."

He nodded slowly. "Not long after her mother took out a restraining order to keep Hartsfield away from them both."

"How long ago did this happen?"

"Three years."

"Was she found?"

"No. She disappeared without a trace. Though no one could prove it—Hartsfield is too good for that—there are those on the San Francisco police force who are certain he's responsible."

"So Easton was on Hartsfield's tail here?"

"I don't know who was on whose. I suspect Easton was following a lead that tied Hartsfield to the disappearances of other young women. I also suspect Hartsfield followed Easton to get rid of him before he uncovered something that would hammer the final nails in his coffin."

"As chilling as it is, I can come closer to understanding a crime of passion that puts a man over the edge—kidnapping and hiding his daughter to get back at his ex-wife. But what would be the motive to go after other young women?"

"It seems they're all from the same school."

The room was ballooning again. "Let me guess. Shepparton College."

"The pattern is clear. Any student who was close to his daughter has disappeared. One by one."

"What was her name?"

Jean's face softened. I remembered he had once lost a daughter, and, somehow, as terrible as Hartsfield's actions were, he understood the love of a father for his daughter.

"Holly," he said. "Holly Hartsfield."

I remembered, then, what Adam had said about his reasons for being at La Vida Pura were more important than life itself. Somewhere within his deranged mind he blamed Easton for the disasters that had rained down on him—lost job, lost family, perhaps even what he'd felt forced to do to cover his tracks after Holly's abduction—and he had been on a quest to balance the scales of justice. To get rid of Harry Easton.

I let out a pent-up breath, aware that Jean was watching me with an expression of compassion and understanding. "So where do we go from here?"

"The most important task at hand is to find your Carly—and Kate, if she is really tangled up in all this."

"I think she is."

He nodded. "That's good enough for me."

"I don't have Kate's note. Adam took it. He said he would give it to the authorities in town."

Jean didn't roll his eyes, but I could see he was thinking the same thing I was. Adam had put the note in his pocket, and it would probably never be seen again. And I had let a solid piece of evidence slip through my fingers. It was gone.

Jean rose, and I did the same. He took my empty glass and set it, with his, near the wet bar. I supposed the chauffeur and jack-of-all-trades assistant would clean it up later.

"I also suggest," he said, opening the hangar door for me, "we get the students back to the ship as quickly as possible. They'll be safer onboard than traipsing around Playa Negra unprotected—at least until we know that Hartsfield is in custody."

"Will he be extradited?" I shuddered to think what might happen to him in a Central American jail—even in a civilized country like Costa Rica.

"Costa Rica has no extradition treaty with the U.S. Crimes like this get messy. If it can be proved that the *Sun Spirit* was within Costa Rican territorial waters when he killed Easton, local law enforcement will prosecute. Believe me, he'll rot in a Central American prison if they have their way. If Interpol gets involved, it's messier still. Jurisdiction issues again." He shrugged. "Either way, he's dead."

I swallowed hard. "Dead?"

"In a manner of speaking."

The chauffeur opened the car door, and I slid into the plush leather backseat. Jean went around the vehicle and got in beside me. I focused on his face rather than the airfield as we glided by.

The shock was wearing off now, and rather than dismay or even sorrow for what Hartsfield had done, the anger that had been hiding in my heart was suddenly making itself known. I felt duped. Betrayed, though I couldn't say exactly why.

I only knew that now I was angry.

"We'll head down to the harbor first," Jean said, "to check on Carly Lowe—just on the off chance she might have come in by canal boat."

The voice of reason. I appreciated it.

Then I remembered the bracelet. "Could she have found a ride some other way? Perhaps gotten someone to fly her here, hired a charter?"

"It's possible, I suppose. Especially if she found the canal closed to its usual taxi traffic. Do you know whether she had her money and passport? That's usually all it takes."

I didn't know, but just at the possibility, I brightened for the first time all morning. I didn't tell Jean about the bracelet for reasons I didn't understand. But I prayed Carly would be waiting at the wharf for her ride to the *Sun Spirit.*

We wound through rolling hills covered with tall grasses, lush vegetation, and scattered banana groves. Inland lay the rain forests and, on terraced slopes in the distance, coffee plantations. To the east a ribbon of ocean glinted in the sun, and after we rounded another curve, the harbor came into sight. The anchored *Sun Spirit,* the size of a toy from this distance, was visible through a low-lying haze.

The car glided smoothly along the main street that led to the harbor. On either side, kiosks were set up to sell flowers, souvenirs, breads, fish, and vegetables. Townspeople, merchants, and tourists wandered among them. As we slowed for traffic, I anxiously searched their faces, looking for Carly or Kate.

Nothing.

Soon we arrived at the wharf where we had disembarked just the day before. There were no tenders. No people waiting.

No Carly.

My heart plummeted. Again.

I met Jean's worried gaze. "We must get to the police station. Quickly."

He spoke to the driver in a language that sounded like Dutch. I wondered why he didn't use English, since the driver spoke it well.

We climbed out of town along a series of short switchbacks to a fortresslike structure that towered above the harbor on a cliff. A thick stone wall ran along the top of the cliff for a mile or so in both directions before turning inland. The car slid through an arched opening, past a guarded gate, and into deep shadow, as if this massive enclosure had swallowed us up. "Impressive," I said to Jean.

He laughed. "It's an ancient fortress built by the Spanish in the 1700s. Of course it's been refurbished inside, but the walls remain. Several governmental offices are housed here, including the local police department and the regional prison."

The barred windows on the bottom level looked like dungeons from the Spanish Inquisition. I shivered and turned away.

The car pulled into a parking slot near some rather faded black-and-white SUVs with ornate REPÚBLICA DE COSTA RICA shields on their front doors. Above a double doorway leading into the stone building dead ahead, letters had been chiseled into an archway: POLICÍA PLAYA NEGRA.

"Were you able to get photos of the girls?"

I shook my head. "So far I haven't been able to reach Carly's mother. When we get back to the ship, we'll get copies of their passports. One of the students—you probably know her, Zoë Shire—works in personnel and is along to take care of the paperwork, health insurance, that sort of thing. I'll have her copy the photos."

"Good plan." He exited the car at the same time the chauffeur opened my door.

We entered the building together, and I stood back as he spoke to the uniformed officer at the counter. The office was dirty, messy, and crowded with tourists filling out what I assumed were forms having to do with crimes committed against them: picked pockets, petty theft, assault, stolen passports. We'd been warned onboard what to expect in these little seaside towns, so I wasn't surprised. But I was disheartened.

I couldn't help thinking again about the travel article. If I told the truth, no one would set foot in Playa Negra.

It got worse. I was soon part of the clipboard-filling-out-forms brigade, standing in endless lines to have the forms stamped by officials, explaining again why I was here, only to be given other forms and told to start the whole process over again. The room grew stuffier, so humid the air almost dripped, as the day grew warmer and more people flocked inside. I heard snatches of disgruntled English, Spanish, Dutch, German, and French. I didn't think anything could be worse than the DMV at home. I was wrong. I'd found the place.

Jean tried to cut through the red tape, and to his credit, he patiently spoke to each official on my behalf. He disappeared into one of the offices about halfway through the process, then returned a half hour later, apologetic for the time and effort it was taking me. He also said he'd asked if Adam Hartsfield had come in—or been apprehended.

He hadn't.

I finally met with a detective who seemed, at best, bored with the report, at worst, hostile toward another American tourist in trouble. It was obvious the red tape was not going to be cut through, no matter what local clout Jean might have. Although the detective promised to look into the matter, he said he needed more documentation from the college authorities and from the girls' parents. And, of course, photos. In the end, I wondered if my visit had moved the investigation along at all.

By the time we left from the dark, dank station, all I could think of was returning to the resort, packing up my things, and heading back to the ship. The cozy comfort of my stateroom, my typewriter, and Gus called to me. My heart needed soothing after all I had learned about Adam. There was nothing like the rumble of Gus's purr to bring me some calm. Or the mundane clicking of old-fashioned typewriter keys and the *ding* of the platen return.

More than anything, I longed to hear some good news about Carly.

Jean wanted to immediately return to the ship to speak to Captain Richter about Adam Hartsfield, so we parted at the wharf, he to board his private speedboat, me to return to La Vida Pura with the chauffeur. I was perfectly content to be alone again. Though I appreciated his take-charge attitude, the urgency of finding the missing girls lay heavy on my heart.

When I arrived at the pagoda, the sun was high, bringing with it an almost unbearable heat and a light so intense it was colorless. Zoë had obviously been out all morning and not bothered to turn on the air conditioning. I flipped the switch and, ignoring the chaotic mess that greeted me, quickly moved into the bedroom to pack my things.

The suite seemed to almost breathe danger, and I quickened my pace to be rid of it. Every creak of the wood structure, every muffled voice carrying from outdoors, caused me to start. I quickly stuffed my toiletries and hiking clothes in my backpack, ran a brush through my hair, and clipped it high off my neck because of the heat.

I reentered the living room, dropped my backpack, then stepped into the girls' room. It was just as we'd left it when Adam and I found Kate's note. I glanced around at Kate's and Zoë's belongings, wondering whether the police would actually show up and treat it like a crime scene or whether I should gather Kate's belongings and return them to the ship for safekeeping. I wondered why Zoë hadn't returned to pack up her things.

I had just finished changing into my trekking uniform, as I was beginning to affectionately call my bermudas and journalist's vest, when a shuffling of feet and a snatch of conversation came from the direction of the front door. At first I thought the cleaning crew had shown up, for it was past checkout time. Then I heard a snatch of English. I recognized the voices—Max Pribble and Price Alexander—and the sounds of a jimmied lock. Without thinking, I ducked into the closet and closed the mirrored sliding door.

Immediately I regretted it. Not only did my claustrophobia rear its ugly head, but I felt more foolish than I had in years. Before I could step outside the closet and demand an explanation for breaking into the suite, they were entering the living room. So I stayed put and waited, straining to hear.

Price and Max came closer to where I huddled, and I could clearly hear their voices.

"Yeah, dude," one of them said. "The guy said to get it back. Didn't matter how we did it, just get it. That's all he said."

I frowned. Get what?

"You sure he said it was in here? This place looks rolled."

The boys' words softened to a muffle, and I imagined they were going through some of the girls' belongings. I heard a zipper open, then close, a soft grunt, probably caused by one of them squatting to look under a bed or beneath a table or dresser.

"Don't see it, dude."

"Gotta be here somewhere."

"The ol' lady probably got it."

The hairs on the back of my neck bristled.

Old lady? Moi?

I stopped myself from flying out of the closet and giving the kid what for. Old lady indeed. I didn't look a day over forty-five. At least that's what I told myself. It didn't matter that most days I felt twice my age. Today was one of those days.

"Hey, I've got an idea. Let's write another one. The dude won't know the difference. He never saw the first one."

My breath caught. Write another what? Were they talking about the note?

Silence fell while they were obviously mulling it over.

"Nah," one finally said. "There was something about the dude's voice on the phone. Not what he said but how he said it. I don't think we ought to double-cross him. Let's just tell him we couldn't find it."

I ruled out Adam as the "dude" they were talking about. As far as I knew, he still had the note.

Who wanted the note? Why did he want it back? And how did the boys get involved?

My head hurt from the whirl of unanswered questions—not to mention lack of food and caffeine. I squeezed my eyes shut, pinching the bridge of my nose, willing my brain to kick into gear.

If I confronted the boys, would they tell me what they knew? I took a deep breath, ready to burst out of my hiding place and demand an explanation.

Then one of the boys said something that chilled me to the bone. And I knew it was Price Alexander.

"You know that cat on the ship?"

"Yeah, the one the old lady had in the carrier the day we boarded?"

"Yeah, that one."

Gus! My heart twisted.

"I got plans for it, man."

"Get-even kind of plans?"

"Yeah, dude. Exactly."

The voices receded, and I willed my heart to stop its erratic beating. As soon as I heard the front door open, then close with a soft thud, I emerged from my hiding place, hurried to the living room, grabbed my backpack, and slipped through the door behind the boys.

I needed to get back to the ship before they did. But how?

They sauntered along the path several yards ahead of me, so I took an offshoot that I knew led to the reception area. I broke into a trot, not an easy thing for a woman of a certain age in the oppressive heat, but I kept thinking of Gus. My heels sprouted wings. Hunger, fatigue, and Starbucks cravings sank like rocks to the bottom of my list of concerns.

The path wound through a meditation garden with fountains and Eastern sculptures. I began to worry this wasn't a shortcut after all, and I picked up speed. I rounded another corner and slowed. Then I halted, midstep, my heart racing.

A figure stood behind a dark tangle of fern and vines. I glanced around, looking for a means of escape. There was none.

He stepped onto the path.

"I was hoping you would come this way."

TWELVE

A dam." The word came out benign enough as I tried to collect my thoughts, decide on my actions—*fight or flight?* Psychology 101 came back to me. Nonverbal signs of the fight-or-flight response: dilated pupils, bristling hair, and increased breathing rate, with either a torso squared for battle or an angling away for flight. I felt my bristling hair and shallow, rapid breathing, and I imagined that my pupils were as black as obsidian and the size of coffee coasters.

I looked down at my torso. My sympathetic nervous system had already kicked into action. It said *fight.* I wasn't going to argue.

I squared my shoulders to match my torso and marched myself toward Adam. Stopped dead in front of him and stared up into his face. "You've got things to tell me."

When his mouth twitched at the corner, I tried not to think of him as a murderer; it wasn't too late for *flight* to kick in. After all this bravado, I didn't want to look foolish. Or feel foolish.

Around us buzzed purplish black bees the size of golf balls. I shuddered as one flew too near my right ear. Another grazed my left ear, and I waved it away.

"I was about to say the same thing to you."

"What do you mean?"

Instead of answering, he turned to lead me away from the flowering bush that attracted the bees. We moved down the path a short ways. A small, three-sided redwood enclosure had been built to one side of the path. A strange sculpture rose from a platform in one corner; a trickling fountain graced the opposite corner. A wooden bench bordered the lattice-work walls. Adam gestured toward the middle section, and we sat.

I perched on the seat edge, ready for flight. I wanted some answers from this man, but I hadn't gotten past fearing for my life.

Adam studied my face for a few seconds before speaking. "What's going on?"

I stared at him. "What do you mean, 'What's going on?' You tell me."

He frowned.

"Why didn't you tell me about Harry Easton?"

"I did."

"You conveniently left out some important details."

Adam dropped his head into his hands and let it hang there. He didn't look up when he started to speak. "You've obviously found out he's the guy who took the photos."

"Yeah, I did. I also found out some other very interesting information."

He was looking up now, but toward the path, not me. The muscles in his jaw were working overtime, his lips were white. "Such as?"

"It seems Easton died of unnatural causes after all."

"How do you know that?"

I didn't answer.

"You seem to be a veritable treasure trove of information. What else?"

"Your marital problems, your daughter Holly's disappearance."

As soon as I said his daughter's name, he whirled. His eyes narrowed and his breathing came out heavy and rapid. "Who have you been talking to? Where did you get this?"

I stood. "It doesn't matter."

He rose and reached for my arm. He held me by the wrist. His grasp wasn't tight. Just firm. No nonsense. "You've got to tell me. It fits with everything else."

"Now you're talking in riddles."

He stared hard at me, then let my arm go. Shaking his head, he said, "I went to the police station this morning."

"And?"

"I ran into so much red tape, forms, that sort of thing, I decided to take the forms with me, fill them out in a café across from the station. While I was there, I overheard a couple of officers talking about an Interpol matter."

I knew what was coming, but said, "What matter?"

"I think you know."

I looked at him, unblinking, then said, "The little matter of being wanted for murder."

"Yeah, that little matter. I don't know a whole lot of Spanish, but I knew enough to pick up my own name and description and why they're looking for me."

"Why did you come back here then?"

"I need your help. You're the only one I can trust right now."

I flew to my feet. "Me? You've got to be kidding. As far as I'm concerned, you're a criminal wanted for murder. Why should I believe otherwise? I have a mind to blow my whistle—" I patted my vest trying to remember which pocket I'd left it in.

The transparent, honest look in his eyes made me stop before I'd ripped open a single Velcro strap. He continued in utter seriousness, speaking rapidly as if he didn't have much time to tell me all I needed to know. He gave me his side of the tragic breakup of his marriage, without glossing over his role. He was brutally honest about how he'd sunk into deep depression after the videotaped beating was broadcast throughout the country—worse, in his hometown—and his life seemed over. His wife and daughter suffered, especially after his wife gave him an ultimatum to get help or else she would take Holly and leave him.

Even then, he seemed paralyzed to get help. Instead, he sank into deeper and deeper despair.

"What about Holly's disappearance?"

"That's the worst tragedy in all of this. I shut her out of my life, thinking she was better off without me. She headed off to college in Florida—the same school these kids are from—"

"Shepparton," I offered.

He nodded. "And I never said good-bye."

I didn't tell him I knew about the restraining order to keep him away from both Holly and her mother.

"Holly was with a group of her friends on a cruise when she disappeared. It was spring break of her sophomore year; fast-track science classes were being offered. She wanted to be a teacher—high-school biology. I was so proud of her." His voice caught, and he looked away from me. "She was in the eastern Caribbean. Disappeared without a trace. She was with a dozen friends, and none of them remembered seeing her go. Her mother and I were devastated. But it woke us both up. We did what Holly wanted us to do all along."

"You got back together."

"It wasn't easy. I had to humble myself first before God, then before my wife. I had been a nominal believer before but had turned my back on God when the troubles began."

He met my gaze, and this time I saw something in his eyes I hadn't noticed before. A peace that went beyond all that had happened to him, all the bad things, the betrayals, the fall into the gutter. There was only one source for such peace. I understood it and touched his hand.

"I promised Jo I wouldn't rest until I found our daughter—or found out what happened to her." He paused. "Jo died not long after."

"I'm sorry."

"I didn't tell you all this to gain your sympathy. It's background for what I need to tell you next.

"They're connected, all the girls who've disappeared—Holly, Carly, and now Kate. And there may be others—from all around the U.S. and Canada. Not many, but they're there if you look."

"What do you mean, 'there'?"

"In the missing persons reports. They're college-age females—mostly nineteen to twenty-one. All northern European heritage, a certain physique, maybe one hundred fifteen to one hundred twenty pounds. No one over five foot six. All pretty and popular with their peers. Not necessarily stellar students, but mostly serious in their studies."

"Serial killer?" I almost whispered the words, not wanting to think the unthinkable. I pictured Carly and Kate. I thought about Holly and the anguish of not knowing what had happened to her. "Do you have a picture of her...of Holly?"

He pulled out his wallet and removed a worn and wrinkled photo. "It's old," he said needlessly. "She was only ten when this was taken."

A pigtailed girl grinned at the camera. Long bangs almost hid her large, intelligent eyes. A smattering of freckles dusted a perfectly formed nose. Two dimples added spark to her personality, even in a still photo— one in the middle of her chin, another in her left cheek.

"Here's the only recent one I've got." He handed me another. I could see his eyes in her gaze, the strong set of her jaw, just like his. Her smile was faint, but she looked happy, content.

He took the photos back from me and returned them to his wallet. "Jo and I tried for years to have kids. We'd just about given up when she got pregnant with Holly. We were both in our forties when she was born. She was a handful, but we loved our new roles, late-night feedings and all."

The lines in his face softened as he talked about his child, then hardened again as he turned the topic back to the missing girls. "I've been on the abductors' tails for two years, and I'm getting close. That's why I'm on this cruise. These are some of Holly's classmates. Some were with her when she disappeared, others were on the periphery. They were all questioned but strangely didn't remember—or admit to remembering—anything."

I wanted to believe him, wanted to trust him. I reached for my handbag, rummaged around inside, and grasped the bracelet. "I found this in the hangar at the airport this morning." I gave it to him, and as he examined it, I told him the story of Carly and Joey.

"She's here, then." He handed the bracelet back.

"And not of her own accord. She would have contacted me by now."

We moved back to the path. "I've got to get back to the ship." I told him about what I'd overheard Max and Price talking about—from the note to their plans for Gus.

"I'm planning to stay nearby—someplace where I can lie low. Though I didn't find anything unusual at the clinic last night, I can't shake the feeling that something's going on there."

"How can I get in touch with you?"

He studied my eyes as if gauging the measure of trust he could place in me. Finally, he said, "The first hairpin curve after leaving the guard gate. There's a two-track road leading into a coffee plantation. I've rented a room from a family. It's out back, attached to a barn. You can't miss it." He paused. "I just ask one thing."

I waited.

"Don't lead anyone there. If you do come, be careful that no one follows you. I'm doing this thing for Holly. I can't fail."

We walked a short distance, then he paused. "You never did tell me how you got so much information so fast."

"Someone besides me remembered the headlines, suspected that you were involved, and had you investigated. Also had enough clout to get an early look at Easton's autopsy report."

"Someone?"

"Dr. Baptiste."

A quick burst of anger lit his face. "The guy has an exaggerated sense of self-importance."

"He's close to discovering a cure for leukemia. I suppose he thinks he has a right to play God once in a while."

"No one has a right to play God, no matter what miracles they think they may hold in their hand." There was no humor in his voice.

He gazed at me one long moment. Around us birds trilled, and in the distance a macaw squawked. He reached for my hand and squeezed it. Then just as quickly he let it go, squared his shoulders, and gave me a half smile and a small salute. Then he disappeared into the foliage.

I hurried to the reception area, and as I turned in my room key, I asked about getting a taxi to the harbor.

Carmen smiled and said, "Oh, I wish you'd been here earlier. Two boys from the Shepparton group had me call a cab for them. They left just minutes ago. You could have shared the ride."

"Max Pribble and Price Alexander?" I hid my annoyance.

"Yes, yes. You are right. Such nice young men."

"Can you call another cab for me? Please ask the driver to hurry."

She glanced at the clock. "I will be happy to, but a van is on its way to take the rest of your group to the harbor. I would say it will be here in ten minutes, maybe twenty. I doubt that a taxi can get here any sooner."

Twenty-three minutes later the van pulled up to reception. By now, those who were left in our group—the Browns, the Doyles, the Quilps, and Zoë Shire—had joined me in the waiting area. Zoë looked more forlorn than usual and barely spoke to the other couples. As the driver pulled away from the resort, she leaned her head against the window and closed her eyes. Before we rounded the third hairpin curve, she was asleep.

I chatted politely with the others, though my mind was anywhere but inside this van. The topic moved from where Kate could possibly have gone to the storm that was forecast for the following day.

"Not a hurricane," Ed Brown said. "Too early in the season. But I heard folks talking about the storm warnings already going out. Small-craft advisories, that sort of thing."

"Hope our captain doesn't play John Wayne and take us out in it," Betty Brown said.

"Especially if he's had a nip or two," Barbara Doyle said.

"Hunh," Adele Quilp grunted.

They laughed, though in reality it wasn't a laughing matter. I remembered what happened to the Exxon *Valdez* several years ago after the captain had a few dozen nips, or more.

I stared through the window, beside myself with worry over Gus. To get my mind off what I planned to do to those two hoodlums if they harmed him, I thought about what I had learned from Adam and how it related to Carly and Kate. But the puzzle bits flew around my mind, refusing to come together in any cohesive manner.

Fact: Carly had disappeared in Parisima and was brought to Playa Negra airport.

Fact: Harry Easton, slightly shady PI and self-proclaimed finder of lost children, was poisoned to death on the same night we discovered Carly was missing.

Fact: Easton had caused Adam Hartsfield to lose his job and his family and had ruined Adam's reputation.

Fact: Adam was about to be charged by Interpol with the murder of Harry Easton.

Fact: Dr. Jean Baptiste portrayed Hartsfield's background information with a certain slant, leaving out important information.

Fact: Adam thought his daughter's disappearance was somehow connected to the spring break cruise run by Shepparton College, the students and/or faculty.

Fact: Adam thought the girls' disappearances might be related to other missing coeds outside Shepparton.

Fact: The last two "facts" were based on what Adam had told me. Had he told me everything he knew? Or had he conveniently left out some important information, just as Baptiste had?

My head ached with the elusive nature of it all. It hit me how much

I just wanted to forget about everything, gather up Gus in his carrier, and go home. Charter a boat to take me north to a U.S. port—any port would do. Catch a train back to California. No flights, no risk. As Captain Richter told me so condescendingly, leave the investigation to the proper authorities, to those who knew what they were doing. It was the easy way out. I didn't care. I was coming close to throwing in the towel.

I could make arrangements in port and be on my way in the morning—before the storm moved in. Contact the FBI with what I knew. Drop it in their laps and go back to preparing a gorgeous rosemary-eggplant napoleon and dancing around my kitchen to "Hey Jude."

My eyes flew open. Captain Richter!

It hadn't taken any of us longer than twelve hours onboard to see the man was barely hanging on to his job. The first officer was at the bridge more often than not. After that first day at sea, I remembered thinking, wryly, Richter must know where the body was buried, so to speak, at the parent company.

Maybe I was right. What if he did know something? I made a mental note to find out how many student cruises Richter had captained. I suddenly wished Adam was here beside me to swap details. Maybe he already knew about Richter and had checked him out.

The van rattled along, and soon the harbor came into sight. I leaned back in my seat, looking out at the *Sun Spirit* gleaming on a sparkling aqua sea. Only five days into this cruise, and it already felt like a lifetime. Except for the clouds building to the northwest, the scene looked as harmless as a Thomas Kinkade seascape, with the blue-green beauty of the ocean, the breakers crashing against the distant shore, the wheeling gulls with their mournful cries.

Even before my gaze moved to the dark, brooding wharf, the seriousness of the girls' plights, even that of Adam, settled heavily on my already burdened heart. I glanced across the van at Zoë, her face relaxed in sleep.

She seemed to feel my gaze and opened her eyes, stretched, then stared at me curiously. For a quick second, our spirits seemed to touch before hers shied away, emotional barrier back in place. But in that fraction of a heartbeat, I saw beyond the thick glasses and the large gray eyes into the frightened, bitter heart of a little girl with great big needs.

In that split second, I decided I couldn't leave Costa Rica. Not yet.

I almost changed my mind forty minutes later. Our small group arrived by tender just as the sun was deepening its descent into a tropical sunset. I hurried to my stateroom, one little creature on my mind.

Gus.

All I wanted was to make sure he was okay, to scoop him into my arms and hear him purr.

My heart caught when I turned down my hallway and saw my stateroom door standing wide open. I picked up my pace and broke into a trot. I shot through the doorway, tossed my backpack on the bed, and cried out, "Gus!"

THIRTEEN

I stared at my empty stateroom. Nothing was out of place. The feeders were exactly as I had left them—one full of water, the other half full of sensitive-stomach cat food, with a few crumbs scattered on the floor nearby. I checked the closet, under the bed, behind the drapes.

"Gus," I called. "Hey, bud, don't scare me this way. Where are you?"

No answering meow. No swish of the elegant tail. No peering at me through those round, wise eyes.

Max and Price. I pictured them laughing somewhere, hiding poor frightened Gus. I hoped that was all that had happened to him. What if they let him go in Playa Negra? Or dropped him overboard? Would they do something so cruel? I sank to the little sofa and dropped my head into my hands, trying not to think the unthinkable. If I had been a little kinder to Price, this wouldn't have happened. My temper had gotten the best of me. I had laid into him, embarrassed him in front of his friends, and now an innocent animal was paying the price. Tears formed, but I refused to cry. I would go after the two bullies, had to go after them, but first I needed to calm down.

I struggled to take a deep and calming breath. It didn't work. Grief pricked at the edges of my heart, threatening to spark into a fury even worse than what had hit me at the rain-forest bridge. That wouldn't do Gus—or me—any good.

I went to the window. The sun had finished its descent into the ocean, and the sky had turned gray; the water, deep navy blue. Lights onshore were flickering on, and in the distance, fishing boats glided across the dark waters on their way back to port.

Then without shedding a tear, I spun and headed for the door. Beware, bullies, I growled to myself as I trotted down the corridor.

"Okay, it's time to fess up," I said. "I know you two are involved, and if I have to, I'll go to Dean Williams."

I had found the boys in the Clipper Lounge. Max sat back in an easy chair, his feet propped on a plastic coffee table. From the far side of the same table, Price shot me an innocent look. An open textbook was draped across one thigh. Biology, I gathered from the photos.

He raked his fingers through his hair, adjusting the tips of his spikes. "What are you talking about?"

"My cat. What did you do with him?"

They looked at each other, seeming perplexed. I didn't trust the look. "Spill," I said. Come on, make my day.

"Dean Williams?" Price sneered. "You know him personally, huh? Just like you know the president of Shepparton?"

Beware, your sins will find you out.

My breath caught in my throat, just as my lie should have the day before. I swallowed hard, deciding on a course of action. No contest. I had to come clean. "Okay, guys. I was pretty perturbed. You scared Zoë to the point she couldn't even move off the bridge."

They stared at me. Sneering.

"It was the first thing that came to mind. I'm sorry. I shouldn't have lied."

"We don't know anything about your cat," Max said.

"I heard you talking about getting even with me. My cat was mentioned as the means."

They looked at each other. It was a look of triumph. I waited for one to give the other a high five.

"I told you it would work," Max said to Price.

"Yeah, whatever," Price said with an indifferent shrug. But he was grinning.

"Didn't I? I told you, man. And it worked like a charm. Just like I said."

Anger was replacing chagrin. Fast. I clamped my lips together and gave them The Look. It had worked on my kids through their teens, but they weren't the immature hoodlums these two were. "Explain what you mean by 'it,'" I said after a long pause, "in the context of 'I told you *it* would work.'"

Again they exchanged glances, then Price leaned forward, hands dangling between his knees. His books slid to the floor with a thud. "Yeah, well, it was Max's idea."

"It?"

"Yeah, well, we saw you go into your room, the pagoda suite, or whatever it's called. Max thought it would be funny if we followed you, hoping you'd do just what you did—hide. Then we'd lay some lies on you." He shrugged. "That's all. We just—"

"—wanted to give you a taste of your own medicine," Max finished for him. His face colored when Price looked at the ceiling. "Well, that's what my mom always says when she's ready to fly at me for some reason or another. 'I'm gonna give you a little taste of your own medicine, mister.'" He laughed at his nasal-toned imitation. The little hoodlum.

I didn't laugh. "And the note," I pressed. "It's important you tell me who contacted you. Kate's life may be in danger."

"We made that up too," Max said.

"So no one told you to get Kate's note?" I frowned. "How did you know about the note, anyway?"

"Easy," Price said. "We overheard Mr. Hartsfield tell the front office manager about you two finding it. He even told him what Kate wrote."

I stared at them, willing my lie meter to kick in. It had never failed with my kids. But that was because I knew their faces well and could read every drifting-over-my-shoulder glance, every over-the-top, honeyed tone, every wide-eyed look of feigned innocence as easily as I read the front page of the *Town Crier*.

"So you didn't intend to kidnap my cat?"

"We may do bad stuff to geeks," Max said, "but we'd never do that to an animal." The meter cleared him.

"Gus is gone," I said. "I found my stateroom door open."

Price looked puzzled and started to speak, but static from the intercom interrupted him. It was the first officer announcing a mandatory gathering in the Clipper Lounge in a half hour.

"You were about to say?" I prompted, focusing on Price as I stood.

They looked at each other, then after a slight shrug, Price said, "I don't know. I can't remember." He pulled his Swiss army knife out and tossed it from hand to hand.

Price Alexander III didn't pass the lie-meter test.

I headed to the bridge to intercept the captain before the meeting. We spoke for a few minutes about Kate's disappearance. He had already met with Dr. Baptiste, so he knew about the Interpol warrant for Adam. I didn't tell him what I knew about Adam going into hiding. Richter might be a key player in the disappearances. I needed to discover all I could about his involvement, and I didn't want to put him on the defensive.

So I changed the topic to Gus and told him what the boys had said at the pagoda. He looked sympathetic, but unconcerned. My heart was growing more achingly hollow with each passing minute. Gus was everything to me. He might be just a purring bundle of fur to some, but to me he was the most unique feline God ever created. I loved him.

"I'll mention it to housekeeping," he said, "but I probably don't need to tell you how often pets disappear on cruise ships. Most don't allow them—except for Seeing Eye dogs and the like. They fall overboard, explore refrigerated sections…you know, slip in when no one's looking, get trapped, and by the time they're found—" It must have been the green hue of my face that made him stop. "I'm sorry," he said. "That was insensitive."

"You think?" I had a sudden urge to throttle him. I decided I'd better leave.

"By the way," he called after me. "Carly Lowe's mother called about an hour ago, ship to shore. I explained that we're worried about her daughter. She asked that you call her right away."

He waited till now to tell me? I almost ripped the phone from his hand.

I stepped to the deck just outside the bridge.

"Tange," I said when she picked up.

"Oh, Harriet. Tell me everything, every detail."

I did, paused to let it sink in, then said, "You need to come."

"I've already made reservations. I fly out tonight, but with connections and the time difference, it will be tomorrow afternoon by the time I get to San José. I'll have to get a charter from there to Playa Negra."

"The last leg may be a problem," I said, hoping I was wrong. "We're expecting a storm to move in tomorrow. The little airport here isn't equipped for an instrument landing. If you can't get out of San José, hold tight and know that I'm doing everything I can on this end. We have the police involved, plus I'm exploring some leads. We're going to find her, Tange."

"I know." Her voice sounded small, not at all her usual robust, go-getter tone.

"It's only been a couple days," I reminded her. "And I think she may be close." I told Tangi about the bracelet.

She didn't speak for a moment, and I thought she might be crying.

"I'm so sorry I couldn't get in touch sooner. I tried to get you at work and at home."

"I twisted my ankle—I was out on a story about some corrupt developers—stepped in a hole. Spent the day in emergency."

"Sounds worse than twisted."

"I broke it. Three places."

"Oh, Tangi, I'm sorry. Are you okay to travel?"

She assured me wild gorillas couldn't keep her from getting to her daughter as fast as she could. We talked a few minutes longer, then she said, "How's Gus taking the cruise?"

I swallowed hard, unwilling to give her any more bad news. "He's handled it well," I finally said. "Not a sign of seasickness."

We hung up, and clutching the phone in my hand, I leaned against the metal rail that framed the bow of the ship. I looked out at the dark water, the sharp whitecaps, and felt the sting of wind in my face. I refused to let myself consider the depth of the harbor waters, the teeming life within them. Or the predators that lurked there.

Jean was standing at the door to the Clipper Lounge, and when he saw me in the hallway, he stepped to my side. We walked into the room together and sat near the aisle in the next to the last row. Several of the older passengers filed by and sat down around us. Students, speaking in worried tones, began arriving in twos and threes. I saw Zoë move to the front of the room. Holding a clipboard in one hand and some files in the other, she sat down next to Dean Williams. He stroked his beard, a habit I had noticed, and smiled at her.

Jean leaned toward me, his hand over his mouth, shielding his words. "I met with the captain and first officer about Hartsfield. Because he hasn't been apprehended, and because of the uncertainties of the Easton investigation, they plan to confine the passengers to the ship for the next several hours." He shrugged. "With the storm on its way, I doubt that he'd pull up anchor anyway."

"Have you seen the official charges against Adam Hartsfield?"

He shot me a strange look. "Do you doubt that they've been made?"

I didn't answer, but yes, I was beginning to have some questions beyond what I'd been told. I wanted facts, not hearsay. I'd been told too much by too many. Some facts jelled, others didn't, and my head was beginning to spin.

Plus, something about Adam's story had grabbed me and wouldn't let go. But I decided to wait for a time other than during a public meeting to tell Jean he was looking for the wrong man. Jean Baptiste didn't strike me as someone who liked to be told he was wrong.

"What about the passport photos of Kate and Carly?" I asked.

He leaned toward me again. "I'm meeting with the Shepparton faculty and dean right after this. I'll ask them to release the photos to the police." He paused. "I'll do my best to make this happen. And fast."

"Thank you." And I meant it.

Captain Richter walked to the podium and leaned toward the microphone.

"Ladies and gentlemen, thank you for so promptly gathering here with us tonight. We are sorry for the inconvenience, but I have an important announcement to make."

To his credit, he sounded perfectly sober.

"As you most likely heard, we are being forced to change our itinerary. Because an alleged crime was committed onboard, we are not being allowed—by Costa Rican authorities—to leave harbor until the investigation is completed.

"This allegation is being disputed by myself and the *Sun Spirit's* parent company. We were in international waters at the time in question, so the jurisdiction isn't clear. It is our opinion that Nassau, headquarters of Global Sea Adventures, should make these decisions affecting our itinerary.

"It is extremely important that we cooperate with the Costa Rican authorities, however, until this is straightened out. As it appears now, the authorities, both local and international—Interpol—will be boarding tomorrow morning at 0800 hours. They want to ask some questions, snoop around a bit, then, we hope, we'll be free to go."

Go?

I sprang to my feet. "Sir, if I may—"

He looked upset but waved for me to proceed.

"Two young women are missing. We know for certain that Kate Rivers disappeared here in Playa Negra, and I have proof that Carly Lowe was brought here as well, perhaps against her will." As soon as the words were out of my mouth, I knew I had tipped my hand. The room fell utterly silent. I felt Jean's hard gaze boring in on me from where he sat.

I forged ahead. "How can you—their classmates, school officials, captain and crew, any of you—think about pulling up anchor and floating away, la-di-dah, as if nothing has happened?"

"I beg to differ, ma'am," Richter said. "As far as we know, the two young women left of their own volition, something college students are prone to do, believe me. One even left a note, according to my sources, telling us not to worry. You are jumping to unfair conclusions. But even so, I assure you, the authorities here in Playa Negra—and truly, in all of Costa Rica—are investigating. They'll find these young women—if they indeed want to be found."

I stared at him, speechless. He had been sympathetic just a half hour ago when I phoned Tangi from the bridge. What had happened to change his mind?

"Please, ma'am, if you don't mind being seated. Save your questions for our Q and A time at the end of our session. Now, please, all of you…"

I felt a hundred pairs of eyes on me. I sat down.

I barely listened to the rest of Richter's spiel. Instead I let my mind race ahead. I needed one thing: to chase down Adam for some answers.

My work in Playa Negra wasn't finished. Not by a long shot.

"You mentioned proof that Carly Lowe was brought to Playa Negra," Jean said when the meeting was over. "Are you sure?"

I wanted to keep the details private, at least for now.

"Of course, I can't be certain," I said. "But I thought I spotted something of hers in town. A bracelet." I laughed lightly and shrugged. "Of course it could have belonged to a dozen different girls. Nothing special about it."

I had the strange sensation that his gaze was boring through me. It worried me that he might have a lie meter of his own. I laughed again and fluttered my fingers, something I've never been good at.

"Now, if you'll excuse me," I said, "I want a word with Dean Williams before your meeting."

"Of course," he said, then hesitated before quietly adding, "You know, Harriet, I'm with you in this. I told you how I lost my daughter. I understand firsthand what these parents must be feeling. If you find out anything, anything at all, please come to me. Don't forget, I want to help."

"Thank you, Jean. I promise I will."

Dean Williams stood with a group of students near the podium. They turned as I came closer.

"Dean," I said, "may I have a moment of your time?"

He glanced at his watch. "I have a meeting right now."

"I assure you it won't take longer than thirty seconds."

He stepped away from the students.

"Do you know if Richter has captained any other student cruises?"

"For Shepparton, you mean?" He stroked his beard.

I nodded.

"I couldn't tell you. This is my first time to head up the program." His expression told me it would probably be his last.

"Who would I talk to about which students are chosen to participate? How they're picked, the criteria, that sort of thing. And is it possible to get a list of previous itineraries and students?"

"Mrs. MacIver, isn't it?"

"Yes."

"May I ask what your interest would be? Why you would require such information?"

"I'm a travel writer."

He frowned. "I can't imagine what that information could have to do with rating the *Sun Spirit* and her accommodations and activities."

"Background," I said vaguely and smiled at him.

He brightened. "The person you need to talk to is Zoë Shire. You've been on all of the cruises, haven't you, Zoë?" She was standing at his elbow, file folders clutched to her chest. She gave me a half smile when I acknowledged her.

"Zoë, you didn't tell me you had anything to do with accepting students into the program," I said when Williams had moved away.

She held up a hand. "Oh, I don't! Not with accepting them. I just process the paperwork, that's all. But I can get student lists and previous itineraries for you." She stared at me from behind her thick glasses. I couldn't read the expression in her eyes.

We walked outside and stood on the deck. The air was heavy with the coming storm. We strolled along the deck for several yards, then stopped by the railing out of earshot of the other passengers.

"I need to ask you some questions," I said once we were alone. "And they're confidential. It's very important that they not be repeated."

"I understand. I work in an area at school that's highly confidential. Student grades, SAT scores, health records, that sort of thing. Administrators trust me. I've never given them reason not to."

"I won't ask you to divulge anything you've been asked to keep confidential."

"Thank you."

"I'm trying to find a pattern of behavior—something or someone—that is linked to the disappearances of Shepparton students."

She looked puzzled. "What do you mean?"

"You do know about the others who have disappeared—I mean besides Kate and Carly." When she didn't answer, I went on. "Holly Hartsfield was the first, I believe. Spring break, her sophomore year." I watched for a reaction, but the light reflected off her glasses, and again I couldn't see her eyes. "Did you know Holly?"

For a moment she didn't answer, then she said, "Everyone knew Holly. She was cute, pretty, popular." Almost the same words Adam used when he described all the young women who had disappeared. "What wasn't to like?"

"And they were all on spring break when they disappeared?"

She nodded. "I don't remember for sure, but I think Holly was on a megaship. One of the biggies. *Empress Catalonia,* I think it was called. Five star. Not anything like this rusty ship."

"This bucket of bolts?" I patted the railing affectionately, and Zoë laughed. "You don't see a connection with any of the students? Or maybe with Captain Richter? He wouldn't have captained the megaship, would he?"

"Are you kidding?"

I laughed. "I guess I didn't need to ask. How about Holly's friends? Are any of them with us on this cruise?"

"She was part of the "in" crowd, just like the girls who were with us. But her friends? The only ones I remember are Carly and Kate. But Holly disappeared so long ago, I can't imagine there's a connection."

We started walking again. The stars were out in full force, their pinpoints of light glinting off the indigo water. A brisk breeze kicked up and lifted the hair from Zoë's face. She closed her eyes, facing into the wind, chin elevated and a hint of a smile touching her lips. She looked pretty. I wondered if she had ever wanted to put aside the Munster-kid demeanor and kick up her heels a bit, try contact lenses, cut and shape her hair, stand up straight without slouching, put on a frilly sundress in place of her tattered jeans. Here I was, playing the mother role again. Seemed I couldn't help it.

"You've never told me about your parents," I said.

"I've got a mom and a grandpa. Mom ran off when I was little. I don't think she knew who my dad was. She pops in and out of my life from time to time, criticizes how I look, always talks about sending me someplace for a makeover. Once threatened to put my name in for *Extreme Makeover,* but she's usually more interested in her latest boyfriend than me. Whatever. I'm used to it, though. And Gramps? He's my hero." She gave me another of her rare smiles. "He's sick, very sick, probably just hanging on till I graduate. It's always been his dream."

"He's a pretty good guy, then."

"The best. He's why I want to go into medicine." She tilted her head and squinted at me. "Hey, why all the questions?"

"We've talked about Carly, about school, about my faux pas in the rain forest, but I've never really asked about you."

She grinned, showing even, perfectly formed, perfectly aligned white teeth. Gramps had spent a bundle on orthodontia. And behind those thick glasses, that feigned indifference, I saw a young woman who would someday be beautiful. Maybe not in a classical sense, but there was something swanlike about her that said, "Just give me time, world."

"Faux pas in the forest?"

"I lit into poor Price the Third like there was no tomorrow. But I had no way of knowing you didn't mind his attention—even though he was about to bump you right off the bridge."

She actually laughed. "Price the Third?"

I glanced around like a spy and murmured, "My name for him. But remember, that's confidential."

She struck a Girl Scout pose with a three-finger salute and said, "I promise."

I left Zoë on the deck, still smiling, and headed to my stateroom. I kept an eye out for Gus, not liking how my heart twisted each time I thought about him. Best-case scenario had him onboard somewhere, frightened and hungry, lost. Worst-case, I refused to consider.

As I walked I again went over the facts as I knew them, trying to figure out what I had overlooked. Harry Easton came to mind, his image bugging me to dig deeper. He was going to the spa resort because he suspected something. Adam was staying nearby because of his suspicions.

I frowned as another name seemed to materialize from the crevices of my brain. Lorenzo Nolan. U.S. citizen—though he spent much of his time in Costa Rica—and wealthy owner of La Vida Pura.

Or not so wealthy? I dug deeper into the crevices, home of the dust bunnies of the brain, those details I picked up from magazines I read in the beauty parlor while waiting for my roots to lighten. All I could remember was that some of Nolan's casinos had gone bankrupt. A few in California, one in Jersey City. That didn't mean his empire was about to crumble, but could it mean he was out to make up for his losses here? Off-shore usually indicated illegal. As in people trafficking. Drugs. Those were the usual suspects.

My head was rebelling from lack of sleep, my stomach queasy from too little food and worry over Carly and Kate. And with each step closer to my stateroom I missed Gus more. That hollow, aching place in my heart threatened to turn me to mush. I blinked rapidly, determined not to cry. Then I pictured Gus—the way he had of purring and eating at the same time, sensitive stomach pellets flying; how he preferred drinking from the bathroom faucet instead of his dish; how he stared at me without blinking as if he knew all of the secret thoughts of my heart—and my eyes filled anyway.

I rounded the corner of my deck. Just when I thought things couldn't get worse, they headed into a nosedive. As I rounded the corner on my deck, I saw Max and Price standing halfway down the railing.

"Yo, Ms. M.," Max said once I was in earshot. "We have something to ask you."

I just bet they did. "And that would be?"

"What you said in there, in the meeting," Price said. "Other people looked at you like you'd gone over the bend, but we believe you."

"Round the bend," Max corrected.

I was tired, still annoyed with them, and if I thought about it too hard, I just might light into them again, despite my earlier promises to myself. "Guys, can we talk about this tomorrow?"

"Sure, whatever," Price said, turning to leave.

"Carly and Katie were—are—my friends," Max said. "I'm offering my services to help you find them."

That wasn't exactly like getting an offer from Saint Francis of Assisi, but I smiled my thanks. "We'll talk tomorrow," I promised.

They started down the corridor, and I reached for my door key.

Then it hit me. What was I turning down? "Hey, guys," I called after them. "You know how to paddle those kayaks?"

They were beside me in an instant.

"What do ya have in mind?" Price asked, his face bright.

I told them.

"Cool," Max said.

ying was bad enough. Stealing was something else entirely. Contributing to the delinquency of minors was even worse. It didn't matter that I considered them half hoodlums already, I was feeling guilty. I looked up at the boys with a frown.

"Kayaking this time of night?" Max's grin stretched from earlobe to earlobe.

"Steal a kayak?" The hoodlum half of Price's personality looked ready to boogie.

"Two," I said. "And one of them needs to be a two seater. One of you can ride with me. The other one's for whoever gets the short straw."

They exchanged a worried look.

Some young people seem to make a point of looking bored. It's cool, I suppose, to be bored, unimpressed, with whatever life throws your direction. I had begun to suspect their faces were permanently frozen in a sunken-cheeked (the girls) or slack-jawed (the boys) boredom.

But Max and Price proved my theory wrong. They looked as if I'd just given them a reprieve from a life sentence of boredom. They were animated, gave each other one of those complicated handshakes followed by a couple of knuckle bumps, then just stood there grinning and talking about how and when they'd pull off their escape from the ship.

"Whoa, guys," I said, shushing them. "Keep it down. I don't want anyone else to know what we're planning." I opened my door and motioned them inside.

They sprawled on the sofa. As I took a seat opposite them, I couldn't help looking over at Gus's feeders, hoping that he had miraculously appeared while I was out. He hadn't. The boys followed my glance and, to their credit, looked sympathetic.

"Hey, Ms. M.," Max said, "we didn't take him. Honest."

I didn't want to get into it again, so I shook my head and held up my hand. "Back to business. I need to get to Playa Negra, the sooner the better."

They both started talking at once, and I did the slice across my neck thing. "We need a plan. First of all, we've got to get off the ship and into the kayaks with no one spotting us."

"Piece of cake," Max said. "Leave that part to me."

"There's the navigation to port—finding our way *toward* shore."

"No prob," Max said.

"Then there's the matter of transportation from port to the spa."

"Hitchhike?" Max suggested.

Price sneered. "In the middle of the night, dude?"

Max shrugged. "Steal a car?"

I shook my head. "Not an option."

"Seriously," Max said, "if we get there early enough, we'll catch a ride. That spa's a popular place. People coming and going at all hours."

"On to the next challenge," I said. "Breaking into the spa itself. And into the building I think is a medical facility."

"Why?" Price frowned. "What's the reason for all this secrecy? Why not just ask the reception desk for a tour?"

"Dude, that wouldn't be any fun."

"Guys, I can't tell you why right now. Call it a hunch. Plus, I just want to have a look around. See if this hunch leads anywhere."

"Like to Kate and Carly," Max said.

"Yeah."

Price sat forward. "What about Dr. Baptiste's boat?"

"Wrong again. I think he'd miss it."

"And probably be p—" Max started.

"Upset," I finished for him.

Price butted in. "Hey, man, we need something with power. We can't be working our—"

"Tails off," I filled in.

"Hey, we owe her, man," Max said, looking away from us. "And she's right. Any kind of powerboat would be noticed. We wouldn't get halfway to shore before the gendarmes would be hot after us."

"How soon can you two be ready?"

They looked at each other.

"It's not like we have to pack anything," Max said.

"How long will we be gone?" Price looked down at his baggy shorts and rumpled tank top.

"Hey, you're cool," Max said. "We're not gonna run into any chicks or anything."

"There are two I hope we do run into," I said.

"Yeah," he said.

"And I don't think they'll care what any of us is wearing."

We arranged to meet near the deck one gangway at midnight. Meanwhile, the boys were going to check out the kayaks and work on the logistics for getting the three of us through the now-closed gangway and into the kayaks. The logistics were making me crazy, so I left them to it. They couldn't have been happier.

I changed into black jeans, black T-shirt, vest, Tevas, and ball cap. "You Go, Girl!" didn't remotely match my spirit when I looked in the mirror. I was tired and cranky, and my eyes burned from lack of sleep. I would have given my right arm to simply go to bed and worry about all of this tomorrow.

But a storm was brewing off the coast, and we might not get off the ship—or across the harbor—if we didn't go now, under cover of darkness. And, more important, the longer the girls were missing, the greater the danger of them not being found alive.

I was ready well before eleven, so I used the extra time to look around the ship for Gus. Not that I hadn't been watching for him since he'd gone missing. But now I tried to imagine where I would go if I were a cat, and I realized I would make tracks to find water and anything that vaguely resembled Kibbles 'n Bits. So I headed to the ladies'—and men's—rooms. Faucets were favorite spots for Gus to grab a quick lap. Toilets if all else failed. But no answering *mew* lifted my heart when I called his name.

I next headed to the darkened kitchen, poked my head inside the food-preparation area and called out. Only silence answered. I did the same thing in the pantry, then checked behind stacks of cereal boxes. I looked carefully on the bread shelf. Gus loved bread, all flavors and colors, but his favorite was sourdough. I examined the loaves, looking for telltale signs that he had chewed through the wrapping.

Every loaf was pristine.

I was just about to return to my stateroom when I heard the roar of a speedboat engine. I hurried through the empty dining room and out to the adjoining deck. It was as I suspected. Jean Baptiste was revving his engine, preparing to leave the ship.

I could easily have hitched a ride with him, but for now I wanted to keep my visit to the spa and clinic to myself. I doubted he would stand aside as I searched for whatever it was my hunch thought was there.

Though I admired Jean and was impressed by his stunning research, I also sensed he had an ego the size of the *Queen Mary II*. I had no doubt that at the first hint I was investigating a clinic he was involved with, he would throw up a roadblock just so his good name wouldn't be sullied. Actually, I wouldn't blame him. His research was too important.

I squinted into the darkness, my focus on the speedboat. Just as it turned away from the *Sun Spirit*, the ship's running lights illumined the back of the speedboat. It was named *Nicolette* after his daughter.

I hoped my hunch about the clinic proved wrong.

Promptly at 11:49, I made my way to the gangway. The running lights had been turned off, and the passageways were nearly dark. The ship was silent except for a few flaps of canvas snapping in the wind and the clanking of metal against metal. Grommets hitting against stanchions, I assumed. Not that I would know one from the other. Until this cruise I thought a grommet was a kind of gerbil and a stanchion was akin to a pelican.

Just before I stepped from the stairs near the gangway, I heard Max and Price talking in low tones. They sounded excited, so I assumed all had gone well with their preparations.

We donned life vests and plastic splash skirts that hung from shoulders to hips and made me look like one of those toaster dolls my mother made for her relatives one Christmas. The three of us then peered over the side into the water where two orange kayaks bobbed close to the ship. It was a vertical distance of about nine feet. Too far to jump.

I swallowed hard. "How does one get from here to there?"

Price jerked his thumb to the edge of the gaping opening. A pair of thin ropes were tied to two metal posts about two feet apart. They dangled over the side, seeming to disappear into the dark abyss below. "Rope ladder," he said proudly. "Found it next to where they keep the paddles."

"I have to climb down that thing?"

He nodded, his eyes abnormally bright. At least it seemed to me they were. I remembered how I'd yelled at him on the rope bridge. Talk about payback time. This might be my undoing. I whispered a prayer, then said, "Let's do it."

"Don't worry, Ms. M.," Max said. "I'll go first; then I can catch you if you fall."

"So you lost—picked the short straw?"

He shot me a grin, then scrambled over the side and descended the ladder with ease. I stepped onto the first rung, wobbled precariously, and decided it was the better part of wisdom to look up rather than into the ink black water below. Unfortunately, I was looking into Price's leering face.

He watched me solemnly. "You're doin' good, Ms. M. You're almost there. That's right, keep going."

I figured that once I was halfway, Price probably wasn't going to let go of the rope. I would have made a bigger splash from the top, something I was sure he would prefer. I gave him a thumbs-up as I stepped into the front opening of the kayak and quickly sat down, stretching my feet out in front of me. Max was already seated in the rear, hanging on to the mooring rope that held the kayak somewhat steady. I remembered to fasten the elasticized splash skirt to the lip around the opening. I wondered how effective it would be at keeping out the waves.

Max handed me a paddle. I dipped each side in the water for a couple of practice strokes. With each movement, the little craft dipped and swayed. I swallowed hard. I'd forgotten how close to the surface of the water you sit in a kayak. I realized too late that I should have grabbed my heart medicine, the little pills that keep my heart in rhythm.

Above us Price silently closed the gangway door just short of latching for easier access when we returned. Then, leaving the rope ladder hanging in place, he zipped down in about thirty seconds and plopped into the opening in his kayak. "I had some practice earlier," he said with a slight scowl. There was something in his expression I didn't trust, but I couldn't pinpoint what it was. I just knew it was there.

The water was relatively calm, and soon we were silently making our way through the swells. The lights onshore twinkled brightly, guiding us to the harbor.

Most of the way we didn't speak. Sound carries across water too easily, and in the event that some passengers or crew onboard the *Spirit* were out for a stroll on deck, I didn't want them getting curious about what they had heard…and launching an investigation.

It took less than an hour to reach the shore. It was a good thing. I'd already worn two blisters on one hand and three on the other. And my upper arms felt as if they were made out of Silly Putty.

"Phase one, successful," I whispered as I unstrapped my life vest. "Now on to phase two."

"Got it covered, Ms. M.," Max whispered back and tossed another palm branch over the hidden kayaks.

"I hired the right guys," I said.

"Yeah, well, you better wait until you see what we've got planned," Price said.

"It can't be illegal," I said quickly. The ambient light was dim, but I saw them roll their eyes. "Okay, spill."

Max stepped closer. "I spotted a police car with a flat tire on our way to the wharf this afternoon. It's right outside town, looks abandoned."

"I bet."

"No, really."

"Why would the local police abandon a car?"

"Actually, it's an SUV," Price grinned. "An older one. It's just sitting in a lot, looking like it needs some work." I noticed his enthusiasm for our caper seemed to increase when something illegal cropped up.

"Maybe it does need work," I pointed out. "Which means…" The thought was too obvious to bother spelling out.

"I can fix anything. And I figure it's fair trade for me to fix the car, drive it to see if it works okay, then drop it by the police station." Price pulled out his Swiss army knife, opened it, and stared at some of the miniature tools. So that was why he fiddled with the thing. Mr. Fixit.

This time I rolled my eyes. "You plan to steal their SUV, then return it to the station?"

"It's not stealing," they both said at once. Max went on, "Call it a test drive."

I couldn't argue with their logic, so I followed them to the lot where they had seen the car. It was still there. A sadder law-enforcement vehicle I'd never seen. It slanted off toward the driver's side with at least one flat tire. With a sigh I sat down on a rock and watched the boys get to work. Luckily, this close to town, I didn't hear the same wild animals I'd been worried about the night before. I tried to relax but too much was at stake.

The hood was up, and the boys, keeping their voices to little more than a whisper, talked about their options. Then one of them kicked a tire while the other rooted around in the back for the spare. We were losing valuable time. I strained to see my watch but couldn't make out the time. I'd never been one for fancy timepieces. Now I wished I had one with a light.

I guessed twenty minutes had passed when they stood back with matching grins. A spare tire had replaced the flat, and when cranked, the engine sputtered to a start. I made a mental note to contact their mothers once all of this was settled and tell them what paragons they had raised. I wouldn't tell them what I'd thought before they showed me what they were really made of.

We bumped along the highway to La Vida Pura, the boys in front. Price drove while Max tried to figure out how to operate the siren and the flashing light bar.

"Got it!" he shouted after about ten minutes.

"Don't even think about it," I growled.

"Hey, we're cool, Ms. M.," he called over his shoulder. "We're cool." But he gave the controls a longing look. Something told me he'd flip on every alarm he could find before the night was over.

We rounded the last bend before the La Vida Pura guard gate. Price drove the SUV off the road and, engine stopped, coasted into some thick undergrowth. We got out and kicked grass over the tracks leading from the main road.

"Looks like we hoof it from here," Price said, sounding nervous for the first time.

"This place has heavy surveillance equipment," I said. They glanced at me, surprised. "On the fence. You didn't notice?"

They shook their heads.

We stopped at the top of a small rise. Below us a smattering of lights from the resort twinkled innocuously. I pointed to the fencing that surrounded the property as far as we could see. Security lights beamed from each fence post, and cameras were in place at the center of each section. I assumed they were equipped with motion sensors.

Max and Price looked at each other thoughtfully.

"You guys into electronics?"

"Not to worry, Ms. M. We've got a plan."

They chose a section of fence hidden on both sides by stands of palms. I stood back while they ducked beneath the camera's field of view. I could hear them whispering about the wiring, fuses, cutting the main, and everything between. Price had his knife out, studying the various tools.

"Another thought," I said after a few minutes, "is that we might cover the lens." I pulled a rectangle of black felt and a small roll of masking tape from two vest pockets.

They gaped at me. I thought I saw a hint of admiration in their slack-jawed expressions.

I swallowed a smile as I handed Max the felt and tape.

We were over the fence in ten minutes. We retrieved the camera cover at the last minute, then, bending low, zigzagged toward the clinic.

I showed Max and Price around to the rear entrance. As luck would have it, the warehouse door was closed. But in one swift movement, Price had his Swiss army knife open again, a variety of tools fanned out. Moments later the warehouse lock sprung open with a resounding *thunk*.

The image of my open stateroom door flashed into my thoughts. I didn't want to believe that either of the boys was capable of harming Gus. But Price did have the tools to open locked doors, and the tools were with him.

Strange. That's how I felt about too many people on this trip. Too many were suspicious around the edges but had something good at heart I wanted to believe in.

The boys worked together to lift the roll-up metal door. I cringed as it creaked and groaned, then slammed into its upper track with a loud *clang*.

For several seconds we waited in silence to see if security had discovered us. I hoped the officers were as lax as they had been the previous night. So far, no alarms. No blazing lights.

Only the night sounds of the jungle.

One minute more, then we scrambled up the short flight of steps to the warehouse floor.

"Mission accomplished," Max whispered.

"Not until we find Carly and Kate," I said.

"Why this place?" Price asked.

We were walking down the same dimly lit hallway Adam and I had trod the night before. "A hunch," I said. "Two people have led me to believe there's something suspicious going on here. The first was Harry Easton—only because he signed up for the spa—and I don't think he was a spa kind of guy. I believe he was onto something and the trail led him here.

"The second was Adam Hartsfield. I came here last night; so did Adam—"

"The guy wanted by Interpol," Max said.

I gave him The Look and said, "Innocent until proven guilty, dear boy. Always. Don't ever forget it."

"Sorry," he said.

"As I was saying, two investigators—people who know what they're doing; one a PI and the other an ex-detective—were on the trail of missing girls. Not Carly and Kate. Others. The trail led here, then seemed to go cold. One of the investigators didn't make it. I want to know why."

We let ourselves in the door leading to a rear corridor and wound through the maze of clinic offices and examination rooms. It was just as I had found it last night. Sterile and empty.

For a half hour we slipped from room to room as I searched for clues. Anything that would lead us to Kate and Carly. In the offices files were locked, desks empty of everything but computers and mouse pads with La Vida Pura logos. The examination rooms were spotless, without a hint of clutter.

I turned on a computer in one of the larger offices, one that I thought might belong to a clinic doctor. But it was password protected, so I quickly shut it down again. The boys lolled nearby, silently watching me but not offering to help. Price seemed especially watchful as he tossed the Swiss army knife from hand to hand. It was as if he knew something more about all this—but wasn't about to tell.

I had just completed a sweep of an upstairs operating room and was about to tell the boys it was time to go when I thought I heard a voice drifting from somewhere down a long hallway. A pinprick of fear stabbed at the edges of my consciousness. I held my finger to my lips. The boys halted midstep.

For a moment the white-noise hum of fluorescent lights reigned. Then, in the distance, I heard the murmur of barely audible voices. Men's voices. A woman's. A child's.

I hesitated, straining to identify any of the speakers. Nothing came to me. I took a step forward. Max and Price followed, their footfalls as silent as mine. We rounded a corner, then stopped again to listen. Halfway down the hall a door stood open, a wide bar of light spilling out on the gleaming linoleum.

This time I recognized one of the voices.

"The procedure from this point on is more difficult," Dr. Jean Baptiste said.

The woman spoke next. Her accent was Scandinavian, and her voice sounded vaguely familiar. "My son," she said, "is so very weak. But we want to do everything we can to save him." Her voice softened as if she was talking to the child. "Erik…" The rest was in a foreign language I thought might be Swedish. Her tone was tender.

The child answered her. Even from the distance between us, he sounded frail. He loved and trusted his mother; I could hear it in his voice.

"The procedure is controversial," Jean said. "Some might say unorthodox. But I can tell you from personal experience, the success rate is promising. And the cure is very close. Maybe even days away. Weeks at most."

"How can we be assured of success?" This from someone who hadn't spoken before.

My mind was busy connecting the dots: The three people with Jean had to be Lorenzo Nolan; his fiancée, Elsa Johannsen; and her son, Erik. I had seen them at the wharf when they arrived. The child was in a wheelchair.

"There is never a guarantee." Jean's voice dropped. "But I am hopeful, so very hopeful, that my work will bring healing—a complete cure— to thousands."

"As we've discussed," Lorenzo said, "money is no object."

"You've been more than generous through the years," Jean said, "and it's you who deserve the thanks. Once I announce my breakthrough cure, your name will be right up there with mine. As to other endeavors near to our hearts, a bright future is ahead. Medical science will move forward by incredible bounds, and you and your support makes this possible." He paused, lowering his voice. "Because of this, I know that what we're here to discuss tonight will go no further than this room."

"That's understood," Lorenzo said.

"Absolutely," Elsa agreed. "You said a moment ago you know first-hand this treatment will keep my son alive while you complete your work on the cure. Is it because of your daughter? Did you have success with this treatment? I mean, until the end."

Once more, I noticed the sorrow in her voice.

Then Jean spoke again. And with his words, the room began to spin.

"Nicolette found complete success," he said. "And is still finding it."

"She is alive?" Lorenzo sounded incredulous.

I drew in a quick breath, my heart pounding. *Is it possible? Jean's daughter…alive?* My brain refused to process the information.

"She is." For a moment Jean didn't speak, and when he did, his voice was gruff with emotion. "I guard the secret carefully because of the, shall we say, experimental and rather unorthodox treatment that has brought about her cure. But you can trust that I tell you the truth. My daughter lives."

I leaned against the wall, unbelieving, my heart still beating double time, robbing me of oxygen. I struggled to breathe. Why would he let the world believe his daughter was dead if she wasn't?

The boys exchanged glances, then stared at me. I noticed a strange look on Price's face, an expression meant to hide something deeper. Something dark. He let his gaze drift away from my scrutiny.

My heart was out of rhythm, and again I wished I'd brought a pill to pop. Second best was a polite little cough to jump it back into normal rhythm. If I didn't cough soon, I might faint. Or worse.

Jean said, "Now we get to the unorthodox treatment I'm going to prescribe for Erik…"

I waited as long as I could, then I turned to the wall, put my hands over my mouth, and let out the quietest cough I could.

Down the hall, Jean fell silent for a moment, then he said, "Did you hear something?"

The others didn't speak, but I heard a chair scrape the floor. I motioned for Max and Price to follow me. We stepped around a corner and, hugging the wall, tried to disappear into the shadows.

"Nothing," Jean said to the others after a moment. The door closed.

"Let's get out of here," I said.

FIFTEEN

s we walked back to the SUV, Max and Price discussed Jean's revelation about his daughter.

"Why would someone do that, dude?" Max said. "I mean, I went to her funeral. Felt bad because of the way we all treated her. Her dad was there, crying and talking about her like she was some kind of saint or something."

While they focused on the deception, I focused on how this latest revelation fit into the increasingly frustrating list of known facts. I came up with zero. It was an oddity. Bizarre even. But Jean was a well known researcher. Perhaps it wasn't so strange to use his daughter as a human guinea pig. He chose Costa Rica so he wouldn't be bothered by U.S. medical regulatory boards. I'd seen in his eyes how much he loved his daughter. I wondered if he'd let everyone believe she was dead, first to keep medical-ethics watchdogs off his back, and second to make a dramatic splash when his cure for leukemia was announced.

"Nicolette is still alive," Price said. "I can't get my head around it, dude."

I knew the feeling.

It took us far less time to make our return trip over the fence than it had to figure out the system first time around, or so I told the boys, gently ribbing them about my felt-and-tape method. We found the car and began the drive back to the harbor. As we neared the first hairpin curve, I told Max, who was driving, to slow down.

Adam had said not to tell anyone his whereabouts, but I'd already decided I had to see him tonight. Besides, if I didn't get to him now, it might not be possible later. I wanted to find out what he knew and tell him the bizarre news about Nicolette Baptiste.

Adrenaline had kicked in earlier, but now I was beginning to feel weary. Both Max and Price were yawning. Now Price was trying to figure out how the flashing lights and siren worked.

"Guys, one more thing before we return. There's a friend I want to visit, and there's no time like the present."

Max craned around to face me. "What?"

"First hairpin, look for a two-tracker. It will take us to a coffee plantation. Get that far, then I'll give you the rest."

With a heavy sigh, Max pressed on the gas. "What's gonna happen when it gets light?" he wanted to know. "We're in a black and white that says Republic of Costa Rica on the side."

"Keep driving, Sherlock," I said.

"Sherlock?" Max said.

"Some dude who lived a long time ago," Price said.

"Fictional dude," I said to both of them.

"Huh?" It was almost in unison.

"Never mind." I was too weary to give them an English literature lesson.

We drove through the coffee plantation, but it was so dark I couldn't make anything out. No farmhouse, no barn, nothing.

"Find a wide spot and swing around," I said to Max. "Do a three-sixty so the headlights give us some idea of what's around us."

"It's after 2:30," Price said with a noisy yawn.

"And it's raining," Max announced. "That's great. Just great."

He stopped, shifted into reverse, then did a perfect three-point turn. His driving instructor would have been proud. The headlights splayed across the landscape, but all we could see were row upon row of coffee trees. Dark and shiny in the rain.

"Head up the road a short distance. If we don't come to the barn, we'll go back toward the main road." I imagined getting lost in this maze of coffee plants and shivered. I loved coffee, but not this much.

Max said, "We won't have the cover of darkness much longer."

The rain was falling in big fat drops now, pattering the roof of the SUV. Standing water on the muddy road glistened in the headlights. Max flipped on the wipers. Mud streaks resulted.

"Does this thing have four-wheel drive?" I asked.

"I hope so," came the curt reply from Max. He clutched the steering wheel and leaned forward, squinting into the rainy night. "Hey, I see something," he said. "Right up ahead. You can barely make it out."

I strained to see through the streaked windshield. A shadowy form emerged in front of us. "That's the farmhouse," I said. "Keep going."

He pressed on, SUV sliding through the mud, wheels spinning, then catching and moving forward again.

"There. Just to the other side of the house. Off to the left."

Max steered the vehicle gingerly toward where I pointed. We neared the barn. It was dark except for a faint light deep inside.

"Who's this friend of yours anyway?" Price wanted to know.

I didn't answer.

Max stopped the SUV just short of a small door leading into what appeared to be the living quarters.

"You two stay here. I'll be back in just a few minutes."

They both yawned, and I figured they would be asleep before I got back. I knew college kids. Once asleep, they were impossible to wake. I didn't want to think about adding that to my list of worries, which included matters like getting back across the harbor in the rain. The responsibility of the boys' physical well-being was weighing heavy on my shoulders. Along with everything else.

I took a deep breath and got out of the SUV. The rain was falling in sheets. I sprinted for the small front porch, knocked, and called out, "Adam?"

I waited a few minutes, then called out again, "Adam Hartsfield?" Suddenly I couldn't wait to talk with him, hear the comforting timbre of his voice, pool our thoughts, and decide on the next course of action.

This latest development had my mind spinning. Even as I stood there, rain pouring down around me, all that was at stake—the lives of Kate and Carly and Holly and the others—washed over me in flood-like torrent.

I rapped on the door again. Harder. "Adam, please! It's Harriet!"

I tried the doorknob and found it unlocked.

The utter darkness, the odor of mud, the almost living, otherworldly splat of the rain on the metal roof all attacked my senses. It was as if the very spores—the atoms—I was breathing had an evil intent. Something evil lurked here. Something was wrong. I felt it all the way to my bones.

My hand shook as I pushed the door open and called out again, "Adam, are you there?"

Girding up every ounce of courage I had, I stepped across the threshold. "Adam?"

A faint light shone from down a short hallway and around a door. The room where I now stood, similar to a studio apartment in the States, seemed undisturbed. A rumpled bed, though empty, was shoved against the far wall. A small kitchenette stood closer to me, just to my right. A round, rough-hewn table near the door held a stack of books with a worn paperback Bible on the top, a small devotional on the prayers of Saint Francis of Assisi to one side, and a wire-bound book that appeared to be a journal of some kind.

"Adam?" I called again, stepping into the hallway. "Adam?"

The door at the end was open a crack.

Fear that had been flitting at the edges of my mind attacked me with a vengeance. Almost quicker than I could process the thoughts, they flew at me. Someone tried to frame Adam, get him out of the way, because he was getting too close to the truth.

He had gone into hiding because of the frame. He had played right into the killers' hands.

This wasn't a game. It was serious. Deadly serious.

The hairs on the back of my neck stood straight as I moved toward the door and pushed it open.

At first I thought Adam had fainted. He was wearing striped pajamas. A toothbrush had dropped to the floor beside him. A partially squeezed tube of toothpaste was in the sink, lid off.

He was curled to one side, in repose, almost as if he had simply gone to sleep.

I ran to his side, knelt, and lifted his limp, still warm hand.

Then I saw the butterfly.

SIXTEEN

Still kneeling beside the body, I stared at Adam, unbelieving.

Emotions threatened to explode from inside out. Shock. Dismay. Panic. Fear.

"Oh, Lord," I whispered, "he's one of the good guys. Don't take him yet. Please, don't take him." Even as I breathed the words, I knew it was too late. He was ashen gray. Saliva and blood had trickled from his mouth and pooled on the floor beneath his head. He looked like he'd taken a beating before his attacker went in for the kill.

I moved my hand to his wrist, held my breath, and prayed for a pulse. There was none. I stared at the blood near the corner of his mouth.

My brain pulled a similar image from the files. Easton. He'd gotten too close to some dangerous truth. So had Adam. They had both paid dearly.

I bowed my head as I released his hand. And for a moment I sat in stunned silence, too overcome with shock and sorrow to run.

Then I heard a door open. And footsteps, sodden footsteps, crossing the room behind me.

Fear shot through me. How stupid to forget that the killer, or killers, might still be here. In a closet, in some deep shadow. I backed away from

Adam's body, half-crawling across the floor to a shallow alcove in the short hallway. I pulled myself against the alcove and waited.

"Yo, Ms. M. You in here?" one of the boys called out.

Letting out a pent-up breath, I unfolded my legs and stood to block either one from entering the bathroom. "I'm here."

"We were getting worried," Max said. He peered at me as he came closer. "You okay?"

I nodded.

He glanced over my shoulder into the bathroom. The body was visible, and even in the dim light that spilled from the small room, I saw Max turn white.

"Hey," he whispered. "What's that?"

"My friend," I said, "didn't make it."

He started for the bathroom, but I touched his arm. "Don't." I wanted to spare him the up-close sight of Adam's body.

Price came through the door just then, shaking the rain off his clothes. "What's going on? Did you see your friend, Ms. M.?"

"Yeah, dude," Max answered for me. "She did. But you don't want to."

Price peered down the hall, then the boys looked at each other, fear clearly etched on their faces.

"Who was this friend?" Price said, his voice shaking.

"Adam Hartsfield," I said. "He must have gotten too close to the truth. Someone poisoned him." Still shaking, I crossed the room and sank into a chair by the table.

"How do you know he was poisoned?" Max asked, dropping into the chair next to me. Price stood behind him.

"It's the same butterfly," I said. "The same species that was next to Harry Easton's body. The blue morpho."

"Order Lepidoptera, family Nymphalidae, genus *Morpho*, species *menelaus,"* Price recited. At my quizzical look, he added, "What can I say? I like science. Stuff like this sticks. I saw it at the butterfly farm. One of the most deadly butterflies in the world."

"A single butterfly can't even kill a frog," I said wearily. "This was left as a calling card by the killer."

"Or a warning," Price said.

I dropped my forehead into my palm and drew in a deep breath. Fatigue was once again setting in, but the night was far from over. Fright and grief had carved a deep pit in my stomach, and I felt sick. When I looked up, I said, "We've got to contact the police. There's that farmhouse down the road. One of you needs to drive there, wake the occupants, and let them know what's happened. Tell them to call the local authorities."

Max stood, jingling the keys. "I guess that would be me."

Price nodded. "Yeah, dude."

"And I think the best thing is for us to wait for the police," I said. "We need to tell them what's happened."

"Who's gonna believe us?" Price asked as Max went out the door. "How do we explain the black and white and why we're out here at three in the morning?"

"Not to mention why we left a locked-down ship," I added.

I reached across the table and almost absently picked up the Bible I'd seen earlier. As I touched the worn cover, the injustice of what had happened to Adam Hartsfield hit me like a fist in the stomach. A man dies alone in a foreign country, chasing after his daughter's abductors, and he comes to this end. It wasn't right. I was still numb, sick, but right alongside the other emotions, anger—deep anger—was taking root.

I opened the cover of the Bible, and a folded piece of paper fluttered out, landing on the floor.

Price picked it up, turned it over, and frowned. "It's for you."

I took it from him. "Harriet MacIver" was scrawled across the top fold. I opened it and read the two almost illegible words. One was a name.

My breath caught in my throat.

It couldn't be. No, he had to be wrong. Or maybe I was connecting the wrong dots.

I examined the paper again. There was no mistaking Adam's intent. He was pointing me to the next dot in my quest.

I stared at the paper.

"What's it say?" Price said.

"Go get Max. We've got to get out of here," I said. "And fast. I'll explain on the way."

But Max was already on his way back. No one was home at the farmhouse, a good thing as it turned out. My plan was to drive to the police department, drop off the car, and get back to the ship as quickly as possible.

As the SUV skidded along the muddy roads, I fought off sleep. I didn't want to think how little time I'd spent head-on-pillow during the past forty-eight hours.

I am woman...

Yeah, right. A very tired, very human, very sad, and very distressed woman. I didn't have a roar left.

Now for the note to the gendarmes. I flipped on the overhead light, pulled out my notepad, and began to write.

Buenos Días, señores y señoras:
We borrowed this vehicle for police business. In exchange,
minor repairs were made to your engine, and your flat tire

was exchanged for the spare at no charge. We hope you
are happy with the condition of the vehicle when you
find it.

However, in the process of our investigation into crimes
we believe are being committed within your jurisdiction, we
discovered the body of a man in the rear house of the coffee
plantation near La Vida Pura. The man's name is Adam
Hartsfield. You will find papers near the body confirming
his identity.

Mr. Hartsfield is wanted by Interpol for crimes he did
not commit. This I will explain to you when we meet. I will
be contacting you within twenty-four hours.
Sincerely,
Ms. M.

We would leave the note on the driver's seat of the SUV, which would be parked in front of the police station. I prayed for two things: (1) for the car and note to be discovered right away, (2) but not before we hightailed it out of there.

Max came up with a brilliant idea.

The boys let me out near where we had hidden the kayaks, then they headed up the steep incline to the fortresslike police headquarters. It was still dark when they passed through the open gate and into the front lot. It was also between shifts, apparently, because (as I learned later) the parking lot and guardhouse were both deserted.

In one quick movement they turned on the siren and flashing bar lights, locked all the doors, and ran like the wind toward a back wall. They waited long enough to see several officers fly out the front door toward the car, only to stand around it scratching their heads when they couldn't get in.

Their flight down the hairpin turns must have caused an adrenaline surge, because when the boys found me by the kayaks—where, I confess, I'd fallen asleep in my life vest and splash skirt—they were as lively as two monkeys in a barrel. I watched mutely as they went through a series of high-fives, knuckle bumping, and "nice goin', dude's." You'd have thought they'd just made an NFL touchdown, but I took no joy in it. Then they pulled the kayaks into the water, helped me in, and started to paddle back to the ship.

The trip was a blur. I paddled by rote in rhythm with Max, barely noticing the blisters. The shock of finding Adam, my deep sadness, and my growing sense of futility threatened to overwhelm me. This thing was rapidly growing bigger than I was. I closed my eyes to pray, but all I could see was Adam's face…and the image of his daughter in the photos. Tears threatened, but I blinked them away.

The anger that had started creeping in earlier surged like floodwaters breaching a levee. This was no time for tears. It was time for guts and savvy. I prayed that I was up to the task. I would see this thing through. For Adam. For Holly. For all the lost girls.

The rain turned to a drizzle, then to a mist, and as the horizon began to pale in the east, the day took on a dreary, deep green gray.

"Hope no one closed the gangway door," Price said as we neared the ship.

We approached the *Sun Spirit* from behind to avoid being seen, but the ship was barely visible in the low-hanging fog. The running lights, still dimmed, cast a pale, unearthly glow across the inky water. The early morning chill, my damp clothing, and the ghostly appearance of the ship gave me the shivers.

I felt as if I'd lived a lifetime since we paddled to shore just a few hours earlier, and in a way I had. Someone I thought was dead apparently lived, and someone else, whose life I was just beginning to cherish, was dead.

We reached the gangway. The rope ladder dangled where we'd left it.

"Way to go, dude," Max said to Price as they glided the kayaks closer to the ship.

"Mission accomplished," Price said with a tired grin.

"Remember, guys," I said once my feet were planted firmly on the deck, "not a word to anyone about any of this. There will be serious consequences if it gets out."

"Like you're going to call your buddy, the president of Shepparton?" Price looked up at me from the kayak. I was beginning to like that baby-faced look of his. He probably had his mother wrapped around his little finger, no matter what hooligan antics he got into.

I smiled. "Just the dean, dear boy."

I left Max and Price to finish their mission, tying the kayaks to the stern of the *Sun Spirit*. We had discussed lifting them by crane to deck two where they had found them. Turned out nothing seemed workable—not without alerting the whole ship. Besides, the boys were too tired to think straight and quite content with my plan to let their discovery remain a mystery to the crew.

Fifteen minutes later I fell into bed, hoping for at least a few hours of sleep before being awakened. As I drifted to sleep, I imagined the Playa Negra police figuring out the identity of Ms. M. and calling Captain Richter. I imagined the officers spotting the boys as they ran away from the police station, following, and with binoculars trained on us, watching us paddle toward the *Sun Spirit.* I imagined detectives dusting the SUV for fingerprints... At that scenario, my eyes flew open. I imagined them showing up at my door to arrest me for the murder of Adam Hartsfield.

Finally, I fell into a troubled, restless sleep. Real images of what I had seen, what I had experienced this night replaced the fantasies whirling through my mind. Frightening, sorrowful, confusing images. Adam's face was at the heart of them.

A knock at my door woke me. Disoriented, I reached for my clock. It was 10:13 a.m. I rubbed my eyes and sat up. My head pounded, and I felt sick. The worst of it was that Interpol and the police detectives had been scheduled to board at 8:00 this morning. I hoped that the storm—and perhaps the confusion over the SUV and the note inside—had delayed them.

"Mrs. MacIver," called the voice, "are you all right?"

Zoë.

I padded to the door, opened it a crack, and peered out. "Hi, luv," I said sleepily.

"Are you all right? You weren't at breakfast, and I was worried."

I stifled a yawn. "I'm just being a sleepyhead this morning."

She hesitated, looking at the floor. "I have something to tell you. Can we talk?"

I had to get to the bridge and fast, but I stared at Zoë's troubled face and remembered my unspoken commitment to her. "Give me a few minutes to get dressed."

A shadow of anxiety crossed her face as she nodded. "Okay."

I closed the door and hurried to the dressing room, passing by the window. The day had turned an ugly gray. Anvil-shaped clouds towered farther offshore, and the chop of the waves had clearly increased. The wind snapped the canvas in that annoying way I often heard, only this time each snap sounded like a gunshot.

Zoë returned fifteen minutes later. I had just finished my shower and, with clean clothes and freshly shampooed hair, I felt human again. Almost.

The coffee was brewed, and I served us each a cup.

Zoë looked solemn. She didn't touch her coffee. Instead, she twisted her long, nail-bitten fingers into a knot and left them on her lap, white-knuckled.

"What is it?" I prompted. I was jumpy, wanting to get to the heart of the problem, so I could move on to the other dragons I had to slay. I was at once ashamed and tried to relax and listen. Whatever was troubling her was weighing heavy.

She looked away from me. "I've done some things I'm not proud of. I wanted to talk to you about them."

"We've all done things we're not proud of, Zoë. We're human."

She turned sharply, studied my face, then said, "None as bad as me." Her expression darkened. Her eyes filled, and angrily she swiped at her tears. "Even the thought, the memory of what I've done, is too much to bear." Her voice was filled with anguish.

I leaned forward, took her hands in mine. "Zoë, whatever it is, you can tell me. I'm a good listener."

"You're the first one in a long time who seems to care, which makes it worse. There's Gramps, of course, but he doesn't have long to live. It feels good to be with someone who isn't out to tell me how bad I am and doesn't ignore me because I don't belong." She pulled her hands away.

"Whatever you've done, maybe just telling another person will help you see it's not so bad."

"It's bad." She hesitated, letting her gaze drift again. This time she looked over at Gus's feeders, seemed to study them. She blinked rapidly. "It hurts to lose someone you love, doesn't it?"

My heart constricted. "Oh, Zoë," I whispered, "was it you?"

She whirled around, frowning. "What?"

"Gus? Is that what you're trying to tell me? You did something to Gus?"

She sat silently for a moment, seeming to be fighting tears. Then, shoulders stiff, she stood and glared down at me. "It hurts, doesn't it? Losing someone feels like somebody twisted a knife into your gut. Now you know what it feels like." Without another word, she stomped to the door, yanked it open, then slammed it behind her.

I stared at the closed door, unable to move. It was Zoë all along? Fresh grief rose to the surface as I thought about Gus.

I dropped my head into my hands.

And my day had only begun.

I wasted no time heading to the bridge to see if Interpol had arrived. Adam's note was in my pocket.

The name he'd written was all the proof I needed. And, if Adam was right, it was the road map that would lead me to Kate and Carly and, I hoped, to Holly.

But first I had to convince the authorities.

I bent into the wind as I climbed the metal stairs leading to the bridge and looked out over the gray horizon. The storm was closer now, whipping the whitecaps into a frenzy. The door to the bridge was closed, and I had to put my shoulder into it to get it to budge.

"Captain Richter?"

He looked up from the desk behind the operating panel. "Yes?"

"Have the investigators been here?"

"Interpol?"

"And the others. Local authorities, I assume."

"I expected them by eight this morning, but with the storm brewing, they've been delayed. Why do you ask?"

"I want to be in on the meeting. I need to talk with them, with the school officials, and with you."

He frowned. "You know, Mrs. MacIver, I once told you to leave the investigation to the professionals." The same condescending tone was back in spades. I had to do something to shake him off his pedestal.

"I have information about the missing girls," I said.

He didn't react, but I could see the skepticism in his expression. I didn't care. It was urgent that he believe me. Now that Adam was dead, I had no allies. I desperately needed Richter to understand, to help. I urged him with my eyes to put aside whatever prejudices he had against me and listen. Just listen.

"Look," I said. "I went into town last night. I've suspected the abductions are related to the clinic at La Vida Pura—"

I stopped in midsentence; Richter's face had turned purple. He stepped close to me. I could smell the liquor on his breath. "You did what?" he shouted.

I leaned back, resisting an urge to fan the air in front of my nose. "I paddled a kayak to shore."

"You disobeyed a direct order to stay onboard?" The clenched muscles in his jaw were working overtime.

"It wasn't a direct order. You said the ship was being quarantined. You didn't say anything about the people on it."

The shade of purple deepened to eggplant. "You paddled to shore all alone."

"You doubt that I can do it?" I wasn't about to implicate Max and Price.

He didn't answer, but the vein on his temple was throbbing visibly.

"Listen," I said. "I can't say why, but I have evidence that Interpol is after the wrong man."

"What do you mean?"

"They shouldn't be investigating Adam Hartsfield."

"How would you know this?"

"Someone else is involved."

"You're making no sense," he said and started to turn away from me.

I thought of Adam's note, the handwriting scrawled in childlike printing, barely legible. Written as if he knew the end was coming.

I spoke the name he'd written. "Dr. Jean Baptiste."

I waited to see him stunned into silence. He wasn't. Again, I wondered whether Captain Richter was caught up in this.

"What's he got to do with it?"

"He's involved."

"You have no idea what you're talking about," he said. "Dr. Baptiste?" He shook his head. "Not only are you skating close to defamation of character, but you'll be made a laughingstock. We're talking about a murder investigation, a poisoning. Linking someone like Baptiste to this crime is ludicrous."

"I'm talking about this and other crimes, including the poisoning death of Adam Hartsfield."

He winced. "What?"

"You heard me."

"Okay, I heard you, but I don't believe it."

"Just let me be part of the meeting," I said, "and I'll explain."

"I'm sure they'll be willing to talk with you one on one after—"

I was sure they would, especially after they realized that Ms. M. equaled Ms. MacIver.

"It must be everyone," I said, "law enforcement, school officials, you, your first officer. It's important, Captain. Lives are at stake." I paused, then added, "Please."

He let out a noisy, irritated sigh. "I'll check with the authorities," he finally said. "But I'm not promising anything."

It was a begrudging concession, but a concession nonetheless. And he hadn't made me grovel. I was in his debt.

The ship was teeming with passengers, and most were disgruntled. Stuck onboard, they milled about the coffee shop, the dining room, and the Clipper Lounge. It had begun to rain again, and the sea looked angry and dark. A pall seemed to have dropped over the ship. The students were conspicuously absent—in classes, I assumed.

I wanted—no, *needed*—to talk with Zoë. For whatever reason, she had been brought into my life. The cruel rejection she had felt from her mother and her classmates made me ache for her. But I was also struggling with what she had all but confessed to me about Gus.

It didn't matter that she was obviously emotionally disturbed. Could I forgive her? I couldn't. Which made me ashamed because forgiveness is at the core of my faith.

Gus. One of the most innocent of God's creatures. Harmed intentionally. I couldn't even begin to consider forgiveness right now. Maybe I never could. But I did need to talk with Zoë and find out what she knew, what she had done. Then maybe I could stop looking for Gus with every corner I turned, at the end of every hallway, in every easy chair I passed.

I found Zoë in a small room set aside as a library. It was little more than an alcove off one of the open areas above deck one.

She looked up as I approached, her face pale, an unwelcome curl to her lips. I sat down across from her. "You're not in class."

She shrugged. "Didn't feel like going."

I glanced at the textbook that lay open on her lap. Chemistry.

"Zoë, what you told me earlier…about Gus, can we talk about it?"

"You're no different than the others."

"What do you mean?"

"You jumped to a horrid conclusion—about your cat. You assumed the worst about me. Poor little Zoë Shire, lonely, ugly, meanspirited, cruel—"

I held up my hand to stop the tirade. "Who has ever said these things about you?"

Her eyes brimmed with tears, and I leaned forward. "Your mother?"

She didn't answer. She didn't have to. I saw it in her eyes.

"Zoë," I said, "you came to me to confess something you felt terrible about. You were staring at Gus's feeders. You said how terrible it is to lose someone you care about… I thought you were talking about Gus and how much I cared for him."

"I was talking about me. About how I'm about to lose someone I care about."

"Your grandfather?"

She was weeping now, openly. I wanted to take her in my arms, but I didn't want to embarrass her. My maternal instincts understood the fine line between comfort and mortification when trying to soothe the feelings of a hurting young woman. And Zoë's hurting was soul deep, deeper than anything my children had dealt with at her age.

"My best friend. If I stop, she'll die."

"Stop what?"

She took off her glasses and stared at me without speaking.

"Zoë, you can tell me."

But something in her eyes, maybe a horror too deep to express, made me wonder if I could bear hearing it. Hope seemed to drain from her, leaving her pale and devoid of emotion.

"Zoë!"

"If you knew," she whispered, "you would hold an unbearable secret. It would be impossible to keep to yourself. Too much would be lost. Lives would be lost."

"What are you involved in? Is it tied up with Carly and Kate? Do you know where they are?"

"It's better you don't know," she said.

"Is someone threatening you? Are people saying that something bad will happen if you tell?" My whisper was hoarse, urgent. "The girls' lives may be in danger. We've got to get to them. Tell me what you know."

"I didn't say I know where they are."

I felt whatever emotional connection I had with her slipping away. I leaned forward intently. "I care about you, Zoë. You've had a burden, too heavy a burden, pressing down on you since childhood. You may have made choices based on that pain. Whatever it is, whatever you came to talk to me about earlier, I'm here to listen. No trouble is too great—"

"Stop it. Please. You don't live in my skin. You don't know the sacrifices I'm making to save another's life. You don't know what it's like to have one true friend when there are no others. Or what it's like to think this one true friend might be taken away from you forever. When you think of her as the sister you never had. When you would give anything to be part of her flesh-and-blood family."

"Nicolette," I said, staring at her. "She is your one true friend. As close as a sister."

"Nicolette is dead." She looked away from me.

"No, she isn't." I paused, watching her expression change. "I don't know how, but I think I know why you're involved in keeping her alive."

She whirled then, her eyes dark with anger. "How did you come to that conclusion?"

Quickly I considered the consequences of telling Zoë the truth. This minute I had a chance to convince her to help me, to help Carly and Kate, if they were still alive. But if her allegiance remained with Nicolette, she would let Jean know I had tied him to the disappearances. He was behind two murders; I didn't doubt that he wouldn't hesitate to kill again.

I looked into Zoë's empty eyes, desperately searching for a flicker of hope. "It doesn't matter how I know," I finally said. "But I know it's true. Nicolette is alive."

I waited for her reaction, then said, "You are helping her stay alive, aren't you?"

"Thousands will be helped in the end," she said. "Soon a child will live because of the sacrifices of many. A child who's never been out of a wheelchair. Soon he'll walk. He has chronic myelogenous leukemia and isn't expected to live another six months. But soon he'll be cured. Completely cured because of the sacrifices."

I leaned forward. "What sacrifices, Zoë? You can tell me."

She reached for her glasses, put them on, then closed her chemistry textbook. "There's no other way," she said, standing.

"I'm going there," I said and rose from my seat.

"Where?"

I knew by her expression I didn't need to answer. "Come with me."

She gave me a small smile. "Don't," she said, sadly. "Please, promise you won't go."

Before I could answer, she walked away.

The storm seemed to have stalled a few miles offshore. Clouds billowed high to the west, but overhead, patches of lighter gray appeared within the murky hues of the deep gray green. At the sound of speedboats heading toward the *Sun Spirit*, I looked through my stateroom window.

Two harbor patrol black and whites, flying Costa Rican flags, circled the ship, then disappeared around the stern, to enter amidships, starboard, I guessed. I assumed Captain Richter would conveniently forget to mention my attendance, so I hurried to meet the entourage, pencil and pad in hand and Adam's note in my pocket. I trotted down two flights of stairs, then headed to the gangway.

Captain Richter, in full dress uniform, stood to one side. The first officer stood beside him, the dean from Shepparton, Guy Williams, directly opposite in crisp khakis and a polo shirt. I looked down at my rather worn jeans skirt and tie-dyed T-shirt, adjusted my "You Go, Girl!" cap and ponytail that jutted through the back opening, and wondered if I should have dressed up for the occasion.

I had pounded the old adage into my kids' heads: You never get a second chance to make a first impression. I might have remembered it myself if I'd not had so much on my mind. Now it was too late. I grimaced, wondering if I was the only one thinking Granny Clampett-does-the-Gap.

The entourage—four men and a woman—stepped onto the deck.

Introductions were made in English and Spanish, then Richter glanced my direction and, scowling, introduced me. He added that I had asked to sit in on the initial debriefing. A few curious looks were exchanged, a few words in Spanish tossed about, then approval given with lukewarm nods.

Ten minutes later we were seated at a large rectangular table in the rear of the bridge. I sat across from the woman, Monica Oliverio, the liaison from Interpol and an expert in human trafficking. Dean Williams was on my right, and Carlos Xavier, lead detective from Playa Negra, was on my left. Captain Richter convened the meeting from the head of the table, then turned it over to Monica Oliverio.

The no-nonsense, dark-haired woman leaned forward, making eye contact with the detectives from Playa Negra. Five minutes into her speech about the cooperation of Interpol with local agencies, I wondered why anyone else needed to be there. Then she got to the point.

"The urgency of this matter is acute," she said. "Let's review the facts: First, a body, a passenger on this ship, was discovered here seventy-two hours ago. Second, another victim, also a passenger on this ship, was discovered just last night, though he was not onboard when he was attacked. Third, both victims were found to have been injected with a substance derived from the deadly blue morpho butterfly.

"The second victim was former law enforcement; the other a private investigator. From what we have ascertained, both were looking for young women who had disappeared sometime previously. Harry Easton, victim number one, had been hired by a young woman's parents in the U.S. Adam Hartsfield, victim number two, was searching for his daughter who disappeared three years ago."

Something she said about the victims had been nagging at me. When she said Adam's name, I knew what it was.

"Excuse me?" I leaned forward, ignoring the scowls around the table. She gave me a hard stare, and I hurried on. "You referred to the first body found, which we know is Easton. When you mentioned the second victim, you didn't say 'body.' You just said 'victim.' Was it a matter of word choice or...?" My voice trailed off as I realized how foolish I sounded.

"You did not know?" Her eyes bored in on me.

"That he died," I said lamely. "Yes, actually I did know. But just now, when you didn't mention his body, I just hoped I was—"

"I won't ask you why you thought he was dead," she said, "when no one on this ship is privy to last night's grim discovery. We will get to that later."

"Please, go on," I said. "I'm sorry I interrupted."

"I'm not finished," she said. "To answer your question, Mr. Hartsfield is not dead. At least not yet. His condition is serious, and he may not recover. I spoke to his doctor before coming here. The toxin caused him to be hypotensive"—she noticed my quizzical look and gave me a tight smile—"an extreme drop in blood pressure. Apparently, following the injection, he suffered a number of seizures, after which he was postictal— a condition that can mimic death." Her tone softened. "He is clinging to life right now."

I fell back into my chair, stunned.

"Now, if you don't mind, I would like to continue."

I nodded mutely, my mind trying to grasp what she had said.

Monica leaned forward intently. "Information about the missing girls has been in our forensics database since shortly after the disappearance of each girl. It is updated from time to time and used by such people as Easton and Hartsfield. We, of course, keep files on inquiries made, by whom, and for what purpose.

"The trafficking of people along the Pacific and Caribbean corridors is rampant, ladies and gentlemen, right up there with the drug trade and money laundering. When people disappear—particularly young women— we are alerted by local agencies in the countries from which they disappear. The young woman in Aruba some time back is just one such example. Our officers provided tireless assistance in the search. We do no less for other missing persons.

"For obvious reasons, it is usually young women who are abducted and sold to crime lords for trafficking in Asia, Russia, Indonesia, the Middle East…the list goes on. These girls disappear without a trace.

"But back to the two recent victims. Though we received information about the ties between the two men, it seems pointless to assume that Hartsfield killed Easton. They were both on this cruise for the same reason. They had both contacted us, asking for any new information about the victims they were searching for.

"Instead, Interpol—rather, our investigators and forensics experts— believes that these two men had come close to finding the source of the crimes committed against these young women. Which leads me to some points worth noting.

"Two young women disappeared while on this cruise. Carly Lowe and Kate Rivers were also both from Shepparton College in Tampa, Florida. So were the two young women Easton and Hartsfield were trying to find.

"From Interpol's perspective, human trafficking was the obvious intent of the abductors. But questions remain. *Who,* of course, is the most obvious. *Why,* we know, at least in part." She leaned forward again. "We need to discuss the other side of that question: *Why* Shepparton students?"

Ms. Oliverio looked around the table, finally resting her gaze on Dean Williams.

He stroked his beard and frowned. "I couldn't begin to answer the question," he said. "The other girls disappeared a few years ago. They were considered runaways. Both came from troubled homes. Not rich by any means. Both girls worked in the cafeteria to make ends meet. It was rumored that they were on their way out." He sat back, shaking his head. "Honestly, until now I never made any connection between those girls and the disappearances of Carly Lowe and Kate Rivers."

I cleared my throat and leaned forward. The captain scowled, but to his credit remained silent as I began to speak.

"I didn't introduce myself earlier," I said. "My name is Harriet MacIver—" I saw the locals raise their eyebrows, so I amended, "some people refer to me as Ms. M." Their brows shot even higher. "With all due respect, Ms. Oliverio, I would like to propose a different scenario."

"And your area of expertise, Ms.— What did you say your name was?" Monica Oliverio gave me a hard stare. Unblinking. I could see that she didn't like having her opinions questioned. And this was my second time to interrupt her.

"Ms. MacIver," I said primly. "Harriet, if you'd like. Yes, well, you see…I don't have any particular area of expertise, except, of course, that which comes from raising three rather rascally children, two of them twins, and propelling a husband up the corporate ladder. And, of course, household management. Volunteering for everything from making potluck soups to selling Brownie nuts. Helping with homework, looking things up in the *Encyclopedia Britannica*—which dates me, I'm afraid. I raised my kids before the Internet explosion."

"Ms. MacIver," the captain said rather sternly. "Please, if you don't mind…"

"Yes, yes, of course," I said. "What I was getting to is this. Raising a family teaches you a lot about life, things like passion for what matters and stick-to-it-iveness to see a project through. You do what you must to get at the heart of a problem, no matter the pain, the sorrow, the roadblocks. And you don't stop until you find the solution." I paused. "Just call me the Energizer Bunny."

"Ms. MacIver?" the captain said again, this time with one of his noisy sighs.

"Yes, well, as I was saying, I do believe my expertise qualifies me to speak to the problem at hand. You see, I got pulled into this because of Joey, my youngest, and Carly Lowe. She's an old friend of the family, and I love her like another daughter. When she went missing, I thought my heart would break…"

"Ma'am," Monica Oliverio said, though this time her tone was gentler. "Please, our time here is limited. You were going to tell us about, how did you call it, another scenario?"

"Yes," I said. "I do have something to add." I pulled Adam's note from my pocket, opened it, and smoothed it on the table in front of me. "The man we need to take a close look at is Dr. Jean Baptiste."

There were audible gasps around the table.

"You see, I left the ship last night and made my way to the clinic at La Vida Pura." I told them what I overheard. The words had barely left my mouth when the mild-mannered dean next to me exploded.

"How dare you make such an accusation!"

I turned to watch him pound the table, one hard hit with his fist. Then he seemed to shudder with revulsion. "Do you know who you're talking about? Dr. Baptiste is being considered for the Nobel Prize. He was one of the pioneers of the Human Genome Project. His work with genetics and hematology is legendary."

The dean's eyes seemed to almost bug out with irritation, his lips clamped with disgust as he stared at me. "How dare you even hint that he could be involved with this…this human trafficking?"

I held up a hand. "I don't deny his brilliance. That isn't in dispute. But please consider why he might be abducting these young women. Consider that his daughter also attended Shepparton at the same time the first two young women disappeared. Consider that he might think the sacrifice of others justifiable not only to save his daughter but to eventually save millions of other lives." I paused. "Is that so far-fetched for this brilliant scientist, who also loves his daughter?"

"Whoa! You've gone on quite long enough, Mrs. MacIver," Captain Richter said. "What kind of proof do you have?"

I didn't answer. I couldn't implicate Max or Price. Neither could I say what I had picked up from my conversation with Zoë. "I only have this."

I picked up Adam's note and read aloud the words he had scrawled across the paper: "It's Baptiste." I looked up. "Adam Hartsfield left this for me to find. My name is written on the front. I found it after I discovered what I thought was Adam Hartsfield's body—on a coffee plantation near La Vida Pura."

"Ms. M., you were a busy lady last night," one of the local detectives said.

"Yes sir, I was."

"You know how to change a tire?"

It was true, I did. I just hadn't needed to for years. "Yes, I do."

"And repair a carburetor?"

He had me there. I fluttered the fingers on one hand and laughed. "My father was a great believer in teaching his daughters everything they would ever need to know about fixing cars."

The two officers across from me didn't smile.

Neither did I when I spoke to the rest of the group. "I can't stress how important it is to question Dr. Baptiste, perhaps visit his island." I paused, moving my gaze around the table. "What if I'm right? What if the untouchable, brilliant Dr. Jean Baptiste thinks he's above the law?"

"We can sit here and ask what-ifs all day, Ms. MacIver," Monica Oliverio said. "But, in reality, Adam Hartsfield could have meant anything by the note. What if he meant for you to ask Baptiste to help you?"

It wouldn't help to argue, so I didn't answer.

She continued as if she didn't expect me to. "We really do need to follow conventional wisdom here. But we thank you for coming forward with this information. We do appreciate citizens who are watchful and want to help."

It was a dismissal. With a heavy sigh I stood and left the room.

wound through the huddles of passengers, some standing in public areas looking out at the approaching storm; others seated in small conversational groups, bent close, speaking in low, worried tones. I imagined they had seen the harbor patrol boats moored near the ship and naturally were concerned about the criminal investigation that was just now getting under way.

The Shepparton classes had apparently been dismissed. Students lolled in the dining area near the soft-drink machine. Notebooks and textbooks had been haphazardly tossed on nearby tables. Their usual animated conversation had quieted, and worried glances on grim faces had taken its place.

I passed through the dining area and picked up a stale roll left over from breakfast, a couple of packets of jam, and a plastic cup of thin, overprocessed orange juice. Then I sat down at a table as far away from the crowds as I could get. My stomach had been complaining all morning from its lack of food, but I didn't realize until I bit into the hard roll exactly how hungry I was.

I had just taken my second bite when a student I hadn't met before approached and stood by my elbow. Mildly annoyed, I put down the roll, dabbed at my mouth with my napkin, and looked up.

"Someone asked me to give this to you." He stared at me for a moment, then thrust a legal-size envelope toward me. I took in his dark hair and acne-pocked face, his unkempt appearance, then focused my attention on the envelope.

It was blank on the outside and sealed. Frowning, I set it down beside the roll while I wiped a smudge of marmalade off one hand. Before I ran my finger underneath the sealed flap, I looked up to ask the student who had given it to him.

He had disappeared into the throng. I stood and looked around, but too many people had now gathered in the dining room, waiting for lunch to be served.

I sat again and opened the envelope.

Dear Mrs. MacIver,
It's urgent that I speak with you. I know the whereabouts of Carly Lowe. I will meet you today at 2:30
p.m. at the Playa Negra wharf to escort you there.
You must come alone, and you must not tell the
authorities.
    Lives will be lost if you do.

The message was typed on a manual typewriter and was unsigned. I couldn't be certain, but I had to wonder if someone had used my old Underwood. Who else onboard would have such a machine?

I stared at the note. I'd made no bones about the fact that I cared for Carly like a daughter and that I was ready to risk my life to save her. Someone knew this about me and was either using it to get me off the ship or was truly concerned and wanted to help.

I stood and rapidly moved through the groups of passengers, wildly searching for the student who had brought me the note. All I could remember was that he wore glasses, had dark hair and a bad complexion, and dressed like most of the others in shorts and a worn, wrinkled T-shirt. He was nowhere to be found.

I returned to the table to finish my roll, though now it tasted like wallpaper paste. Dried wallpaper paste.

"Yo, Ms. M.," Max said as he approached. "Mind if I join you?"

"No, not at all. Please sit down."

He sat across from me, lunch tray piled high with something that vaguely resembled spaghetti. Three pieces of bread sat atop the ubiquitous iceberg-lettuce-and-grated-carrot salad. This wasn't the time for such a thing to hit, but I couldn't help thinking about the humdinger of a travel article this trip was going to make. Especially the gourmet cuisine. I almost laughed.

"Please don't tell me it's canned spaghetti," I said to Max as he took his first bite.

"What's wrong with canned spaghetti?" He stuffed in another bite, chewed, wiped his mouth with his napkin, then said, "I grew up on SpaghettiOs. Nothing better."

"Unless it's Pop-Tarts," I said.

"Mmm, love those too. And that little blue box of macaroni-and-cheese fixin's. Great stuff."

"And Twinkies?"

He took a gulp of milk. "Nah, can't stand 'em. Not after that guy said they made him go on that killing spree. Never touched them after that."

He put down his fork and squinted across the table. "Hey, Ms. M., you look a little pale. Are you okay? I mean, especially after what you went through last night." I pulled the note out of the envelope and handed it to him. He scanned it, then said, "You gonna go?"

"If I can get transportation."

He didn't hesitate. "Count me in."

I leaned forward. "If you let me off a distance from the wharf, I can walk there and talk to whoever it is while you wait. The note says I must be alone."

"Only if we're close enough to hear you holler if you need us."

"You think Price can make it?"

"Not sure. I saw him earlier. He said he's gotta talk to the investigators this afternoon."

My heart stopped for a half beat. "I've kept your names from the authorities. I hope it doesn't have anything to do with last night."

"And I hope we didn't miss any fingerprints when we wiped the car. But not to worry, Ms. M., we can do it without him." He checked his watch. "I'll have the kayak waiting at 1:30. It'll take some doing to make sure we're not seen and stopped, but I'll figure out something. Maybe Price can help with that part."

"Hey, Max?" I said as I stood. He was winding another forkful of spaghetti but looked up. "You're the best."

He grinned and gave his corn-silk hair a small embarrassed toss.

Lost in thought about the task ahead, the glimmer of hope about Carly, and the worry over worsening weather conditions, I almost didn't see the entourage heading toward me. I had just stepped into the corridor outside the dining room, when they turned a corner and I was directly in their path.

"Ms. MacIver," said the captain in the lead. He passed without another word.

The others followed suit, almost acting as if I wasn't there. Monica Oliverio walked slightly behind the others and had the grace to at least give me a curt nod as she passed.

"Ms. Oliverio," I called after her, unwilling to let her go by without at least a word.

She turned and didn't look pleased. "My time is limited," she said. As if I had all the time in the world and how I used it didn't count toward anything important.

"Did you make a decision about investigating Dr. Baptiste?"

She frowned. "I thought it was clear when you left—"

I interrupted her. "There was obviously no interest in going to the island, but I thought Interpol, perhaps even the local authorities, might see the value of at least looking into how the abductions, the poisonings might lead back to him."

"When I get back to my office," she said vaguely, "I'll definitely make a note in the file."

"Note in the file?" I almost shouted the words. "By then it may be too late."

She held up a hand. "Please, Ms. MacIver, let the experts take care of this. You've been a great help, really. But let us take it from here." Her expression held something akin to pity. Along with having all the time in the world on my hands, she probably thought I didn't have anything better to do than poke my nose into matters far beyond my comprehension.

"Ms. Oliverio," I said, "one of the missing girls is very close to my family. Her mother asked me to keep an eye on her while I was onboard. I feel responsible—"

"Ma'am, there wasn't anything you could have done to prevent this."

"I'm not going to give up," I said, "even if it means confronting Baptiste myself."

"Stay out of this, Ms. MacIver. Leave it to the authorities to investigate."

I was still seething as I returned to my stateroom to get ready for the rendezvous.

At 1:24 precisely, I proceeded to the gangway amidships. Though we were in the tropics and the rain might come in torrents, wind chill probably wouldn't be a factor. Nonetheless, I had changed into jeans, wadded up a sweatshirt and tucked it in my backpack, and grabbed a waterproof windbreaker to wear over my travel vest. I thought about taking an umbrella, then I remembered it would only serve as a lightning rod. Which brought up another set of worries—as if I didn't have enough to start with.

I knew the dangers we were about to face, but how could I not go if it meant saving Carly? Her mother would be flying in as soon as the storm cleared. What better gift than to greet her at the airport with the news that Carly had been found?

Thunder. Lightning. Fog. Wind. Torrential rains. Any of it, all of it, might be just ahead. How could I let Max face those dangers? It was one thing to take the risk myself; it was quite another to ask this good-hearted student to risk his life.

"Hey, Ms. M.," Max said as I approached the gangway.

The corridor was empty. "Where is everyone?"

He pointed to three signs, one blocking the end of each passageway that led to the gangway. They were the bright-yellow, A-frame, caution signs similar to those you find on freshly mopped floors or in front of rest rooms when they're being serviced. Each had a polite notice on it:

PARDON US WHILE

WE CLEAN FOR YOU!

A mop and bucket stood near each sign.

"Good thinking," I said.

"It was Price's idea. He took them from a utility closet he found open." He turned back to the open gangway door. "Your chariot awaits, Madam."

"Max?"

"Yeah?"

"You don't have to do this, you know."

He looked at me. "I know."

"You can get me started, pointed in the right direction, and with the wind to my back, I'll get to shore in two shakes."

He rolled his eyes. "Yeah, right."

I stepped closer, touched his arm. "Hey, bud. Look out there. This storm is moving in. I'd rather you didn't go. I'm serious. If anything happened to you—"

"Not a problem," he said. "My dad's an attorney."

"Now that's something to worry about." I donned my life vest and splash skirt, then he helped me position myself at the top of the rope ladder. Warily, a step at a time, I descended until I could drop into the kayak. As soon as I slid into place, the craft rocked with the choppy waves.

I watched Max scurry down the ladder, my chin resting on the thick foam-encased vest surrounded by an equally bright and bulky splash skirt. A fluorescent orange abominable snowman. Nothing like trying to blend in with the surroundings.

Max unfastened the tether, and in tandem we paddled away from the ship. I glanced up to see if anyone was watching us, wishing I'd thought to bring a dark blanket to drape over our neon-hued selves. Because of the storm, the decks were deserted, and it was impossible to see faces inside the glassed-in areas. I needn't have worried because we hadn't gone more than a few yards when we disappeared into thick fog.

"I hadn't counted on this," Max said, his voice sounding small. "Bummer."

"Just hold a steady course," I said.

He pulled the oars, fell into a rhythm, and we were once again gliding across the water. "I just hope we're going the right way."

"We are," I said.

"How do you know?"

Truth was, I didn't. The kayak rose and fell, and the waves seemed higher than before. The wind picked up again. Then, just as quickly as we entered it, we were clear of the fog. We had drifted slightly off course and were farther from shore than when the fog had first enshrouded us. Max said to hold off on my paddling while he made a correction, turning us to the left. Then we counted out a rhythm and started to paddle again, dead-reckoning for the wharf.

"That's odd," he said, after a few minutes.

"What?"

"We're paddling hard, but we don't seem to be making any progress."

I cast a worried look at the approaching storm. Suddenly it quit the stall.

Dark rain poured from the distant clouds, perhaps only a few miles from us. Bright flashes of lightning cracked open the dark skies. The rumble of thunder echoed across the water.

My knees were shaking beneath the splash skirt. If the wind hadn't been so loud I was sure I would have heard them knocking against the sides of the kayak. We were helpless out here. And the storm was on the move. How long could we keep the waves from flipping the little craft, filling it with water, and pulling us under?

"How's it going?" I asked, willing my voice to sound calm.

"The current's against us. We're still not making any progress."

"Okay, what if we go back? There's got to be another way. Get back to the ship, ask the harbor-patrol officers for help. We can still get to the wharf, find out about Carly."

"No good," Max said. "Look where the ship is."

I turned, my heart sinking. We had been carried south of the ship, and in the deepening fog and drizzle, it was barely visible. "It still may be our best shot," I said.

A jagged bolt of lightning lit the sky, then a rumble of thunder reverberated across the water. "We've got to get to shelter," I said. Talk about an understatement.

Max looked around again, obviously estimating distances. "The current is carrying us south, maybe we should just go with it—"

"Right into the storm."

"We'll head for shore before we get into it. There seems to be a small peninsula or something jutting out. With luck, maybe we can hit it."

"With prayer," I amended.

In truth I hadn't stopped praying since I'd slid into my end of the kayak. But my ways weren't God's ways, and judging from the happenings on this cruise, he had brought me here by design. For what purpose, I didn't exactly know. What I did know was that being in the heart of his will didn't necessarily mean that I would be in an easy place. That's the way it is with God. I thought about what Mr. Beaver said about Aslan in C. S. Lewis's book *The Lion, the Witch and the Wardrobe:* "Safe? Who said anything about safe? 'Course he's not safe. But he's good."

Right now I prayed for God to shower us with his goodness even as the rain fell.

The sky grew darker, and the drizzle turned to a steady, fog-shrouded rain. The kayak lifted with the waves, higher than before. Max knew enough about boating to point us into the waves, hitting each swell head on so we wouldn't flip.

I held on to the handles on each side of the little craft, my hands clenched so tightly they were numb. My knee-shaking had moved up to include all of my insides. I thought I might be sick. We didn't speak now, each of us lost in our own thoughts. I looked for the peninsula Max had pointed out earlier, but it was obscured by clouds. My heart fell.

A lightning bolt danced across the black sky, followed by a loud clap of thunder. Too close.

Max and I looked at each other, and I read his thoughts as I was sure he read mine. We were human lightning rods waiting for a strike.

A larger wave than we'd yet seen rose up before us, seeming to hang majestically in place before crashing down on us. A whirling surge of foam and water covered us, sucked us down, then suddenly it was gone. I came up gasping and spitting, still in the kayak, and miraculously, so was Max.

"Whoa," he said, white faced, then he looked down and grimaced. "My paddle! I just lost my paddle."

"Not to worry," I said calmly. "I've still got mine." Then I felt a cold slosh of water at my feet. Ankle deep. My voice wasn't quite as calm when I shouted, "We're taking on water!"

"I know."

"Do we have anything to bail with?"

"You can't bail from a kayak."

I turned to look at Max. His face was paler than before, and now his hair was plastered to his head, and water was dripping from his eyebrows.

I touched my own head and realized that my "You Go, Girl!" ball cap was gone. Funny how you focus on small things during times of catastrophe. Suddenly I wanted that cap almost more than life itself. I scanned the waters, ready to dive for it if I saw it floating nearby. But I could see only the dark, foamy sea raging around us, whipped up by the howling winds.

I tried to remember what I'd read about kayaks being unsinkable. I didn't want to put it to the test. If we were in calm waters, we could get out and tip the kayak to get rid of the water. But these waters were far from calm. And if we were hit by another wave? I didn't want to think about it. At least we had the life vests—and I would never again complain about the color. But who would know to look for us? And how would they know where to look? We had drifted a long ways from the harbor.

I didn't have time to voice my thoughts. From a distance, the sound of a boat engine rose above the wail of the wind and rain.

"You hear that?" I yelled to Max. "Someone to the rescue already!"

"How will they see us?"

He was right. The rain was heavier now, sheets so thick I couldn't see farther than a few yards in any direction. "You bring a flashlight?"

He shook his head. With a grin I reached into my soggy travel vest, yanked open one of the Velcro pockets, and pulled out a high-intensity emergency light. I flipped it on and held it up in triumph.

It had a flashing strobe light on one side, a red light on top that cast a powerful beam straight into the heavens, and a regular incandescent flashlight opposite the strobe.

Max was grinning. "Cool," he said.

I listened for the engine to come closer, ready to yell and wave my arms. At first the boat seemed to travel away from us, then it circled around and made its way back. I held the light higher, waving it slowly so that whoever was coming to rescue us would know it was being held in human hands.

"Please, oh please, oh please," I whispered. "Come closer. And hurry."

With each wave that crashed, the kayak took on more water. I thought about toeing off my shoes, knowing they would weigh me down if I had to swim. But help was on the way, so I decided to wait it out.

The sound of the engine grew louder, and I lifted both hands to cheer.

Then Max said, "Wait! Get down! What was that?"

I sat, frowning. "What?"

"Turn off the light. Hurry!"

"Wh—?"

"Turn it off!" He was screaming and crying at the same time.

Then I heard the sound. I sat in stunned disbelief, paralyzed, afraid to move. Max dived for the light and grabbed it out of my hands. Then in one quick movement, he put the kayak into a roll.

Another hail of bullets slapped the water around us.

EIGHTEEN

The whine of the boat engine receded. Then the boat seemed to circle and idle, as if waiting. The kayak was upright again, though water sloshed at my feet. Max and I sat up and looked out into the storm-roiled waters. We would soon turn into two fluorescent corks bobbing in the waves. I didn't want to think about our smallness in comparison to the sea. It was too much like my nightmare.

Instead, I concentrated on the young man behind me. He had a lifetime ahead of him compared to me. I didn't mind so much that mine might be over, but I hated knowing that, because of me, his might be too. And I hated to abandon the search for the abducted girls. No one had connected Baptiste to the crimes, and if Max and I perished out here, no one would know how it happened. No one but Adam—if he survived.

"Someone really wants us dead," Max said, stating the obvious.

"Makes me think I've stepped on some toes."

"Big time."

Around us the rain fell steadily. The kayak was filling fast. It was time to toe off my shoes, except my feet were numb with cold.

"It's about time to go to plan B," I said.

"And that would be?"

"Getting in the water. Flipping the kayak so we can have something to hide under if they come back. This thing's bulletproof, right?" It was futile if we were fired at again, but it was the best plan I could come up with.

"Yeah, right."

I looked back at him, and with a nod of agreement, we unlatched our splash skirts from the lips of the openings and slithered from the rocking craft. As soon as I plunged into the water, a series of waves pressed me under. Then I popped up like a cork and felt the rain pouring over me. I coughed, sputtered, and looked around for Max. He was already by the kayak, leaning over the front opening.

"You forgot your flashlight," he said and tossed it to me.

I missed, but it surfaced only a few feet away, so I paddled awkwardly toward it between waves. "A lot of good it did us," I shouted.

"Hang on to it. You never know," he shouted back.

I stuck the light in a pocket, then tried to move through rolling waters to the kayak. Max reached out and pulled me toward where he clung. "Think we can turn it over?" I yelled above the whine of the wind.

"We've got to move fast. Otherwise, it will take on more water as we flip it."

"That's a happy thought."

"It won't sink. It's made to stay afloat."

"Okay, on three," I shouted cheerfully. *"I am woman; hear me—"*

Max frowned and held up a hand. Something had changed. We both felt it and clung to the kayak, not moving.

A heavy, pregnant silence settled over us. It was more frightening than all that had come before. More frightening than the crash and wail of the storm, this silence pressed down on us, pricked our senses, and caused us to stop talking.

The eye of the storm was over us now. I could sense it. Whether at the center of a tropical depression or a hurricane, the eye is utterly, eerily silent. The winds dead calm. The waves without a chop. It was like this now.

If we could get back into the kayak, we could make it safely to shore before the storm picked up again.

But instead of moving out of the water, we stared at each other, and in our fear, each of us knew the other was feeling the same sudden hopelessness.

Max identified the source of that fear first. "They're listening," he mouthed.

Of course. Sound travels exceptionally well over water. The calmer the sea, the better sound travels. In restricted visibility, the sound is amplified. In the eye of the storm, conditions were just about perfect to amplify any sound we made.

The motorboat had not left, as I'd hoped. Whoever was in it was waiting, engines cut, in utter silence. Waiting for us to make a sound.

Unless they had heard us already.

They had.

The engine sputtered, revved, came to life. I clung to the kayak, closed my eyes, and prayed. Beside me, Max whispered a prayer of his own.

The boat engine seemed to scream toward us.

"Go under!" Max yelled and yanked my arm. "Take off the vest and dive!"

My fingers fumbled with the ties. Max worked his, ripping and pulling, trying to wriggle out of it. A zinging spray of bullets cut through the water around us. The kayak splintered, and I thought I heard Max scream. I flung off my life vest, swam to him, and saw blood.

He gave me a weak grin. "Dive," he said.

"You ready?"

He nodded.

I grabbed his arm and dived. He kicked, trying to help. Another hail of bullets slapped the water around us.

More bullets, more blood. My lungs were ready to explode.

A spotlight beamed above the water, sweeping, searching. I knew that all was lost.

woke in a hospital. At least that's what I thought it was. It might have been a clinic. The thought froze me. La Vida Pura!

I was hooked up to an IV, and my head was wrapped in some sort of gauzy bandage, low enough to cover my eyebrows. I tried moving my extremities one at a time. Toe, fine. Both feet, arches okay. I wiggled my fingers on both hands—left side, restricted somewhat because of the IV; right hand, apparently sound enough to pound keys on the Underwood.

I probed my forehead with my right hand and winced when I reached my left temple. It felt like someone had gone after me with a baseball bat.

I looked up at the IV, considering what was running through my veins. If this was La Vida Pura, it might be poison. But if this was La Vida Pura, why would they bother to take care of the head wound? Knowing their record, all they needed was to give me a giant injection of vitamin butterfly.

Or they could have finished me off in the ocean.

Then it all came rushing back to me. The gunshots. The boat. Max!

I looked around for the buzzer to call for a nurse. Found it. Pressed it frantically. Then I looked toward the door and saw a guard just outside. All I could see was a few inches of his right shoulder and torso, but I could tell he was in uniform. Playa Negra police. I breathed easier.

A young, dark-haired woman brushed past him and hurried to my bedside. She spoke in rapid-fire Spanish, and I said, "I'm sorry. I don't understand."

She stepped closer. "Señora, I speak a little English. How can I help you?"

"Where is the boy? Max?"

"I'm sorry. No one by that name was brought in."

I turned my head away, remembering the blood. He didn't make it.

"There was another man who came in at the same time."

Great. If it was one of the assailants, I'd get out of this bed, no matter what shape I was in, and give him a taste of some vitamin butterfly of my own. The nurse touched my shoulder, and I wearily turned back to her.

"This other man's name is Maxmillian. Señor Maxmillian Pribble. He is also from your country." She pronounced the double *l* with the Spanish *y* sound, but I knew who she meant. I had never heard such a beautiful sound.

I grinned. "That would be him. Is he okay?"

"Never better," Max said from the doorway. He wore a hospital gown and was holding the back closed with one hand, maneuvering his portable IV with the other. Even so, he kept his back to the wall as he came into the room. He was much too tall for the baby blue gown they'd put him in, and his knobby knees stuck out from underneath.

He almost fell into the chair by my bed, looking weary beyond words. "So, what's new?" He gave me a weak smile.

I laughed. "Some vacation we're having." I paused, solemn thoughts penetrating the temporary emotional wall I'd already erected. "What happened? Do you know how we got here?"

"I was told that the Interpol liaison was part of the rescue, and she'll be here later to fill us in on the gory details. All I know is that the harbor patrol was out looking for us, heard the gunshots, and headed there just in time to save us."

"Sound amplified over water," I said.

"Yeah." He looked thoughtful, probably thinking the same thing I was. That amplified sound had almost done us in. It had also saved us.

"How about the assailants? Were they caught?"

"They got away clean. Harbor patrol boats roared to the rescue with spotlights, sirens, all the bells and whistles going full force. Gave the bad guys plenty of warning they were coming."

"Also saved our lives. A few seconds longer and…" I didn't finish. He knew. "Max, were you hurt? I thought I saw blood."

"Nah, just dehydrated they tell me. The blood was yours." I must have looked confused, because he added, "Grazed," and tapped his temple.

I didn't have time to contemplate the difference a fraction of an inch would have made.

There was a knock on the doorjamb. "May I come in?"

We both turned to see Monica Oliverio standing in the doorway. The nurse scurried past her on the way out.

"Of course," I said. "Please do."

She pulled up a chair from the empty bed space next to mine. "Do you feel like talking?"

"Other than feeling like I've been run over by a 26.9 ton combat earthmover, yeah, I'm ready." Ms. Oliverio might have been instrumental in saving my life, but I was still annoyed with her.

"How are you feeling? You've been through quite an ordeal."

No kidding. "It's good to be back among the living. Let's leave it at that."

"Amen," Max said.

She gave him a nod, then focused on me again. "You've been filled in on what happened out there?"

"How you came to the rescue, yes." I should have sounded more grateful, but the truth was, I wouldn't have been out there—endangering my life and Max's—if the authorities had paid attention to what I had discovered about the grand Dr. Baptiste and acted like they were the least bit interested.

"Look, I know you're upset about what happened at the meeting yesterday, but we had no reason to believe there was any truth in what you told us."

"And do you now? Have reason to believe me, that is?" Now that I've almost had my head blown off? The more I thought about what we'd been through, the madder I got.

"Someone thinks you're too close to the truth. In my book, if it's Baptiste, then he's just dug his own grave."

I tried to lift my head, grimaced, and fell back against my pillow. Ms. Oliverio hurried to give me a sip of ice water from the pitcher on the bedside table. I took a sip, enjoying the moment.

"We've met again—the same group that convened yesterday—and we're taking preliminary steps to do a full investigation of Dr. Baptiste, including a visit to his island."

"Preliminary steps? What does that mean?"

"In Costa Rica, as in the U.S., a search warrant is required. We have to prove just cause." She paused. "We'll need to depose you about what you overheard in the clinic. It's not much, especially because there are no other witnesses, but it's a start for building our case."

"What about the people who tried to kill us yesterday?"

"There's no proof that Baptiste was involved. And how would he have known you were on to him? We have no direct link from you to his actions. My gut feeling is yeah, the guy is somehow linked to all this, but there's no concrete proof. We're building this thing on hearsay."

"I was there," Max said. "So that part of it is no longer hearsay. I'm a witness."

Ms. Oliverio turned to him. "You were where?"

He glanced at me, then back to her. "La Vida Pura. The night Baptiste was telling a patient's mother that he was keeping his daughter alive through—how did he say it?   through 'unorthodox medical practices.'"

Ms. Oliverio frowned at me. "Is this true?"

I nodded. "I didn't want to implicate him in our own rather unorthodox means of getting to the clinic or disclose that he was with me when I found Adam Hartsfield's note." I paused. "I went to see Adam that night to tell him what we had discovered. That's when I found he'd obviously made some discoveries of his own—'It's Baptiste.'"

She looked thoughtful, then said, "That helps, but what you—what we—have put together is still based on hearsay. But I'll do what I can. I promise." She stood to leave.

"One more thing," I said.

"Yes?"

"I want to go to the island with you. I need to see for myself what Baptiste has done to the girls." I couldn't keep the bitterness out of my voice. "What he's done to them in order to keep his own daughter alive."

She stared at me for a moment without speaking, then said, "You are in grave danger, Ms. MacIver. You may not take the threat seriously, but believe me, we do. If Baptiste knows you're with us, and if he is indeed behind some sort of ghoulish plot, your presence could send him over the edge. Your life would be at risk. We can't properly investigate and watch over you as well. I hope you understand."

She stepped closer to the bed. "The U.S. government is breathing down our necks because of yesterday's little incident." She glanced at Max, then back at me. "Suffice it to say, we are committed to keeping you both safe until the investigation is completed, arrests made, and you are safely back in your own country. Whichever comes first."

I lifted my head from the pillow, trying not to wince. "I understand all that, and now that you've said what you needed to, let me say this: I still want to go."

Ms. Oliverio surprised me by laughing. "Anybody ever tell you how stubborn you are?"

I smiled. "You might ask my kids."

"One more thing," she said from the doorway. "Adam Hartsfield is here—in ICU. He is still on life support, but his vital signs are stabilizing."

I fell back against my pillow. "Thank you," I said. "That's good news."

But her somber expression didn't match the news. There was something she wasn't telling me.

must have slipped into a dreamless sleep right after Max and Ms. Oliverio left my room. When I awoke after what felt like only a few minutes, beyond the window I could see that the sun was on its downward arc. I had obviously been out for hours.

I tried to sit up. The pain was less intense than before, so I swung my feet over the side of the bed and padded to the bathroom. I peered into the mirror and almost laughed at my image. Feeling like I'd been run over by an earthmover was one thing; looking like I'd been run over was something else entirely. I lifted the gauzy bandage, touched the bruise around my eye, and drew in a sharp breath.

My ball cap was often reserved for bad hair days, but it was going to take more than a ball cap to camouflage this shiner. Besides, my favorite cap had probably floated all the way to South America by now.

Behind me, the door to my room was open a crack, and I froze, remembering Ms. Oliverio's warnings. The door was closed when I awoke, and I assumed that the guard was still outside. What if he wasn't?

I backed farther into the bathroom, closing the door. I stood with my back to it, almost afraid to breathe.

"Harriet?" came a voice from the other side of the door. "You in there?" The words were followed by staccato taps.

Relief flooded through me. Only one person I knew would be so bold as to knock on an ailing person's bathroom door.

I threw open the door. "Hey, Tange."

She stared at me, clearly shocked at my appearance. Finally she said, "You're looking good, Harriet."

"So are you." I looked pointedly at the cast covering her broken ankle.

We both laughed, then she started to cry, and I wrapped my arms around her. "We'll find her, Tange. I promise you."

"Or die trying," she said, pulling back to blow her nose. "You look like you're halfway there."

"Did you hear the details?"

She nodded. "Everyone feels terrible about it. Dr. Williams and Zoë Shire picked me up at the airport this morning. They filled me in—at least on what they knew." She hobbled to the bed and patted the mattress. "You look like you've been run over by a Mack truck. Better climb back in bed, then you can tell me everything."

"Earthmover," I amended, "make that a combat earthmover."

She laughed as she dropped into a chair and propped her crutches nearby. As she wiped her eyes again, I noticed how her laughter and tears seemed indistinguishable from each other. We'd known each other for decades. I knew of her heartache when her marriage broke up and she faced raising Carly by herself. She knew about mine when Hollis's plane went down. She knew of the mysterious circumstances surrounding his death, yet she had never printed a word of it when she covered the news of his death.

On our mantels we had matching photographs of Joey and Carly taken on their prom night—Joey in his black tux, Carly in a fuchsia tux of her own, the silk-lapelled jacket draped over a peach-lace camisole, her short red hair spiked and gleaming.

I studied Tangi as she struggled to get her emotions in hand, thinking how like Carly she was. Her daughter had let her hair grow out, and now it was Tangi who wore the messy, bird's-nest spikes. But their smiles had always been the same. Dazzling. Until now.

It would be some time before Tangi smiled that way again. Right now the only smile she seemed capable of was filled with soul-weary sorrow. She looked like she hadn't slept in forty-eight hours. With her cast and crutches and my bandaged head and black eye, we made quite a pair.

"Tell me everything that's happened…everything you know about the case, everything you suspect," she said.

And I did.

"You've put this all together, Harriet," she said. "And already you've risked your life. Thank you."

"I'm going to the island when they go out with the search warrant. I want to be there when they arrest Baptiste."

She hesitated. "It's still not all that certain, is it?" I must have registered my surprise because she quickly added, "I spoke to the Playa Negra authorities before I came to see you. They are still looking at other suspects." Her eyes filled. "Neither option is good. They're looking at 'human trafficking,' as they call it. You're looking at medical experimentation…" Her voice broke and she looked away. "I'm not going to think the unthinkable. I'm not going to consider what the local police told me. I'm pinning all my hopes on your hunch, Harriet."

Unspoken were the words *don't let me down.* I could see the pleading in her eyes.

"I can't be wrong," I said softly. "I can't be." She met my gaze, and I felt every burden of her heart weighing heavily on mine.

By ten the following morning, the two Costa Rican doctors who had admitted me—one a heart specialist, the other the ER doctor—signed my release. I asked the ER doctor to clear the way for me to visit Adam.

My guard, a young man named Rodolfo, was at my side as I made my way to ICU. I asked Rodolfo to wait in the hall, and he grumpily nodded his okay. I left him standing woodenly next to Adam's armed guard who sported an identical uniform.

I stepped through the door, then stopped to let my eyes adjust to the dim light. After a moment I walked over to Adam's bed, trying to ignore the beeps and whirs of the monitors he was hooked up to. He was pale, deathly so, and his breathing came in shallow puffs. He lay utterly still. He was on an IV, but not a respirator. For that I was thankful.

I touched his forearm just above his wrist. "Adam, it's Harriet. You don't remember, but I'm the one who found you. And I found your note. You're quite the hero in my book. You've put all this together, and I know you're right. I'll give you all the details when you wake up."

I smiled down at him. "You wouldn't believe all that's happened. I really misconnected the dots about you and that morpho. You gave me quite a fright. That dot business of mine may not be so reliable after all.

"But I'll tell you all about it later. You've got to get strong fast and wake up. It's not fair. I'm having to keep all this intrigue and excitement to myself. And hey, I'd really rather be sharing it with you. After all, you're the expert."

I patted his arm. "I don't want to wear you out with our conversation. But I'll be back to chat tomorrow. It's not often I don't have to worry about being interrupted." I chuckled and glanced at his face, hoping to see one of those tiny twitches at the corner of his mouth.

Nothing.

My eyes stung, and I started to turn away, then stopped, remembering all those old black-and-white movies with heroes in comas. It was worth a shot. "Hey, big guy," I said, "if you can hear me, blink an eyelid. Left or right; it doesn't matter."

Nothing.

I lifted his hand, held it between both of mine, and squeezed it gently. "Okay, let's try again. It you can hear me, squeeze my hand."

I waited, praying for a response. There was nothing but the solid, still warmth of his hand in mine. "That's okay," I whispered. "We'll try again tomorrow."

Outside the door to Adam's room, Rodolfo joined me and we walked to a back entrance of the hospital. Max had been released the night before and had already returned to the *Sun Spirit*, still at anchor.

The local authorities had given me the choice of taking accommodations in town or returning to the ship. I chose the ship even though Tangi and Kate Rivers's parents were staying in Playa Negra. I hadn't given up hope that I would find Gus.

The students welcomed me like a hero returning from battle. The reception by the *Sun Spirit* crew and Shepparton faculty was a different matter. I had barely settled into my stateroom when I was summoned to the bridge.

Captain Richter stood waiting for me near the control panel. Dean Williams was next to him, his expression grim. I knew I was in trouble the moment I saw their faces. I was escorted to the captain's office just behind the bridge. Rodolfo waited just outside the closed door.

I took a seat in front of Richter's desk. Dean Williams sat to one side and back a ways, legs crossed.

"You endangered the life of one of our student passengers," the captain said. "He could have died out there."

"I'm well aware of that, Captain," I said. "Believe me."

Dean Williams sat forward. "I think you don't know, or perhaps aren't capable of understanding, the gravity of what you did."

Capable of understanding? As in brain capacity? I felt the hairs on the back of my neck begin to rise. I didn't dare speak for fear of saying something I would regret.

"You have put the entire program at risk," Williams said. "We could be sued. Max Pribble's father is an—"

"—an attorney," I snapped. "I am aware of that as well. He understood the risks. I tried to get him to stay on the ship, but he would have nothing of it."

"Excuse me, Ms. MacIver," Williams thundered. "But who is the adult here?"

"Max is legally an adult. I couldn't stop him from coming."

"You didn't have to continue your pursuit of this supposed scheme," Williams said. Then he dropped his voice to a patronizing tone, which was worse. "I know you meant well. We all heard your reasons. You are certain Dr. Baptiste is behind these unfortunate abductions. You were out to prove you were right—no matter what the authorities concluded. No matter whose life you endangered."

I didn't answer.

The captain leaned forward. "Legally, I must inform you that as of seven o'clock tomorrow morning—our estimated time of departure for the next port—you will be escorted off the ship. You, ma'am, have proven to be a danger to our passengers—and now, of course, even more so." He glanced at the closed door where my guard waited on the other side. "I don't believe it is necessary to list your offenses. They will be written up and delivered to your room for your signature. It is a legal document, binding on all parties—Global Sea Adventures, Shepparton College, and, of course, you."

"You seem to be forgetting that someone is out to kill me, presumably because I got too close to the truth. And neither of you has mentioned any sadness or concern about the man who died or the one who remains in a coma—both passengers on this ship—or about the two young women who were abducted. You're more concerned about covering your tracks in the event there is an inquiry, likely from those in upper management. Perhaps from an insurance carrier." I leaned forward, seething, my tone barely civil. "You, gentlemen, are covering your tails. You don't care about justice." I stood up and glared at Richter, then moved my hard-eyed gaze to Williams. "You, gentlemen, should be ashamed of yourselves.

"As for leaving this ship? You couldn't pay me enough to stay onboard. I will have my things ready for departure at six o'clock in the morning. And you'd better believe me, gentlemen. I am a travel writer, and your lack of concern for the safety and well-being of all onboard will be covered in my first article."

I turned and strode out the door. I had taken only a few steps when I stopped, leaned against the wall, and closed my eyes. The pain in my temple was intense. I needed to rest.

Rodolfo was by my side in an instant. "Señora, you are unwell?" He took my arm and helped me back to my stateroom, then took his position outside my door.

I glanced about for Gus as soon as I entered, more out of habit than expecting to see him. But suddenly I was surprised by fresh grief over his disappearance. Feelings of helpless sadness, combined with fatigue, the wound on my head, and the discouragement of the moment made me want to throw in the towel.

My problem was that I cared too much. What had I said to Ms. Oliverio at the meeting? "You do what you must to do to get at the heart of a problem, no matter the pain, the sorrow, the roadblocks. And you don't stop until you find the solution." A lot of good all those "qualifications" had done me. Passion, I'd said. Stick-to-it-iveness. Ha!

I was just getting ready for a grand pity party when I heard a knock at the door.

"Who is it?"

"Monica Oliverio."

I opened the door. She thrust a little bouquet of flowers at me as if embarrassed. No one had brought me flowers since Hollis died. I felt a sting at the back of my throat and swallowed hard. If Ms. Oliverio was embarrassed to bring me this gift, she'd be downright mortified if I teared up.

"Well, my goodness," I said cheerily. "This is a surprise."

"How are you feeling?"

"Better. Really. Would you like to come in?"

She shook her head. "I pulled some strings to get you a place with the team."

"What team?"

"Our people are on the way to Baptiste's island. Sometimes we allow press along—for PR purposes, you understand. Not to interfere in the investigation in any sense."

I wanted to punch the air with my fist and holler "YES!" Instead I gave her a quick, professional nod.

"You have an international press pass, don't you?"

"Yes."

"A badge?"

"Of course."

"And you're feeling up to it?" She glanced at my bandaged head.

I grinned. "We're going by water?"

She gave me a quizzical look. "Yes, of course. There is an airstrip, but in this case, harbor patrol works best. Too many of us for a conventional private plane."

I relaxed. "Can you give me a few minutes to freshen up?" And take some extra-strength aspirin.

"We need to speak to one of the students. But that should take only about twenty minutes."

"I'll be ready."

In fifteen minutes flat I had changed into fresh clothes. In another three I arrived at the gangway, Rodolfo at my heels.

I rather liked having my own personal bodyguard. He was twice my height, with shoulders the size of watermelons. His mother must have taught him well; one minute he was looking snarly and dangerous to any-one who approached and the next he was politely opening doors and standing back to let me go first. I daresay he would have fixed me a cup of tea with two lumps had I asked. I was thinking about adopting him.

Rodolfo stepped into the harbor patrol boat first, then took my hand to help me in. There were ten of us all told. I was the only civilian with the others, a mix of Playa Negra police, detectives, and Interpol.

We faced into the sun as the boat glided away from the ship, changed course slightly, then revved the engines and sped across the water. I had replaced the gauzy bandage around my head with a smaller adhesive patch, then covered the whole thing with a ball cap, this one with an Oakland A's logo. The sun reflected off the water and intensified the headache pain, so I pulled the cap low and closed my eyes.

"You're here as an observer only," Ms. Oliverio said at my elbow.

I opened one eye. "I know that."

"Not everyone is convinced that Baptiste had anything to do with the crimes. Some are convinced not only that we're pursuing a wrong lead but that the trail of the real perpetrators—people traffickers—is getting colder by the minute. They are also acutely aware that if we're wrong, a search warrant is the greatest insult that could be dealt a distinguished man like Dr. Baptiste."

I swallowed hard. What if I had connected the wrong dots?

Ms. Oliverio looked out to sea and said no more.

It took a little over an hour to reach the island. It was large, perhaps the size of Catalina Island off Los Angeles. Dark, rocky cliffs jutted from the black sand beaches on the only side I could see. The pilot had done his homework and announced we were heading for the only natural harbor suitable for mooring the boat. Unfortunately, it was the island's only harbor—that belonging to Dr. Baptiste. The pilot cut back on the throttle, and we idled slowly toward the dock. Three boats were moored in the half-dozen or so slips. One of the boats was a Glastron GX185, the same speedboat I'd seen Baptiste pilot near the *Sun Spirit*. As we idled, I read the name on the back: *Nicolette*.

The pilot pulled close to the dock, but before we could disembark, a golf cart headed down a small incline toward us.

It was Baptiste.

"Well, well." He gave the group a tight smile as he got out of the cart. "What a surprise." Without hesitation, he strode over to the captain of the Playa Negra police force and pulled him aside.

They conferred for a few minutes, then the police captain turned back to the waiting group. "Dr. Baptiste has generously granted us permission to visit his facility. He says a search warrant is not necessary. We are welcome to come in and look around. The entire facility is open to us. He has nothing to hide. He will give us a tour, if we like, and then we can put our forensics teams to work independently."

The team's relief was palpable. When they started up the short incline, I fell in behind. Though Jean looked toward me several times, he didn't acknowledge me in any way. I assumed someone had let him know I was his accuser. I wondered who. The thought chilled me.

He was the consummate, professional host. We came to a small rise affording a view of his home and the buildings behind it, which I thought might be labs. Farther still stretched the runway for his private jet with a hangar nearby that matched the one at Playa Negra.

His home was an adobe, Southwest style, one of the few like it in Costa Rica. From here it looked just like an adobe from Santa Fe or any other upscale community in the American West. But the sun's deepening shadows gave it a cold, gray look instead of the usual warm salmon or rust hues. It looked dirty, like moldy soil.

I shuddered, even in the warmth of the sun. The uncertainty of what might greet us was as murky as the color of the walls.

With Baptiste leading the way, the team walked down the rise toward the austere house. Now it took on the look of a fortress, with high walls and small windows. Architectural efforts for authentic adobes concentrated on the interior, with the house itself surrounding a central courtyard. In Spain the style was developed centuries ago for security.

I wondered if this house had been built for the same purpose.

Baptiste led the team through his home, pointing out features that had been photographed for *Architectural Digest* three years earlier. Nowhere inside was there any evidence of a young woman's bedroom, or any sign that she lived here now or ever had. An oil painting of Nicolette at about sixteen hung above a massive stone fireplace in the library. That was the only sign of her.

We toured his labs, met his two assistants, and heard the pride in their voices as they talked about the great strides Dr. Baptiste had made in his research.

He ended his tour in his prize gardens and butterfly preserve, also highlighted in *Architectural Digest*. Standing near a large boulder, he invited the team to examine any part of his home or grounds.

He paused. "I know you all are simply doing your jobs, but it saddens me that in today's world, anyone can dirty the name of another. I suppose that's the price we sometimes pay for democracy. I don't know who my accuser is, so I can't respond directly to that person. But I want you all to know that I have nothing, absolutely nothing, to hide.

"My life is an open book. I know suffering and loss, I know how these emotions can shade rational thinking. I know how misguided people can make mistakes in the throes of such emotional upheaval. They grasp at straws, wanting to see justice done, even if they're pointing a finger at the wrong person. It happens.

"But I need you to know that I'm on the brink of discovery. After years of working on the Human Genome Project—experimenting with the genetic relationship of the disease to its victim, identifying the gene missing in victims suffering from chronic myelogenous leukemia, introducing that missing gene into a human stem cell—I am literally days away from a cure for this, the deadliest form of leukemia, a disease that kills children and adults in their prime.

"Each interruption sets me back. Each interruption means this cruel disease claims one more victim." He looked at his watch. "Even as we stand here, one more victim has died, thousands more are dying.

"I believe in freedom of speech. I believe in the freedom to act when one is on a quest for truth. When one is passionate to see that justice is done.

"But I beg of you, all of you, please do not interrupt this important work. I will be most happy to arrange for your investigative visits. As many as you like. Whenever you like. But even as I say that, I know what these investigations can mean—the disordering of files by well-meaning people who don't know research techniques, ripping apart files and taking computer programs that contain data that if contaminated or destroyed would set back the discovery of this cure by decades."

There wasn't a sound in the garden except for a single bird calling mournfully in the distance.

"Please," Dr. Baptiste continued, his voice choking, "please, search if you must. But I beg you to remember the lives that are at stake if you disturb or interrupt my work in any way." He smiled again sadly and gestured, his palms outstretched. "Please, help yourself. Do what you must. I leave you to it."

Without another word he turned on his heel and strode down the path toward his house. The investigators spoke among themselves and decided their next course of action.

I knew before they did what it would be.

We headed back to the harbor patrol boat just as the sun was dying to the west. No one spoke to me as we headed back to the *Sun Spirit*.

TWENTY-ONE

t didn't take long for the word to spread: Dr. Baptiste was back on his gold-plated pedestal, and Mrs. MacIver was relegated to the Winnie-the-Pooh status of a bear with very little brain. Not only that, but she was to be escorted off the ship like a criminal. She had endangered a student, led him down a path of crime, and made libelous accusations against one of the finest, brightest, most upstanding citizens of the United States. A man who would someday give hope to those dying of chronic myelogenous leukemia and be awarded the Nobel Prize.

No one said anything openly, but from what I read in the other passengers' expressions, I imagined all sorts of disparaging remarks being passed behind my back: The old girl's gone barmy. Daft as a dervish. Even Adele Quilp's "hunh" as she looked me up and down seemed to contain an unpleasant assessment of my very little brain.

Then again, maybe it was just my own insecurities filling me with doubt. They had a way of rearing their nasty little heads and attacking my self-confidence with yammering nonsense when I failed at something so colossally important.

Worse than my own worries was the knowledge that Baptiste was guilty of heinous crimes and was getting away with it. Law enforcement saw him as some sort of savior of humankind. Untouchable.

The trail was cold. Dead.

I should have been hightailing it back to my stateroom to lick my wounds. Instead, I was angry. Livid. Spitting-barbed-wire livid. This monster would not get away with what he'd done, not as long as I was on the right side of the grass, as Hollis was prone to say. People might be looking at me as having gone round the bend, but I was far from turning that corner.

I needed a new plan. And fast. I wasn't going to let this arrogant criminal continue to masquerade as some Jonas Salk or David Livingstone. No siree. Not on my watch.

I stomped toward my stateroom filled with new resolve.

Then my stomach growled. Some things can't wait. I ducked into the dining buffet to pick up a cold sandwich to eat in my room. Too much planning to do, no time to waste chitchatting.

I was about to push through the door to the outside corridor when something caught my eye—a flash of dark hair, the side of a young acne-scarred face, shoulders that seemed permanently hunched. They were the shoulders of someone who spent too much time in front of a computer. This student was strangely familiar.

Curious, I made a detour toward his table, threading between the clusters of students and passengers. He stood, preparing to leave, and I faded into the background to watch. He picked up his tray and carefully sorted the dishes and flatware from the garbage. He helped his seat partner, whose back was to me, do the same.

As he turned slightly to take his tray to the trash receptacle, I got a better look—and identified him. Chatting, sharing snickers, and seeming thick as thieves, Zoë and the young man—the same young man who'd delivered the note that almost got me killed—continued along the corridor.

Even more surprising, Price Alexander stepped out from the shadows and joined them. The three spoke, then disappeared around a corner, heads bent in earnest conversation.

I had seen enough and let them go.

Rodolfo was waiting for me outside the dining room. Above the din of conversation and clinking china and glassware, I told him I no longer needed his services. Having a bodyguard, much as I liked him, would only slow me down. Plus, I guessed he reported my every move to headquarters.

My plans had to be mine and mine alone.

It took three tries in my broken Spanish to get him to understand. His replacement was due to arrive for the night shift within minutes, and I insisted they both return to port by harbor patrol boat. I gave him my most brilliant smile, hoping I reminded him of a beloved grandmother, and thanked him for his help, assuring him I was perfectly safe now. Then I turned on my heel and hurried to my room before he put up a fuss.

I closed my stateroom door and leaned against it, listening for Rodolfo's footsteps. I had bluffed my way through sending him away, and so far he was buying it. I hoped. In reality, either the Costa Rican authorities or Interpol could send him back—this time with handcuffs—to haul me into police headquarters.

After a few minutes passed with no sign of Rodolfo's return, I sat down to eat my sandwich, which had an odd, overly spiced ham taste and was a bit gristly to chew. Gus's feeders were in my line of vision, which spoiled my appetite even further. I put the sandwich aside after only a few bites. I missed him and wondered if I would ever find out what had happened—if one of the students had played a cruel joke, taken him just out of sheer orneriness. Maybe it was better if I never learned the truth.

I hadn't yet received the captain's letter listing my "grievous offenses," but I would be off the ship by early morning. So I pulled together my clothing, my duffle, my typewriter case, and finally Gus's carrier.

After tonight there would be no chance of ever seeing him again.

I held the carrier in my arms and, sinking to the sofa, rested my forehead on the plastic top. "Well, bud," I whispered, "I guess this really is it. I should have left you home. A cat-sitter wouldn't have been all that bad. But I thought I needed you. Well, I didn't just think so. I really did, bud. And truth is I still do."

I put the carrier down, reached for my duffle, and got on with my packing.

A rap at the door interrupted me.

I pulled the door open, and Max stood there grinning at me. "Where's the big guy?"

"I fired him."

"And the reason being…?"

"Don't need him."

He stepped inside and zeroed in on the partially eaten sandwich. "Hey, can I have some of that?"

"Help yourself."

He sat down and took a monster bite. "And that would be because…?"

I sat down opposite Max. "Number one, the captain has ordered me off the ship. Number two, I like to travel light—no excess baggage or bodyguards."

"Not a good enough reason," he said around another bite. "Hey, you got anything to drink?"

"I can make you a cup of herbal tea."

He rolled his eyes. "How about water?"

I gave him a bottle from the minifridge. "Didn't you go to dinner tonight?"

"Too busy talking to the captain."

"One of my favorite people."

"You may like him better now."

"Since this morning? I don't think so."

He took another bite and chewed thoughtfully before washing it down with half a bottle of water.

"He's about ready to come down here with an invitation to stay on-board the ship."

This time I rolled my eyes. "Yeah, right."

"No, I'm serious. I've been on the bridge talking to him. Heard him making the decision while he was on that fancy satellite phone of his."

"Who was he talking to?"

Max took another bite, chewed, wiped his mouth, and grinned. "My dad."

"Wha—?"

"My dad was explaining some of the finer points of litigation law. Heard him say something about age discrimination, how suit can be brought against companies for the minutest details. Such as not allowing an elderly passenger to complete her cruise, especially after said passenger has been injured while on said cruise."

"Elderly?" I sputtered.

"Hey, my dad can speak legalese with the best of them. You should have heard him. It was great. The dude didn't know whether to whistle or to wind his watch."

"Whistle or wind his watch?"

"Or he didn't know whether he was on foot or on horseback, if you prefer." He leaned forward, looking serious. "There's something else."

"I'm almost afraid to ask."

"I heard what happened at the island today, and we can't let Baptiste get away with this."

"Max, don't go there. This guy is dangerous, chillingly dangerous, yet he masquerades as a medical miracle worker. I saw how the authorities reacted to his talk of the cancer cure. They turned tail and ran. And think about it; we almost died out there because of him. The closer we get to unmasking him, the more determined he is to see that we don't. No matter the cost. And the cost is clear—our lives. Next time he may not miss."

"When I talked to my dad today, he said the abductions are all over the news in the States. Constant coverage. Cable news, all the major networks, are in Playa Negra. Reporters broadcasting live from all over the place. Dad said it's a feeding frenzy. The media is running on the assumption that it's people trafficking."

"A wild-goose chase."

"I asked Dad about just going to the networks and putting the word out there about our suspicions."

"Can't," I said. "I'm sure he told you about libel laws."

"Yeah."

"So where are you going with this?"

"Me and you are the only ones who heard Dr. Baptiste tell those people about his daughter."

"And Price," I said, suddenly wondering why he seemed to have disappeared from the ship.

"Yeah, Price. But I was thinking about me and you talking to that guy, what's his name?"

"Lorenzo Nolan. And it's you and me."

"Huh?"

"Never put yourself first in conversation. Ungrammatical, plus impolite. It's always you and I or you and me."

"Yeah, well. Okay."

"Max, I appreciate the thought, but I can't expose you to any more danger. Plus, Nolan may not know anything that would nail Baptiste, or if he did, he might not be willing to tell, especially if by telling he'd incriminate himself."

"He's got to know what the 'unorthodox' procedures are that they were talking about the other night. It's his girlfriend's kid who's sick. If you were her, wouldn't you want to know everything they're going to do? I mean, every little detail?"

Bingo.

"You're brilliant, Max!"

"Huh?"

"You've just given me an idea, but it's something I've got to do alone."

His face fell. "I can't come?"

"Sorry. Plus the ship is sailing tomorrow, and you'd miss the rest of the cruise."

"That's the other thing I had to tell you. We're not sailing tomorrow. My dad says every law-enforcement agency on the planet that thinks they've got jurisdiction has ordered the captain to stay put. Even the FBI is getting involved. So it looks like we're stuck here for a while. I heard some of the parents are flying in, and there's talk that the rest of the passengers are already demanding a refund."

"Captain Richter has his hands full."

Max grinned. "That's why the hint about discriminating against the el—"

"Don't say it."

He laughed as he stood. "Hey, Ms. M., send up a holler if you need a lift to shore. I have some ideas."

"I've got it covered."

The next morning, clothes back in the closet and duffle tucked away, I headed down to the kitchen before breakfast was to be served. The chef was standing over the stove, stirring a pot of oatmeal. I was surprised it wasn't instant but didn't say so.

He looked up with a scowl as I entered.

"I never did get my tour of the galley."

He grunted and kept stirring.

"Bet it's hard to get supplies when the schedule is bollixed up this way." I looked around the stainless countertops, openly admiring the mixer and copper-bottomed pans. I could see him softening.

"Yes," he finally said with a noisy sigh. "This cruise is the hardest I've worked. We haven't made a single port where I'd preordered supplies. I've had to resort to cold cuts and SPAM. I had hoped to shop here in the open market, then the storm ruined everything."

"SPAM?" Ah, last night's sandwich.

"You didn't recognize it?" When I shook my head, he went on to tell the variety of ways he had camouflaged the canned delight since the cruise's inception. "I bet you thought yesterday's breakfast was chipped beef on toast."

"It wasn't? Really? I wouldn't have known!" Luckily I was still in the hospital for yesterday's repast. But I couldn't wait to write this up in the travel article. "How would you like me to shop for you in town?"

He put down the two-foot-long spoon and gave me an incredulous look.

"I'm serious. I need to get into town, and it may be difficult to get past the harbor patrol boats swarming the ship. If I'm with a crew member—you, perhaps, or an assistant—I could help."

I could see he wasn't going for it. "Well, I just thought I'd ask," I said lamely and started for the door.

"Wait," he said. "Could you pick out some local fruits? Citrus? Especially lemons. Maybe find some lettuces? Sweet red peppers?" He kissed his fingertips, already salivating.

"Of course," I said with a broad smile. "And the biggest, reddest, juiciest tomatoes I can find."

"I'd kill for a rutabaga."

Somehow that didn't surprise me. "How many should I get?"

He was literally dancing around the kitchen, a regular Emeril Lagasse, as he opened and shut cupboard doors. He flitted into the pantry and out again, scribbling on a notepad all the while. I prayed he wouldn't open the Sub-Zero. I really didn't want to imagine Harry once being inside.

"You will send someone with me to oversee the transport of all this back to the ship?"

"Yes, yes," he called to me from the pantry again. "Don't want you gobsmacked by the ordeal." He poked his head out. "And believe me, shopping for this boatload of passengers is an ordeal, maybe delightful, but still an ordeal. I'll take care of everything. Just be at the gangway in two hours."

I returned to my room, wondering what I'd gotten myself into.

Two hours later I stepped into the tender. I was back in my jeans, ball cap, Tevas, and travel vest, which was looking no sorrier than usual for its dip in the ocean. Its pockets were, in my usual style, crammed with pencils and pads, camera and film, money clip, nail file, small hairbrush, and other odds and ends.

The vest weighed heavy on my shoulders as I settled into a seat on the starboard side. Only two others were onboard—the pilot and the crew member the chef promised. Only he wasn't crew. And I wasn't happy to see him.

"I thought I told you I had this covered."

Max ran his fingers through his corn-silk hair, then gave it a flip. "I heard the cook needed someone to help get supplies. I volunteered. What can I say?"

"You must have bugged the kitchen."

He grinned. "I have my ways."

"Seriously, how did you know?"

"We've got some real geeks onboard. You pay 'em enough, they'll run wires anywhere. In fact, most of what they do is wireless. That's the beauty of it."

The pilot started up the engines, and we circled around, then headed to the wharf.

"A little different than paddling a kayak," Max said.

"Why would you want to bug the kitchen?"

"Isn't it obvious? Midnight raids to the pantry." He was quiet for a moment as we glided across the water. "Truth was, the geek came to us after it was done."

"Came to whom?"

"Me and Price." He cleared his throat. "Price and me. Seems he was bugging something else and picked up the kitchen by mistake."

"What's this kid look like?"

He told me. Before he finished the description, I knew it was the boy who'd brought me the note. "What's his name?"

"I don't know his real name. Everybody calls him Chip."

"Let me guess—as in microchip?"

"You're good, Ms. M."

I sat back in my seat and closed my eyes, thinking about Chip. He'd cropped up twice, and now a third time. He was a kid who was into computers. A gofer for someone who wanted to get rid of me. A kid who spent time with Zoë, who happens to work in administration at Shepparton. And he'd obviously had something important to say to Price Alexander.

Why was the kid involved? Hacking? But for what purpose?

I started to ask Max if he knew anything about a relationship between Zoë and Chip. Or the two of them and Price, then decided to keep my suspicions to myself. For now.

The sunlight glistened off the water, but as we neared the wharf, I felt a sudden chill. And a distinct sense that someone was watching us. There were more people milling about now than I'd seen here before. I assumed some were media related, though no camera crews or reporters were in sight.

I scanned faces as we moored, then lifted my gaze to the hillside and its scattering of small, tile-roofed homes. No telltale glint of field glasses.

A few fishing boats were moored at the wharf, and farther out, the same yachts I had seen previously. I fixed my gaze on the largest of the yachts anchored apart from the others—Lorenzo Nolan's *Sea Wolf*.

The disquieting feeling of being under surveillance chilled me again as we disembarked, and my own sense of hypervigilance grew more intense with each step. Beside me, Max chatted, seeming oblivious.

Playa Negra's main street was alive with vendors and shoppers. I recognized the upscale dress of La Vida Pura guests, Americans more obvious than the Europeans. The shoppers were mostly locals, all business, as they bargained for the best prices on breads, cheeses, fruits, and vegetables. Flies buzzed around the fish counters, and the odor wafted throughout the rest of the street market, threatening to bend me double. The sun pressed its suffocating heat down on us, increasing the smells and discomfort.

I gave Max the list, and we hurried from vendor to vendor.

I was standing at the tomato counter when I saw her.

I had guessed that the storm might keep boaters aboard their crafts, and today's first open-market day would be a draw. I was right.

She wore dark glasses and a shoulder-wide lavender raffia hat. Her blond hair was tied back in a low chignon, and large gold hoops hung from her ears. She carried a straw bag, already laden with fruit. Stately and tall, she moved with the grace of a gazelle, even while performing the ordinary task of shopping for her family.

She was speaking to a vegetable vendor in fluent Spanish when I approached. She sensed my presence and turned.

"I need to talk with you," I said.

She frowned as if she didn't understand me and turned away.

"About your son," I called after her. She halted, and for an instant she stood with her back to me.

"It's about life and death," I said gently, walking closer. "And it's about a mother's love."

TWENTY-TWO

What do you want?" Elsa Johannsen spoke English fluently with little hint of a Swedish accent.

"I know you are in Playa Negra for your son's treatment."

"How would you know this? Our doings here are confidential." She leaned toward me suspiciously. "Do you work at the clinic? Is this how you know?"

"Please," I said gently, "there are others involved in your son's treatment."

"Of course there are others—doctors, nurses, lab techs. There are many people involved in saving his life."

A chill shuddered up my back, and I looked around, certain we were being watched, perhaps being listened to as well. When I saw no one turned in our direction, I looked back to Elsa. "Please listen. I may not have much time, but you need to know that young women have been abducted. I believe they're somehow connected to keeping Nicolette Baptiste alive."

"You know Nicolette is alive?"

"Yes, I do."

She stared at me without speaking for a moment, then she said, "You are a crazy woman, and I do not need to listen to you." She turned to go.

I fell into step beside her. "The mother of one of the missing girls is here in Playa Negra. We are both convinced that her daughter was taken by someone working with Dr. Baptiste. She loves her daughter, Carly, as much as you love your son. But not to know where she is or whether she is alive is breaking her heart.

"Just think how precious your son's early years are to you. She also remembers rocking her baby daughter to sleep, watching her first wobbly steps, hearing her cry out 'mama' when she was hurt. My friend would agree there is no greater pain than to know your child is suffering. She would gladly trade places with her daughter if she could. If she knew where Carly was."

Elsa remained utterly silent as I spoke, then she fluttered her fingers. "Ludicrous. You have made this up. You are probably a reporter trying to get a story. Do you know who you are talking about? Dr. Baptiste is known throughout the world for his advances in cancer research. He is so close to a—"

"Cure," I finished for her. "Yes, I know."

Around us the babble of the vendors continued, mixed with the hubbub of shoppers, the cries of the gulls overhead, the roar of motorbikes speeding through the streets. One sped close, slowed when it came near us, then revved its loud engine and took off again.

"I have one question," I said.

She stared at me, and I got the distinct impression she was desperate to escape. Not from my physical presence; she could walk away at any moment. But from the truth of what I had told her.

"I really must be going," she said.

"One question, please."

"I'm sorry. I can't help you." She adjusted her hat, pulling the brim low.

"How is Baptiste going to keep your son alive while he works on the cure?"

"Bone-marrow transplants—the stem cells in the marrow."

"The match has to be precise. Genetics and blood type are only two of the factors for long-term success. Are you a donor?"

Her mouth quivered slightly. "No, I'm not a match."

"Then who are the donors?"

"I didn't ask."

She started moving away from me, and I called out, "What is your son's blood type?"

She turned, looking at me quizzically, and said, "Type O."

"Fairly common," I said, "but still necessary for a match. What if Carly Lowe is type O? And Kate Rivers? Holly Hartsfield and all the rest? Will you believe me then?"

She gave me a hard stare, and then she was gone.

Max arrived with a cartload of vegetable and fruit boxes.

"Move them to the tender," I said, "then wait for me. I'll be back as soon as I see Adam, then find Tangi."

Playa Negra's main street ran parallel to the Canal de Tortuguero and formed the center of the small fishing village. The regional hospital stood on a sloping hillside opposite the fortresslike police headquarters, a fish processing plant, and a Spanish church that was centuries old. Three small hostels—Casa del Azur, Hotel el Sueño, and Casa del Pescador—were lined up like flowerpots on the bank of the canal.

I headed to the hospital first and gave my name to the receptionist. She recognized me from the previous day and waved me past ICU and Adam's guard.

Today I didn't hesitate and walked over to Adam's bed. His eyes were closed, and the beeps and whirs kept up their rhythm, just as before. His color was better, and for that I was thankful, even though all signs said he was still comatose.

I pulled up a chair and sat down by the bed, opposite his shoulder. "Adam," I said softly, "it's Harriet. I told you I'd be back, and here I am."

I waited for a response, but there was none.

"I've got a plan now, and I sure wish you'd wake up and give me your thoughts. Believe me, I could use them.

"Truth is, I'm scared. This is the hardest thing I've ever done. But too much is at stake not to do it, if that makes any sense. I know I'm heading into dangerous territory, by the most frightening means possible—at least for me.

"I know you're a praying man. I wish you'd open your eyes and let me know you'll pray for me, pray for the lost girls, pray that justice will be done."

I waited, hoping to see his eyelids flicker. They remained as still as carved stone. So with a sigh I stood. "You better believe I'm praying for you, Clint." I laughed softly. "Someday I'll tell you about this Clint business, but hey, you gotta wake up for that part."

I took his hand, nestled it between my palms, and squeezed it gently.

"I'm not going to do the melodramatic movie thing again and tell you to squeeze my hand if you hear me. But I just want you to know I'm here, and you've got a friend. And the other thing is, I'm doing my best—for you—to find your daughter."

I whispered a prayer, then laid his hand down and patted it. "I'll be back tomorrow to let you know how the story ends, my friend. Besides, I'm getting used to these one-way conversations. Love it that you can't interrupt me."

At that I thought I saw the tiniest quiver at the corner of his mouth. I waited, utterly still. "Adam?" I whispered, willing him to do it again.

He didn't. Minutes later I strode into the Hotel el Sueño, the hotel Tangi had mentioned, and was greeted by a school of piranha masquerading as journalists, all vying to get to the check-in desk. So much for my plan to quietly find Tangi and ask her about Carly's blood type. If I so much as whispered Tangerine Lowe's name to the clerk, the media feeding frenzy would begin.

To save Tangi's privacy and sanity, I backed away from the desk and trotted down the steps, glad to be out of the cacophony. In front of the hotel, a dozen or more satellite trucks had thrust their dishes overhead, cameras rolled, strobe lights glared off inverted silver reflectors, and reporters tested microphones. I hurried past, stepped onto the crowded street, and made my way through the curiosity seekers, grips, gaffers, producers and their assistants.

The crowd thinned out, and after a few minutes, I saw Max standing at the wharf. I waved and started across the street. The azure sea beyond the wharf caught my eye. A glittery light spread across the harbor, looking like a million brilliant diamonds scattered by a giant hand. But it was only my perception, an illusion. Just as Baptiste had shown the world his brilliance, his gift of healing. Perhaps there was substance there. Perhaps it was all sham. Someday I hoped to know.

I was still watching the changing light of the ocean when I heard a noise behind me.

A motorbike. It came roaring down the street. I turned as the driver— bent low, helmet covering his head, dark visor hiding his face—swerved the thing toward me.

I ran to the side of the street, jumped to the walkway.

The beast kept coming, vaulting to the walkway where I stood. Louder. Snarling. Careening wildly.

I turned and ran. But the thing seemed alive, seemed to anticipate my every move.

There was nothing to duck behind, no shelter. People stared as I ran, parting like the Red Sea as I came nearer.

I heard Max shouting from a distance. Sensed he was running toward me.

I slipped, lost my footing. Slipped again. Fell.

The motorbike was only yards away. I rolled to one side. Pulled my knees into a fetal position. Wrapped my arms around my head.

The motorbike roared closer, swerved again, and skidded to a stop next to me.

Each breath I took was agony, like a knife slicing into my side. My heart thundered. I couldn't look up.

A paper-thin object brushed across my hand. Then the monster roared and was gone.

Max knelt beside me. "Yo, Ms. M., that was a close one."

With a groan I unfolded my arms from around my head and sat up. An insect lay dead on the ground beside me. I stared at it, then looked up at Max.

He lifted the blue morpho into his hands. "The driver could easily have killed you, but instead he throws this thing."

"Obviously to scare me." I struggled to get up, and Max helped me to my feet. "But I don't scare. Ever." Too bad someone hadn't told my knees. I brushed myself off, and we headed for the tender. Even from this distance, I spotted the fruits of Max's shopping. It was piled high with cartons of fruits and vegetables. And at least a bushel of lemons.

We arrived at the wharf, and I stopped Max before we boarded the tender. I'd been finalizing a plan in my head, and now that one more card had been laid down, I had another of my own. One that would end this treacherous game. Or my life.

"Hey, bud?"

He was standing by the tender admiring the produce. Inside, the pilot had started the engine and was letting it idle while he waited for us to board.

"I've got a big favor to ask you."

"If it has anything to do with kayaking, the answer is no."

I laughed. "I'm not going back with you."

"Hey, Ms. M., it's not safe for you to be here alone. That's why I came along. And even so, look what happened."

I held up a hand. "I know, I know. And I'm grateful to you." I moved closer and dropped my voice. "But this is extremely important. I need you to get Zoë and bring her back here."

He ran his hand down his face. "Zoë Shire?"

"Is there another?"

He let out a heavy sigh. "It's just that Zoë is stubborn. Zoë doesn't do anything Zoë doesn't want to do. Plus, she doesn't trust any of us. Always thinks we're out to get her."

"For good reason, from what I've observed."

He looked embarrassed. "You need her here?"

"I need to talk with her, and it's got to be away from the ship and anyone she might be in contact with. Tell her I need her. You can mention the motorbike accident, but don't give her any details. And whatever you do, don't let her bring anyone with her—especially that kid Chip." I didn't know how, but I suspected he was involved. Maybe he was Baptiste's computer hacker extraordinaire. Tampering with blood banks. Students' health records. But he was a piece of the puzzle I would deal with later. For now I just needed Zoë.

I hoped that whatever emotional connection we'd made would bring her to me. Maybe if she thought I needed her, she would come—no matter how close her connection with Baptiste's daughter.

Max nodded reluctantly and asked where we would meet. I scanned the street, noting the gaggle of taxis and hired cars. Media related, no doubt.

"Taxi," I said to Max. "When you get here, look for a taxi that will be waiting specifically for you. I'll leave instructions with the driver where to take you. I need to get away from the town center—I hope, without being seen. I'll be waiting for you in a safe place."

Max rubbed his face again, frowning. "Can you at least tell me where you'll be—well, in the event something goes wrong?"

I shook my head. "It's better you don't know yet." I paused, resisting the urge to reach up and pat his cheek the way his mother would. "And Max?"

"Yeah?"

"You're pretty good at getting people across the harbor. I have no doubt you can do it again."

He grinned. "I've already got some ideas."

"Don't take any chances…or lift any kayak paddles to get her here."

"You got it, Ms. M." He grinned, then turned and clambered into the boat. "Price Alexander," he called as the tender backed away from the wharf. "I'll get him to help me."

"No! Not Price," I called to him.

But he didn't hear me.

I hailed three taxis before I found a driver who spoke English. The cabby I settled on was taking fares only until sundown when he needed to start back to his home base in San José. We negotiated the fare, and after a few minutes of required haggling, I hired him for the rest of the day.

I settled into the backseat and told him to take a route that would take us by Hotel el Sueño first. We slowed as we passed the hotel. The media frenzy continued, but this time—behind a bank of microphones toward the entrance—I saw a flash of spiked flame hair.

"Wait!" I said, and the driver stopped. "Stay here. Park if you must. But wait for me."

He nodded and pulled to the side of the road, and I got out.

Tangi, flanked by an FBI agent and Monica Oliverio from Interpol, was just finishing her statement. When the FBI agent began his report, she fought her way through the reporters and headed my direction.

"You look terrible," she said.

I gave her a weary smile. "Thanks." I gave her a hug. "How about you? How are you faring?"

My gaze followed her gesture to the crowd. "This is awful. I can't get out of the hotel without getting hounded. It's bad enough being frightened to death over Carly, but this just makes it worse."

"I've got a taxi. Do you want to drive somewhere? Maybe find a place far from the madding crowd?"

"I can't, Harriet. I need to stay near the FBI. They've become lifesavers in all this."

"You heard what happened yesterday? About the warrant to search Baptiste's island?"

"I was fully briefed. The feeling is that Baptiste isn't behind it, can't be behind it."

"And they're looking at people trafficking."

Her eyes filled, and she shrugged. "That's the latest assumption."

"What do you think, Tange?"

Her eyes met mine, and I could see a spark of fierce stubbornness in them. The same spark that flashed in Carly's eyes. "Everything you've told me fits," she said. "I still believe you're right. He's as guilty as sin."

I smiled. "Good, because I'm not ready to give up."

"What do you have planned?"

"You'll be the first to know—if I'm successful." I laughed lightly. "If I'm not, well, then you can send out a search party." I was sorry not to tell her my plan, but if the FBI got wind of it, they would make sure I was on the next flight to San Francisco. I couldn't have that; I was afraid to fly.

"I'll be the first to volunteer."

"I'll be in touch," I said. "And you'll be in my prayers. And Carly. Always Carly."

"I know," she said. "I've always loved that about you."

Hard-as-nails Tangerine Lowe loved something about me? "Prayer?"

She nodded. "Pray without fanfare. It's never meant so much to me as right now."

"He's a good friend, and he's always there, always listening. And there's no limit to who gets his ear, if you know what I mean." I gave her a gentle smile. "It's not like you've got to get up earlier than everyone else to get his attention. You can tell him all that's on your heart anytime, anywhere."

She nodded and blinked rapidly. I wrapped my arm around her shoulders and whispered a quiet prayer for us both, gave her another hug, and hurried to my taxi.

She stood watching me as I opened the door and climbed in. I rolled down the window and leaned out. "By the way, what is Carly's blood type?"

"Type O," she said. "Why?"

"I'll explain later." Then I called up to the cabby, "To the airport. And make sure we're not being followed."

didn't want to consider what I was about to do, couldn't consider it. First of all, my heart felt like it was ready to flutter right out of my chest. Second, my legs were inclined to run the other way as soon as we pulled into the Playa Negra airport. And third, just looking at a plane, any plane, made me want to upchuck.

"Let me out over there." I pointed to the hangar.

The driver guided the car to the smaller of the two doors.

I gave him half the money we had agreed on, then I said, "You need to pick up two people at the wharf within the next hour or so." He took the money, nodding as I described Max and Zoë. "Bring them here." I glanced at the sky, gauging the hours until sundown. "Please hurry."

He drove off, leaving me standing alone. Swallowing a knot of apprehension, I glanced around, again feeling the eerie sense that someone was watching me. I had checked a dozen times through the taxi window and had seen no one, at least no one close enough to be concerned about. Now I double-checked, scrutinizing each private plane, each corporate jet.

Nothing.

More planes were tied down on the field than before. For my plan to work, I needed charts, a flight book listing radio frequencies for the area, and, of course, a plane. I had flown a Cherokee, but I was most comfortable in a Cessna. Not wanting to take any more chances than I already was, I needed to stick to the Skyhawk.

Though the Cessna was the most familiar, it was also the most frightening to go near. Still standing by the hangar, I scanned the field. There were two Skyhawks, one toward the end of the field, the other just two planes down from where I stood. Both red and white.

First things first. I dug around in my vest for a metal nail file and stuck the cuticle end into the lock on the hangar door. I quickly stepped inside, closed the door, and leaned against it.

I looked around the dimly lit room. Stacks of pigeonholes lined one wall, and I hurried toward them. I moved from one to the next, thumbing through files, charts, and maps. I knew from my harbor-patrol trip to Baptiste's island yesterday that it lay in a southeasterly direction. But it was one of a half-dozen or more islands in the same area. Once I was at cruising altitude, finding the island would be like trying to find a needle in a haystack.

Conscious of the time and acutely aware that someone could walk in on me any minute, I dug and discarded, rapidly moving along the wall. Four large pigeonholes high and at least a dozen long meant a total of forty-eight, each with a half dozen files or so, some having to do with the airplanes that were owned by Baptiste's corporation, others having to do with privately owned planes apparently tightly controlled by the corporation.

I was nearing the end of the row when I pulled out a file stamped Cessna 172 Skyhawk on the tab. I flipped it open, held it to the light from the window, and smiled. Everything I needed to know about the Cessna tied down nearest the hangar, including maintenance records. It hadn't been serviced for several months, but beggars can't be choosers. In an envelope was the key that unlocked the cowling. I pocketed it.

Whoever flew the Cessna last had flown it to Baptiste's island, because the charts and radio frequencies, usually in a binder, had been pulled and left in the folder. At least that would save me time looking for the binder.

At the end of the room stood a row of metal filing cabinets. Curiosity got the best of me. Because of Carly's bracelet, I suspected that the abducted girls were flown here before being taken to the island. The charter fleet in Playa Negra would be the most logical to use for the abductions. They provided an easy cover since they were chartered often by the guests for trips in and out of the spa. It also kept Baptiste's name off the paperwork.

I wanted to get my hands on those records. It didn't make sense that Baptiste, or whoever was assisting him, would keep them in plain sight. But I also knew that the brighter the person, sometimes the more arrogant, and the more arrogant, the more prone to slip up. Power does that sort of thing to people. It can corrupt, it can also make one feel indestructible.

I pulled out my Swiss army knife. Price wasn't the only one who had experience picking locks with this handy tool. I worked the lock on the cabinet closest to me. It opened on the third try, and I pulled the drawer out. Judging from the yellowed folders and faded handwritten labels, they were simply dusty, obsolete files. I pulled one out toward the end of the section. It was at least three years old and listed the flight records for Baptiste's planes going back even further in time.

Adam had said that his daughter disappeared three years ago—right after Nicolette Baptiste's supposed death. I checked the date, and with my index finger, traced the meticulous list of takeoffs and landings and reasons for the flights.

One flight caught my eye. A specially equipped Cherokee had flown from an unnamed island in the Caribbean near the time Holly Hartsfield disappeared and had arrived in Playa Negra four days later, following a route that took the pilot partially over land, partially over water. A note to one side—the letters *HH* circled—made my breath catch in my throat.

I put the file aside and thumbed through the folders, desperate to find one nearer to today's date. To find more initials matching the latest disappearances.

A prickling at the back of my neck stopped me cold. Someone was aware of my presence in this room, watching my every move.

A small whirring sound, a click, a barely audible buzz, made me turn. In the corner of the room, a minute camera stood guard. Either it had been on since my arrival and I hadn't noticed, or it was trained on the file cabinets and triggered by motion. In this case, my motion. I only hoped it was film and not live.

If it was live feed, I had no chance of getting away from the airport. Heart racing, I tucked the flight records into my vest and, holding the Cessna file in one hand, quickly exited the hangar.

The Skyhawk stood in the distance. Without warning the sorrow hit, rolling over my heart in waves. The memory, as acute as if it were happening this moment, came back to me. I remembered the slant of the late afternoon sun that day, the painful clarity of the sky, the long shadows cast by the men who walked solemnly to my door.

I remembered watching their faces for a flicker of something that said they understood my shock, my profound grief. But there was no such emotion. Later I imagined that they had made such calls before and needed to protect their hearts. Or perhaps they were afraid I might break down and they wouldn't know how to comfort me.

Such a pity that too often we all do the same. Hold back our comforting arms, afraid of our own vulnerabilities, afraid we won't know what to say, when maybe all someone needs is a look of compassion, the touch of a hand.

I stared up at the little plane. It looked airworthy enough, and in spite of the maintenance records I hoped it would serve me well. I thought of the times I had circled our Skyhawk, testing fluid levels, hoses beneath the engine cowling, movement of the ailerons. It really didn't matter today. I was throwing caution to the wind anyway. But old habits don't easily die, so around the plane I went, testing and prodding.

I had just finished letting the condensation drip from the fuel tanks when I heard a vehicle approaching. I hid in the shadow of the plane until I saw a taxi moving slowly toward the hangar. I stepped away from the plane and waved it over. As soon as the cab stopped, Max and Zoë got out of opposite back doors, Zoë scowling. I paid the driver, gave him a generous tip, and asked him to wait a few more minutes. He shrugged and drove off the field to wait by the hangar.

The three of us stood staring at each other, and then Zoë said, "What's going on? Max said you'd had an accident."

"I did. I've had some close calls lately—one that almost killed Max and me. Today's was more a cruel trick to scare me off."

"What's that got to do with me?"

I glanced at Max who got the hint and moved away so that Zoë and I could speak privately. He walked along the row of small planes, kicking tires, and fiddling with flaps and ailerons.

"Zoë, we don't have much time. That's why I asked Max to bring you here."

"What are you talking about?" Her look was defiant, and my heart fell. I'd hoped she had softened. I didn't want to think too long about her mental state or her reaction to what I was about to say. All I could think about was getting to the abducted girls before it was too late.

"The sacrificial ones," I said, "that you told me about. They don't have much time to live, do they?" She didn't answer, so I went on. "Their lives are being sacrificed—their blood, their marrow—to keep your friend alive. You admitted to this. You also said you wanted it to end. Do you still, Zoë, do you want it to end?" My voice was low, urgent, as I spoke.

She swallowed hard and nodded slightly.

"Does Nicolette ever plead with you…plead with her father…to let her go?"

She gave me a sharp look. I knew I had hit a nerve. I led her closer to the plane, and we stood in the deepening shadow cast by the wing. "What is her life like, Zoë?"

"She is bedridden now—but once the cure is found, she'll be back to…good health." Tears filled her eyes.

"Does she know about the others, about those who are giving their lives for her?"

She shook her head. "I promised I wouldn't tell."

"You promised her father?"

She hesitated slightly, then said, "Yes, of course. Dr. Baptiste. Who else?"

"I told you I planned to go there—go to the island."

"You went yesterday."

"And found nothing because no one knew where to look." I paused. "You're the only one, Zoë. You're the only one who can stop the sacrifices, stop choosing the ones who give their life's blood to keep Nicolette alive. I'm not going to ask you how you got the right blood type or genetic markers, how you chose exactly which girls would be abducted, but I think I know." This wasn't the time to bring up Chip's involvement.

She stared at me. Silent. I couldn't fathom what was going on behind those thick glasses, behind those large gray eyes. But I thought there might be an equal measure of regret and defiance.

"You're the only one who knows the dark secrets of the island. Please, Zoë. Come with me."

She looked up at the Skyhawk. "You know how to fly this?"

"I'm a certified pilot, yes. And I'm familiar with this aircraft. I flew one just like it for more than twenty years."

"I'll take you there," she said. She glanced at Max, now at the end of the runway. "But not with him. I'll take you if no one else comes. No cops, no Interpol."

"The girls are being held on the island, is that right?"

"Yes," she whispered, already looking like she regretted her decision.

"And they are still alive?"

She looked away from me.

"Zoë, are they alive?"

Her voice was barely a whisper. "They're very sick."

My heart twisted; I didn't want to think about their suffering. "But alive?"

She turned back to me. "I don't know...I don't know."

I fought tears as I signaled Max to come back to the plane. He trotted toward us, blond hair blowing in the wind.

"Yo," Max said when he arrived.

"We're flying to the island."

"Can I go?"

"No."

"You're flying this thing?" He watched me open the doors and motion for Zoë to sit in the right-hand seat. "Way to go, Ms. M.!"

Zoë climbed in, and I stepped back to the ground. "I need to ask a favor," I said to Max.

"Shoot."

I handed him the records I'd taken from the file cabinet. "See to it that these are taken to Monica Oliverio. Place them in her hands only. No local police, got it? They're too enamored with their own celebrity. Tell her where I've gone and who I'm with. We finally have the proof we need. And we have a witness."

He stared at me solemnly as I climbed back into the plane. "What if it's a trap, Ms. M.?"

I motioned for him to get away from the plane.

"Clear!" I yelled and started the engine.

I adjusted the engine rpms and taxied to the end of the grass runway. My fear was so intense my knees were shaking as I checked the instruments and adjusted for altitude.

I looked over at Zoë. "You ready?"

She nodded solemnly.

"Let's do it then."

We raced down the runway. I said a little prayer. The airspeed hit sixty-five. Seventy-five. Eighty-five.

Another little prayer.

Then I pulled back on the yoke, and the Cessna rose into the air. The ground fell away below us.

TWENTY-FOUR

We climbed to six thousand feet heading due east, for a short time at least, facing away from the sun. For that I was grateful; this was difficult enough without the sun in my eyes, glaring off the ocean, blinding me. The minute we lifted off, all those old flying instincts came back to me. My knees still felt weak, but the sick feeling in the pit of my stomach had passed.

I scanned the skies for other aircraft, but so far we were alone at our altitude. I kept a vigilant eye on scattered clouds to the southeast, worried they might build into something I didn't want to deal with. I kept watch behind us as well; I remembered the feeling of being watched and didn't quite trust that I had foiled any attempt to tail us.

"You okay?" I studied Zoë's profile. Clearly she was a troubled young woman. Now that we were in the plane I wondered if she might be pushed over that line between reality and fantasy, knowing there was no way to back out now. She already lived in a shadowy land, and I suspected Baptiste had brainwashed her into helping him find his "sacrificial lambs." Would she sacrifice herself—and me—to save him? And her best friend?

The thought all but stole the breath from my lungs. I whispered a prayer and willed my heart to quit its racing beat.

Zoë had been quiet during takeoff, but now, as if reading my mind, she turned to me and said, "I don't know what's ahead."

"You mean what we'll find?"

She nodded. "It scares me."

"Are you worried for your safety?"

"Oh no. I'm Niki's best friend. Dr. Baptiste would never hurt me."

I bit my tongue to keep from asking Zoë her blood type. I was willing to bet it wasn't type O.

She was quiet a moment, then she asked, "Why are you doing this? I heard what Max asked you. What if you're walking into a trap? You don't really know me." Her eyes were large behind the thick eyeglasses. "I could have set it up."

"So, am I walking into a trap?"

She stared straight ahead.

"To answer your question, because it's the right thing to do. There is no doubt in my mind about that. And when I feel passionately about something being right, I act. It also has to do with my sense of justice, I suppose. But beyond that, I'm doing it because I care about Carly. Her mom, too. But Carly's always been special to my own family."

"You don't even know Kate, yet she's part of what you're doing too."

"She's someone's daughter, someone's granddaughter, someone's friend. I know how I would feel if someone abducted my daughter or one of my sons. I would give my life to get them back. I can do no less for these kids—all of them. Even Holly—and I don't even know her."

"Holly isn't there."

"Where is she?"

"She hasn't been there for over a year now."

"Where is she, Zoë?"

"I don't know."

"Don't you care?"

"Like all the rest, she probably gave her life so that others might live. No one tells what happens...well, after...you know." She shrugged and put her head down.

"Oh, Zoë. You can't mean that! It sounds like someone drilled it into you." I blinked back angry tears.

"Soon others will give their lives as well." She turned to me, watching, as if gauging my reaction. "I can't imagine what that would feel like—to have someone care enough to give her life for me."

"I hope that's not what's required tonight," I said quietly, adjusted the vector signal, and turned the plane due south. "I'm willing to do it, but I also have a lot of living left ahead of me. I won't go quietly into the night."

She smiled wistfully. "My gramps says that a lot."

"Would you give your life for him?"

She nodded.

"Then you understand."

"In a way I'm already giving up my life for him," she said, surprising me. "What I'm doing is for him, too. You know about the transfusions and bone-marrow transplantation, but you don't know about the rest of it."

I glanced at her. "The rest of what?"

"The embryonic stem cell experiments."

"Baptiste said something yesterday about his work to identify a missing genetic marker and plant it within a human egg—but he was talking specifically about the missing gene in CML victims."

"His plans go far beyond what you or anyone else can imagine. His plans for embryonic stem cell transplantation are already in motion."

If Baptiste had no qualms about sacrificing the lifeblood of young "donors" to save his daughter, I shuddered to think how he would go about getting the hundreds of thousands of donor eggs for his embryonic stem cells. He was a madman.

"You mentioned your grandfather. What does he have that makes him so ill?"

"Parkinson's disease—the form that causes its victims to lose their minds."

"Oh, Zoë. I'm so sorry." Her grandfather was all she had, and someday he would not even remember her name. She was clinging to another family—to a best friend, who was like a sister, and her friend's father, who was promising a cure for her grandfather. No wonder Baptiste was able to blur the lines between good and evil.

She turned to me, her eyes hard. "That's why I still haven't decided what to do."

"To let Dr. Baptiste go on with his research—or blow the whistle. Tell what you know so he'll be stopped." I tried to remain calm, though my knees were shaking again. The closer we got to the island, the more vulnerable I felt.

"He'll go to prison if I testify against him," she said. "Thousands who would be saved will die."

"I can't make your decision for you," I said sadly.

"I know," she said, her voice sounding very small. "That's why I'm scared."

I reached for her hand and held it tight. She smiled, tears filling her eyes. Then she pulled her hand away and wiped her glasses.

❧

I scanned my charts as a group of islands appeared on the horizon. "Do you recognize where we are?"

"It's the second island from the left. The largest in the group."

"The chart shows the runway laid out north to south just behind the main complex."

"That sounds right. There's a hangar there—just like the one at Playa Negra. It sits parallel to the runway."

I throttled down to lose altitude. I turned north to keep out of sight of Baptiste's home, circled back to the south until we were about a thousand feet off the ocean, then turned directly north for a straight-in approach. I scanned for other air traffic in the event Baptiste or his colleagues were taking off or landing.

Everything was quiet. I put down the flaps and cut the power.

The sun was setting now, casting a shadowy pall across the island. A light haze had moved in off the ocean, blocking the view of the harbor side. But high on the cliffs above the harbor, Baptiste's adobe was in full view. Its gray walls looked squat and thick from above, prisonlike, surrounded by shrubs and plants partially obscured by the same ocean fog.

I adjusted the flaps, thankful we'd be on the ground before the fog settled in thick and deep.

"I want to bring the girls back with us," I said as I lined up with the runway. "We need to get to them fast, get them into the plane, before we're socked in."

"I told you, if they're still alive, they're too sick. They'll never make it."

I peered ahead and adjusted the engine power. We seemed to almost float toward the runway. I kept a sharp lookout for Baptiste, expecting him to run out of the hangar to block us from landing. His Citation was tied down just to the left of the runway, but there was no sign of him.

A crosswind caught us, lifted one wing, then just as quickly changed direction. The little Cessna swerved and dipped precariously. Zoë gasped. I added power and fought to keep it on course, heading straight for the quickly approaching runway. We touched down with a strong bump, followed by another. Then another. I never was great at greasing it on, as Hollis called it. But we were down, and for that I was grateful. I powered back to slightly over idle, and we taxied to tie down near the Citation.

I climbed out of the plane, and Zoë followed, jumping to the ground. Then she stopped and stared, her face white.

Striding toward us was Dr. Baptiste.

TWENTY-FIVE

r. Jean Baptiste moved toward us with the power and grace of one whose self-confidence knows no bounds. The grace of a venomous reptile. His eyes glinted with amused interest as he neared, which frightened me more than if I'd seen anger seething in their depths.

"Well, well, right on time," he said. "I was worried you would disappoint me, Mrs. MacIver. I've been admiring your courage from a distance—via the miracle of electronics, and now I get to experience it up close and personal. And here you are on my little island."

I remembered the camera in the hangar and glanced at Zoë to see if she was surprised he knew we were coming. She was focused on Baptiste, her expression hopeful.

"Yes, here we are," I said lamely.

"Ah, I can see you are wondering how I knew exactly when to expect you. I'll let you in on a little secret. My island is electronically monitored and controlled. No one arrives—or leaves—without my approval."

"I did assume you had a system of some sort."

"A system?" He laughed with the same belittling amusement I'd heard in his voice earlier. "How charming, Mrs. MacIver. Utterly charming."

"I had already determined you are a master of systems," I said, ignoring his tone. "I'm impressed with the little empire you've set up. The systems for capturing unsuspecting young women. Systems for identifying them by blood type and genetic markers—probably by hacking into blood-bank records. And, of course, leaving the final choice of your victims to others so you don't have to dirty your hands with something as abhorrent as kidnapping."

"I am as impressed by your powers of deduction as I am by your courage, Harriet. Or should I call you Ms. M.?"

I glanced at Zoë again, hoping she could shore up her own courage and give me some support. But she still seemed as mesmerized by Baptiste as before.

"I came on behalf of Kate and Carly. I want to see them."

He shrugged. "I suppose it's a moot point, since none of you will be leaving the island in quite the same way you arrived."

At this Zoë gave him a sharp glance. "You don't mean me, Dr. Baptiste, do you?"

He touched her cheek gently. "No, little one, you are the exception. You are too valuable. I have other plans for you."

Her answering smile was almost worshipful.

He led us to the hangar, and as soon as he opened the door, I realized what the inspectors had missed yesterday: the largest, most obvious building in the complex. No one had suspected that the lab and clinic might be housed in the airplane hangar.

I stepped into the state-of-the-art hospital, and my mouth dropped open. Three hospital beds, privacy curtains, heart monitors, defibrillators, IV stations. The works.

"Surprised?" Baptiste said at my elbow.

"Stunned, but where are your patients?"

Zoë had gone on ahead of us and was pressing against the large double doors at the end of the room. They clicked open, and she disappeared inside.

"Obviously through there," I said and started after her.

But Baptiste reached for my wrist and held it fast. "Not yet."

"You won't stop me," I said. "The authorities know where I am. They know I have a witness."

"There will be no witnesses by the time they arrive, only the unfortunate news of your demise in a small plane as you attempted to land on my island. Miscalculated the fuel onboard, apparently." He tsk-tsked, shaking his head. "I will be as horrified by the accident as anyone else, especially because dear Zoë was once my daughter's best friend."

Knowingly or unknowingly, he had touched on my greatest fear. I backed away from him, my mind skittering in every direction—but always coming back to dying the way Hollis did: the twisting spiral into the ocean, the jarring slam into the rolling breakers, the surge of water filling the cockpit, the frantic attempt to get out. Doors jammed. Windows unbreakable. Then sinking…sinking…helplessly dragged downward. I had pictured it a thousand times, my dearest Hollis living through those final, horrifying moments, only to die as his beloved plane sucked him into the sea's murky graveyard.

"You would sacrifice your daughter's friend? You would let her die after all she's done for you? She's given you her soul, and you've trampled it. You've destroyed what innocence she had left. Now you would take her life as well?" I stepped toward him, my anger replacing fear. "I once gave you credit for saving lives. Though I thought your methods detestable, I thought you were doing it for the good of humankind."

The glint was back in his reptilian eyes. "Indeed I am, Ms. M. That has never changed, but you see, my methods are, shall we say, unconventional. Pedestrian minds, even the most brilliant scientific minds, don't understand the sacrifices that must be made. There are secrets that must stay on this island. No one finds out my methods. No one."

"You will be found out," I said, "no matter how you try to cover your tracks today. I left proof. It's already in the hands of Interpol—"

He laughed, interrupting. "Oh that? That little shred of evidence you picked up out of my file? I'm afraid, dear Ms. M., that it is gone. Poof. A little puff of smoke is all that remains. I had it set afire."

I almost forgot to breathe. "What do you mean? How?"

"The young man you've taken under your wing?"

Max!

"I had his taxi run off the road. It was a terrible accident. I'm afraid the cabby didn't live through it. Max, you'll be happy to know, was uninjured. He is being held by my associates."

"What good can he do for you?"

"Ah, my dear. His worth is great. For, you see, he holds the key to a very important decision you must soon make—just as you hold the key to whether he lives or dies."

Icy fear skittered up my spine.

He seemed to enjoy my reaction. "You might have wondered how I was going to get you to, of your own accord, take off in the Cessna with our little Zoë at your side? It's a beautiful plan, really. Max Pribble is at the airport in Playa Negra. A Cessna Skyhawk, identical to this one—the irony of which I thought you would appreciate—is awaiting takeoff. Your friend, hands and ankles bound, is about to go for a ride. We won't blindfold him, however, for we want him to have the full sensory experience of his ride…and his free fall into the ocean.

"Unfortunately, it will be dark by the time his plane takes off, so he won't have the full visual effect. Perhaps some coastal lights in the distance, a few stars—because fog is forecast to linger just off the coast. All in all, it will be the experience of a lifetime." He laughed at his own joke. "Now, let's continue with our tour, shall we? Your plane is being prepped and should be ready in just a few minutes. You will find it adequate for your journey. You will have enough fuel to get airborne."

"And if I don't, Max dies."

He escorted me through the double doors, then halted. A hallway stretched before us, flanked by four closed doors on either side.

"A quick study," he said, laughing. "He'll also go for this ride if you attempt a crash landing, say on a beach somewhere, or even glide to another island. Your fuel will take you only as far as I can keep you in sight with my field glasses. The deal is, you are exchanging your life for his. You go into the water, and disappear without a trace."

I fought the rising panic that threatened to overwhelm me and nodded mutely.

"And should you think the approaching fog will shield you," he laughed quietly, "you're wrong. It will only work in my favor. Sound travels extremely well in these conditions." He paused. "So have we struck a bargain?"

"With one exception. Let me take the Cessna out alone. Please let Zoë live. If you have no regard for her, think of your daughter. What would she do without Zoë? They're as close as sisters."

His face softened for an instant, and I thought he might agree, then he said, "My daughter has slipped into a coma."

"You said she was responding to treatment."

"She is. This is a temporary setback. She will revive."

I bargained for Zoë's life, desperate to save her from such a cruel death. "Wouldn't hearing Zoë's voice make a difference for Nicolette? Maybe bring about a response?"

"There can be no witnesses. She betrayed me, betrayed Nicolette, by bringing you here."

This wasn't what I had planned. Suddenly the weight of the nightmare I'd brought about—for Zoë, for Max—pressed on my heart. I had to convince this madman to let Zoë live. I touched his arm. "I tricked Zoë to get her into the plane. I sent Max to pick her up without telling her why."

He seemed to consider my words, then he shook his head. "My life's work is built on sacrifice. One life given for the greater good. It's time for Zoë to sacrifice hers so she won't be tempted when the next opportunity comes along to betray my work—to betray the thousands of men, women, and children who will benefit from my research. It's simpler that way. Less messy."

"Aren't you playing God? You've already made great strides in finding a cure for CML. Your research is known throughout the world. Isn't that enough? You are dedicated to saving lives, yet you are equally willing to snuff out the lives of others. Why?"

"You know why. They are keeping my daughter alive."

"But why these particular girls?"

We walked a short distance down the hallway, and he paused in front of the first door. He rested his hand on the stainless-steel handle. "You haven't figured it out, have you? I'm surprised."

"I know about the genetic markers, the blood type needed. I also know these young women all are from Shepparton. I know how it was discovered that they had the precise qualifications to be donors. What I don't know is why Kate and Carly and Holly were chosen over other girls. What was it about them?"

He stared at me, almost thoughtfully. "I suppose one could call it 'revenge of the nerds.' My daughter wasn't well liked, you see. Many weekends when she flew home from school that first year, she spent hours in her room crying. The things said to her were disgusting. The tricks played on her, cruel. She went through months trying to ignore the hurtful, venomous, and unforgettable barbs and taunts. They imitated her stutter, injuring her to the core. They damaged her psyche, sent her into a deep clinical depression. Some victims of harassment act out in anger. You remember Columbine?"

I nodded.

"But, you see, my Nicolette didn't have a mean bone in her body. She took the insults, the ribbing about her looks and dress, her stutter, and eventually convinced everyone she didn't care. I am certain, though, that what happened at Shepparton, the vitriol she internalized, caused her immune system to shut down. Weakened her. Left her susceptible to disease. Genetically, she was predisposed to CML, but the depression, her sense of worthlessness, triggered something that couldn't be stopped."

"So you kept a list."

"Yes, I'm not ashamed to say I did. And there is a system—yet another system—in place at Shepparton." He smiled at his own cleverness. "Zoë handled much of the targeting. She knows what it feels like—and Nicolette was her best friend."

"I suppose there will be others," I said. "And you'll have to develop a separate list having nothing to do with Nicolette. But the profile will be the same: the beautiful, the popular, the in crowd, the clever—your sick retribution for what you think the in crown did to you daughter. And let me guess how you will bring this about. Computer geniuses, moles in the admissions department, files tampered with, admission offered to people whose health records are a match. Blood type. Genetic markers."

He started to speak, but I held up my hand. "You can't stop. You have a seven-year-old boy to keep alive while you work on your cure. So you need fresh blood that's a better match; bone marrow that's closer to the victim's genetic makeup.

"And I suppose that because the donors aren't blood relatives of your patients, the bone marrow is rejected after a few weeks, making more transfusions necessary, requiring more bone marrow."

Baptiste's smile was condescending. "A simplified version of something more complex than you can imagine. I do admire your courage, Ms. M., your tenacity, your cleverness. But I'm afraid it's time to say good-bye. You and Zoë are due to take off in less than ten minutes." He opened the door and stood back so I could enter. "You may also want a few last words with the young women you came to save."

The stark room held a single bed, a table with a lamp, and a stainless-steel-and-faux-leather chair. The drapes were drawn against the falling darkness, and the lamplight cast deep shadows across the room. The décor was stark, without a television, radio, stereo, or even a stack of magazines or books in sight.

The only relief in the gray and white room was a colorful print in a shadow box that had been hung directly across from the bed. As I drew closer, I realized it wasn't a print. It was the real thing—a collection of vividly colored butterflies. Each pinned through, each with bright wings frozen in flight.

It was positioned so that Carly had nothing else to look at.

I turned to Carly and reached for her hand. Her eyes fluttered open. For a moment I didn't think she recognized me, then she gave me a weak smile.

"Hey there," I said.

"You here to spring me?" Her voice was hoarse.

"I'm going to try my best, sweetheart." I smoothed her forehead. "Your mother is here—still in town, though."

"I've got a lot of questions…"

"I know. We all do, and I hope we'll have the answers soon."

She closed her eyes. "I'm thirsty."

I reached for a water pitcher that sat on a small wheeled table positioned near the head of the metal-frame bed. I poured a glass, then supported her head while she sipped. She lay back, exhausted from the effort. "Tell Mama I need her…to hurry…" After a moment her breathing slowed, and I could tell she slept, probably sedated.

I squeezed her hand before letting it go. "Good-bye, dear one." Then I stooped and kissed her cheek.

Shaking with anger, I turned back to the doorway where Baptiste waited. His look was scornful, as if he'd enjoyed witnessing the scene between Carly and me. He gestured to the next room down the hall, and without a word I brushed past him to enter.

I recognized Kate, who slept soundly, her skin the color of parchment. Her room was furnished the same way—gray and white. Stark. Designed to draw the eye to the one bright spot in the room—the butterfly collection on the wall.

I wondered if in their drugged states, Kate and Carly dreamed of the pinned butterflies, dreamed of flying again. Dreamed of freedom—only to wake and realize they couldn't move.

I whispered a prayer for Kate and bent to kiss her cheek.

"Satisfied?" Baptiste said from the doorway.

"Let them go," I said as I approached him. "You have no right to play God. Let them all go, including your daughter." I paused. "I'll bet she has begged you to release her from this sick form of bondage."

The corner of his eye twitched, but he said nothing.

"I want to see her," I said.

"It's time for you to go."

"Let me see her."

He inclined his head toward a room at the end of the hallway. His face was expressionless as he escorted me to the door, opened it, and stood back for me to enter.

The room was large and luxuriously furnished in a French Country style of multicolored pastels. Roses and violets and baby's-breath adorned the wallpaper, and at the far end of the room, ceiling-to-floor windows were covered with matching drapes, swagged on both sides, with gathered pastel sheers underneath. It was a room designed by someone who assumed this was what a young woman might want, when, in actuality, it was a little girl's room, complete with a teddy-bear collection, elegant porcelain dolls, and Mickey Mouse knickknacks on glass shelves.

A queen-size, canopied bed was positioned close to the window, where, I assumed, Nicolette could see the ocean. A stereo system was in place with high-tech speakers in each corner, and a flat-screen plasma television was attached to one wall. There were no butterflies in this room.

Beside Nicolette's bed, Zoë kept vigilance. I could see she had been crying.

I walked quietly to the bed. Zoë looked up, but it wasn't my eyes she sought; it was Baptiste's, who stood behind me.

"Why didn't you tell me?" Her words, spoken slowly, deliberately, reflected as much rage as I felt toward the man, the same rage I imagined she had stored up through the years. "She's not responding. She's comatose, isn't she?" When Baptiste didn't answer, she stood and repeated, "Isn't she?"

She circled Nicolette's bed to stand in front of him and said, "You lied. All this—all I did to help—was to keep Niki alive, to help her get better, restore her to full health. Now"—she gestured helplessly toward Nicolette—"you've done this. You've turned her into a vegetable. How long now, huh? How long will you keep her like this while you work on your miracle cure? She was already begging you to let her go. Now she can't even speak."

Zoë was crying openly now, tears running down her cheeks. She swiped angrily at them. "How long will you let this go on?"

Baptiste took a step toward her, and she backed away. "Let Niki go," she whispered. "Have compassion on your daughter. Please, just let her die."

Baptiste turned to me. "It is time for your return flight." Then he said to Zoë, "I will consider your words, but for now, you must return to the mainland with Ms. M."

A shadow crossed her face, and she looked at me, frowning. "Is this true?"

It made me sick, but I nodded. "Yes," I whispered. "A crew is preparing the plane now."

"Carly and Kate? Are we taking them with us?"

"They are needed here, my little one," Baptiste said. "Ms. M. and I have reached an understanding about all involved. She will tell you about our agreement during your flight."

Again, Zoë looked to me, and I confirmed his words with a nod.

"You must be on your way. Let's go." He gestured to the door in a gentlemanly manner and stood back to let us exit the room.

When Zoë reached the doorway, she stopped, then ran back and hugged Nicolette. I watched, tears in my eyes as she kissed her friend's forehead. "Good-bye," she whispered, then joined Baptiste and me in the hallway. His stride was long and rapid as he led us to the exit.

The Cessna was where I had left it next to the Citation. No crew was in sight, and I hoped, for a brief moment, that Baptiste had been bluffing.

Heavy-hearted, I started toward the little aircraft, Zoë trailing behind me. The runway lights had been turned on, casting a surrealistic, eerie glow on the airfield.

Zoë looked at Baptiste when we reached the plane, her face almost white in the garish light. "I wish you would change your mind." Her voice was unnaturally calm, and the worshipful, affectionate expression was lighting her face again.

Only this time I saw through the facade. I wondered if the earlier glimpse of the same emotion had been false as well.

"I do wish you'd change your mind about Niki…" Still smiling, she stepped toward him. "I feel like I've awakened after a long, horrid nightmare. I thought you loved your daughter, but now I see it wasn't love at all. It was self-indulgence, self-love. You didn't want to save her life as much as you wanted the glory for pulling it off. You didn't want to save the victims of leukemia as much as you wanted the glory for the discovery.

"For some time I've suspected you didn't care for anyone but yourself, but I didn't know for sure." Her eyes were dry and clear as she stared at him. "Not just Niki, but me. All I wanted was a family. A sister. A dad." She laughed bitterly. "Look who I chose."

"Get into the plane," Baptiste said, his voice low and threatening. "Get into the plane before I call the guards."

"Like I'm real scared," she said, mocking him.

I wanted to cheer her on, but I stood dumbfounded, my mouth hanging open. This was a side of Zoë I hadn't seen.

For a moment Baptiste seemed as shocked as I was. I wondered if anyone had ever defied him so openly. "Get in the plane," he repeated finally.

"I promise you, this plane will take off," she said, smiling. "But I won't be in it."

My heart beat erratically. She meant for me to take off alone. Any change in Baptiste's plans meant we would all die. He would never let Zoë defy him. He would probably kill her here and stuff her body in the plane with me. She would die anyway, even if she refused to board the plane.

I was powerless to warn her; it would do no good anyway.

Zoë was sneering at him now. "I think you should be the one to take this lovely evening flight," she said. She looked up at the sky. "The stars will be beautiful tonight."

He stared at her, hard. "What are you talking about?" He took two steps toward her.

"That's far enough," she said.

She pulled out a gun.

I don't know anything about guns. They make me nervous. Some people keep them in a bedside table for protection, something I don't agree with. I was always worried I'd shoot Gus by mistake.

I could tell that this gun was an automatic, not a revolver, but that was about all I knew. I could also tell that it was big, though in the shaking hand of a slight young woman, it probably looked bigger than it really was. I imagined Baptiste thought so too.

"Get in the plane," Zoë growled at Baptiste, "or I'll blow your head off."

TWENTY-SIX

Surely you can't mean this." Baptiste's face had turned a ghoulish gray in the ambient glow of the runway lights.

"With all my heart." She waved the gun around awkwardly, which made me catch my breath.

I tried to see if the safety was on or off, but I couldn't tell. Mostly because I wasn't sure what to look for.

"Go!" She waved the gun at Baptiste. "Get in the plane."

Frowning as if he didn't understand, he started for the Citation, his private jet.

"Wrong move," she said. "Wrong plane." The gun was trembling in her hand. "Get in the Cessna. You've got a short little flight to take tonight…in the starlight."

He turned to her, hands outstretched in supplication. "Honey, you don't know how to shoot a gun. Who do you think you're trying to scare with that thing?"

"You don't think my gramps taught me how to shoot?" She smiled at him. "One more step, and I'll show you." She waved the gun again.

She looked brave, but I could see her knees shaking. No doubt Baptiste saw it too.

"You've got my gun, an automatic," he said, "and you've probably never seen a gun like that." He took another step closer. "And you've never shot a man. I don't think you've got the guts to pull the trigger. "

Zoë hesitated, a quick frown crossing her brow. In the silence I thought I heard a noise. At first I could barely make it out, then the noise grew louder.

Neither Zoë nor Baptiste seemed aware of it. They stared at each other as Baptiste moved closer. Step by step, cautious at first, then with more confidence, he moved toward her.

"Get back! I'm warning you. I'll shoot." The hand holding the gun trembled. Tears trailed down her cheeks. "Get back!"

Baptiste lunged for her, and time seemed suspended.

They struggled. I heard Zoë cry out. Baptiste grunted. Then the gun went off, with a concussion that made me jump.

It echoed through the night.

Then all was quiet. I stared, afraid to move. Afraid to breathe. Two bodies down. A cry. A moan. And blood. Too much blood.

I ran to Zoë and knelt beside her. Sobbing, she threw herself into my arms.

Just then a jackhammering *whump* seemed to rise up from the sea behind us.

I wrapped Zoë in my arms as the helicopter landed. The troops rolled out. FBI, Interpol, or Costa Rican law enforcement? I couldn't tell in the dark. And it didn't matter.

Monica Oliverio, in full uniform, ran toward us. Immediately behind her was a couple I assumed to be Kate's parents. And Tangi Lowe. The troops spread out across the compound.

Monica knelt by Baptiste's body, looked at the sobbing Zoë, then met my eyes. "The girls are here?"

The others waited expectantly.

"Yes," I said. "Inside, through the double doors, and down the hallway. First two doors on your left. They've been sedated, and they're extremely weak, but they are alive."

Tangi started to go, then turned, knelt down and wrapped her arms around both Zoë and me. "Thank you," she said.

"You'd better get in there. I think Carly's expecting you."

She grinned, blew me a kiss with both hands, and ran for the hangar.

TWENTY-SEVEN

The following morning I was just beginning to pack my Underwood in its hard case when I was interrupted by a knock on my stateroom door.

It was Max.

"Hey, bud."

"Ms. M." He smiled. "You okay?"

"None the worse for wear. How about you? Did they hurt you?"

He shook his head and plopped down on the little sofa. "A bit of duct tape here and there, nothing serious. I could've taken the guy, but the others helping him surprised me. After the accident and all…"

"By the way, if Baptiste's thugs nabbed you before you reached Monica Oliverio, how did you get word to them about where I'd gone?"

He grinned. "I have my ways."

"Seriously."

"I had a backup plan, thanks to Chip."

"Chip helped you?"

"He didn't know he did. He was hangin' with Zoë at the Clipper when I got back to the ship. Showing off a satellite phone he'd ripped off from somebody in Playa Negra. It was cool—did everything from—"

"Hey, back to the story," I said.

He laughed. "I sort of borrowed it from his backpack before Zoë and I left for port. Neither of them knew I had it." He shrugged. "With my luck these past few days, and knowing you had something big planned, I thought it'd be a good idea to have it along. As soon as you took off, I got through to some main number for Interpol. Said it was an emergency. They connected me to Monica."

"You're a good guy, Max. You saved some lives yesterday."

"Aw shucks," he said, his cheeks coloring. Then he looked up. "How's Zoë? She's been through a lot."

"She's been taken into custody and will eventually be returned to the States for trial." I told him what Baptiste had told me about the donor list and the chilling reasons for the abductions.

Max looked down. "I'm as guilty as anyone. It's cool to come up with barbs—the crueler, the funnier. I'm pretty bummed about my part in all this."

"Maybe you should talk to Zoë, tell her how you feel. She's an emotionally disturbed young woman with a lot of years of recovery ahead. It might help her to hear how you feel. Nicolette, too, if she regains consciousness. But I think this would have happened anyway even if you and the other kids hadn't done what you did. What began as honest, ethical research had become a megalomaniac's personal vendetta and experimental lab. He was using human beings instead of mice."

"Do you think he really was close to a cure?"

"Someday we may find out. I'm not sure who will end up with Baptiste's research. There may be years of litigation over this. Whatever's on his computers and in his files may never be read—or used—by other scientists and verified."

Max took a deep breath. "Meanwhile, little kids die—like the boy at La Vida Pura. What if Baptiste was close? He kept saying he was days away from a cure. What if he was telling the truth?"

I felt the sting of tears and looked away. "Research is going on in other places. South Korea, Europe. I hope researchers who have been following Baptiste's work will fight to get the records released."

"That'll take years."

"I know." It was another of those sorrowful things I would push into those hidden places in my heart, but someday—and probably, often—it would hit me afresh: What would've happened if I'd waited just a few weeks before blowing the whistle on Baptiste?

I might be standing at my sink washing dishes, walking down the frozen foods aisle to reach for a box of éclairs, or sitting in my Chevrolet at a long stoplight, but I knew my tears would flow again. I had caught a glimpse of him only once—and that was from a distance. But now every time I saw a thin little boy with a shock of blond hair, I would think of Erik. His image was tucked permanently in my heart.

"What about La Vida Pura? Do you think Nolan had any connection to Baptiste?"

"We can assume from what we overheard that Nolan has funded some of Baptiste's research. Though because of Nolan's financial difficulties, I wonder if even that was about to come to an end."

I reflected for a moment on the good Baptiste had set out to do before power and ego got in the way. "We've got to remember—even in light of the tragedy here—there is great hope in scientific research conducted in view of the public. But it's got to be subject to peer review, to the ethical safeguards medical science has set up. I was reading somewhere recently about pluripotent stem cells…"

Max leaned forward, elbows on his knees, hands dangling. His eyes weren't quite glazed over, but I could tell I'd lost him somewhere between *peer review* and *pluripotent.*

"Well, hey, I'm just glad it's over," Max said. He paused. "What about the captain? Did he ever apologize?"

I laughed. "You should have heard him. As soon as I boarded, he made a beeline to intercept me. No summons to the bridge this time. And he couldn't have been nicer, bless his heart."

Max grinned. "Bless his heart?"

"Oh yes. He's offered me free passage on any of his ships, any line he might work for, at any time." I laughed again. "His reputation is pretty shaky in the industry already, and after the cruise being scrutinized by every media outlet around the globe, I have to wonder if he'll ever get another job as captain."

"How will you handle the review for your article?"

"With humor and grace, of course!"

Another knock interrupted us. Max jumped up to get the door.

It was Price, smiling sheepishly. Behind him stood the couples who had gone with us to La Vida Pura—the Doyles, the Browns, and the Quilps.

"You all think you're going to fit in here?" I laughed and stood back to let them in.

"It's a party!" Ed Brown declared in his inimitable Oklahoma accent. He held up a bottle of sparkling cider. Behind him, his wife, Betty, was carrying a plate of hors d'oeuvres that looked suspiciously like little balls of SPAM scattered among sliced cucumbers, celery, cherry tomatoes, and mushrooms. "Just a little something to say we're sorry you're leaving the ship early."

"Thank you, but I've got plenty of material for my article. It's time to go home."

"Of course we don't know the half of all you were involved in," Barbara said, "I would bet the rest of the cruise will be pretty boring." She bit into a SPAM ball and frowned. "I bet this would be better rolled in caviar."

"Boring is good," Don Doyle said. "And you're right about the caviar." He reached for a cherry tomato.

Price took a sip of cider and watched me over the rim of the paper cup.

I gave him a playful punch on the arm. "Hey, bud, I haven't seen you around. You only got in on half the excitement—our first foray into the life of crime." I told the Doyles, Browns, and Quilps about the boys getting me to shore in the purloined kayaks and then to La Vida Pura in a "borrowed" police SUV.

"Hunh," Adele Quilp said.

Orris squinted, speared a piece of SPAM with a celery stick, then popped it into his mouth.

"Speaking of boring. Here we thought you were a boring travel writer, not one primed for a life of crime," Betty Brown said with a laugh. "We should've been hanging around you, girl. It would have been much more exciting than being trapped on this ship."

"We even went into town to shop for the chef's vegetables," Max said. "Though now I kinda miss the SPAM sandwiches."

"Have an hors d'oeuvre," Barbara said, handing him the platter. Behind her, Ed poured the sparkling cider into paper cups, then handed them around.

"To the best travel writer I've ever met," Ed said, holding up his drink.

"To the *only* travel writer we've ever met," Betty said, bumping her cup against mine.

"And to the girls whose lives you saved," Barbara added solemnly.

Don lifted his cup toward mine. "To following your heart no matter how rough the seas. There are some happy parents tonight who are glad you did."

They all cheered, and I looked at Price, who had been abnormally quiet since entering the room. "So what've you been up to, bud? I got sort of used to having you around, paddling for me, that sort of thing, during our crime spree."

He shrugged. "Homework. Papers due for my onboard classes, that sort of thing." He paused, looking at Gus's feeders, which I hadn't yet packed. He frowned at me. "Hey, did your cat ever come back?"

The pain was still fresh and almost took my breath away. "No. It's one of those unsolved mysteries." I explained to the others the circumstances surrounding Gus's disappearance. "I thought it might have been one of the students, maybe someone whose toes I'd stepped on." I glanced pointedly at Price, but he didn't react.

Across the room, Ed Brown gasped. "You lost a cat, darlin'?"

"Yes, I did. A big gray tabby with Elizabeth Taylor eyes."

"Violet eyes?" Adele Quilp said. "Really?"

"I meant the eyeliner she wore as Cleopatra."

"Oh, darlin'," Ed said again and stood, looking stricken. "I've got something I need to show you." He headed to the door. "Now, don't you move. I'll be right back."

I heard a sound outside my stateroom almost before I could wonder. The door opened only wide enough for something small to squeeze through. I didn't dare hope. I didn't dare look. I almost turned away.

It couldn't be.

I stood and moved around the bed where I could better see what had just entered my room. And I held my breath.

A gray, black, white, and rust tabby entered, sat down, and washed his foot. Gus obviously wasn't as ecstatic about his reentry into my life as I was. With a yelp, I ran to him and scooped him up.

Of course, cats being cats, he would have none of the hugs-and-kisses business. He squirmed to get down, cast a superior look at the others in the room as he headed to his feeders, tail waving elegantly. He sat, his back to me, in front of his empty dish. Waiting.

He'd trained me well. I rummaged around for the bag of sensitive-stomach cat food, poured some in, and waited to see him dive in.

Gus just sat there staring at the dish.

Meanwhile Ed told me how he'd found Gus meowing outside their stateroom several days earlier. He brought him in and fed him scraps from the kitchen, thinking he was the ship's mouser. Gus had occupied his days outside the stateroom, then showed up every evening for dinner. I tried not to feel jealous.

Gus sauntered over to his dish, took one sniff of the cat food, and walked away, his nose in the air, his tail swishing.

"He seems to prefer SPAM," Ed said.

When the room was empty, I scooped Gus into my arms and went to stand by the window. Now that I was alone, a strange sense of something unfinished, something I'd overlooked, nipped at the edges of my mind. I should have felt elated that Baptiste was out of the picture, that the girls were safe and getting the medical help they needed. But instead it was as if something I hadn't thought of, something I'd missed, was out there, lurking, waiting for me.

Gus purred, and I laughed at myself. I was getting a bit barmy after all. Obviously my overactive imagination, probably because of the excitement and dangers of the past few days, had put my emotions off kilter. It would just take time for me to recover.

I stared out at the harbor. In the distance the tall and beautiful silhouette of Lorenzo Nolan's yacht caught my attention. From here it looked like a toy rather than the magnificent vessel it was. I wondered about the child and his mother, about Lorenzo himself, the billionaire who was about to lose his empire.

Lose his empire? My breath caught as I remembered the conversation between Nolan and Baptiste that night in the clinic. Baptiste had made reference to funding from Nolan. If Nolan poured money into Baptiste's research, he'd be looking for more than a cure for his girlfriend's child, more than the profits that might be had from a cure for CML. To bring the kind of money he needed into his coffers, it had to be something bigger. Much bigger.

I stared at the distant yacht, possibilities flying into my mind.

The dangerous game wasn't yet over.

At two o'clock I boarded the tender, accompanied by Max who was heading to the airport to meet his parents. Gus was beside me, protesting the hated carrier.

"How do you think Gus got out?"

"Pretty ordinary escape," I said. "I think maybe the cabin attendant left the door open and turned her back just long enough for him to make a run for it. I don't know why she didn't lock up when she finished with my room. Maybe she thought the cat might return."

We spoke of the remaining days of the cruise, the interruption of coursework, how Shepparton was going to handle the demands for refunds, and the inquiry into Baptiste's connection with the school.

"My dad's already talking about me transferring to Florida State next semester."

"What about you? What do you want to do?"

"I'm still crazy about science—oceanography—and Shepparton's got a strong program. There are some good people there in spite of this bad publicity Dr. Baptiste has created." He shook his head. "He was such a cool guy. Who would ever have known?"

"The first recorded blood transfusion—in 1492—was performed on Pope Innocent VII. The blood of three healthy little boys was transfused into the dying pope. The children and the pope died not long after." We were just pulling up to the wharf, and I paused while the pilot bumped against the siding and tossed the rope to the crew member assisting him. As soon as the tender was secure, I stood and picked up Gus's carrier. "Guess what the doctor's given name was?"

Max shook his head as he gathered up my typewriter case and duffle. "Jean Baptiste."

"You're kidding. How do you know?"

I laughed. "Just one of the bits of trivia that has stuck with me."

We stepped onto the wharf. I tipped the pilot, then looked around for a taxi. Max hailed one that was parked up the street, and a few minutes later we were settled into the backseat, Gus's carrier between us.

Max looked across at me. "Do you think our Baptiste is related?"

"It was a given name. The last name was Denis—so no relation. I suspect he assumed the name after he went into the field of hematology."

The cabby drove slowly through Playa Negra, dodging media vans and pedestrian gawkers. With the breaking news from the night before, many stations were giving minute-by-minute updates. Portable satellite dishes—three times as many as before—seemed to have sprouted up like oversize mushrooms after a rain.

"To the hospital," I called to the taxi driver.

Around us the usual sounds of the bustling seaside village filled the air along with the underlying whine of motorbikes. I shuddered at the memory of my close call with the butterfly bearer on this same street.

Minutes later the taxi pulled up in front of the hospital. I headed to ICU and looked in. My heart caught. Adam's bed was empty. I almost ran back to the nurses' station.

"Adam Hartsfield? Can you tell me, *por favor*, where he is located?"

The nurse smiled and beckoned for me to follow her. Moments later I was shown to the door of a room on the second floor.

"Adam?" I whispered from the doorway.

His bed was elevated, and he was sipping water through a straw. He turned toward me and gave me a weak smile as I entered the room.

"Welcome back," I said.

"It's good to be back." His voice was raspy and soft, as if it was too great an effort to speak.

I sat down beside him and for a moment I was silent. Then he surprised me by letting out a weak laugh. "I actually liked it better when you were holding my hand," he said.

"You knew?"

He nodded. "I also liked hearing you talk. Tell me what happened."

And I did. At the end of it all, he seemed exhausted, but I knew one question remained unanswered. Holly.

I took his hand and squeezed it. "We still don't know the answers, Adam. She wasn't there; neither were the other missing girls. Only Carly and Kate, his most recent victims." He turned away from me but didn't let go of my hand. "The authorities are searching the compound for medical records, for anything that might lead them to the others."

I stood and leaned closer. "It's not over, Adam. There's still hope." But in my heart I doubted my own words.

His voice was thick with weariness and emotion when he spoke again. "My search isn't finished. If I have to keep looking till my dying day to find my daughter, I'll do it."

"I know," I said softly.

He fell silent. His back was still to me, but after a moment I could tell by his breathing that he had fallen asleep again.

On a whim I rounded the bed, stooped, and kissed his forehead. This time I was sure I saw that tiny quiver at the corner of his lips.

I stopped at the nurses' desk and asked to use the phone for a local call. Ten minutes later I settled into the backseat of the taxi, Gus and Max at my side. The driver cut across to a side street on the inland side of the canal. The traffic thinned, and as we headed to the outskirts along the same route Max, Price, and I had taken in the police SUV, we were alone on the road.

Behind us, though, mixing with the sounds of the cab's muffler and engine noise, something else caught my attention. The hair at the back of my neck stood on end.

The whine of a lone motorcycle.

Max and I glanced at each other, then looked back as it came closer. The colors of the bike were the same. The rider's helmet, green and black with a dark visor, matched that of the biker who'd run me down. He probably had a dead butterfly in his pocket.

The bike pulled dangerously close to our bumper, and our driver cursed and swerved.

Anger, hot and quick, shot into me. "Pull over," I said to the cabby.

"You *loca*, Señora?"

"Please, do as I say."

He found a wide spot and pulled to the side of the road, gravel crunching beneath the tires. The motorbike skidded to a stop behind us. I reached for the door handle.

"What are you doing?" Max had turned pale. "That guy almost killed you."

"He wanted to scare me."

"But now? Why's he coming after you now?"

"I don't know, but I've had about enough of all this."

The kid on the bike was waving a gun. I didn't know this one from a muzzleloader. I only knew it was smaller than the gun Zoë had been waving around last night.

"Game's over," I said to the biker. "You can take off your helmet. I know who you are."

He didn't make a move to put down the gun or take off his helmet.

"Okay, play it your way," I said. "Let me tell you what I know, and if I'm right, then you can do the dramatic unveiling. If I'm wrong, then you can put away the gun and head on up the road on your bike, and no one will be the wiser. The mystery will go unsolved."

In my peripheral vision, I could see Max's very pale face.

"Now I don't know what you're doing out here—you could be heading to the airport or to La Vida Pura. This road leads to both places. But I would assume that you were hired to give me a final scare, try to run us off the road, shoot at the car if all else failed, perhaps toss a dead butterfly at me as a parting shot to ensure I never visit this lovely part of Costa Rica again. Or look any further into the crimes in Playa Negra."

"Who'd hire him?" Max muttered. "Baptiste is dead."

"Ah, who indeed?" I said. "You see, we still have one unsolved murder. And Baptiste, in spite of his murderous heart, had his own agenda. Murdering Harry Easton wasn't part of that agenda. Baptiste was focused on his research. Oh, he took his share of lives, but they were to serve a sacrificial purpose. He used them for one thing alone—to keep his daughter alive."

"There's someone else," Max said.

"You're good, Watson."

"Who's Watson?"

"I'll tell you later."

I looked again at the still helmeted biker. "You're not a killer. But you've got a connection to the real killer. Let me guess. He's your uncle? *Or* maybe your dad's fraternity brother? Your godfather?"

No response.

"No matter," I said. "The important thing is that you've known the desperate measures needed for Lorenzo Nolan to rebuild his empire. His losses have been enormous, in the billions of dollars, I've heard. I suspect that you, maybe your family, stand to gain from these riches someday. So

Daddy sent you down here to help Uncle Lorenzo in any way you could. Maybe as a gofer? Maybe just to spy so you could report back to Daddy how the family finances might be enhanced?

"And Uncle Lorenzo, bless his eighteen-karat gold buttons, was more than delighted when you showed up. He needed someone onboard the disastrous cruise of the *Sun Spirit* to feed him information. He likely suspected that Easton and Hartsfield were on to him, had connected him to Baptiste. He had to get rid of them. Too much was at stake."

"How is he connected to Baptiste," Max wanted to know, "and what's the crumbling empire got to do with it?"

"Do you want to tell him? Or shall I? Or maybe he guessed, just as I did the night we broke into the clinic. You were the only one of the three of us who didn't seem surprised by the conversation we overheard. Oh, surprised about Nicolette, I'm sure. But you knew about the connection between Nolan and Baptiste, didn't you, Price?"

"Price? You're kidding!"

Price removed his helmet and shrugged. He still held the gun, but he didn't look serious about using it. "Embryonic stem cells for fighting disease. Lorenzo poured a ton of money into Baptiste for the development of offshore clinics. The plan was to harvest eggs and offer medical solutions to people who can't get the same help in the States. Cloning. Transplantation."

"Let me guess," I said. "The eggs would be harvested from more kidnapping victims, only this time, I suppose, the women would be pulled out of the ghettos of Central America." Max frowned at me, and I shrugged. "Hey, I read about this stuff in the *Economist.*"

Price's expression told me I'd hit the target.

I explained to Max. "Their families don't have enough money to search for them. They would simply disappear. No media frenzy, no tearful parents' images being beamed across the world. Just lost and forgotten girls."

"You don't know what you're talking about," Price said. "The advances are already astounding. If Baptiste could have lived—"

"Does the end justify the means? What about the ethics? The moral values Baptiste and others like him have discarded? What about the intrinsic value of a human life, whether it's a girl from the jungles of Guatemala or an unborn fetus?"

"Fetuses are unnecessary in Baptiste's work. Only the unfertilized egg from the donor."

"And so that 'donor' becomes a machine, for this much I know: tens of thousands of eggs must be harvested in order to have one successful cloned cell." I paused, feeling my anger ready to erupt. "Then what? You create a 'butterfly farm' to keep these young women available, producing for the purposes of the rich who can afford the innovative medical treatment?"

He shrugged. "So what are you going to do? There will be more Baptistes in the future. You can't stop medical advances."

"But Lorenzo Nolan will be stopped from looking for the next Baptiste."

Price waved the gun my direction. "Nobody knows. If I take care of you, then no one will ever know."

The hand that held the gun was shaking, and for a moment I felt sorry for him. "Too late, bud. I called Interpol from the hospital a few minutes ago. They're on to Nolan." I checked my watch. "They may already have arrested him for the murder of Easton and the attempted murder of Hartsfield."

Price turned white and dropped the gun. "Did you tell them about me? About the motorcycle incident?"

"No. I don't think you're in so deep that you can't get out. My advice is to hightail it back home and steer clear of Uncle Lorenzo till your dying day." He stared at me. "If you don't steer clear, and I hear of it," I added, "I'll always have the option of making that phone call to Interpol."

"I got a phone, dude," Max said, patting his pocket.

Price shoved the gun in his pocket, climbed back on the motorbike, skidded into a U-turn, and raced off toward town. We listened until the whine of the bike faded to silence. A macaw squawked in the distance. Birds chirped, bugs buzzed, and the air was heavy with building thunderheads. I was ready to go home.

Max and I got back in the taxi. I patted the carrier, and Gus gave me a growling meow to again protest his confinement.

"To the airport," I said. "And hurry. We don't want to be grounded because of the storm."

"Somehow, Ms. M., I think it might take a lot to ground you," Max said with a grin.

An hour later I was circling Playa Negra, looking down at the little town, its harbor, the coffee plantations, and the jungles beyond. The *Sun Spirit,* looking like a toy boat in a sparkling, azure sea, disappeared as I turned northeast and climbed to a cruising altitude of five thousand feet before crossing a low range of mountains.

The rental plane, one of the few that didn't belong to the Baptiste Corporation, was another Skyhawk. The engine purred along at about 145 miles an hour, 4,500 rpms. The winds were from the southwest, which gave me a bit of a tailwind—and a smoother ride. I looked down at the charts and recalculated the time to reach San José, factoring in the tailwind. I had recaptured my love for flying, but I wasn't hankering to fly this baby all the way to California. Give me an airbus any day for a long international trip.

No, this short flight was a gift I was giving myself to say, "I'm alive!" To say that I may be scared sometimes, I may be confused or angry or overwhelmed by the injustices in the world. I may be all these things mixed together. But when it comes right down to it, "I am woman…hear me roar!"

Grinning, I picked up a small package that Max had given me just before I climbed into the Skyhawk. Holding the yoke with my knees, I tore off the paper…and laughed.

It was a black ball cap with "You Go, Girl!" embroidered in silver letters across the front.

I put it on, flipped my ponytail out the back, and adjusted the brim to keep the western sun out of my eyes.

Dear friends,

I hope you've enjoyed accompanying Harriet on the first adventure in her new mystery series. She is one of my favorite characters of the many I've written. She literally jumped into my mind full blown, capturing my heart with her gutsy, quirky, and fun-but-flawed nature. She soon became so real it almost seemed as though she sat by my side as I wrote, telling me her story—a rare and delightful thing for an author! Also a bit barmy, as Harriet would say.

I'm already at work on book two, *Those Sacred Bones,* which will take Harriet, Adam Hartsfield, and Max Pribble on a new adventure, this time to the Mediterranean on a luxury cruise with ports of call that include Barcelona, Spain; the French Riviera; and Rome, Italy. The story opens when a monk is murdered at a rugged mountaintop abbey in Montserrat, Spain. Max is the only witness, and fearing for his life, he comes to Harriet for help. She is quickly drawn into a web of international deceit, ancient cover-ups done in the name of religion, and dangers aboard ship that are more chilling than she could ever imagine. The stakes are high, the clock is ticking, and Harriet's feet itch to run away from the danger. But her heart won't let her. Watch for *Those Sacred Bones* in May 2007.

Thank you to those readers who have followed my writing journey over the years, from the days I wrote under the pen name Amanda MacLean to the present with my newest adventures with Harriet. And a heartfelt "Welcome to my world" to those of you who have just discovered my books. If you have difficulty finding any of my earlier books (listed at the beginning of this volume), please contact me at the following address:

diane@dianenoble.com

or

PO Box 10674

Palm Desert, CA 92255-0674

Blessings and God's peace to all!

Diane Noble

ACKNOWLEDGMENTS

Heartfelt gratitude to all those who've been instrumental in the development of the Harriet MacIver mystery series: First of all, Don Pape—dear friend and agent—who came to me a few years ago with some what-if questions about placing a mystery series aboard cruise ships. The e-mails flew back and forth, a few phone chats ensued, and the idea for the series began to take form. It wasn't long until I sat down at the computer, and Harriet came to life. I also want to thank my brother, Dr. Dennis Hill, who—as he's done so often—explored with me more of those what-if questions, this time having to do with stem cell research, bone marrow transplants, and difficult issues involving medical ethics. A very special thanks, too, to my husband, Tom. I couldn't do any of this without him. Besides being both resident historian and chef extraordinaire, he's an early reader who critiques the manuscript through every stage, giving me invaluable input. I must also mention two beloved members of our family—two felines named Kokopelli and Merlin—who provided endless ideas and inspiration for Gus.

Writing is by nature a lonely life. What would I do without my online friendships and support network of other authors? We pray for one another, weep and rejoice together, run book ideas and titles and characters by each other. Mostly, though, there's comfort in knowing these buddies are there to listen, console, and support. At the top of the list are three very special authors: Annie Jones, Lynn Bulock, and Sharon Gillenwater. As always, a special thanks to my dear friend Liz Higgs, whose prayers, friendship, and support never waver—even in the midst of the tightest deadlines.

I'm happily in debt to all!

ABOUT THE AUTHOR

DIANE NOBLE is the award-winning author of nearly two dozen books, including historical and contemporary women's fiction, romantic suspense, novellas, and nonfiction books for women. *The Butterfly Farm* is the first book in her new Harriet MacIver mystery series. Diane is a three-time recipient of the Silver Angel Award for Media Excellence, has been double finalist for RWA's prestigious RITA, and has been a *Romantic Times* Lifetime Achievement Award nominee. Diane makes her home with her husband, Tom, and their two cats-who-think-they're-people in Southern California. You can visit Diane's Web site at *www.dianenoble .com,* where you can catch up on her latest releases and works in progress and hear about Harriet's upcoming research trips. You may also write to Diane at:

PO Box 10674
Palm Desert, CA 92255–0674